SAILORS TAKE WARNING

By Malcolm Torres

This is a work of fiction. Any resemblance to real people or actual events is purely coincidental. The narrator assumes responsibility for tampering with anything that does not match the reader's version of reality. To discover things that will aid you in understanding this dark tale, and to find free stories and chapters by the author, please go to www.malcolmtorres.com.

For George, Hannah & Benjamin

SAILORS TAKE WARNING

Captain Reginald Fox, USS Nimitz *Commanding Officer*
Captain Samuel Brandt, USS Nimitz *Executive Officer*

Medical

Commander Sternz
Medical Officer

Kate Conrad
EMT

Gutierrez
Corpsman

Crew

Commander Bradmore
ECM Lead

Nikki Thompson
Admin

O'Malley
Fire Marshall

Donna Grogan
Fork Lift Driver

Larry Burns
Cook

Stanley Comello
Flight Deck Worker

Grady Dutro
Supply Runner

Darnell Ratcomb
Deckhand

Legal

Mr. Keef
Detective

Commander Shakley
Investigator

Lieutenant Gallagher
Sea Lawyer

Lieutenant Jones
Sea Lawyer

Stingers

Commander Aronson
Stinger CO

Lieutenant Gould
Pilot

Lieutenant Rhodes
Pilot

Chief Crenki
Maintenance Chief

Trueblood
Weapons Lead

Terrance McDaniels
Plane Captain

Danny Jenks
Plane Captain

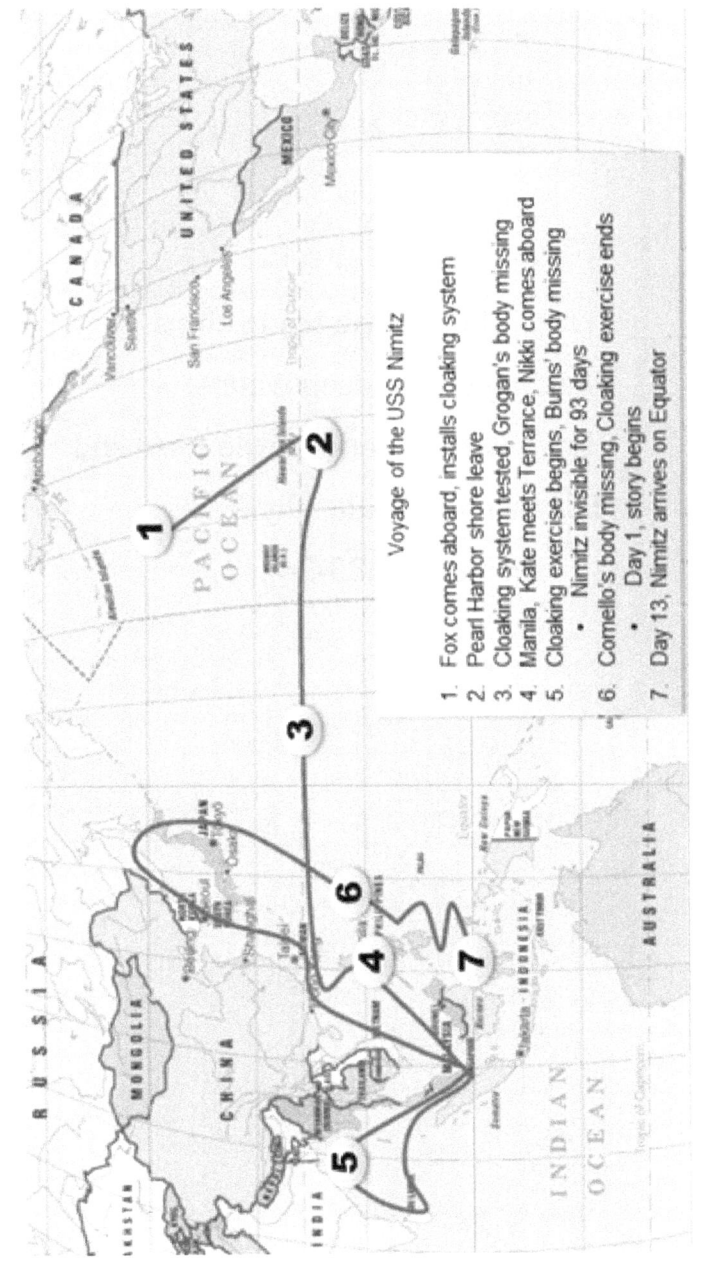

Voyage of the USS Nimitz

1. Fox comes aboard, installs cloaking system
2. Pearl Harbor shore leave
3. Cloaking system tested, Grogan's body missing
4. Manila, Kate meets Terrance, Nikki comes aboard
5. Cloaking exercise begins, Burns' body missing
   - Nimitz invisible for 93 days
6. Comello's body missing, Cloaking exercise ends
   Day 1, story begins
7. Day 13, Nimitz arrives on Equator

They who sail the sea in ships,

Trading on the deep waters,

They see the works of the Lord and

His wonders in the abyss.

Psalm 107.23-24

PART I

ABOARD THE USS NIMITZ

CHAPTER ONE – Day 1

Kate Conrad leaned out the pharmacy's dispensing window and handed the man a tube of medicated cream. She was about to tell him to apply it twice daily to the affected area, when the alarm bell rang.

At twenty, Kate was tall with short-clipped sandy hair and blue eyes. Second thoughts about leaving the University of California at San Diego to join the Navy still haunted her, but as a member of the ship's Flying Squad, she never thought twice when that alarm bell rang.

"Follow the directions on the label," she said hurriedly while locking the pharmacy. She ran from the medical department, calling back over her shoulder, "And don't scratch no matter how itchy it gets!"

In the main deck passageway, Kate waited and listened to the bell's incessant clangor.

It rang from waterproof speakers throughout the ship—a bone-rattling metallic din, threatening to perforate eardrums.

Thousands of sailors looked away from computer screens, set aside power tools and paused conversations. Throughout the multilevel maze, eyes turned toward speakers mounted on bulkheads. Those asleep in narrow bunks under white sheets and scratchy wool blankets startled awake—eyes suddenly open in air-conditioned darkness.

A squeal of feedback squashed the clanging bell, and a computer-generated female voice announced, "AWAY THE FLYING SQUAD. THIS IS NOT A DRILL. FLAMMABLE SPILL ON THE AFT HANGAR DECK, FRAME TWO FOUR FIVE. AWAY THE FLYING SQUAD, AWAY." The bell resumed its urgent call to action, reverberating against every bulkhead.

Kate Conrad ran aft inside the main deck passageway, shouting at sailors walking ahead of her, "Gangway! Coming through!" After weeks of endless boredom, Kate relished the adrenaline shot as she ran to the accident scene.

The eight-foot-wide corridor was the Nimitz's main drag compared to so many other narrow passageways, but sailors crammed in, walking two and three abreast. Fluorescent lights glared off the polished green Formica. Bundles of cable, ventilation ducts and myriad pipes carrying water, jet fuel and sewage crammed into the low overhead. Bulkheads marked with weld scars and rows of rivet heads. Fire hoses stowed in compact racks. Watertight doors, battle lanterns and fire extinguishers flew past in Kate's peripheral vision.

They were the shipboard equivalents of ambulances screaming along crowded boulevards. In passageways throughout the ship, sailors squeezed behind pipes and doors, flattened themselves against bulkheads, like cars pulling to the curb, as Flying Squad members ran past, their black boots booming on the steel, their cries of "Gangway!" and "Make a hole!" punctuating the boredom of shipboard routine.

Frequent drills tested her ability to locate damage control lockers and emergency medical stations hidden away inside the Nimitz's 1,000-foot-long and 17-deck-high hive of compartments and passageways. She'd studied 3-D schematics of the ship and proved she could find any location blindfolded during blackout and smoke drills.

Jet fuel mist swirled down around a ladder angling at 45-degrees through an open hatch in the deck above. The smell seared her nose; Kate pulled a gas mask tight against her face and exhaled hard to clear it.

Fire Marshall O'Malley emerged from the jet fuel fog. A

human tree trunk with the bark peeled off, he shouted orders at sailors distributing extinguishers, mops and buckets in a disciplined frenzy. O'Malley's fierce eyes stared out through his face shield. "You and you," he roared, pointing a thick finger at two boatswain mates. "Grab oxygen bottles and a stretcher. Follow EMT Conrad!" O'Malley stared at Kate and shouted, "There's one serious injury and several overcome by fumes on the fantail. Move it."

She grabbed her bulky EMT kit from the damage control locker and a fresh shot of adrenaline pulsed into her limbs as she climbed the ladder into the mist. At the top, in the aircraft hangar, she came face to face with the cause of the current emergency.

Jet engine shipping containers—steel cans, each the size and weight of a minivan—were normally stacked three-high and chained to the deck in this area. As best Kate could tell, one container had fallen over and landed on several wooden crates, reducing them to splinters. A second shipping container had fallen over, rolled across the deck and smashed a pipe against the bulkhead.

A fountain of fuel—creating an asphyxiation, fire and explosion hazard—squirted in multiple directions across the hangar, splashed on several cargo containers and misted in the air. Kate saw the cloud of vapor billowing through the open space packed with jet aircraft and aviation support equipment.

Sailors scrambled about dropping bails of rags and tearing open bags of absorbent granules, dropping them on a growing puddle of fuel that sloshed this way and that as the ship rolled on erratic ocean swells.

A jet mechanic in blue coveralls and a scuffed yellow hardhat shouted, "Over here," hailing Kate and the boatswains.

They splashed through the jet fuel puddle, and followed the mechanic through a shop crowded with partially assembled jet engines. "A shipping container fell on the poor guy," the mechanic explained. He swung open a big metal door and led the way out onto the fantail, an open deck on the aft end of the ship where sailors throw trash overboard, go fishing and occasionally bury a shipmate at sea.

Passing from the ship's air-conditioned interior to the

scorching humidity, here a few degrees north of the equator, Kate broke a sweat instantly. She pulled off her gas mask and took a deep breath. The oppressive claustrophobia of the ship's cramped interior fell away. Blue ocean and boundless sky expanded to the horizon.

A crowd stood gawking at the accident victims.

"Give us room here," one of the boatswains ordered in a thick Boston accent.

"Let's go, move it," the other boatswain shouted as the crowd shuffled toward the far side of the fantail.

Kate went directly to the injured man lying on the deck, while the boatswains administered oxygen to several sailors who were soaked with jet fuel and overcome by fumes.

She knelt and placed her hand on his shoulder and saw his grease-streaked brown jersey soaked with jet fuel and blood. She opened her kit and noted his head cocked at an odd angle and his eyes open in a dead-ahead stare. Between baby-fat cheeks, his lips twisted in a grotesque kiss.

She found no pulse at his wrists or neck. She pulled on a pair of Nitrile gloves and a facemask, stuck two fingers between his teeth and pulled his jaw down to reveal a mouth filled with blood. She grabbed a pair of surgical scissors, and in one smooth motion cut his brown turtleneck jersey from collar to hem and pealed back the wet fabric.

Blunt force trauma had crushed the entire left side of his chest. A malicious purple bruise covered his smashed torso. Blood flowed from punctures where fractured ribs pierced skin. Kate pictured the shipping container tumbling over, knocking him down and crushing him—causing massive thoracic trauma. Flail chest— she remembered from training—when ribs are broken in so many places that the shattered sections detach from the ribcage and play havoc with the diaphragm, making it impossible to breath. Fuck, she realized, he's already dead!

Examining his neck, she found it wasn't broken. She turned his head to the side. She grabbed a suction device from her kit and tried to clear his airway, but too much blood flowed from his mouth. She dropped the suction device, grabbed a tracheal tube, inserted it in his mouth and pushed it down into his lungs.

"Oh-two," she shouted.

The kid from Boston connected an oxygen bottle to the tracheal tube and let it flow.

The victim's chest raised a little.

Kate thought maybe, held her breath for a few seconds hoping, but his busted chest contorted and collapsed. Blood flowed from the torn skin where his broken ribs protruded.

"Gentle pressure," she whispered.

The kid from Boston grabbed a towel from the kit. He pressed it against the guy's chest, trying to hold the ribs in place, so Kate could get him breathing, but his torso was all Jell-O and broken bones.

Oxygen filled the victim's lungs and contorted his ribs. A large blood-blister bulged through the skin on his shattered breastbone.

Flail chest with hematoma. Kate knelt on the steel, helpless with her first responder kit. He needs a team of specialists and a thoracic surgery suite, Kate thought, as air and blood gurgled out of him.

The mechanic squatted beside her. "A shipping can weighs over two tons," he whispered. "It took eight of us to lift the corner of it just so we could pull him out."

Kate closed the dead man's eyes. She gazed across the ocean and noticed a ship cruising a ways off. It looked strange riding in the Nimitz's wake. It had spinning satellite dishes and high towers with long antennas. She wondered if the people on that ship could see the Nimitz.

* * *

In the medical department, the sheet came off the second the dead body hit the examination table.

"Owwww!" Gutierrez groaned when she pealed back his jersey and eyed bone splintering through bruised-black flesh. Her brilliant white teeth bit her lower lip.

Kate snipped the dead man's laces and pulled off a boot.

Gutierrez bucked up and began snipping his pants.

Kate tugged at a silver Navy ring on the dead man's left

hand but his fingers were pudgy and it wouldn't budge.

"Try this." Gutierrez handed her a tube of petroleum jelly.

The chief medical officer, Commander Sternz, entered the room. A stout woman with a freckly, olive complexion and dark eyes, Sternz wore her black hair in a bun so tight it looked painful. A smile rarely stretched her lips and never reached her eyes.

Kate tugged at the ring and said, "A shipping container fell on him, ma'am. He died from internal bleeding before I got there."

Sternz glanced at the caved-in chest and said, "Finish stripping this cadaver and lock it in the morgue. Meet me back here at nineteen hundred for an autopsy." She glanced mechanically from Kate to Gutierrez. "This gives us a training opportunity," she said. "We'll explore his thoracic interior." Then Sternz left the compartment, oblivious of the door banging shut behind her.

"She's colder than this guy," Gutierrez said.

Kate dropped the Navy ring into a Ziploc bag along with the dead man's wallet. They slid a thick, black plastic body bag under him, folded his arms and legs inside and zipped it shut.

Kate rolled the gurney across the hall to the morgue. She typed the combination on a keypad lock. She held the door with her foot as she maneuvered the gurney into the small space.

Vertigo wiggled behind her eyeballs and her knees wobbled. She stepped forward to prevent herself from stumbling. Wondering if a rogue wave had hit the ship, she glanced at the rows of shiny stainless steel drawers.

She thought about Donna Grogan with a broken spine, fractured skull and covered with sticky maple syrup. Grogan went into the morgue, but then where'd she go, Kate wondered. And Larry Burns, the cook who died of a heart attack while pulling a tray of dinner rolls from an oven in the bakery. Somebody put him in here, just like Grogan, but where'd his body go? Kate glanced at the drawers, wondering which ones Grogan and Burns had occupied.

She positioned the gurney and prepared to put this guy, whose name she didn't know yet, into cold storage.

*   *   *

Kate grew up on the beach in Ventura, California. Muscles rippled on her long arms and legs. In high school, she was fiercely competitive in volleyball and track, so dragging a 170-pound corpse from a gurney to a morgue drawer wasn't a problem.

She grabbed the body bag, braced her legs and out of nowhere a shadow of doubt flitted across her mind: What am I doing? I should be in college!

After months at sea, these thoughts intruded several times a day. I'm filling penicillin prescriptions for sailors with the clap, when I should be in a pre-med program or at least at a Friday night keg party with friends!

"Okay, cool it," she reminded herself that the University of California at San Diego volleyball scholarship had only covered one-third of her tuition bill. She remembered the start of every semester, standing at the financial aid window signing a student loan promissory note. She still felt the anxiety and depression that swelled in her chest after several terms; after she did the math and calculated her growing mountain of student loan debt.

One night at the library, cramming for an Anatomy exam, a panic attack hit. Owing so much to Bank of America, she feared, would prevent her from ever buying a car, a house, or having kids. Shoving the textbook aside, she tallied what she'd owe by the time she earned a medical degree. The six-figure number gnawed at her during lectures and labs. She awoke in her dorm room in the middle of the night with such dread it was difficult to breathe. I'm too young for this kind of debt, she told herself as she sank back into a troubled sleep.

A few days later, with sunlight streaming through the library windows, she was surfing the web and saw, under a banner ad for Clearasil, a picture of a female sailor dispensing a prescription over a pharmacy counter.

The next day, she rode her bike off campus to meet with a Navy recruiter.

* * *

With fists that spiked their way to a high school volleyball championship and a UC San Diego scholarship, Kate dragged the body bag onto the cold drawer.

Outside the morgue, she double-checked the lock.

In the records office, she dropped into a chair, touched color-coded menu options on a screen to open a fatality report. Reaching into the Ziploc for the dead guy's wallet, the ring slipped around her finger. She pulled it out, examined the blue gem and read his name, Stanley Comello, inscribed inside. Her mind flashed on his chubby knuckles and out of nowhere, tears brimmed on her lower eyelids. She dropped the ring back into the bag, and opened her eyes wide and inhaled deeply through her nose to make the tears go away. In Comello's wallet, she found his ID and glanced at his picture. At 19, he hadn't burned off the baby fat. His chubby cheeks and toothy smile gave him a slow moving, good-natured look.

She swiped his ID and his record started downloading.

She glanced at a whiteboard where they kept track of the number of days they'd been at sea. Across the top, someone had written "DAYS ON AN INVISIBLE SHIP . . ." and below that, a big number 93 in the middle of a dark smudge where someone erased and updated the number every morning.

She remembered the ship cruising behind the Nimitz and wondered if it was the Hayward. Had it finally found them?

She filled in the fatality report and clicked save.

Before meeting Terrance McDaniels for dinner, Kate checked the lock on the morgue one last time.

CHAPTER TWO – Day 1

Terrance McDaniels treated his freshman year at the University of Nebraska like a social event. He knew after graduation he'd return to the farm and work there for the rest of his life, just as his parents and grandparents had done. He earned passing grades in agribusiness, drank brews on the weekend. On sunny days, he played ultimate Frisbee on the quad.

During finals week, Terrance answered a call from his mother and she told him to come home immediately because his father had died of a heart attack.

That afternoon he stood on the sidewalk outside his dorm glancing down the street, keeping an eye out for his brother's red dual-rear-tire Chevy pickup. The trees full of spring leaves and the smell of cut grass wafting across the campus distracted him, as he tried to remember exactly what his dad had said the last time they talked.

A tiny white car pulled up and the driver's window lowered to reveal his brother crammed into a bucket seat behind the steering wheel. A ball cap tipped back revealing a crew-cut and a lower lip swollen with Skoal. Big arms stretched the white t-shirt.

"Where's your pickup?" Terrance asked.

"Hop in," his brother sighed, "and I'll tell you."

Heading east on Interstate 80, his brother explained, "All the way here I've been thinking 'bout how I'm gonna tell you and I figured the only way is to just say it." He spat in a Mountain Dew can. "Dad borrowed against the farm and against his life insurance and now he's dead and mom's got nothing."

"I don't get it—" words wandered from Terrance's mouth.

"The bank already repo'd the pickups and combines."

"What about the farm?"

"It's in the final step of foreclosure, little brother."

Tears blurred the headlights of oncoming cars.

*   *   *

They qualified for food stamps and a subsidized apartment in Lincoln.

Terrance was the first McDaniels to ride on a city bus and apply for a job, and he earned both distinctions on the same day. Upon entering Kentucky Fried Chicken to fill out a job application, his stomach flipped at the smell of grease.

Since seeing his dad's coffin lower into the ground a few days earlier, he was constantly trying to catch his breath, especially inside the tiny apartment.

On the sidewalk, outside the KFC, nervous anxiety tied his stomach in knots, making it impossible to take a step.

Surrounded by glass and concrete, adrift in a sea of parking lots and shiny vehicles, Terrance felt lost among the fast food joints and big box stores.

When he saw the Navy recruiter's office at the end of the retail strip, he made up his mind.

*   *   *

They met at a beach barbecue in Manila, while playing volleyball on opposite sides of the net. Kate spiked on him with devastating power. Embarrassed, Terrance made a point to block her next shot. But later in the game when she leaped off the sand and blocked his spike, their friendship officially began. They sat cross-legged on a blanket under the palm trees, eating potato salad and ribs slathered with spicy barbecue sauce. They filled tall paper cups with beer from a cold keg and drank until the sky was black and full of stars. A positive energy pulled them together from the start. Kate was competitive and talkative. Terrance was easy going and liked her bubbly California accent.

He admired her high cheekbones, how they glowed with a peach hue, and the way her bright eyes opened wide when he told her about his dad's farm. Her nonchalance in a bikini on that beach in Manila disarmed him.

She admired his flat, hard stomach and wide, square

shoulders. He kept his hair in a crewcut to honor his dad, who gave him and his brother crewcuts every Saturday when they were boys. She heard the subtle Midwestern twang in his voice and looked from his arms to his honest eyes and she couldn't resist the powerful crush.

The ship left Manila and they met for lunch and dinner almost every day. During that long 93-days at sea, they talked for hours and became more than friends.

* * *

Deciding not to wait in line for pot roast with gravy and vegetable medley, they went to the salad bar and piled their trays with mixed greens, Garbanzos, hard-boiled eggs, croutons, shredded carrots and bacon bits. They stood amid a thousand eating sailors and waited for two seats next to each other.

He asked about the alarm he'd heard earlier and paused with his fork in front of his mouth, a crouton impaled on the tines, while she told him about Stanley Comello. Color drained from her cheeks, and her lips, usually full and smiling, were pinched and listless.

"Rattled you?"

She glanced aside, not wanting to say anymore here, under the florescent lights, among so much loud-talk.

He touched her hand and she saw genuine concern in his eyes.

They took their trays to the scullery and walked aft along the main deck.

"Let's get some air." She led him past the damage control locker and up a ladder into the hangar. They stopped next to the dented shipping containers, restacked and secured with extra tie-down chains.

"Here's where it broke." She pointed at a section of new black pipe, welded in place.

Terrance saw a foot-long scrape and a mean looking dent on the gray painted bulkhead. He glanced at the containers stacked three high.

"Is this where," he paused, "you know, like, you worked on

him?"

"Out here." She tugged his sleeve.

They emerged on the fantail. The sun sank in the ocean and the humid equatorial air wrapped them like a moist blanket. Somebody had hosed the blood off the deck.

A shadow came over her face. "I tried to resuscitate him."

Terrance almost made a consoling comment but bit his lip.

A guy on watch, wearing a headset and a life vest, stood at the railing watching swells roll past. Another couple stood nearby whispering. Terrance wanted to ask the guy on watch about the ship on the horizon but decided to wait. He stood behind Kate and rubbed her shoulders.

"I couldn't help him." She tilted her head, letting Terrance work on a tight spot.

While she grappled with the toughest part of her job—death at an accident scene—he felt a powerful impulse to tell her how to deal with it, but he rubbed both big hands over his crewcut and went back to massaging her shoulders. That's how it is with girls, he remembered his mom saying, they just want a strong man to listen.

A voice boomed from loudspeakers on the flight deck above. "MAKE A READY DECK. STAND BY TO LAND AIRCRAFT."

A Prowler jet screeched in behind the ship. Kate pressed her fingers in her ears. The jet descended on its final approach, a hundred feet off the water, engines roaring. It was so close they could see lights on its nose landing gear blinking green and red. A deafening roar as great gusts of burnt air blasted from the aircraft's engines and rippled the water behind the ship. It screeched in right over their heads. A HOWL and a WHIRRRRR, like a metal animal colliding with the ship, filled the air as the Prowler grabbed an arresting wire in the landing area above.

"I gotta go," Kate said. "Sternz wants to do an autopsy." She looked at Terrance's dirty brown turtleneck, his canvas pants, and realized Stanley Comello died wearing the same thing.

"If the body's still there," Terrance chided.

"If it's missing," tension tightened around her eyes, "I'll dive overboard and swim for land."

Terrance glanced at the water. "It's only a twenty foot

jump." He smirked and pointed his chin toward the man on watch. "Be sure he's not looking when you jump, because he'll call in a helicopter to pluck you out of the water."

"There's an investigator snooping around," Kate countered Terrance's skepticism, "so it's not just rumors."

"What if the body isn't there when you get back?" Terrance played it straight.

"Sternz'll have an explanation."

"Then why all the rumors?"

"They're not rumors." She pinned him with a stare. "You haven't worked for Commander Sternz. She's an Annapolis grad'. She shines her shoes, presses her uniforms, everything by the book. There's no way a body leaves the morgue without her knowing."

"So—"

"So," Kate squashed his interruption, "when the first body went missing, Sternz ordered everyone to look for it, and like an hour later she said it was buried at sea."

"That's not possible?" Terrance challenged.

"No. It's not possible." Kate shook her head. "Someone in the medical department would've known where it went. Sternz would've known."

"She didn't know?"

"She had us looking for an hour," Kate's voice rose.

"Maple syrup girl, right?"

"Yes," she exhaled, exasperated at his unwillingness to take her seriously.

"You should have followed the trail of sticky footprints," Terrance couldn't resist.

Kate ignored him. "The second time—"

"Mister hot buns?" he interrupted.

"It's not funny." Kate regarded his sly grin. "Larry Burns had a heart attack while taking dinner rolls out of the oven."

"Burns got burned, huh?"

"Everyone in the department knew Burns was missing from the morgue," her tone impatient, "and nobody knew where he went, and out of the blue Sternz tells us he was sent to a storage freezer down below." Before Terrance made another wise crack, she said in her most serious tone, "No one knew anything about either body

17

being taken out of the morgue."

"So, who's snooping around?" he remembered to ask.

"I'm not sure," a frustrated pitch in her voice. "Some big dude from Texas."

"One second," Terrance changed the subject. "Hey," he called to the man standing watch by the railing.

He looked their way.

"Is that the Hayward?" Terrance pointed at the ship on the horizon.

"Sure is," the watch smiled. "They finally found us after ninety-three days."

Terrance and Kate set their hands on the railing.

The Hayward's tall antennas and spinning radar towers stood out against the orange sunset.

They faced each other with bright eyes and big smiles.

"We'll pull into port," he said.

"That'd be awesome."

"Maybe we could find a place to stay on the beach."

She imagined walking around an open-air market, holding hands like tourists but instead she said, "Let's not get our hopes up."

"They'll probably want to keep us out here for another ninety-three days," he agreed with a resigned sigh.

"I gotta get back to work."

He led her toward the door into the ship.

In the dark passageway, he stopped and put his hands on her hips. She touched the back of his neck.

They kissed and for a moment forgot they were aboard a battleship on a nameless ocean.

*   *   *

Kate wondered what it might be like dating Terrance if they weren't in the Navy. She was falling in love with his mix of manners and irreverent humor, his handsome face and broad shoulders. A clean cut guy from the wide-open spaces of Nebraska she mused as she stood in the washroom running hot water and scrubbing her hands with soap. She pulled on a surgical robe and imagined living with Terrance in a tiny apartment in a college town, cramming for exams late at night in the library, waiting tables part time, riding bicycles to class, buying plates and glasses at Goodwill, sleeping together in a twin bed on sheets that didn't match.

"The body's gone!" Gutierrez burst in, shattering Kate's daydream.

"No way," she whispered.

"It ain't in the morgue," Gutierrez insisted. "The drawers are all empty."

Kate charged out of the washroom.

A small crowd gathered outside the morgue, everyone speaking at once.

"Where's the body?"

"Another one missing?"

"Sternz'll shit her pants!"

Kate barged in and saw the body bag, flat and zipped shut, lying on the open drawer. It looked odd, as if the body had evaporated. She wondered why anyone would zip the bag back up and leave it there after taking a body out of it. She did an about face and walked right into Commander Sternz.

"The body—" Kate said.

Blood drained from Sternz's face as a cold vacancy enveloped her. The thought of standing in front of the ship's executive officer, Captain Samuel Brandt, trying to explain how she'd lost another body made her blood run cold.

CHAPTER THREE – Day 1

High in the USS Nimitz's superstructure, Captain Reginald Fox, the ship's commanding officer, stood on his weatherdeck looking through binoculars. A stiff breeze ruffled his pant legs and shirtsleeves. He braced his elbows on the rail and watched the scene unfold. Disappointment filled him as the USS Hayward approached on the ocean's rolling blue surface.

"Dammit!" Fox wanted to call his electronic-warfare team into his office and ask how the Hayward could possibly have found the Nimitz after only 93 days.

Here came the Hayward, cutting a wide turn on the sea a few miles to starboard, moving swiftly into position alongside. Her masts bristled with spinning arrays and satellite dishes. Her sleek bow rose out of the water, exposing black paint on her keel, then plunging beneath and scooping a big splash out of the sea.

He didn't have to think back over the entire 93-day mission. He knew things started going wrong on the seventy-second day, when his reconnaissance pilots returned from a scouting sortie to report the Hayward's position. His analysts, always crunching data and plotting colorful charts, had determined that on six of the past ten days the Hayward was closer to the Nimitz than at any other time since the exercise began. They didn't seem to know the Nimitz's precise location, but they were obviously drawing a bead. Suspecting that the Hayward had intercepted his encrypted messages requesting jet fuel replenishment, Fox slashed the flight schedule and ceased all communications. But the Hayward continued closing in.

And now here she was coming alongside.

Fox lowered his binoculars, because now he could clearly see faces smiling at him through the windows on the Hayward's bridge. A helicopter lifted off from the helipad on the Hayward's stern. It sped over the ocean, circled toward the Nimitz and came in for a landing. A string of colorful signal flags on the Hayward's mast caught Fox's eye. He frowned as he read the message, "Tag you're it."

He did not appreciate the joke. He curled his fingers into a fist and pounded lightly on the rail. "I can hide from you for more than ninety-three days, by God," he muttered, "and I'm determined to do it."

The instant he moved toward the door leading into the Nimitz's bridge, his armed marine bodyguards snapped to attention. One opened the door and stepped inside. The other followed him through and latched it behind.

* * *

Five months earlier, Captain Fox first came aboard the Nimitz during a storm on the Northern Pacific Ocean. He and his team of electronic warfare technicians and TenRay Corporation engineers, arrived in six Sea Scorpion jet-propelled helicopters, loaded with a dozen crates, each marked TOP-SECRET in red stencil. Rather than pull into Pearl Harbor and hold a formal change of command ceremony, Fox relieved the previous captain immediately and kept the Nimitz at sea for several extra weeks.

Rumors ran wild among the crew as their aloof new captain, and his cadre of techs and engineers, unpacked the mysterious crates.

One day Fox and his team were in the bowels of the ship upgrading the sonar equipment, and the next they were studying blueprints in a compartment crowded with high voltage equipment outside the reactor plant. Along the main deck passageway, they hoisted steel plates and laid cable alongside the ship's circulatory system of ventilation ducts and pipes. They installed cameras in the catwalks, and pointed them out at the sea.

From the flight deck, where aircraft launched and landed around the clock, men and women craned their necks to observe workers high atop the Nimitz's towering superstructure. In hard hats and fall protection harnesses, they assembled tall scaffolds and draped them with white canvas sheets.

All hands wondered what their new captain was doing to

their ship.

At night, the canvas sheets were backlit by cutting torches as workers cut away the old antennas and radar arrays. The metal pieces were hand-carried down ladders, taken aft to a garbage chute and dropped, with a splash, to the bottom of the sea.

Communication specialists pulled miles of fiber-optic cable, connecting the new cameras to a light-speed network. And finally, in an air-conditioned compartment in the Nimitz's superstructure, they booted up the TenRay supercomputer.

After a few weeks at sea, Captain Fox ordered all hands to stand down for a special announcement. His voice came from speakers throughout the ship while the crew of over 5,000 listened attentively. All ears prickled with curiosity as they heard his voice for the first time.

"This is Captain Fox speaking. I want to chat with you because my staff tells me you are buzzing with rumors about the new system we've installed, but you don't have to wonder any longer, because I'm here to tell you that the Nimitz is now equipped with a cloaking system that can make the ship invisible." Fox relished the fact that he could reveal mysteries to seafaring men and women. "You heard that correctly," his dignified voice a bit nasally and full of authority, as he spoke into a hand-held microphone while standing on the bridge. "We now have the capability to make the ship invisible. The way it works is quite simple. Fifty cameras mounted around our outboard perimeter feed a three hundred and sixty degree panorama to a computer that fits the incoming video together and sends it to a projector atop the superstructure. The projector is a new piece of technology that casts a pyramid-shaped holograph that conceals the entire ship. The easiest way to explain it is that anyone or anything looking in our direction sees right through us. We also have new arrays in the sonar bulb below the water line and atop the superstructure capable of detecting anyone looking for us and deceiving them with electronic misinformation."

Every person listening tried to fathom the idea that they were on an invisible ship.

"Right now the system is fully operational, and the next step is to train our electronic warfare team to use it, but first we will stop in Pearl Harbor for a few days of much deserved shore leave."

A cheer arose from all hands, and Fox relished the adulation before speaking again.

"After we leave Pearl Harbor, we will spend several weeks training our team to operate the new system, and then we will be stopping in Manila Bay for a few days."

Another cheer arose from the crew.

"After we leave Manila we will make the ship invisible and the USS Hayward, a ship with powerful electronic tracking capability, we begin hunting for us. Normally, we sail with a task force of other ships, but while the Hayward is attempting to find us, we will be sailing alone. I anticipate that the exercise will last in excess of one-hundred days." Fox paused to let that cheerless message sink in. Then he continued. "Our goal is to prove that the TenRay cloaking system is ready for installation on ships across the fleet. I want everyone to understand that we are embarking on a voyage of discovery. Our ability to make this ship invisible will shape the art of naval warfare for centuries to come."

* * *

Unlike the anemic sailors working below decks under fluorescent lights, Captain Fox had a healthy tan. A touch of gray at his temples contrasted with his neatly trimmed dark hair, giving him a dignified look that worked to his advantage when directing often cocksure and occasionally timid young officers. He projected a dignified demeanor, from his regal profile to his shined black shoes. His pressed khaki shirts precisely fit his tapered waist and square shoulders, providing a commanding palette for the golden eagles tacked to his collar points and the stacks of ribbons above his chest pockets. High-wasted pants showed off his long legs, and his lengthy stride made it difficult to keep up with him as he moved quickly through the ship's passageways. An action-oriented disposition prevented Fox from sitting behind his desk for more than a few minutes. He exited boring meetings and darted off to the bridge or the electronic warfare command center.

* * *

23

A technician wearing a headset stood at a large touch-sensitive, see-through screen that showed a 3-D image of the ship with the cloaking system components glowing green. Rows of technicians wearing headsets with wrap-around microphones sat at banks of computer monitors managing data in the ship's electronic war-fighting systems. At the back of the dimly lit compartment, behind floor-to-ceiling Plexiglas panels, tiny green lights blinked on the TenRay supercomputer where it sat running in air-conditioned darkness for the past 93 days.

Fox stared at the tiny green lights wondering if the supercomputer had an unknown vulnerability—or had one of the technicians made a mistake.

His bodyguards maintained a tight perimeter around him as he stepped across the compartment toward Mr. Bradmore, his cloaking project team leader. "Prepare to shut it down, Bradmore," Fox said with an angry sigh.

"Yes, sir," Bradmore replied, and raised his voice so everyone in the compartment could hear. "Prepare for shut down."

They stepped over to the 3-D display. Bradmore removed a key from his pants pocket and slid it into a keyhole on a panel covered with dials and glowing green lights. On a touchscreen, he entered his user-ID and password.

The green lights blinked and then turned a steady yellow.

"TenRay report," Bradmore ordered.

"Null spectrum," a tech shouted back.

"Video?"

"Cameras idle, sir."

"Radar and sonar?" Bradmore shouted.

"Minimum capacity, sir."

"Holograph lasers?"

"Ready to go offline, sir."

Fox slid his key in, then entered his user-ID and password, and watched the yellow lights switch to a steady red.

A subtle hum that had filled the compartment for the past few months, a noise nobody seemed to notice anymore, wound down until an awkward silence filled the entire space.

The game of cat and mouse between the Nimitz and the Hayward was over, but Fox's mind burned with the question: How did they find us after only 93 days?

* * *

Cryptographers, intelligence analysts, meteorologists and pilots sat around a big Mahogany table strewn with coffee cups and tablet computers.

"Attention on deck," someone yelled.

Everyone leaped to their feet and stood at attention.

"As you were." Fox sat and his marine guards took their places, standing at ease behind his chair.

A tall, thin lieutenant with short black hair and gold wire-framed glasses stood at the far end of the compartment. He'd come over on the helicopter from the Hayward to brief Fox and his team.

Surprised at seeing none of the Hayward's senior officers, Fox made a mental note to inquire about that.

"Well," he said to the Hayward's lieutenant, "Tell us how you found us."

"We used satellites to search for the unique wake the Nimitz leaves on the water's surface," the lieutenant explained.

Mr. Bradmore bolted forward in his chair, put his big elbows on the table and said, "The rules banned the use of satellite cameras." One of his hands curled into a fist the size of a softball while the other wrapped around it as if he was going to hurl a fast pitch at the scrawny lieutenant.

"Your wake is a unique fingerprint, and satellite cameras enabled us to find it," the lieutenant replied.

"I'm crying foul," Bradmore objected.

"You can file a complaint with the Pentagon planning team," the lieutenant shot back, "but I think you should consider your mission a success—"

"A success?" Bradmore was incredulous.

"Mr. Bradmore, I share your objections," Fox said, "but, let's discuss it later."

Bradmore sat back and crossed his muscular arms. "The mission parameters clearly stated the Hayward could use technology only available to other nations," he said, "not US satellites."

"That's not how we read the rules," the lieutenant quipped.

One of the recon pilots chimed in, "We'll never be able to safely cloak this ship from US satellites."

Fox thought about how he was going to shut down this lively dialog without deflating the team's enthusiasm.

"Every day we took a billion pictures of the ocean's surface," the lieutenant explained. "Then we fed all the pictures into a pattern recognition software package that searched for every ship's wake."

It dawned on Fox that the Hayward's senior officers had skipped this briefing to avoid the conversation that was about to happen. Everyone knew, but no one wanted to admit, that there was only one way to cover the Nimitz's wake from satellite cameras. As the lieutenant spoke, a bubble of unease swelled until one of the analysts finally said, "The only way to cover our wake is to put a mirage projector on our stern."

"I appreciate the enthusiasm," Fox glared at everyone around the table, "however, we will not have this discussion now."

"Ninety-three days is a long time to hide from the Hayward," the lieutenant continued. "We had technicians inspecting pictures of every wake across Southeast Asia. They searched for a picture of a wake without a ship, and most of the time we had no idea where you were."

"The Russians and Chinese don't have access to US satellites," Bradmore fired another objection and turned toward Fox. "So why should the Hayward?"

Fox looked at Bradmore's piercing eyes and big hands. Voicing the groups' concerns, he was leading with courage and hedging against the installation of a mirage projector on the Nimitz's stern.

"I appreciate the question," Fox said, "but please, let's have this conversation after this briefing."

"To make the TenRay cloaking system a success," Bradmore said, "the Hayward must be banned from using satellite cameras."

"Agreed." Fox's patience began to ebb. "As I indicated, we will discuss this in another meeting."

"Sir," Bradmore said, his voice bold with concern, "the only way to prevent overhead cameras from seeing our wake is to install a mirage projector on our fantail."

Every person at the table nodded in agreement.

"Is that so, Mr. Bradmore?" Fox gave up his effort to prevent this confrontation.

With a thin layer of nervous perspiration forming on his brow, Bradmore pushed ahead. "A mirage projector will generate unstable levels of static electricity—"

"Are you worried about static?" Fox interrupted.

"Yes, I am," Bradmore said, "as we all should be."

"We will begin another cloaking exercise in a few days," Fox said. "Therefore we should not allow him," Fox pointed at the Hayward's lieutenant, "to hear us discussing our technology options. Do you understand, Mr. Bradmore?"

"Yes, sir," Bradmore conceded.

"Please continue," Fox told the lieutenant as he set his mind to figuring out how he would focus Bradmore's passion and creativity. Fox decided he'd get to know Bradmore a lot better in the next couple of days.

The cloaking system's success meant unprecedented warfighting advantages for the US Navy, but for Fox personally it meant admiral's stars on his collars and a plum executive position at the TenRay Corporation after he retired from the Navy in about a year.

Before adjourning, Fox cleared his throat and said, "Mr. Bradmore, draft a memo listing your concerns, and we'll discuss it before sending it to the exercise planners at the Pentagon."

CHAPTER FOUR – Day 1

"This better be important, Sternz," Captain Brandt growled, as he stepped awkwardly away from Seaman Nikki Thompson, who scrambled to button her blouse.

Commander Sternz averted her gaze and studied a portrait of an old sea captain hanging on the wall. She wished she'd knocked before bursting into Brandt's office.

The door opened and closed as Nikki Thompson, Brandt's personal executive assistant, slipped out.

Rattled and blushing, Sternz took the seat across from him. Part of the problem, Sternz knew, was that Thompson styled her hair, wore cosmetics and a push-up bra. She herself, pulled her hair back in a tight bun, flattened her breasts with a sports bra and never put on makeup at sea. Glamorizing herself was unfair, she reasoned, because it caused sexual frustrations for the male sailors.

Brandt's desktop looked like an acre of lacquered hardwood stretching between them.

"A shipping container crushed a man in the hangar today. We put him in the morgue and—"

"Not another missing corpse," Brandt interrupted.

Sternz nodded.

"Dammit!" He stood and pounded a meaty fist on his desk. Short-sleeves exposed old tattoos on his brawny forearms; a faded hula girl on the right and a tiger on the left; markings from years as an enlisted man. "That's three, Sternz!"

"Correct, sir." She prepared for a brutal reprimand.

"Are you certain this one is missing?"

"We locked him in the morgue an hour ago and now we can't find him—"

"Shit!" Brandt sat down. His taciturn face concealed a mind methodically tracking the paper trail he'd created to cover up the first two missing bodies.

*   *   *

Donna Grogan, a petite brunette from Lawrence, Kansas, died of internal bleeding after she drove her forklift into an open elevator shaft while moving a pallet stacked with five-gallon buckets of imitation maple syrup. The buckets fell 35 feet to the bottom of the shaft and burst open, creating a sticky mess. The forklift flipped over, and Grogan fell out of her operator's seat. The buckets broke her fall, but the forklift crushed her against the elevator's mechanical equipment. In the medical department, they pronounced her dead, zipped her inside a body bag and stuck her in the morgue. A few hours later, an autopsy team, intent on cleaning the maple syrup off her, found the drawer empty. A frantic search couldn't locate her body.

A few days later, Mr. Keef, an undercover detective from the Naval Criminal Investigative Service (NCIS) arrived to conduct a secret investigation. He posed as a medical inspector and proceeded to examine computer records, interview medical staff and tour the department spaces, including the morgue. He found nothing amiss. The phrase "lost at sea" went into the report, and the case remained open with Mr. Keef assigned to stay on board and secretly investigate.

Sternz speculated that a man or a group of men took Grogan's corpse from the Morgue to perpetrate an unspeakable perversion. Perhaps they planned to return her body but someone discovered it missing. With their prank gone awry, they likely slipped her remains overboard—an unceremonious burial at sea.

About a month later, several weeks after the official cloaking exercise started, Larry Burns died of a heart attack while pulling a pan of rolls from an oven in the ship's bakery. And several hours later, his body inexplicably vanished from the morgue. At that point, even though she had no proof, Sternz decided there was a necrophiliac, a cannibal or some other psychopath loose among the crew. Her suspicions ran to every member of her medical staff. She shivered when she imagined what might have happened to the corpses.

"What about the next of kin?" Sternz asked.

"You keep track of the bodies," Brandt replied. "I'll keep track of the paperwork."

Brandt, a master of the Navy's myriad miles of red tape, had ordered Nikki Thompson to take dictation while he fabricated the story of Donna Grogan's disappearance. "High seas during a hurricane, 800 nautical miles west of Hawaii, washed your daughter over the side," Brandt had said while Nikki Thompson typed, "and after an extensive search and rescue effort, we were unable to recover her body." He included instructions to print the letter on fine cotton bond paper, stamped with the United States Navy's seal in color foil. He sent along orders for officers in crisp dress uniform to hand deliver the letter to Grogan's parents in Kansas. That communication had left the ship right before the 93-day cloaking exercise began.

To Larry Burns' wife in San Diego, Brandt tactfully explained, "Lawrence died of smoke inhalation while valiantly attempting to rescue a shipmate during a fire in the galley. In accordance with the instructions in his service record," Brandt lied again, "Lawrence received high honors before his burial at sea."

Brandt took a big step toward softening the bad news and allaying suspicion when he had Nikki Thompson backdate Serviceman's Group Life Insurance policies showing that Grogan and Burns had increased their coverage to $1,000,000; the maximum available to enlisted personnel. Nikki prepared the policy changes; Brandt signed them and sent them to the Pentagon with the death reports.

Sternz didn't dare ask how Brandt planned to prevent a congressional inquiry. She knew that the ship's commanding officer, Captain Fox, had delegated administrative and disciplinary control over the crew to Brandt, and she knew he could hide the truth with a little administrative sleight of hand.

* * *

Now, with the cloaking exercise paused, message traffic started flowing again. Brandt would soon find out if the next of kin had made an official inquiry, but he hoped that a check for a million bucks would be salve enough to silence their suspicions.

Although Sternz distrusted Brandt, she had no time to waste with his scheming behavior or his unpredictable shifts between roaring anger and icy calm. Although she had a department to run, she still wondered if he informed Captain Fox about the two missing bodies—now three she reminded herself.

When he glared at her, she lowered her gaze, but she knew that behind his cold blue eyes, his brain calculated the intricacies of a heartless scheme.

"What's the missing dead man's name?" he asked.

"Stanley Comello," she replied.

"Send over Stanley Comello's personal belongings," Brandt ordered. "I'll see that everything is handled appropriately."

"Will you notify NCIS?" Sternz asked, suspicious about the investigator left behind after Grogan vanished.

Brandt rounded his desk in two strides and got in Sternz's face. "For Christ's sake," he snapped, "NCIS is why good men like me serve alongside girls and queers." He snatched a pack of Parliament off his desk and lit up. "I'll handle this my damn self!"

Even though policy called for her to bring serious problems to him, this third moral compromise made her jaw clench and tightened the muscles in her back like ropes. She worried that simply following the Navy's process wouldn't provide her with legal cover if a scandal erupted.

"When we get stateside," Brandt consoled her, "my man in Washington will get you an operating table anywhere you want, and he'll do it so your record stays clean."

CHAPTER FIVE – Day 1

During Mr. Keef's illustrious career as a naval investigator, he chased down bar room brawlers, drug smugglers, thieves, sodomites and bigamists.

He was tall, had a remarkably large forehead and a great abdomen atop spindly, preposterously long, skinny legs. A discoloration, something between freckles and liver spots, speckled his skin.

Any time a superior officer pressed him to explain the particulars of a case, which happened frequently in his line of work, he exhibited a ponderousness that rendered him unconvincing. In the back of his mind, he had ideas, but when asked pointed questions, his lips parted to reveal straight rows of unusually large, white teeth between thick, mottled jowls, and his eyes opened so wide his forehead corrugated. This facial distortion happened while thoughts traveled from his brain, through a low-bandwidth bundle of nerves to the back of his mouth where they converted into words that he slowly enunciated in a folksy Texas twang.

* * *

Mr. Keef had come aboard the Nimitz to investigate the disappearance of Donna Grogan's body. After the initial investigation came up clueless, Keef received orders to continue looking into the mystery of the missing dead girl covered in imitation maple syrup.

Keef reported directly to Captain Brandt.

During the past three miserable months, he scrutinized every serious crime. He searched hundreds of lockers, and interrogated everyone sentenced to brig time. Fancying himself a hard-boiled detective, he'd lock a suspect in a dimly lit compartment and leave them to stew for half an hour before bursting in, turning on a bright overhead light and assaulting the individual with a barrage of questions. When the interrogations got him nowhere, he turned to eavesdropping in the galley, in living quarters, in passageways. He caught thieves in the supply division. He stumbled upon fire control technicians brewing ale in a rocket launcher. In his evidence locker, he had a confession written by black supremacists, a moldy box of hash-cookies and numerous vials of suspicious looking pills. He took credit for busting a marijuana sales ring working out of the ship's laundry. He was closing in on the ringleader of a ship-wide cigarette and chewing tobacco distribution network. And yet, Keef remained painfully aware that his investigation into the disappearance of Donna Grogan's syrup-covered corpse remained clueless. To make matters worse, Larry Burns had gone missing shortly after Keef came aboard, and he had no clues in that investigation either.

After countless hours poring over dates and times of the disappearances, physical characteristics and causes of death, Keef developed a tentative criminal profile. His suspect was crazy enough to snatch a corpse from the morgue and calculating enough to pull it off more than once. Accusations of occult activity, cannibalism or morbid fetishes were likely correct, but years of investigating sailors' most abhorrent predilections taught Keef not to speculate on motives until he'd discovered some clues, and to his severe disadvantage in this case, there simply were no clues.

While tracking leads for three months, Keef fell into a routine where he woke up around 0930, ate breakfast until 1100 and stopped in at the Master at Arms (MAA) office to check the activity blotter before lunch.

* * *

Keef's brow furrowed as his thoughts made their way down from his brain to his mouth.

Brandt stood behind his desk, cutting Keef to bits with his razor tongue and burning holes in him with his icy stare. "I'm tired of hearing you don't have any evidence—"

"Well, I reckon this case," Keef interrupted, "it's a one-of-a-kind situation, requires more than a single individual investigator." Keef inhaled and his eyes closed under the strain of speaking and thinking in tandem. "If I had someone to run leads, pull surveillance and like that, I reckon—"

"A necrophiliac or a cult of devil worshippers is loose aboard my ship!" Exhaled smoke punctuated Brandt's speech. "If you were competent you'd have caught this freak and I'd have 'em locked in the brig."

"I reckon that's accurate, sir," Keef said.

"Keep your ears open because this monster will be talking backwards," Brandt blustered.

"I remain ever vigilant, sir."

"And you're watching for anyone with a dead body slung over their shoulder, right?"

"Absolutely." Keef detected a bit of the criminal element in the old man. "Sir, I'm fixin' to get back to work about now. Beg your pardon, but may I be dismissed?"

"Not so fast." Brandt dropped a coil-bound report on his desk. "This says someone is sabotaging engines in the Stinger squadron."

"Sabotage?" Keef was ignorant on jet engines, but a sabotage allegation got his attention.

"Yes," Brandt said gloomily. "Somebody's tossing bits of steel down the aircraft intake ducts, tearing up jet engines."

"A little bitty piece of steel wrecks a jet engine?" Keef couldn't believe it.

"Yes, it does." Brandt pinched the bridge of his nose.

"But a jet can fly through a flock of birds and spit out feathers," Keef said.

"Birds are soft," Brandt speculated, "but a nut or bolt is hard—it ruins the whole engine, costs the Navy millions of damn dollars." A headache pulsed across Brandt's forehead. "Just read the damn report!"

"I reckon if they put a screen over them intake ducts it would solve this here problem," Keef said.

"I'm not asking you to redesign military aircraft," Brandt said. "First, read this report and then go see Commander Aronson, the Stinger commanding officer. Tell him I sent you."

"What am I gonna do for him?" Keef asked.

"With your investigation into the medical department going nowhere it's time you earned your keep around here."

A dreadful funk came over Keef and left him feeling an acute need to solve the missing-body mystery, get off this ship and away from Brandt. "Sir," he said, "my assignment is to investigate the medical department, not—"

"You work for me," Brandt snapped.

"But, sir, I've been—"

"You help the Stinger squadron figure out who's sabotaging their airplanes."

"But, sir, as I—"

"I don't care what you—" Brandt pinched the bridge of his nose and pointed to the door. "Get out, Keef," he said. "Just, get the fuck out."

CHAPTER SIX – Day 1

    The Nimitz's anchor chain lockers are steel wells, each 12 feet wide and 59 feet deep, located far forward in the bow of the ship and slightly inboard. While underway, a dogpile of heavy gauge steel chain sits piled helter skelter in both locker bottoms. Deep in the port chain locker, three sailors sat on a scrap of plywood teetering atop the tangle of 300-pound links.

    The ship rode on gently rolling swells.

    Many years prior, a sailor, whom none of those present ever knew, carved a pentagram into the plywood scrap, and since then it served as an altar for many satanic services. That night a black candle burned at the center of the pentagram. It fizzed and dripped and added more wax to the dribbles already hardened there. The flickering flame cast frightful shadows of the three young men inside the deep steel well. Hanging above them, the chain creaked and swayed as the ship forged across the rolling ocean.

    The men held hands in a circle and chanted.

    "In the name of our ruler, Satan, we call the dark forces of evil. Rise from the depths. Open the gates of hell. Come forth and answer to your names. Oh hear your names."

    Danny Jenks whispered, "Baphomet."

    Darnell Ratcomb whispered, "Diabolus."

    Grady Dutro, a novice Satanist, whispered, "Nergo."

    "You idiot," Danny Jenks blurted and tore his black hood back. "It's not Nergo! It's Nergal, Ner-gal, not Ner-go. Get it right, dumbass!"

    Grady Dutro cowered.

    "It's about good and evil, Grady," Danny Jenks said. His pimply complexion shone in the candlelight. "God and Satan are locked in combat and you gotta pick a side."

    Jenks restarted his rhythmic chanting, trying to heighten his awareness, attempting to achieve the familiar hallucinatory state of demonic possession, but no matter how ardently he concentrated, no matter how hard he tried to detach himself from his immediate surroundings, Grady's trembling hand distracted him.

Grady gazed at the flickering candle and listened to Jenks and Ratcomb chanting. He tried to calm down but couldn't stop his hands from shaking.

The squabbling didn't faze Darnell Ratcomb. As he chanted incantations, a green luminescence swirled around him.

"I am prepared to meet the deathless ones," Darnell whispered. He floated among sparkling particles in empty space. "Clear my eyes, Satan," he whispered. A yellow beam passed through the murk and vanished. Another yellow beam shot past like a flashlight searching. Something rubbed against Darnell's leg. "Reveal mysteries to me, Satan," he whispered.

At the sound of Darnell still chanting, Danny Jenks looked under his hood and saw only the whites of his eyes. Then he glared at Grady and said, "You're holding me back, you jerk!"

In the blurry darkness, Darnell saw orange and black fish sliding past him. Their yellow eyes glowed. Their slippery scales rubbed his legs.

"I ain't risking brig time to sit in this hole mumbling at a candle, you pussy!" Danny Jenks fumed.

"I'm trying," Grady whispered, "but it's scary."

Darnell Ratcomb touched one of the slime-coated fish as it swam past. He marveled at its bright orange and black stripes. Instantly, squirming curlicue microbes appeared on his finger and burrowed beneath his skin. Quickly, it spread to the back of his hand and up his wrist.

"Release me from your grip," Darnell demanded. "Return me to the realm of life."

Danny Jenks put his ear to Darnell's hood.

"Release me from your grip," Darnell mumbled.

"Holy fuck!" Jenks knew immediately that Darnell was stuck in some bad shit. "Get out of it, man," Jenks bawled, trying to break the spell. "Get out of there, Darnell!"

Darnell's pupils rolled down. He blinked and gasped.

"Shit," Jenks exclaimed. He grabbed Grady Dutro around the neck with one hand and slapped him hard across the face with the other. "You held me back, you pussy!"

*   *   *

While eating pizza in the galley, Danny Jenks asked Darnell Ratcomb, "Did you see them same orange and black fish again?"

"I touched one," Darnell said.

"I didn't see shit because Grady held me back."

Darnell stared at his fingers where he'd touched that fish.

"We should make a sacrifice of that punk," Jenks said.

Darnell dropped his pizza on a paper plate. "What the fuck is this?" He started scratching the back of his hand.

"What the hell?" Jenks asked at the sight of bumps on Darnell's dark skin.

"That fish did some shit to my arm."

PART II

THE STINGERS

CHAPTER SEVEN – Day 2

Chief Crenki put down the day's thirteenth mug of black coffee, held a radio to the side of his grizzled face and barked, "Are you telling me Terrance McDaniels left the cockpit open on three zero seven and we just steamed under a raincloud?"

"Roger, chief, this aircraft is all fucked up," a technician said through static. "Most of the electronics gear in the cockpit is wet and has to be replaced before it can fly again, so we're taking this bird down to the hangar right now."

"Dammit!" Crenki slammed the radio down on his desk and grabbed the phone. He hit speed dial for the line shack with a trembling finger.

"What do you want?" a raspy voice answered.

"Identify yourself," Crenki demanded.

"Danny Jenks, now identify your-damn-self!"

"This is Chief Crenki!" He knew Jenks, a shitbird in the Stinger line shack. Jenks joined the squadron a couple years ago, a newly minted electronics tech, but got into a scandal and they shit-canned him to the line shack.

"Send McDaniels to see me right now," Crenki ordered.

"Gotta find him," Jenks said.

"Well, go find him," Crenki said.

Danny Jenks, a thin, tall 20-year-old with a sharp jaw and a bad haircut, cursed the oily jet exhaust that made his face break out with tiny pimples. He didn't want to see McDaniels because he owed McDaniels money.

"Who doesn't owe that hay-bailer money?" Jenks wondered as he looked at a whiteboard showing the location of each Stinger aircraft. He read, "McDaniels 309 hangar" scribbled in black Sharpie. "Three oh nine?" He could've sworn Crenki said 307.

In an uncharacteristically conscientious gesture, Jenks called Crenki back.

"You want Terrance McDaniels, right?" Jenks asked.

"Correct, send him to me on the double."

"Whatever you say." Jenks exited the line shack—a cramped steel compartment under the flight deck where the Stinger line crew kept tiedown chains.

At the top of the ladder, Jenks grabbed the railings and leaped so high his knees hit his chest and he slid on his hands down to the next level. The soles of his steel-toed boots slapped the metal deck. In one fluid move, he took two quick steps to the top of the next ladder and threw himself down again. He knew the safety rule required three points of contact—two hands and one foot at all times—while descending ladders, but he didn't give a shit.

* * *

Danny Jenks could have had good grades in high school, if he wanted, but he played X-Box and never turned in homework. His apathy wasn't due to a lack of intellectual curiosity, but the result of a shitty home life. He'd never met his father and his mother introduced him to a new roughneck boyfriend every few weeks—the monthly man of her dreams. One gave Danny a fat lip, black eye combo when he woke up and caught Danny stealing coins from his pants pocket. That soured Danny on being a tough guy and taught him that the main problem with stealing was getting caught.

After earning the highest military entry exam scores his recruiter had ever seen, Jenks left home without even saying goodbye to his mother. After boot camp, he attended aviation armament systems training. Back then, he wore a crewcut, starched his shirts and polished his boots. His interest in weapons systems went beyond the Navy's electronics curriculum. Sure, he studied the textbooks, but then he read graphic sci-fi and horror novels, before turning his attention to defense contractor magazines where he read about particle beams and rail guns. He loved the technical specs, color photos and diagrams. He thought he understood it just fine, but the fiction and the military technology mixed up in his head, and he started believing there were weapons systems engineers hiding in underground labs, plotting the end of the world, like bad guys in a special edition Marvel Comic book.

About a month after arriving at the Stinger squadron, Lieutenant Gould approached Jenks. "You know everything about the Hornet's armament systems," Gould began, "so you're a perfect candidate for a special assignment."

For the first time in his life, Jenks felt wanted.

Gould said the Stingers had an elite weapons loading team, "just in case we're called on to carry out a nuclear strike."

They sent him to a nuclear weapons training on Nevada's high desert, where brown mountains rose above the sage-dotted plateau. Nine hours a day for 30 days, Jenks and a small group of other sailors studied nuke weapons loading, arming, circuitry and trigger mechanisms. The instructors taught with classified textbooks, simulation software and mock-up missiles. It fascinated Jenks that a garbage-can-sized device could incinerate a densely populated urban area.

* * *

In the cavernous hangar, a breeze mingled the industrial odors of polyurethane paint, jet fuel and grease. Yellow lights overhead cast shadows under jet wings. Pneumatic wrenches and airbrushes, wielded by overall-clad mechanics, clattered and hissed.

A tow tractor clamped to the nose wheel of Stinger 309 and a gang of deckapes scrambled around, pulling wheel chocks and unsnapping tiedown chains. Terrance McDaniels sat in the cockpit, riding the brakes.

"Cranky wants your ass," Jenks shouted.

"What for?" Terrance asked, but a siren whooped as the aircraft elevator lowered on dozens of greasy cables. The tow tractor pushed 309 onto the elevator, where the deckapes chocked the wheels and chained it to the black metal grid.

Terrance climbed down and asked. "What's Cranky want?"

"I don't know," Jenks replied, "but he's pissed."

Something sour kicked the back of Terrance's nostrils, and he wondered if it was Jenks' breath or his filthy body. Probably both. Terrance exhaled sharply and walked to the edge of the elevator. A refreshing breeze blew against his face. Whitecapped waves covered the sea, clear to the horizon.

The siren whooped as the elevator rose smoothly and became a seamless part of the flight deck. Terrance kept his head turning so he always knew what was going on around him. He'd seen thousands of jets scream in out of the sky and try to catch an arresting wire at 200 miles per hour, but miss it and bolt back into the sky with afterburners spitting 50-foot licks of flame. Helicopters and prop planes took off and landed constantly. The crew regularly serviced aircraft with potentially explosive liquid oxygen and flammable fuel. They prepared jets for missions by loading them with bombs and rockets. Adding to the danger there was no railing on the flight deck.

Jenks and McDaniels pulled sound attenuators on their helmets down to protect their ears. Terrance lowered his goggles.

Just in case anyone fell in the water, there was always a chopper hovering nearby the ship, ready to swoop in for a rescue.

A mechanic in the cockpit of an A-6 Prowler pushed the throttles forward, and the aircraft roared like thunder.

Terrance put his mouth to Jenks' right ear cover and said, "You owe me money."

Jenks wanted to knock McDaniels to the deck, but knew the big farm boy wouldn't go down easy. "I'll give you a few bucks on payday," Jenks said.

Terrance pulled a tiny notebook from his back pocket, flipped it open and checked his figures. "You owe me four hundred and seventy-five dollars."

"Don't worry," Jenks said. "I'll get it to you."

"Watch my bird while I go see Cranky," Terrance said.

"Sure," Jenks replied, "I'll keep an eye on your bird."

CHAPTER EIGHT – Day 2

On her 19th birthday, Nikki Thompson raised her right hand at a recruiting station in Detroit and swore to defend the United States while serving in the US Navy; then she flew to sunny San Diego for eight weeks of boot camp and two weeks of HR data systems training. After that the Navy sent her to the Philippines to meet her ship—the USS Nimitz.

When Nikki arrived at the Manila International Airport, the place was a zoo. Throngs of people waiting in lines and hordes of hawkers selling flowers, cigarettes, candy, bottled water and pre-paid phone cards, none of which Nikki wanted. She took a bus to the waterfront where the Nimitz sat tied to a long concrete pier.

Pride and intimidation compressed like a powerful spring inside her chest as she trudged up the gangway with her overloaded seabag strapped on her back. Overwhelmed by the sheer size of the ship looming above her, she feared she wouldn't be able to speak when she reached the quarterdeck. The superstructure towered into the sky. Ropes as thick as her leg crisscrossed from the ship to the pier. Tied off to big metal bits, the ropes kept the ship from floating away. In Detroit, she'd seen plenty of mile-long factories, but never this much steel. The ship hummed and steam hissed and water gurgled from pipes along its metal sides. Sailors on the pier looked tough, standing around in tight T-shirts, exposing tattooed arms. Handsome officers in crisp uniforms, some with gold bars on their shoulder boards and hats.

These were fleet sailors.

Red, white and blue bunting and bright white ropes tied in elaborate knots festooned the top of the gangway. Under the glaring sun, a man in dress whites stood behind a podium staring at her.

"Nikki Thompson, reporting for duty, sir," she chirped. But the man just stood there, and she knew she'd forgotten an official gesture or a required phrase. Embarrassed, she started digging in her purse for her orders.

"Salute the ensign," the man said with a wink.

Then she remembered her boot camp training and popped to attention. Her right hand rose in a crisp salute, she pivoted to face the aft end of the ship where she knew the American Flag was flying and proudly said, "Request permission to come aboard, sir."

"Permission granted," the man replied.

* * *

Inside the ship, like an ant underground, Nikki made her way through cramped passageways, among pilots in flight suits and dress uniforms, sailors in colored jerseys, and hunky marines in tan camouflage and shiny combat boots. She never knew what deck she was on or if she was heading forward or aft while trying to find her way around. She figured out how to get to the galley for meals and to her tiny cubicle in the ship's personnel office, but that was it.

On her second day aboard, a shrill whistle blew from a speaker above her desk. Startled, she jumped to her feet. She listened to an announcement and recognized the phrase "weigh anchor" which meant they were leaving Manila, but the rest of it made no sense and she wondered where they were bound.

The ship barely swayed and it felt like they weren't moving at all. A few days after they'd supposedly left Manila, she discovered a ladder tucked behind a big pipe near the main galley. She climbed it and found an open door to the aircraft hangar. Venturing into the enormous space, she picked her way carefully between strange machines and metal containers stacked to the ceiling. Wandering around, she checked out the airplanes, impressed by the sleek lines along their cockpits and wings. The strong smell of grease and spray paint dissipated as a fresh ocean breeze blew in. She walked over to the oblong opening in the side of the ship, stood near the cable railing and gazed at the sun shining on the ocean. Surprised at how the water whisked by so fast, she felt the deck grumble in the soles of her shoes. Sunlight on the silky waves worked like a tranquilizer. The clatter of power tools and humming air compressors faded in the background as she listened to the ship plow a splashing wake through the sea.

An authoritative male voice boomed from speakers on the flight deck above. She heard "make a ready deck" and "stand by to land aircraft." A SHRIEK, followed by a CLANK and a BANG and a jet engine growling so loud she plugged her fingers in her ears, reminded her that there really was an airport on top of the ship.

* * *

After three weeks at sea, life aboard stopped revealing little surprises, and Nikki Thompson's days fell into tight predictable routines, each an exact duplicate of the one before. The day, the month and the time of year had no significance. She was bored. Each day she woke up, got dressed, ate breakfast in the galley, and at 7:15 she sat down at her desk, in her cubicle at the back of the ship's administrative office, staring at her computer screen. She quickly figured out how to complete all her data entry, scanning and filing. She asked her supervisor for more work, hoping for something interesting, but he piled on payroll corrections and promotion processing, which she quickly mastered. She started taking two-hour lunches and working out in the gym, where she did crunches and curls and hit the rowing machine. One night in the library, looking at a world map on the wall, she figured if the rowing machine were an actual rowboat, she could have stroked her way from Manila all the way to Sri Lanka by now. She tried reading to pass the time but romance novels pricked her libido. She started flirting with guys and that led to an even more depressing level of frustration, because none of them could pull off anything even remotely resembling a date. A technician propositioned her with a hook-up in a ventilation duct, and she seriously considered it. That's what it came down to, because there was no privacy. People were jammed into every inch of the ship. To make matters worse, any public display of affection could bring disciplinary action. She worked in the HR department, after all, and they'd drilled it into her during human resources training in San Diego that she had to be a role model of the Navy's many policies, especially the one that stipulated no sex at sea.

* * *

One day her supervisor invited her to a department staff meeting. She sat close to the head of a long wooden table and waited for the meeting to start. Suddenly a door opened and someone shouted "Attention on deck!" Everyone jumped to their feet and stood up straight. She'd learned about this in boot camp, but it was exciting to do it for real.

Captain Samuel Brandt stepped to the front of the room.

His confidence and seriousness were palpable, especially the way he told everyone to sit down, but he stayed standing throughout the meeting. He wore khaki pants and a short-sleeved shirt, shined shoes and captain's eagles on his collar points. Nikki thought he looked like a total stud with short-cropped hair and a rugged, clean-shaven face. A crafty kind of intelligence sparkled in his eyes. He kept everyone keyed up, like a trigger cocked and ready to shoot, because nobody knew when he'd fire a question at them. The old-school tattoos on his brawny forearms—a savage tiger tearing the skin on one and a hula girl shaking her hips on the other—were so unlike the nerdy instructors who taught the data entry classes back in San Diego. Everything about him, from his staccato questions and orders, to his occasional irreverent snip of a joke, turned her on.

She'd never met a man whose presence intimidated younger, stronger guys—literally made them jump to attention when he entered the room. The power oozing off Captain Brandt had her daydreaming about ways she might get close to him.

* * *

Brandt saw Nikki the second he entered the room. She somehow made her uniform look like a slutty Halloween costume. He liked that blend of youthful innocence and Rite Aid sophistication. He wanted her.

At the end of the meeting, as everyone filed out, he startled her by gently grabbing her forearm and whispering, "Excuse me, miss. I'm Captain Samuel Brandt, the ship's executive officer. Please introduce yourself."

Nikki's heart banged out a series of irregular beats. His

warm hand lingered gently on her forearm and his causal grip caused her heart to settle into a slow steady throb. She heard words blabbering from her mouth as she introduced herself. At some point she stopped speaking, unaware of what she'd actually said, and realized they hadn't broken eye contact and neither of them wanted to. His cool blue gaze melted wonderfully into her hazel green eyes.

He licked his lips and stared at her smooth neck and silky blonde hair—inching closer to her every few seconds, all the while asking about her training, and seeming unusually interested in what they were teaching back in San Diego.

Her mind relinquished decision-making power to her burning body when she realized that they were alone in the compartment.

He continued to punctuate his interest in what she was saying by occasionally touching her forearm or shoulder.

She caught a faint whiff of manly body wash from his open shirt collar.

CHAPTER NINE – Day 2

As Chief Crenki berated Terrance McDaniels in the narrow passageway outside the Stinger maintenance office, Terrance studied Crenki's whiskered face. The stink of cigarettes—like dried-out dog shit moistened with cold coffee—blasted through Crenki's yellow teeth and drilled deep into the back of Terrance McDaniels' nasal passages. Crenki had been trying unsuccessfully to nail McDaniels for a long time, but this rain-in-the-cockpit disaster gave him license to rip McDaniels a new asshole. The over-caffeinated circuits in Crenki's brain fired excitedly.

"I know you don't want to pay for the black boxes that were ruined when you left the cockpit open, although we both know you can afford it with all the money you make." Crenki hinted that he knew about McDaniels' sales and loan sharking operation.

Terrance watched a vein in Crenki's forehead wiggle like an earthworm under a rock.

Crenki searched McDaniels' eyes for any sign of guilt. "Sometimes I wonder if you're the scumbag who's sabotaging my engines."

That very morning an engineer in the jet repair shop gave Crenki a report that proved someone had placed bits of stainless steel in six aircraft intake ducts, and when those engines sucked them in, it caused severe damage to their compressor blades and rendered them useless. Those incidents grounded all six aircraft while Stinger mechanics replaced their engines.

Although Crenki enjoyed tearing into McDaniels for leaving his cockpit open, a vague uncertainty lingered, because McDaniels had never botched anything this badly. Nevertheless, Crenki laid into McDaniels, trying to provoke insubordination, maybe nail him with dereliction of duty. Crenki wanted McDaniels confined to his bunk during the upcoming equator-crossing hazing ritual. Nothing infuriated him more than the thought of having his ass paddled by Terrance McDaniels when the Nimitz crossed the equator in the next couple of weeks. Blood boiled in Crenki's stomach. During 20 years in the Navy, he hadn't crossed the equator aboard ship, and therefore hadn't crawled before King Neptune's Royal Order of the Deep and therefore couldn't call himself a Trusty Shellback.

"Exactly what do you have to say for yourself, McDaniels?" Crenki's growl filled the narrow passageway.

Terrance stared blankly into Crenki's gnarled old face.

"Well, chief, I don't know." Terrance put his fingers to his lips. "You sure you're talking about aircraft three zero seven?"

"Yes, your jet. The one taken down to the hangar after the cockpit got rained in." Death threats rode on Crenki's stare. "And where the hell were you anyway? Probably out peddling contraband when you should have been tending your aircraft?"

Over Crenki's shoulder, Terrance saw Commander Aronson, the Stinger's commanding officer, in flight suit and crash helmet, coming down the passageway. Terrance rolled his shoulders back and put a self-righteous expression on his face.

Crenki thought McDaniels might take a swing. The sensation excited him.

"Well, Chief," Terrance said, trying hard to push one of Crenki's easily accessible self-destruct buttons. "Three zero seven is not my aircraft. Three zero nine is my aircraft, and it's a go on the next launch."

Blood seeped through the ulcerated lining in Crenki's stomach and nerve endings short-circuited in his brain. A torrent of foul language bottlenecked in a vision-fuzzing spark behind his eyeballs. "Do not lie to me, McDaniels. Your Hornet is side number three zero fucking seven."

Terrance exaggerated his Nebraska farm-boy accent. "Chief, I ain't lying. I got three oh nine." And when Crenki opened his mouth to speak, Terrance said, "You got bad information, chief."

"Who is the plane captain on three zero seven?" Crenki snapped his mouth shut, as another electric spark of hot plasma and digestive acids rose into his esophagus.

Terrance cringed at Crenki's stinky breath, and studied his

eyes, now pulsing out of their sockets on detrimentally high blood pressure. Terrance retreated against the bulkhead. "I don't know who's got three zero seven," he lied. Crenki could find out for himself.

Commander Aronson strolled up behind him.

"Chief Crenki, has this man caused a problem?" Aronson asked in an authoritative tone, tempered by years of hearing his underlings call him sir.

Crenki clenched his fists at his sides and turned to Aronson. "Well, uh, McDaniels, or uhm, rather—" Crenki stuttered as he patted McDaniels on the shoulder. "No, sir, uh, one of our cockpits got rained in and, uh, a mechanic told me—"

"Rain in one of our cockpits?" Rage radiated along every nerve in Aronson's body. That very morning he'd met with Captain Brandt to discuss a new engineering report that proved Stinger engines were being sabotaged! "How did a cockpit get rained in?"

"I'm trying to find out, exactly," Crenki stammered, "uh, sir."

"Get to the bottom of this, Crenki, and report back to me." Aronson's stare, like a laser, almost burned holes in Crenki's face. "Sabotage on Stinger engines," Aronson shouted, "and now rain in a cockpit! Unacceptable!"

CHAPTER TEN – Day 2

After being chewed out by Chief Crenki for something he didn't even do, Terrance McDaniels returned to the flight deck.

"So, when you gonna pay me the money you owe?" he asked Danny Jenks.

But Jenks just smirked and slinked off because they both saw Commander Aronson approaching across the flight deck. Aronson walked up to McDaniels and asked gruffly, "Is this Hornet ready to fly?"

"Let's do a walk around and make sure," Terrance said.

Commander Aronson wore combat boots, a green flight suit with the Stinger insignia—a fierce Hornet poised to plant its needle-sharp stinger—and an American flag sewn on the sleeve. The crash helmet's dark visor obscured his eyes, so Terrance could only see his chin, speckled with whiskers.

Circling the aircraft, they checked the engine oil and hydraulic gauges. They examined the tires. At each air intake duct, Terrance crawled down headfirst to inspect for structural integrity and ensure no foreign objects were present.

When running, the engines inhale thousands of cubic feet of air each second. They inject the air with fuel, compress it and ignite it in a series of chambers that creates a constant highly-controlled explosion. The resulting thrust propels the Hornet across the sky at up to 1,500 miles per hour.

With his head and torso jammed inside the duct, Terrance ran his hands over the smooth throat, inspecting for loose rivets and cracks. He burrowed down close to the compressor blades and shined his flashlight on each while spinning the fan slowly. He squinted but didn't see any nicks or cracks. He wondered about his shipmates on the Stinger line division who'd gone down the intake ducts on every engine that had been damaged over the past few months. What had they missed? None of them had found anything unusual, but after each of those aircraft started, something went wrong. Either the engines sucked in a small bit of metal that tore their insides apart, or a foreign object, like a loose nut or bolt was already down inside each engine before it started.

Terrance spun the blender-like fan there in the dim light and recalled a few weeks earlier watching a Stinger Hornet taxi to the steam-powered catapult. Deckhands attached the launch bar and signaled the pilot to push the throttles to full power. He watched in awe as the Hornet's engines roared and flames burst from the afterburners like a dragon breathing fire. Suddenly sparks shot from the jet's exhaust. Something had broken loose. The pilot shut it down, because anyone standing nearby could have been injured or killed if the engine came apart.

"How do they look, McDaniels?" Aronson asked after McDaniels dove both intakes.

"Ready for flight, sir."

A metallic voice announced from the deckedge loudspeakers. "ALL UNNECESSARY PERSONNEL CLEAR THE FLIGHT DECK AND CATWALKS. ALL REMAINING PERSONNEL GET IN THE PROPER FLIGHT DECK UNIFORM. SLEEVES ROLLED DOWN, FLOATATION VESTS, CRANIAL HELMETS, GOGGLES AND CHIN STRAPS SECURELY FASTENED. START THE GO AIRCRAFT."

A moment later the Hornet inhaled a continuous flow of air through its intake ducts and blasted hot exhaust from its tailcones.

With hand signals, McDaniels told Aronson to lower the tailhook and flaps. He checked them and gave Aronson a thumbs-up. Then he stuck his head inside the landing gear wheel well to check the pressure on the hydraulic gauges.

He took off the chains holding the main landing gear to the deck and swung them over his shoulders. Weighted down with 60 pounds, he saluted Aronson and made his way to the catwalk, between taxiing jets and spinning propellers. As they hooked his jet to the catapult, he felt the ship accelerating and shuddering. He stepped down a narrow ladder into the catwalk and entered the ship through a door in the hull. He turned away from the screaming engines, the stifling heat and the crackling sun, as he stepped inside the ship. He did not want to watch his aircraft take off. It had never gone down on the launch, and he did not anticipate it would now.

In the line shack, plane captains sat on metal folding chairs, smoking and carrying on a dozen conversations.

"What're you doing here?" Jenks asked.

"They got Aronson on the catapult now." Terrance said. "There's no way he's going down."

"HEADS UP BEHIND CATAPULT ONE. HORNET SHOOTING SPARKS."

"Shit!" Terrance ran to the catwalk. Several plane captains followed.

Did the Stingers fod another engine?

The directors attached a tow tractor to Terrance's jet and pulled it off the catapult. They parked it in front of the superstructure. Terrance scrambled around chaining it to the deck, and then he lowered the cockpit ladder.

Aronson climbed down. He raised the dark visor, stared hard at Terrance and demanded, "Did you see anything out of place when you went down those intakes?"

"No, sir," Terrance replied.

"Go explain that to Chief Crenki."

Terrance hesitated at the thought of facing Crenki again.

"Move, McDaniels."

*   *   *

"Shit! Another fodded engine," Crenki's screamed. "That's it. Every Stinger is under suspicion." He sucked a big drag that sharpened his cigarette to a glowing orange pencil-point. He gulped scalding black coffee and grinded his molars. "Who the fuck is sabotaging my Hornets?" he demanded as Terrance McDaniels appeared in the doorway.

CHAPTER ELEVEN – Day 2

A broiled T-bone steak and lobster tail, broccoli with melted cheddar and a baked potato slathered with butter and sour cream sat on a plate in front of Mr. Bradmore, sending a delicious, steamy aroma into his face. He wanted to dig in but minded his manners, because Captain Fox, who sat across from him, hadn't touched his utensils yet.

"What are your plans after the Navy?" Fox asked.

"I should give it more thought than I do," Bradmore admitted, "two more years and I can retire."

"So you've been on active duty for eighteen years?" Fox asked.

"Yes. How about you? Any plans after the Navy?"

"I'll be joining the board of directors at TenRay Corporation," Fox said.

With such a big stake in TenRay, Bradmore wondered, how could Fox report to the Pentagon on the system's performance with any objectivity?

When Fox picked up his fork and knife and began sawing into his steak, Bradmore did the same. He chewed, swallowed and attempted to change the subject. "My wife and I have a condo in Chula Vista, she's a teacher there," Bradmore said. "Whatever I do after the Navy, I'll be staying in San Diego."

"What a coincidence," Fox said warmly. "TenRay's headquarters are in National City, right down the road."

"Interesting." Bradmore sensed strings attached to the delicious dinner.

"You know, Mr. Bradmore," Fox said, making eye contact with a quick glance across the table, "after you and I figure out how to make this cloaking system a success, the Navy will purchase millions of dollars' worth of TenRay gear over the next several decades."

54

"Amazing technology," he said.

"Yes it is." Fox put a medium-well piece of steak into his mouth and chewed vigorously.

"Big hurdles to overcome though," Bradmore said.

"The static?" Fox snapped.

Regretting his comment, Bradmore said, "We'll figure it out, the team's working on that risk mitigation plan."

"I'll be candid with you," Fox said. "Your technical skills got you where you are, but they're not going to get you where you want to go."

Bradmore paused with a cheesy broccoli bud halfway to his mouth. Eighteen years in the Navy, and no one had ever spoken to him like that. Sure, he'd had feedback during annual reviews, a few commendations along the way, but he was a working guy; rotating between sea deployments and shore duty. He'd never thought much beyond the work-a-day life, standing watches, managing projects. "What do you mean, sir?" he asked earnestly.

"The static from the mirage projector does present some risk but it's just that—static. Turn it down and tune it out, because I want you to hear a different message now. Can you do that?"

"I'm all ears."

"We'll work out the bugs, trust me, but right now I want you to think about the big picture." Fox sawed into his steak. "You and your wife have children, don't you?"

Thrown by the question, Bradmore asked, "Excuse me?"

"You have kids, right?"

Bradmore didn't see where this was leading, but realized he didn't have time to analyze it. He said, "My son is sixteen and my daughters are nine and seven. How about you?"

"Mine are twenty-eight and thirty-one. Have you thought about how you're going to pay for their college?"

"We've set a little money aside." Bradmore's brow furrowed. "But, it's not enough. I worry about it."

Fox leaned over the table, a sparkle in his eye, and said, "Make the cloaking system a success, and then come work for me at TenRay."

"Seriously?" Bradmore asked, pleasantly surprised.

"Yes." Fox smiled again. "You won't have to worry about

paying for your kids' college."

Bradmore's brain lit up like a Christmas tree. He saw his wife and kids splashing in an in-ground pool. Palm trees and flowering shrubs around a lush green lawn. A brick ranch house with a tiled roof. Through a sliding glass patio door, he saw right through the living room and out a big front window where the San Diego skyline shimmered in the afternoon heat a few miles away. The ocean sparkled in the distance.

Fox and Bradmore stared into each other eyes. Fox chewed and swallowed a mouthful of buttery lobster. "I need you to help me make the TenRay cloaking system a success, Mr. Bradmore."

"I can see that, sir," Bradmore said dreamily. "I see it clearly."

CHAPTER TWELVE – Day 2

Silk boxers and clean pants after a hot shower would have to do, because a splash of cologne was out of the question. That would arouse the suspicion of Terrance's shipmates.

He walked to the library and sat on a wooden chair between the stacks.

Kate studied titles on books lining the shelves, pretending to search for something particular. Hooking up this way had gone according to plan several times. She'd wink and they'd leave the library separately, taking different routes.

Kate's Flying Squad duties included keeping remote medical station 12 ready. In an emergency, like a fire, an attack or a plane crash, station 12 was equipped to provide trauma care.

Kate arrived first and flicked on the red emergency battle lantern. Terrance arrived a moment later and padlocked the door from inside. She folded an operating table down from the bulkhead. Backpacks full of emergency response gear hung on hooks. Several metal drums on the floor crowded the tiny space.

Kate slid onto the padded operating table. Terrance stood between her legs. They kissed in the battle lantern's dim red glow.

The steady hum of machinery rose through the deck.

"You look nice," Kate whispered.

He handed her two foam earplugs.

"I thought you liked me greasy," he said.

They rolled the earplugs between their fingers.

"I like you better cleaned up."

"TIME FOR ALL UNAUTHORIZED PERSONNEL TO CLEAR THE FLIGHT DECK AND CATWALKS," the voice boomed outside, "ALL REMAINING PERSONNEL GET IN THE PROPER FLIGHT DECK UNIFORM—"

Kate pressed the earplugs in. Her hands trembled as she unbuttoned Terrance's shirt.

"—SLEEVES ROLLED DOWN, CRANIAL HELMETS AND GOGGLES PROPERLY FASTENED—" blasted across the darkened deck above.

Terrance's belt buckle jingled in her frantic fingers. Their attempt at slow romance and seductive disrobing abruptly ended.

"—FLOATATION VESTS SECURELY SNAPPED."

Boots clunked in the red-lit darkness.

Clumsily they shed their clothes.

"NOW START ALL THE GO AIRCRAFT. START ALL THE GO AIRCRAFT."

They embraced and kissed with their tongues as jet engines hummed to life a few feet above their heads. The sound exploded like an army of ferocious air compressors. Entire squadrons of jets burned fuel and air furiously. Kate pressed her earplugs in further and lost herself as the blast rose to a static roar.

Catapults, firing after sudden injections of compressed steam, whistled as they shot pilots in their sleek machines into the night sky. Every few seconds another distinguished itself above the howl, as it rose to full power and rocketed from the deck. The compartment shook like a roller coaster on metal tracks.

In the red glow, they kissed and caressed. The steel plates and I-beams around them rang with a colossal CLANG each time a catapult shuttle reached the end of its stroke and launched a jet into the sky.

In nearby compartments, crewmembers who weren't working the launch, sat and listened to the raucous machines. Covered by the roar of launching aircraft, Kate and Terrance made reckless, noisy love.

Afterward, they cuddled on the narrow operating table. The deckedge loudspeaker shattered the silence. "WRAP UP THE CATAPULTS, LAUNCH COMPLETE."

They scrambled to find their clothes.

Kate finished dressing and flipped on the lights.

Terrance pulled up his pants and sat on one of the metal drums to lace his boots. "What are these?" He slapped the top of one of the drums. "Doesn't look like medical supplies."

"Liferafts. They're supposed to attach them to the railing outside." She pointed over her shoulder, toward the flight deck catwalk beyond the door at the end of the passageway.

"Who?" Terrance asked.

"Deck division."

"They have access to this space?" Terrance asked.

"Sure."

"You mean someone might bang on the door while we're in here?"

"That could happen." Kate smiled mischievously. "That's why we lock it from inside."

Terrance almost said they should find somewhere else, but nowhere else existed.

"We have no choice," Kate said.

"Nothing could stop me from being with you, especially the way you wink at me," he said.

"You keep me sane," she said. "I get so bored in the pharmacy, I start hoping for an alarm, even a drill, anything to break the monotony."

"I don't know how you do it. I'm outside breathing fresh air all day."

"I feel like an ant underground," she said.

"Awhile back they sent me to work in the supply department," he said. "I didn't see the sun for two weeks."

"We just sit around gossiping about missing bodies."

Her missing-body stories seemed a lot more serious lately, he thought.

"I don't believe Commander Sternz," she said. "When I told her Stanley Comello's body was gone, her facial expression said it all. She went in her office and came out a minute later and told us flight ops had put Comello on a cargo plane off the ship."

"Maybe they're turning into ghosts," Terrance suggested.

"That's what people are saying. I mean come on," Kate said. "Everybody knew two bodies already disappeared, so they had an eye on the morgue. Nobody took Comello's body. Sternz is hiding something."

CHAPTER THIRTEEN – Day 2

Darnell Ratcomb climbed carefully down the anchor chain into darkness. As he stepped off onto the teetering plywood scrap at the bottom, a match sparked into flame. Danny Jenks lit a candle. Without a word, they pulled their hoods on, joined hands around the candle and began chanting.

"What the hell?" Jenks tore his hood off and looked at the bumps, scratched raw, on Darnell's hands. "That shit better not be contagious." Jenks wiped his hands on his pants.

"It's itchy as hell." Darnell reached over and grabbed Jenks' hands.

"You better see a doctor," Jenks said. "That shit looks like poison ivy."

They began chanting and right away Jenks entered a variant state.

Green serpent-like kelp twisted on the ocean's surface. White foam sizzled on the surging waves. Below, in greenish murk, orange and black striped creatures swam up from the abyss.

"Reveal secrets of the netherworld, almighty Satan." Jenks vision penetrated the murky water.

An orange and black fish the size of a refrigerator darted past—a yellow eye as big as a bowling ball glowed in its profile. Another shot by and another and dozens more in a swarm of orange and black stripes as vibrant as Bengal Tigers sliding by with troubled ease. Thousands of them moved in the same direction, their orange and black sides flickering in shafts of sunlight penetrating from the surface.

"Tigerfish," Jenks whispered.

He marveled at one. It was massive with pulsating lips that opened to reveal jagged teeth set in a powerful jaw—clearly capable of taking off his leg in one bite. That thought scared him, so he chanted for protection, and his vision shifted, revealing frothy whitecaps sizzling on the ocean's rolling surface. Small tigerfish skipped across the waves. Larger ones slid quickly through the depths. The sun was down and Jenks saw the lights of a ship twinkling in the distance. He recognized the Nimitz's flight deck and the towering superstructure. A half-moon glowed against a backdrop of sparkling stars.

He found himself inside the ship walking through a deserted living compartment.

He opened the curtains on one bunk after another but found them all empty. He ran along the passageway, opening and closing doors, and found himself alone. He climbed a ladder and headed toward the anchor chain locker to see if he could spy on himself and Darnell. He imagined meeting himself inside his own satanic ritual, and realized that would be a total mind fuck.

He pushed in behind the anchor chain locker, expecting to see the little hatch, but instead saw a metal door with the words DEAD CREW stenciled on it.

"What's the dead crew?" he wondered aloud.

Grabbing the doorknob without hesitation, he pushed inside, where he found a cramped, fluorescent-lit compartment with a black floor. Small square doors covered one wall. He grabbed a handle and pulled, revealing a long empty drawer. "A morgue," he whispered, slamming the drawer shut and yanking open the next. His anticipation rose at the possibility of seeing a corpse, but disappointment followed as he found each drawer empty. The last drawer wouldn't open. He pulled and pulled. He even braced one foot against the wall, grabbed with both hands and yanked as hard as he could. Finally, he stopped and leaned in close to examine the latch. That's when he heard something rustling. He pressed his ear to the cool, shiny metal.

A dog barked from inside the drawer.

"What the fuck?"

He rapped his knuckles on the drawer and the dog yelped.

He rapped harder and the dog barked louder. It scratched furiously, as if trying to dig through. He stepped back, wondering if the agitated mutt would bite him if it escaped.

A loud bang from inside as it crashed against the door. A dent appeared on the outside. Another crash and a piece of the metal latch clattered on the floor.

A sudden ache in his wrist made Jenks wonder if he'd pounded the door too hard. He glanced at his sleeve, careful not to take his eyes off the drawer, and saw the fabric turning black. A curl of smoke told him his arm was too close to the candle and his sleeve was about to ignite. This was the most realistic trip he'd ever had.

Violently, the thing in there smashed again. The latch rattled loose and the drawer opened a crack.

That mutt's guarding the gateway to hell, he realized. A lean hound with sharp claws, he imagined a choke chain around its neck and teeth capped with silver tips.

"Bad ass," he whispered.

Pain flared in his wrist. The scene flickered.

"Lord and Master protect me." The vision came back into focus. Greasy smoke curled from his sleeve and a red blister formed on his wrist. He knew he might burst into flames if he didn't break away now.

"Bring the fire, Satan!" he squealed as flame seared his arm.

A snarling snout, covered in short black fur, snapped at him through the narrow opening. He grabbed the edge of the door and pulled. "Come on you fucking mutt," he shouted. He didn't care if it devoured him, he wanted to go down into hell and meet the man. But the pain in his wrist and the greasy smoke and burnt hair made the vision flicker. He pulled with all his strength.

In that final second before Darnell Ratcomb slapped him across the face, the metal handle broke off and Jenks dropped it clanging to the floor. The drawer burst open with a BANG. Flames rose from his sleeve. A salacious grin stretched his rat-thin jaw.

A man with saggy jowls like a bulldog lunged out of the drawer and came right at him. Jenks froze in amazement. The dog-faced man burst from the morgue drawer, snapping its sharp teeth in his face.

* * *

"Crazy shit," Darnell Ratcomb said after Jenks told him about seeing the words DEAD CREW on the door and the dog-faced old guy in a locked drawer.

"That mutt was guarding the entrance to hell," Jenks blurted.

But Darnell was too busy scratching the rash on this arm.

CHAPTER FOURTEEN – Day 2

Captain Brandt brushed Nikki's forearm when he leaned over her desk to sign papers. He summoned her to his office several times to explain trivial payroll corrections. He called her around behind his desk, where she had to lean over to see as he pointed to a spreadsheet.

Within a week, he appointed her as his personal assistant. He planned to put her on top of something that required special attention.

One evening he called her to his office and while working late, squeezed in behind his desk, the sexual tension was practically crackling.

She knew it was inappropriate but she didn't care. Life aboard ship was boring and she was hornier than she'd ever been. A minute after he put his hands on her hips and planted a wet kiss on her lips, she unhitched his pants and watched them drop down around his ankles. The delight she experienced at the sight of his cock popping out of his boxers, right in her face, almost overwhelmed her. And, when he sat back in his cushy office chair and she climb on top of him, a warm buzz hummed in her loins, shot through her belly, swirled around her heart, and grounded out like a hot electric spark in her brain. Nikki loved the feeling of Captain Brandt's power pulsing deep inside her. The first few times with him, a new, exciting energy filled her. After each of their special meetings, her skin glowed as she wobbled out of his office.

He called her to his office six times in two-weeks, and each time her crush on him charged with greater intensity. Memories of their bold escapades kept her awake at night in her bunk. And when she dozed off, she dreamed they were driving along a mountain road in a red convertible. They stopped for a picnic of wine and sandwiches on a grassy hillside. While sitting at her desk during boring days, she imagined him in dress uniform, leading her in a waltz at a grand reception. A flowing white dress swirled about her as she floated across a parquet floor, beneath crystal chandeliers, surrounded by a crowd of smiling friends and relatives. She awoke in her bunk at night acutely aware that he was an officer and she was enlisted and that made their tryst illegal; a clear-cut violation of naval regulations and they both knew it.

One afternoon she entered his office, and said, "Hi, Sam," using his name for the first time, but he pressed a finger to her lips.

He pulled her behind his desk, sat in his swivel chair and quickly unbuckled her belt. Moments later, her panties were around her ankles and he had her bent forward over his desk. She grabbed the hard wooden edge, bit her lower lip and groaned as he tried to penetrate her, but she was too dry and he was too rough. She wanted to talk to him, make eye contact, run her hands over his chest and kiss him on the mouth. She knew that would get them both in the mood.

Instead, he sat down, spread her vagina and poked a few times with a wet finger. Then he stood up and forced himself in. She reached around and grabbed the front of his shirt, but he put a big hand on the back of her head and forced her face down on his wooden desk.

In a husky whisper he said, "Don't make a sound."

The violated feeling dissipated after a series of long, steady strokes that slowly built toward an explosive moment. He held her hips at a perfect angle and probed her exquisitely until they both came.

Afterwards, she realized she'd never felt such a wonderful sensation before.

They might have both screamed when they came together, but Brandt couldn't be sure. He reminded himself to stuff something in her mouth, her wadded-up panties perhaps, and bite his tongue next time. He certainly didn't want anyone who happened to be walking by in the passageway outside to overhear cries of unbridled pleasure.

He uncoupled and zipped his pants, fastened his belt and sat in his cushioned chair with a contented sigh.

She turned around while tucking in her shirt and fastening her pants and looked him in the eye. She opened her mouth, but he shushed her again. "Don't ruin it," he said.

"You're dirty." She placed a hand on his brawny forearm, stroking him there, hoping for some lighthearted conversation.

"Go back to work," he said, exhausted, "I'll call you some time ... soon."

* * *

She squirmed in her chair until their sex dried on her thighs and boredom took over again. No breeze, no sunshine, no trees, no sitting on the back step at her mom's house petting the cats, no talking on the phone, no cruising to the mall with friends in her little car. Every few minutes she looked at the clock on the gray-painted wall.

Her heart sang at the thought of a relationship, but then it ached because she knew he was using her. Yet she kept glancing at her phone, wanting it to ring, wanting to hear his voice beckoning her to his office.

Hour after agonizing hour she sat at her little desk doing data entry. During long minutes, she strengthened herself with contentious thoughts, like not answering the phone if he called. She contrived to make him jealous. That's it, I'll play around with someone, she told herself. Thousands of guys on this ship will kiss my ass, and I won't even have to give them the time of day. But when anger and resentment saturated her, the pendulum swung the other way and she glanced at the phone, yearning to hear it chirp and see his name on her caller-ID. Oh, if it rang right now she'd snatch it up. Deep in her heart, she knew she'd run to his office if only he'd call.

* * *

Her phone finally rang and she saw his name on the caller-ID. Her heart leaped and she hoped he loved her, but even if he didn't a few minutes in his office was better than data entry.

Her hand went for the receiver, but she let it ring two times before answering with her most perky hello.

"I need you in my stateroom," he said.

"Your stateroom?" Nikki asked, surprised. "What if someone sees me go in there?"

"No one will see you," his tone impatient. "I've got a splitting headache."

"Poor baby." Nikki bit her lower lip and curled a lock of hair around a finger. She shifted nervously on her chair as the ship heeled into a steep turn. She let silence stretch for several seconds between them while thinking about how she might make his headache go away, all the while stalling so it wouldn't be too obvious that she really wanted to go to his stateroom.

"Whatever you're doing can wait," he coaxed her.

"I'm writing your monthly report," she said. "It's due tomorrow."

"Just put a new cover on last month's report," he growled. "I never read the damn thing anyway."

"What if rumors start?" She surprised herself.

"Don't worry," he assured her, "this is top-secret."

"What about Sternz barging in on us yesterday?"

"She has enough problems," Brandt said. "Pretend you're going to lunch," he whispered, "and head over there."

"Oh my," Nikki said, realizing that this would raise their involvement to a new level. She wanted to win him over into a respectful relationship, but a devilish mix of caution and excitement swirled in her heart. He'd have a bed in there. It would be like the first time at a new boyfriend's apartment.

"You know you want to, Nikki," he prodded after hearing the exquisite tremor of fear and desire in her voice when she'd said "oh my" through the phone—that playful coo had deflated the pressure of his headache just a little.

CHAPTER FIFTEEN – Day 2

       Lieutenant Gould held two envelopes in his right hand as he made a beeline to his stateroom. The letters, from his pregnant wife, made his heart ache to be with her, to see her, to place his hands gently on the bulging baby bump swelling on her lovely belly. He glanced at the letter with the older postmark and noticed the curly cursive strokes. He sniffed the paper and swore he could smell her perfume. He quickened his steps in anticipation of seeing the photos that he could feel inside. He adored everything about his wife, Sarah, but she was in Delaware on the opposite side of the planet, living with her parents while he made this endless cruise. All he had now were her written sentiments and the pictures she'd sent. He dashed along the passageway, resisting the temptation to open the letters. He wanted to lie in his bunk and savor them in private.

       As he walked along, his attention went to the coil-bound report in his other hand. His boss—the commanding officer of the Stinger Squadron—Commander Aronson had told him to read it. He glanced at the cover and remembered Aronson saying it contained proof that someone had sabotaged several of their aircraft, but the letters from his wife would come first.

       He glanced at her name, Mrs. Sarah Gould, and the memory of her in a beautiful white wedding dress popped into his head. And there she was, holding her father's arm gliding down the aisle. Her radiant beauty blew him away. Her delicate jaw, perfect nose between pronounced cheekbones and her cool hazel eyes—she was a gift from heaven.

       He hadn't seen her since leaving Pearl Harbor five months ago. She'd flown there to meet him and they spent two nights in a hotel overlooking Waikiki, ordering room service and only leaving to lie on the beach in the afternoon and dance in the hotel disco each night.

Sara swore she was still taking birth control even though they hadn't seen each other for months. But, pill or not, they conceived a child in that hotel room. He figured that she hadn't really been taking her pill, or his super-high sperm count—after so many weeks at sea—overpowered the pill's active ingredients. Either way, they hadn't planned to have a baby for a few years, but when he heard Sarah was pregnant joy overflowed from his heart.

He wrote to her every day even though no mail came or went while Fox kept the ship cloaked behind the invisibility shield.

* * *

When he got to his stateroom, Gould tossed the report aside and laid down to read the letters. A quick glance at the postmarks and he opened the oldest. It was the first he'd heard from her since the cloaking exercise began. Sara wrote about how much she missed him, how her pregnancy was going. Her boobs were getting larger and her complexion glowed. Would he be home when she went into labor? The doctor said it was a boy.

Gould smiled. Yes! A little man!

The stateroom door opened and Lieutenant Rhodes, Gould's roommate, stepped into the compartment. With the exception of a handlebar mustache curling across his cheeks, Rhodes looked a lot like Gould, the composite Navy fighter pilot—a handsome jock in a green flight suit.

"It's a boy," Gould blurted.

"I thought she wasn't due for another few months," Rhodes said, his mustache bouncing on his cheeks.

"The doctor did an ultrasound and saw his pecker."

"Got a name picked out?" Rhodes asked, absentmindedly curling his mustache.

"I don't know." Gould rolled onto his back, wet-eyed with the news. A son!

* * *

Gould fantasized about being with Sara for his son's birth. Since she got pregnant in Hawaii, he knew she was almost four months along. That meant she had several months until she went into labor. He had no idea where he'd be. This cruise, unlike other's he'd made, was open ended. They'd stay out until Fox proved his cloaking system worked. If only the ship would pull into Singapore or Hong Kong, he could hop a flight home. But that wasn't going to happen, so Gould resigned himself to the fact that he would not be there when Sara went into labor.

Damn this cloaking system!

"I have three kids but I only saw one pop out," he recalled his boss, Commander Aronson, explaining the facts of Navy life. "Just be glad you were there when your wife got pregnant, Gould."

Yet he still imagined catapulting off the flight deck and flying all the way around the world to be there when his son was born.

* * *

The second letter didn't smell like perfume. He pulled out a single sheet of paper and a jolt of panic twisted his heart when he saw the photo.

The alcohol-flushed face was a little blurry, but unmistakably his. The girl was 13, maybe 14. His tongue flicked at her nipple. She cradled his Ivy League head in her skinny, brown arms; crumpled pesos clenched in a delicate hand. Her long nails, painted brilliant pink. His hairy chest pressed against her smooth brown tummy. Beneath her pastel eyelids, a forced party-girl smile. At the bottom of the photo, his lecherous hands clutched her bare, adolescent buttocks.

—months ago, the ship visited the Philippines, right before they started the 93-day cloaking exercise. He and several other Stinger pilots went out drinking at a bar in Manila, and he got so shitfaced that he woke up with two naked girls on a dirty futon the next morning. A lumberjack smashed at the inside of his skull with a dull ax.

When he returned to the ship, the guys chided him. "Gould, you wild man," they'd hooted. "Your little girlfriends were cute." and "You're out of hand, Gould. Dancing on the bar with that chick's panties in your teeth! I thought I knew you, brother!" He remembered those stunts, but he couldn't remember what happened afterwards. Five or six hours remained unaccounted for—locked in a booze-induced stupor— somewhere between playing around with the strippers at the bar and waking up with them.

He'd regained consciousness scratching itchy mosquito bites—shit, mosquito welts were more like it—and stumbling around looking for his clothes. His anus was sore—damn, how drunk was I, he remembered thinking at the time.

He'd had a few nights like that over the years, but the memories always came back like post cards from his subconscious.

But not that night—he figured it was never coming back.

How wrong he'd been, because that night was back on this glossy photo in the mail from his wife. Dread punched a hole through his gut and everything good drained away. He read the letter and winced as his thoughts completed the circuit—Some asshole, probably an enlisted guy, snapped this photo and sent it to Sara. With proof of my cheating, she got an abortion and filed for divorce.

The photo prompted a vague memory of a camera flash, and he tried to recall which of his crooked shipmates had snapped the picture and sent it to his wife.

Ex-wife—the word burned as he rolled onto his stomach, buried his face in his pillow for fear that Rhodes would see the tears bursting from his eyes.

CHAPTER SIXTEEN – Day 2

Popping the clasps on his steamer chest and lifting the lid, Brandt hoped Nikki would enjoy what he had in store. He turned to her and smiled.

She sat on the edge of his perfectly made bunk, nervously running her fingers along the scratchy wool blanket. She'd expected a luxury cabin or a bachelor pad, not this gray box with a narrow mattress, a chair and a desk folding down from the wall.

The sparkle in his eyes and his up-to-no-good smirk made him look like a sneaky boy about to prank her. The shift away from his stern demeanor soothed her. She tried to peek around him to see what he was hiding.

"I want to share my toys with you," he whispered.

Nikki moved towards him, but his broad chest blocked her view. He usually grabbed her roughly and kissed her forcefully, but this time he wrapped her gently in his arms and hugged her. She threw her arms around his neck and they kissed.

"What's in there, Captain Brandt?" she asked.

"Call me Sam," he said.

"Okay, Sam, what's in there?"

He stepped aside.

She looked into the steamer chest with a mix of trepidation and curiosity.

Silver tacks held a black velvet lining in place. Her eyes roved over a tangle of padded handcuffs, rubber items like kitchen utensils with metal studs and leather fringes. A riding crop and an apparatus with chrome rings and black straps. Several whips. An impossibly long, thick purple dildo with fake testicles. Several tubes of lubricant and a bondage mask with a golf-ball sized gag. A lot of clips—like the clothespins her mom used to hang wash on the line—she figured he must like those, whatever they were. A sexy pair of black leather gloves caught her eye. A black rope snaked through the tangle.

"Curious?"

She almost said no but instead asked, "What if it hurts and I want to stop?"

"Before we start, we tell each other a safe word," he said.

"What's a safe word?"

"It's a word you say when you want to stop."

"It's that simple?" she asked, wondering what the point of torture was if all the victim had to do was say one word to make it stop.

"Yes," he said. "I'm making a sacred promise to stop when you say your safe word."

Their eyes met.

"A sacred promise?" she asked.

"Yes," he agreed, "a sacred promise."

"My safe word is love," she told him.

"I promise to stop when I hear you say love," he assured her.

"What's your safe word?" she asked.

"Fire," he said.

"Ok, when you say fire, I'll stop." A wave of tension fell away. She fiddled with one of the clamps, grimaced and asked, "What's this for?"

Brandt took it and slid the little ring up and down. The clamp opened and closed. "It's a pleasure clamp," he said. "We put them on each other and it creates a tingling sensation."

"I don't want it on my boobs," She forced a laugh.

"It can go anywhere you want, or nowhere," his voice oozed patience.

Nikki picked up a latex bustier, dropped it and wondered how many other girls he'd used this stuff with. She picked up a mask that would cover the eyes. Setting it aside, she found a triangle of chrome-studded leather. Stretching its elastic waistband, she shot it at him. "Put this on," she ordered playfully.

Brandt stepped into his little bathroom and closed the door.

Nikki stripped quickly and squeezed into the bustier. The tight fit flattened her breasts. She grabbed a whip and struck a pose.

When he stepped out, wearing only the banana hammock,

she cracked the whip, and sternly said, "Get over here."

He knelt on the deck in the middle of the compartment. She cracked the whip again, louder than expected.

"What should I do?" he asked.

"I'm thinking," she replied.

"I could be your slave," he suggested. "Try ordering me around and punish or reward me depending on how I do."

"You'd go for that?" She cracked the whip then wondered if someone walking by outside could hear.

"That's the idea," he said. "You train me to please you."

She snapped the whip hard. It lashed the back of his leg. He groaned—half pain, half pleasure. "Oh no," she cringed, bent over, touched the rising welt softly. "I'm sorry."

"You're not supposed to apologize."

"But I didn't mean to do it."

"Let's just play," he said. "I'm the slave, you're the master."

"It feels kind of stupid," she said.

"It's a game."

"Then I can say I'm sorry and you can't argue."

"The master's always right."

"Then I'm sorry. I didn't mean to hit you with the whip."

"Try the paddle," he suggested.

She tossed the whip on the bed and grabbed a foot-long crop with a thick leather flap at the end. She whacked her hand a couple times and found the leather surprisingly soft and supple.

"I want a foot massage," she said as she reclined in his cushioned chair and crossed her legs.

He rubbed her foot with both hands.

She pressed her toes under his chin and made him look her in the eyes. "You should offer to use lotion," she said.

He went into the bathroom and returned with a bottle of moisturizer.

"You're lucky you have that," she said playfully.

"Anything you desire, my mistress."

Her entire body went limp as he slid both thumbs along her arch. Tension melted from the backs of her leg, left her limp in his chair.

"What's a good pet name for me?" she whispered.

"Anything you like."

She put the whip handle under his chin and made him look at her. "You should make suggestions."

"Dominatrix," Brandt worked lotion into the dry skin around her heel. "Queen, bitch goddess, latex lover?"

"I'll need a lot of practice before I'm a bitch goddess, don't you think?"

"We'll have several more months at sea for you to practice."

After he rubbed both feet, she asked, "What else should I make you do?"

"Anything you like."

"You're a bad boy," she said sternly. "When I ask a question, you make suggestion, understand?" She leaned forward, got face to face with him. "Now, what else can I have you do?"

His eyes sparkled and that mischievous smirk curled the corner of his lips. "Anything you like," he said defiantly.

"You, disobedient man!" She rummaged through the toy chest, thought about lubing up the dildo, doing him from behind. Instead, she grabbed a paddle that looked like a spatula. "You better suggest something."

"Yes, mistress," he said submissively raising his bottom.

She whacked twice as hard as she could. "Suggestions!" she demanded. "I said make suggestions."

"Anything you like, bitch goddess."

She paddled his buttocks until they glowed a rosy red. "You enjoy that, you freak!"

He purred—his headache obviously gone.

"Then call me goddess from now on," she growled. Something inside let go as she unleashed a volley of hard smacks.

CHAPTER SEVENTEEN – Day 2

With a cardboard box under his arm, Terrance entered the Stinger living compartment. It was the middle of the day so the compartment was empty. He went straight to the garbage and pulled out an empty 7up can. He set it on the floor just inside the closed door. This way, if he heard the can knocking across the deck, he'd know someone had entered the compartment. He walked quickly to his cubicle and tore open the package that had just arrived from his brother back in Nebraska. It was the first package he'd received in over three months. He looked at the new merchandise and thought about all the cash he was going to make when he sold it—six cartons of Marlboro, three of Newport and 25 cans of Skoal. As he wrote numbers in his little notebook, he heard the pop can clatter across the deck. He tossed the goods into his locker, closed it and slid back against the bulkhead.

Footsteps approached.

Peeking over the lockers, Terrance saw Danny Jenks creeping along the narrow passageway between the cubicles. Jenks breathed heavily, nervously. He smirked. His eyes shifted comically from side to side. Terrance watched him remove a shiny silver ring from his pocket and slip it onto his right hand. Jenks scratched at a red rash on his forearms and cursed under his breath.

Jenks entered a cubicle and slid the curtain open on the middle bunk. Petty Officer Trueblood lay there with his head resting peacefully on a pillow. For a second Jenks studied Trueblood's face, and then he cocked his right elbow back and drove his fist into Trueblood's nose.

Trueblood groaned.

Terrance winced.

Jenks ran past but stopped and jumped back. He sneered at Terrance and then he bolted from the compartment.

"Get back here you bastard," Trueblood hollered as he

rolled out of his bunk and stumbled after his assailant.

But Jenks was gone.

Trueblood saw Terrance. "Who was it, McDaniels? I know you saw 'em!"

Blood dripped from Trueblood's nose and splattered on the green Formica in quarter-sized red spots. Terrance grabbed a white towel and held it to Trueblood's broken face.

"I didn't see anybody," Terrance said.

"You're lying, McDaniels. Either that or you hit me."

* * *

Commander Aronson and Lieutenant Gould sat in cushioned chairs in the Stinger ready room. Terrance wished they would offer him a seat, but that wasn't going to happen.

They kept asking him, "Who hit Trueblood?"

"I didn't see anybody," Terrance lied.

He'd lied to the MAA when they came to take a report.

He lied to Crenki before helping Trueblood down to the medical department, and he lied again to the corpsman who put six stitches in Trueblood's upper lip.

Trueblood was sitting in one of the cushioned chairs. Terrance thought about stepping over and sitting in one of the empty seats, but decided not to, because he really wanted to beat feet out of there as soon as possible.

A bruise like raw meat framed Trueblood's eyeballs. Rolled up, bloody gauze stuck from his nostrils.

"How did you not see the person who did this?" Gould asked.

"I heard somebody run out of the compartment," Terrance explained, "but I didn't get a look at 'em." He wished they would quit asking him so he wouldn't have to lie again. An eternity passed, and finally Terrance asked, "May I be dismissed?"

"Go on and get out of here," Aronson growled.

CHAPTER EIGHTEEN – Day 3

"I received a message from the Pentagon." Captain Fox glanced at the team around his conference room table and caught Mr. Bradmore's eye.

They exchanged a private nod.

Fox took a slip of paper from his breast pocket, read silently, then paraphrased, "The Hayward may only access cameras on US satellites through unauthorized means." He looked around and said, "The rationale is that any foe might do the same."

"So," Bradmore said, "the Hayward can hack US satellites to hunt for us."

"Correct," Fox replied.

Several at the table wanted to jump into the conversation but held back, allowing Bradmore to lead the challenge.

"The last time we met I asked Mr. Bradmore to lead this team in the development of a risk mitigation plan."

"We met twice and both times the team got stuck on the same issue," Bradmore said.

"And that is," Fox asked.

"With a holograph projector running atop the superstructure and a mirage projector running on the fantail, a dangerous level of static will build up around the ship," Bradmore's voice rose to a mild yet respectful challenge.

"And the concern is?" Fox sounded impatient.

"The static will magnify the intensity of a storm," Bradmore said. "Of particular concern are rough seas, extreme winds and high voltage lightning."

"Don't allow fear of static electricity in the air to influence your decisions." Fox played the bad cop in keeping with their plan to build the team's trust in Bradmore.

"Sir," Bradmore forged ahead. "The Bristol Cove had a mirage projector and we all know what happened to her."

"Do we?" Fox asked. "Have rumors revealed what became of the Bristol Cove?"

"The Bristol Cove had the same cloaking system we have," Bradmore's dark eyes hot with challenge, "and she had a mirage projector on her stern to cover her wake. We know the Hayward was hunting for her on the South Pacific. And we learned from that exercise that combining a holograph projector atop the superstructure with a mirage projector on the stern will cause dangerous levels of static to build up around our ship."

Fox and Bradmore both knew that everyone at the table shared this concern, and that the best thing was to get it out in the open and deal with it. They'd contrived this little ruse to do just that, and in the process, they'd solidify Bradmore's position as the team leader.

"I heard the Bristol Cove's mirage projector threw off so much static it didn't just attract an electrical storm," a technician interjected, "it pulled lightning down from a clear blue sky."

"Dozens of sea spouts," another technician added, "and gale force winds."

"Thousands of lightning bolts."

The investigation remained open. The few known facts remained classified. When the Navy's top brass recruited Fox to put the TenRay project back on track, he demanded full access to the secret report.

"Some believe the static electricity ran so high," one of the recon' pilots said, "it caused hundreds of lightning bolts to strike her simultaneously."

Bradmore glanced at Fox and saw a barely perceptible nod. "The speculation is that the Bristol Cove's crew was electrocuted to death," Bradmore said.

"Speculation," Fox said with thinly concealed contempt.

"The fact that the Bristol Cove is missing," Bradmore said, "is a warning to us."

"I heard huge waves swamped her," a technician chimed in.

"That makes no sense," another of the recon' pilots countered. "If she sank, there'd have been a radiation leak that would of led search and rescue divers to the wreck."

"At least debris," another tech added.

79

"It's all classified," the pilot said. "Without an official report, like the captain says, this is speculation."

"The Bristol Cove could still be out there," the technician said, "hidden by her cloaking system, sailing with a dead crew."

"Captain," Bradmore said, right on cue, "is there any truth to the rumor that the pentagon has an emergency response plan in case the Bristol Cove reappears?"

"It's true," Fox said to everyone's surprise. "The Bristol Cove could be out there and she could run aground or collide with another ship or worse I suppose, her reactors could melt down. On the other hand, her autopilot could keep her running even with her crew electrocuted to death. She could remain invisible for years."

All eyes were on Fox.

They knew he had the classified file, and were amazed to hear him revealing its contents.

"Her mechanical systems will eventually break down, but her reactors could run for decades." Fox paused, savoring his ability to captivate these seafaring men and women. "But as long as salvage subs are searching for wreckage speculation will continue." Fox shared these secrets in order to win them over. He'd decided that they had a need to know. What he neglected to tell them was that the Pentagon brass refused to call the TenRay cloaking system a failure even after the Bristol Cove's disappearance, because a debacle of that magnitude would force several admirals into early retirement. Rather than kill the TenRay project, they doubled its budget and assigned him to make it a success.

Now he had his team's attention. He looked around and made eye contact with each pilot, meteorologist, engineer and technician sitting at the table.

"The Bristol Cove," he explained, "sailed with a crew of less than a hundred when she should have had three-hundred. Being that shorthanded could have led to a catastrophe totally unrelated to the cloaking system."

Bradmore scowled because he knew the mirage projector was dangerous. It would generate high levels of static that could pull lightening out of the sky. But he relaxed his brow and let his gaze wander around the table. Along with steak and lobster, he'd swallowed his resistance and resigned himself to the fact that Fox would drive them all toward perilous extremes in his effort to make the cloaking system a success. Bradmore sipped his lukewarm coffee and fondly recalled the vision he'd had when Fox offered him a job at TenRay. He saw his wife and kids splashing happily in a swimming pool, and the flowering shrubs surrounding the house with the view of San Diego and the ocean. All he had to do was make the TenRay cloaking system a success.

"We must remember the Hayward closed in on the Bristol Cove in the corner of a restricted operating area in a remote section of the South Pacific," Fox had explained to Bradmore over one of several dinners they'd eaten together, just as he explained to the team now. "When that storm came up, I believe she ran off course, and that explains why they have not found the wreck yet."

As he spoke, Captain Fox stood and threw his shoulders back. He hardened his eyes and said, "We are testing a revolutionary technology."

As if on cue, his marines snapped to attention.

"The most effective way to evade the Hayward," Bradmore said supportively, "is to install a mirage projector to cover our wake."

"Absolutely correct," Fox said. "So gather this team and develop a mitigation plan."

Bradmore saw that their ruse had eased the team's concerns. He said, "We'll meet later today and get on with our risk planning."

"Very well then," Fox concluded the meeting. "At this time we'll replenish supplies and stand by for orders to reactivate the cloaking system."

CHAPTER NINETEEN – Day 3

Darkness spread across the ocean. A warm, salty breeze buffeted the ship's steep sides. Silver starlight twinkled above the drifting clouds. In the catwalk, a match lit and a cigarette began to glow.

"Are you crazy?" Terrance whispered. "This is a fueling station. Put that out so we don't get blown up."

"Did you see me hit him?" Jenks smiled as he took a drag.

Terrance wanted to call him a coward for hitting Trueblood in his sleep, but didn't want to complicate the fact that Jenks owed him money. "I told Crenki, the MAA, Commander Aronson and Lieutenant Gould I didn't see anything."

Jenks took another drag. "Did you know Gould's in charge of the nuke loading team? Him and Trueblood are tight."

"That why you hit him?"

"That's between me and him," Jenks said.

"No it ain't, because he don't know you hit him," Terrance was quick to point out.

"You gonna tell him?"

"Look, Jenks, you're into me for nearly five-hundred bucks." Terrance's irritation grew as he watched Jenks' cigarette glow again. "Start paying me and I got nothing to say to anyone."

"You threatening me?"

"Just pay up. That's what I'm telling you."

"You're threatening me."

Sparks flew as Terrance's palm flattened the cigarette against Jenks face. In an instant, he was on his back with Terrance's knee pressing on his chest. "Half of what you owe me by next payday," Terrance demanded, "or you're gonna be swimming with the fish."

Jenks shook his head, trying to get the burning ember off his cheek, but banged his forehead on a metal pipe. "You're breaking my ribs." He grabbed Terrance's wrists and struggled feebly.

Terrance remembered the nasty redness on Jenks' arms, and feeling those rash-eaten hands clutching at him almost made him let go.

"You gotta pay me back." Terrance pinned Jenks firmly against the steel. "Do you understand?"

"Yes!" Jenks whined. "You're hurting me."

Terrance walked away.

Jenks muttered curses at his back.

* * *

Terrance loaded cigarettes and dipping tobacco into his laundry bag and pulled the drawstring tight. He slung it over his shoulder and left the Stinger living quarters to make his evening rounds.

First he went forward and then outboard. He entered the deckape living quarters. They worked irregular shifts, so he never knew who might be around. A few guys sat in folding chairs, staring at a TV. Terrance waited a moment before walking down a narrow aisle toward the back door. Sure enough, they followed.

He loosened the drawstring and reached into the bag.

The first guy said, "Marlboro," and handed Terrance a twenty.

He gave the guy one pack. No change.

"Two cans of Skoal," said the next man.

Terrance pocketed a fifty.

He sold a few more items before disappearing out of the compartment and down a ladder. Content with their favorite brands, his customers didn't care where he came from or where he went.

Like an ice-cream man cruising suburban neighborhoods, Terrance walked his route inside the labyrinth of compartments and passageways. He hit the deck division and the aft galley, the Prowler squadron's line shack. He knocked at officers' staterooms and charged them double. Officers earn more money, he figured, so they pay extra.

He wasn't doing anything wrong, he reasoned, just demonstrating entrepreneurial initiative, something the military sorely lacked. When he first came aboard the Nimitz a few years earlier, he heard that the store ran out of Marlboros, Newports, Copenhagen and Skoal after a few weeks at sea. So, he wrote to his brother and asked him to send a couple hundred dollars' worth of cigarettes and chew. Several weeks later, a care package arrived and Terrance started selling. Since then, he'd had a steady stream of packages from his brother—right up until the cloaking system shut his business down. But now with the 93-day exercise over, he was back on his sales route.

He figured out that he had to enter a living compartment or office and sell a few items quickly, and never do business in the passageways because roving MAA could walk up at any moment. He reduced risk by selling in the shadows and slipping away.

Over time, he accumulated a large bankroll, and once his shipmates found out he had excess cash, they started asking him for loans. It was their idea to pay high interest—not his.

CHAPTER TWENTY – Day 3

"Now I make the rules," Brandt said as he yanked Nikki's wrists behind her back and clamped on handcuffs.

"Hey, you said we made the rules together." She forced a chuckle, tried to keep it playful.

"The first rule is shut the fuck up!" He whacked her ass with a riding crop.

"Ouch!" She wobbled on too-high stilettos he forced her to wear. She banged her shin on the edge of his bunk.

"No talking." He cracked the back of her thighs.

"You're too strict." Fear swirled in her belly.

"On your knees!" He fastened a collar around her neck.

She stumbled on the stupid heels. It was impossible to get to her knees gracefully with her hands cuffed behind her back. She was about to insist that he remove the cuffs when he roughly wrapped a leather mask around her face. A hard plastic ball forced into her mouth. She bit her lip. He fastened Velcro straps on the back of her head.

She pleaded for him to stop, but her words were garbled nonsense around the gag.

He shoved her down and she landed with her hands stuck behind her back. Pain jolted through both arms as the cuffs cut into her wrists.

Through slits in the mask, she could barely see him grabbing a handful of those metal clamps.

"What are you doing?" her words indecipherable.

His sinister laughter cut like razors in her ears.

A clamp pinched on the soft side of her breast.

"LOVE," she shouted, her tongue striking the gag. "Love! Love!" she whimpered. "Love!"

"What?" he asked, laughter cackling from his throat. "I can't understand a word you're saying."

CHAPTER TWENTY-ONE – Day 3

The handlebar mustache bounced on Lieutenant Rhodes' cheeks as he delivered the flight plan. "Wooden tank targets are set up on the south shore of an uninhabited island," Rhodes explained, "and each pilot will make three passes, taking out one target on each pass."

Lieutenant Gould, consumed with grief over the news of his wife's abortion, listened to Rhodes review the techniques for guiding a missile to the target with the Hornet's joystick. He half-heartedly scribbled notes on a kneeboard Velcro-strapped to his right thigh.

When he arrived on the flight deck, Gould looked at the Stinger logo on his aircraft's tail. A vengeful Hornet with its wings swept back, its abdomen slung forward, a sharp stinger aimed at unseen prey.

Gould imagined the stinger smashing his helmet, piercing his skull and pumping venom into his brain. He imagined a painful purple welt on his scalp as the damn insect flew away. That's how it felt to think about his wife. His EX-WIFE!

He went through the preflight checks with Danny Jenks leading the way. Gould followed thoughtlessly, while Jenks scratched the backs of his arms and mumbled the whole time.

A second before launching, Gould looked at the catapult crew and realized his payload included an armed laser-guided missile. In a woefully ineffective attempt to set aside his guilt and misery, he gripped the control stick. The catapult shuttle tugged at the launch bar as he eased the throttles forward. He glanced across the gauges and rested his helmet on the headrest. He thumbed the afterburners as the catapult engaged. Instantly, the jet accelerated to 175 miles per hour.

At 20,000 feet, Gould lowered his aircraft into the echelon formation outboard of Rhodes. He couldn't shake the image of his wife's face, her crying eyes red with scorn.

For the thousandth time he knew his life was ruined.

"Do you have a problem, Gould?" Rhodes' voice in his helmet.

He saw a white ring of sand surrounding emerald palm trees and fuzzy hills far below. Gould snapped back, tried to stop brooding over his broken marriage. He knew that flying with emotional junk clogging his thoughts could get him killed.

What did Rhodes say about the targets? Were they trucks? Tents? Take out three tenks? He smiled for the first time since opening that dammed letter—fucking tenks! He'd mixed tents and tanks. "Tenks," he chuckled.

He keyed his mic' and said, "Ready to attack."

"Zero niner, expedite," Rhodes said. "Follow Gould in for the kill."

Shit, Gould thought, I'm leading this raid and I don't even know what I'm supposed to shoot at. Nosing into a steep dive, he figured an aggressive attack might cover for anything he did wrong. Leveling off at 300 feet above the water, he flew directly at the island. When he started north, Rhodes' voice crackled, "South, Gould. Tanks are on the south shore." Gould tweaked the stick, worked the rudder and flew in over the breakers. On his kneeboard, he'd written, "Vulcan, Vulcan, LG missile," so he'd fire in that order. When the first wooden tank came into view, he backed off the throttles and nudged the stick forward. Palm trees filled his windscreen so fast it spooked him. He watched the target slip from his crosshairs, but he pulled the trigger on his Vulcan cannon anyway. A burst of bullets pruned the tops off a grove of palms, and one fell on the plywood tank.

"Nice job camouflaging the enemy, Gould." Rhodes snickered in his headset. "Pull back and let a real attack pilot show you how it's done."

Gould peeled off and rejoined the formation just as Rhodes' bullets turned a target into a blur of smoke and splinters.

On his second pass, Gould still heard his wife sobbing at the abortion clinic. His bullets cut down more palm trees. He pursed his lips and shoved his marital problems aside. Time for a third pass. Time to deliver a laser-guided missile.

After switching the heads-up display to the laser-guided missile, he saw his second tank target still standing on the beach beneath him. On impulse, he pulled back on the throttles and tweaked the trim tabs. The Hornet nosed over. Gould didn't flinch when a fuzzy green hilltop filled the windscreen. The wooden tank appeared in his cross hairs. He squeezed the trigger, expecting a burst of bullets to spray from his Vulcan cannon and disintegrate the target into a blur of smoking wood chips. Instead, a tail of fire screeched from the missile under his port wing.

Oh, shit! He'd already switched over to the laser-guided missile.

He accelerated away from the beach as the missile burrowed into a sand dune. The fireball threw lava boulders, tree trunks and palm fronds hundreds of feet into the air. Debris sailed over the pristine white sand and splashed in the transparent blue breakers.

"What are you shooting at?" Rhodes barked. "Climb to twenty-thousand feet and circle until we complete this run."

* * *

How can I minimize the damage? Gould wracked his brain, hastily deciding to make it look like an electrical malfunction. He pulled out his Swiss Army knife, plucked open the screwdriver and loosened four screws holding a black box in the armament panel. He broke the safety-wire on the cannon plug and removed it with a twist. He folded out the pliers and broke two copper pins out of the plug. As he pressed it back on, replaced the box and tightened the screws, he tried to formulate a story. Shit! If Rhodes saw me nose over and take aim, he'll know I tried to fire the Vulcan cannon, not the laser-guided missile, Gould thought frantically. "Okay, no problem," he reassured himself. "I'll say I wanted to go back again with the missile." Shit, this story leaks. If an inquiry is ordered, they'll detect a pattern of mistakes. This'll get me grounded, he thought dismally.

Red warning lights blinked in his control panel as panic took over. Shit! What did removing those pins do?

The smell of melting wires filled the cockpit, and a wisp of smoke curled up from the black box he'd sabotaged.

*   *   *

After Gould flew off the ship, Jenks went below for a glass of cold water. The smell of baking bread filled the galley. Jenks held his glass under the spigot and glanced at his reflection in the fountain's shiny backsplash. Above his pimply, soot-speckled cheeks, he noticed his eyes were red and watery. For a moment, he saw a dog's snout and saggy jowls. He stepped back so fast water splashed from his glass.

He refilled, sat down, and while guzzling cold water he considered the progress he and Darnell Ratcomb were making since ditching Grady Dutro. "Tigerfish and guard dogs," he whispered between gulps of cold water. "We're gonna meet the man, I know it."

He left his dirty glass on the table and headed forward along the main deck. He climbed a ladder and cut through a living compartment, leaving footprints on a freshly waxed floor.

The smell of wet Comet and glass cleaner filled his nostrils as he slipped through the door, walked past a bank of spotless sinks and mirrors, and entered a stall at the back. He shut the latch and enjoyed the privacy for a second. He unbuckled his belt, dropped his pants and looked at the red bumps that recently appeared on his thighs. "Fuck it," he whispered as he pulled a small tablet computer out of his vest.

As he whacked off, swiping through pictures that barely did it for him, he hoped the rash on his hands wouldn't spread to his dick.

Afterward, he stood at the sink and rinsed his face. He looked in the mirror and noticed tangled gray hairs sprouting from his head and deep wrinkles spreading out from the corners of his eyes. One of his upper front teeth turned black and another sparkled gold. He chuckled but it sounded like chains rattling beneath his ribs. Tattoos, like the ancient mariner's art of scrimshaw, covered his neck, and on his chest, a skeleton danced atop a treasure chest heaped with gold coins. Mesmerized, he watched the skeleton transform into a moving cartoon as it juggled pentagrams.

"What's happening to me?" he asked, startled at the sight of a pirate staring back at him through the mirror.

He bolted out the door and climbed ladders and walked through narrow passageways. He flattened himself behind the anchor chain locker, a round steel silo that rose through several levels. He looked at the small oval door welded into the steel and remembered the vision he'd had of this exact place. It was the door with "DEAD CREW" stenciled on it. What the fuck was that about, he wondered.

He swung the door open and climbed into the dark. He stood on a narrow shelf and sensed the death-fall in front of him. With one hand, he shut the door behind him, but a pair of tattooed hands pulled it open again. An old man with translucent skin and wispy hair climbed in beside him. "Who are you?" Jenks asked, but the old man smirked in the dim light, then reached out, grabbed ahold of the anchor chain hanging in the darkness, swung himself out and climbed down.

"Are you with the dead crew?" Jenks whispered, but there was no reply.

He looked down into the darkness. The old man was gone. Jenks wondered if he had been there at all. Then he reached out and grabbed one of the anchor chain's large, cool links. He swung out, worked the tip of his boots into the links and began climbing down, hand over hand. At the bottom, candlelight flickered.

As he descended, he heard air circulating units whirring, the propulsion plant humming and the steady hush of the ship cutting through the water.

Down below in the chain locker bottom, he heard his fellow Satanists chanting as another ritual began.

* * *

Jenks trudged along, absentmindedly looking through the catwalk grating at the water eighty feet below. A jet howled on the flight deck a few feet above him as it launched from one of the bow catapults and another screamed as it touched down in the landing area.

He'd been working on deck for several years and enjoyed

the controlled violence that occurred there. The air vibrating with the fury of roaring engines, hurricane gales of exhaust, clanging catapults shooting jets into the air and a crashing whirr of the arresting cable each time a pilot slammed his aircraft to a stop in the landing area.

Jenks held the metal turnbuckles close to his chest so the chains wouldn't slip off his shoulders. They weighed about sixty pounds, and since he'd been carrying them, his muscles were bulking up. He hung the chains on the scupper, and stood by to recover his aircraft when Gould came back.

A siren, like a fire truck trying to break through city gridlock, whooped from the deckedge loudspeakers. "ALL CRASH AND SALVAGE TEAMS REPORT TO EMERGENCY STATIONS IMMEDIATELY. THIS IS NOT A DRILL."

Jenks looked forward and aft, wondering if there'd been an accident or a fuel spill. Maybe there was a problem arming a weapon.

Then he saw Terrance McDaniels running toward him in the catwalk yelling excitedly, but Jenks pointed to his ear and shrugged. And then McDaniels put his mouth to Jenks' ear protection, and said, "Gould's got an electrical problem!"

"What are you talking about?" Jenks asked.

"Your bird, Jenks," McDaniels shouted. "The radio said Gould has an electrical problem—"

Horrendous SHRIEKING and the WHOOSH of an explosion blotted out McDaniels' voice. The catwalk shook so hard Jenks' chains rattled loose from the scupper. Both men grabbed the railing. McDaniels ducked and threw an arm over his head.

The Hornet's severed landing gear tumbled end over end across the deck, followed by the fuselage, smoke pouring from the cockpit. Its nose and the tip of one wing scraping against the deck, shooting a rooster tail of sparks. Flames erupted from the wreckage.

A tire bounced high in the air, slammed down on top of a Prowler, bounced again and splashed in the water.

"FIRE ON THE FLIGHT DECK," the voice announced. "FIREFIGHTING TEAMS AND CRASH CREWS RESPOND. ALL HANDS TO BATTLE STATIONS. THIS IS NOT A DRILL."

A crash and salvage crew in silver fireproof suits ran to the burning fuselage, discharging burst of white fog from their extinguishers.

* * *

The mangled remains of Lieutenant Gould's Hornet sat chained to the hangar deck behind yellow and black tape printed with the words: CRASH INVESTIGATION -- DO NOT CROSS.

Rumors spread and sailors came to the hangar from below like ants venturing from an anthill. Everyone wanted to see the wreckage. They leaned over the tape to glimpse inside the cockpit, but a scowling marine ordered them back. Those who did get a peek were disappointed because there was no gore. They saw only charred electrical components.

The howl of jet aircraft on the deck above filled the air all about the ship with a constant rumble. It threatened to deafen the gawkers in the hangar.

* * *

Some told stories about crashes they'd seen and fires they'd actually battled, while others retold stories they'd only heard but embellished them so well listeners felt they were at the center of the action.

One tale claimed Gould ejected several miles aft of the ship, but the raft on his ejection seat failed to inflate, so he sank like a rock before the chopper could swoop in to rescue him. The story went that even after Gould ejected, the autopilot was bringing the jet in for a perfect landing, but the ship swayed at the last second and the Hornet's wheels hit the round down on the aft end of the flight deck. The impact caused the landing gear to break off, which sent the jet into a fiery crash.

Another rumor told how Gould rode the plane all the way in even with a fire in the cockpit, but they didn't find his body in the wreckage because he'd burnt to ashes.

That's how sailors behave—always telling outrageous tales to entertain each other.

Outside the Stinger Squadron, among the crew of over 5,000, not one person knew Gould personally.

The entire hubbub didn't cause a minute's delay in the flight schedule. After all, there were pilots who wanted flight hours, there were bombs to drop and jet fuel to burn.

PART III

NAVY JUSTICE

CHAPTER TWENTY-TWO – Day 4

Crammed in among cardboard boxes and mailbags, Commander Shakley sat buckled to a jump seat in the back of a tiny cargo plane on a flight from Hong Kong. He listened to the engines humming and the cargo creaking under bungee nets as the plane bounced through the sky. The acrid odor of burnt fuel saturated the tiny space, and with all the boxes piled around him, Shakley worried the plane might catch fire and crash in the ocean.

Through a tiny window, he saw water twenty-thousand feet below, spreading all the way to the curvature of the earth.

"Commander Shakley," the pilot's voice crackled through a speaker somewhere behind the cargo, "we'll start our descent in a minute and FYI the Nimitz is a few ticks north of the equator."

Shakley had never crossed the equator, but he'd heard plenty of stories about what happened aboard a ship when it 'crossed the line' as they said. The most common tale told of sailors dressed like pirates forcing pollywogs like him down onto their hands and knees for an ass paddling. A pang of dread shot through his thick midsection as he imagined a gang of twenty-somethings forcing him to wear his underwear outside his pants and making him roll in garbage as part of an ancient hazing ritual.

Shakley removed his glasses, closed his eyes and massaged his hairless scalp. The tiny plane buzzed and bounced and descended through the brilliant blue sky.

After landing on the ship, the plane taxied to a spot in front of the superstructure. The entire rear end of the aircraft folded down and a burst of hot exhaust filled the compartment. Jet engines howled, and the flight deck director's amplified voice barked orders through the air. A gang of deckapes tossed boxes out of the plane. Shakley disembarked and met Captain Brandt, who wore a crash helmet with a dark visor covering his eyes. Brandt ordered a deckhand to carry Shakley's bag, and led the way into the ship and down a ladder. They zigzagged through passageways. Every few seconds, a jet landed on the steel plates above their heads, and a loud CLANK and a tremendous WHIIIRRR shook the walls.

All the ambience of a medieval castle under siege, Shakley thought.

"This is your private stateroom," Brandt said as he pulled his helmet off and handed Shakley a key.

Shakley unlocked the door and saw a Spartan cell, with a narrow bunk, two plastic chairs, a flat panel TV and a small door partially opened, revealing a cramped sink, toilet and shower.

"VIP accommodations," Brandt said seriously. "Normally, as the ship's executive officer, I wouldn't get involved in a crash investigation, but Captain Fox has delegated this matter to me because he's busy with a special exercise."

"I see," Shakley said.

"The pilot was missing from the wreckage," Brandt explained, "so I'm concerned."

"I'm sure there's a logical explanation," Shakley replied.

"I'm sure there is," Brandt agreed.

An awkward silence ensued. Brandt waited for Shakley to volunteer something, but Shakley only glanced from the outlandish tattoos on Brandt's forearms to his blue eyes where he saw schemes and calculations brewing.

"I want you to work with Mr. Keef," Brandt said. "He's already investigating the Stinger squadron—"

"I'll do an initial assessment alone," Shakley said.

"Hands to help you sift the wreckage," Brandt insisted.

"I'm capable," Shakley cut him off again.

Brandt didn't like the hard little eyeballs behind Shakley's wire frame glasses. And he didn't like the shine coming off Shakley's dome either.

"I'll have Keef check in with you," Brandt said, determined to monitor the investigation.

Shakley didn't want Brandt's mole burrowing into his business, because evidence got messy when a guy like Brandt and his lackeys weighed in.

"There is one thing I need," Shakley said.

"What's that?" Brandt asked.

"Flight deck DV."

Brandt grabbed the phone and pressed a few buttons. "Brandt here. I've got Commander Shakley with me and he requires access to flight deck DV." He handed the phone to Shakley and said, "This guy'll get you through the firewall."

* * *

Shakley opened his canvas seabag and pulled out a tube of scalp cream. He turned on his laptop, touched the colored tiles, opened a new crash investigation file. He clicked through the multipage form, scanning the empty fields, each waiting for him to enter the appropriate code.

For Shakley and his Pentagon counterparts, a code existed for every variable that occurred between the time an aircraft started and the time it became a pile of twisted wreckage. The Pentagon regularly kicked back reports that lacked the appropriate codes. He avoided narrative explanations because they made him uneasy. They were subjective, and sometimes loaded with innuendo and opinion. He liked codes.

With a few fuselage fragments, Shakley could determine the exact codes for anything that had gone wrong. During almost two decades of crash investigations, he'd codified the tragic ends of more than 100 aircraft and many pilots.

His counterparts at the Pentagon would only accept codes, not words, never mind sentences, in their data-crunching computer programs. They wanted codes like AQ-43-R: Aircraft depleted fuel supply in flight; or KH-90-E: Foreign object damage to engine in flight; or FC-22-L: In-flight collision with terrain.

Codes kept the Pentagon's information management systems flowing with programmed precision.

People like Brandt, Shakley knew, could prevent him from reporting the proper codes. Brandt had an agenda, Shakley was certain.

He decided to look at the wreckage and examine the flight data recorder right away.

He pulled a pair of Latex gloves and a handy 10-in-1 tool from his bag, locked his stateroom and went down to the hangar.

* * *

Crash and salvage crews had chained the twisted fuselage and a bent section of the main landing gear to the deck. They spread several hundred pounds of absorbent granules, like cat litter, to soak up hydraulic fluid, oil and jet fuel still dribbling from broken hoses and mangled components.

Shakley handed his orders to a marine who examined them before allowing him to pass under the tape.

What's missing, Shakley asked himself. Several fuselage panels, the cockpit canopy, the nose radome and a tailcone off one of the afterburners.

The fuselage had started to come apart, but the airframe held together because the Hornet's tailhook had grabbed an arresting cable. Shakley worked his way along the mangled heap, examining every inch. He couldn't stop thinking about Captain Brandt. He knows he should stand back when a crash investigator arrives. I can report him if he interferes. Shakley pondered Brandt's comments about sabotage and the pilot's body missing.

He had to determine the facts.

He pulled on the Latex gloves and climbed onto the fuselage, between the twin tails. With his pocket-sized 10-in-1 tool, he unscrewed fasteners holding a panel over the flight data recorder. Setting the panel aside, he noted the small compartment was clean and dry as he unclamped and unplugged the recorder. He held the orange metal unit, the size and shape of a stuffed FedEx overnight envelope, in one hand while carefully climbing off the wreckage. Continuing his inspection along the fuselage, he noticed the ejection seat still in the cockpit. Gould had unbuckled during flight. Odd, Shakley thought, and a big mistake because it prevented him from ejecting.

On the badly burned side of the cockpit, he tapped the melted buttons and cracked LEDs. His gloves prevented soot from contacting his skin. He noticed scratches in the paint on the heads of several fasteners on one of the armament black boxes. Shakley folded out his 10-in-1 tool's straight-slot screwdriver. Had someone tampered with the cockpit's control panel? He unscrewed the box and looked closely at the cannon plug on the back. What do we have here? A twist of safety-wire that should have secured the plug in place was broken.

As he unscrewed the cannon plug someone behind him said, "You must be the sabotage investigator."

Shakley craned his neck around and saw a chief petty officer standing beside him next to the wreckage.

Immediately the marine guard stepped between them.

"Stand down, marine," Crenki said. "This is my airplane."

"You are unauthorized in this area," the marine said.

"I need to speak with this man," Crenki objected.

"Unauthorized personnel are not permitted inside the perimeter."

Crenki backed up a few steps and ducked under the tape.

"I'm Chief Crenki, head of Stinger maintenance," he said from a few feet away. "I've got a report for you. It shows the data on the sabotaged engines. Boy, am I pissed they didn't get you out here sooner, but the invisibility shield prevented that, I'm sure."

A missing pilot, Shakley thought with dismay, and now sabotage and an invisibility shield. He wondered how many other kooky ideas would try to attach themselves to his investigation. "I must get back to work," Shakley said as he turned away.

"I'll help you interrogate suspects," Crenki said, "and search their lockers. We'll nail the dirty saboteur, you'll see!"

"Thanks, Chief." Shakley looked back into the cockpit and picked up the black box. He examined the cannon plug and the broken twist of safety wire. When he looked inside the plug, and saw that several copper pins were broken off, a word formed in his mouth before he could stop it.

"Sabotage!"

CHAPTER TWENTY-THREE – Day 4

Flickering candlelight cast eerie shadows of two young men inside the narrow steel well. The big chain, hanging from the darkness above, swayed each time the ship rose and fell.

"You piss me off, E-darg!" Danny Jenks spat the words.

"I ain't into this, Jenks," Grady Dutro said, wishing he hadn't come down here.

"You prevented me from communing with Satan, E-darg!"

Grady stumbled and wrapped an arm around the big chain to steady himself.

Their shadows flickered on the steel walls.

Jenks bit down on his cigarette and took several quick puffs, turning his face into a sinister, black and orange mask. "Do you want to join the dead crew, E-darg?"

The burn on his face, where Terrance McDaniels had flattened a cigarette, still stung. Now he wanted to pass that insult along. "Do you want to join the dead crew, E-darg?" Jenks asked again.

"I don't know what you're talking about," Grady said. He wanted to climb out of there without further antagonizing this psycho. "Who's the dead crew?" Grady tried to distract his tormentor. "I never heard of them."

Jenks lurched forward, touching the cigarette's hot cherry to the cowering man's face.

Sparks sprayed.

Grady yelled.

"Don't you want to join the dead crew, E-darg?"

"Come on, Jenks. Stop it, please."

"Do you know why I'm calling you E-darg?"

"No." Grady ached for the courage to fight back.

"Because E-darg is your name backwards," Jenks said, certain he had Grady paralyzed by fear. "It means I'm gonna

99

sacrifice you to Satan. Listen," he shouted. "Don't you hear him calling you to join his dead crew now?"

Grady mustered a spark of courage. "The hell with this," he muttered under his breath.

Jenks puffed his cigarette and lunged, attempting to burn Grady's face again.

But Grady braced his feet on the pile of big links and shoved Jenks as hard as he could with both hands.

Jenks shrieked in surprise and grabbed franticly for the anchor chain, but tumbled backwards empty handed. His head struck one of the links and he fell silent.

"Jenks?"

Nothing.

The candle had fallen over and gone out.

The hush of the hull slicing through the sea and the faint whir of machinery filled the black space.

"Jenks?" Grady called a little louder.

No answer.

Grady climbed the chain as fast as he could.

* * *

Scratch.

Scratch.

Scratching the infernal itch.

Clawing at his thighs, Jenks regained consciousness. The damn rash drove him nuts. He waved his hand in front of his eyes but saw only blackness. Chain links, lumpy and cool, pressed against his back. He groped around and tried to sit up, but pain jolted along his spine. He lay back with his head between two links, his arms and legs splayed at odd angles. He remembered Grady shoving him. He wondered how long he'd been lying there and realized he must have hit his head.

He stood up, scratched hard at his thighs and began climbing.

As he made his way to the Stinger living compartment, he knew it was past lights out. There was hardly anyone roaming the passageways.

Jenks removed his boots. He usually slept in dirty clothes, but now he had to wash.

In the shower, cold spray from the nozzle numbed his itchy skin. He lathered his torso with a bar of soap and reflected with sick pride on the tattooed, rash-ravaged thing he'd become.

* * *

Reveille's bugle blares woke him.

Jenks rolled out of his bunk, opened his locker, pulled on a pair of canvas pants, a brown jersey and his flotation vest. He tied the laces on his scuffed black boots.

Since his jet had crashed, he had nothing to do.

He went to the line shack to show his face and grab a tool pouch and the boom room key.

In the boom room, a tiny steel compartment under the flight deck in the front of the ship, the Stingers stored bales of rags and drums of aircraft soap. Jenks unlocked the padlock on the tiny door, climbed into the cramped space and locked the door from inside. There wasn't enough room to stand, only to lay with his legs scrunched across several wire-bound bails of rags.

He pulled the flashlight from his tool pouch, turned it on and set it on a beam. The boom room rose as the ship climbed a swell and then slowed for a moment, filling him with a weightless sensation, like an elevator reaching a skyscraper's top floor. Drums of aircraft cleaner creaked beneath him. Then the boom room fell as the ship slid down into a trough between the waves.

He removed his float-coat and pulled his jersey off over his head.

He squeezed forward in the cramped space and reached down against the ship's outer skin, feeling around for a bag of joints he'd smuggled aboard in the Philippines. He lit one and smoked it half way and then set it on a drum of aircraft cleaner. He pulled his Phillips screwdriver from the tool pouch and put the tip in an angle in the I-beam.

For an hour, he worked the tip quickly back and forth against the steel.

Occasionally he took a toke to maintain his buzz.

If he returned the screwdriver to the line shack, someone would see that he'd sharpened it. "Damaging government property," he snickered. "I'll get in trouble for that."

He poked his fingertip with the fine point, but it had to be sharper, like a needle, so he continued honing it against the steel.

Another hour passed before he was satisfied with his handiwork. He set the shank down and took a big toke off the roach. Then he stabbed a bail of rags with his new weapon.

"Messy work," he whispered.

He pinched some skin on his chest and pressed the point there. It hurt, but he recited a little incantation and pressed harder.

After a year of practicing dark arts, he'd arrived at a place where pain felt good. The metal point pressing against his skin sent a chill through his ribs.

Pulling the skin out harder, he pressed the shank there and gritted his teeth so tight enamel chipped.

He'd ventured beyond his mother's abuse. He no longer wondered about a father he'd never met. He sensed a dark voyage ahead, one that would open realms of mystery.

He wanted to stand before that door again and read the words DEAD CREW. He'd fling the door open, burst into the morgue, grab the drawer handle and pull with all his might.

He imagined it sliding open and the dog-faced sailor barking ferociously, lunging at him.

"I'll stab that fucking mutt," he whispered. "It won't stop me from climbing into that drawer!"

Chanting had gotten him this far. Now, through deeds, he had to demonstrate a new level of devotion. It wasn't enough to light another candle and chant.

"If I want to meet the man," he whispered, "I gotta pierce the mutt!"

He pulled hard on the flap of skin on his chest and exhaled slowly.

And with a smooth upward stroke, the sharp tip pierced his flesh.

CHAPTER TWENTY-FOUR – Day 5

Rubbing moisturizer into his bald scalp with his fingertips, Shakley stretched his husky legs under the table. He turned the words sabotage and pilot error over in his mind, speculating that the case ran in both directions. The flight data recorder had revealed that the armament system experienced an electrical failure, wires melted and smoke filled the cockpit. Gould sent a mayday and flew back to the ship but came up short on his final approach. That was all obvious. It was the broken safety wire on the cannon plug and Gould's missing body that had Shakley rattled.

But those weren't the only things knocking him off his game. Being close to the equator worried him too. He'd heard about the barbaric initiation rituals, and dreaded the thought that a gang of young-buck sailors would paddle his ass and force him to crawl through garbage.

Sabotage and pilot error; he forced himself to focus as he opened a crash investigation form. His fingers scrambled over the keyboard while browsing codes. Thirty minutes later, he had a scenario worked out: Someone vandalized the cannon plug causing an electrical short, which led to sparks under the control panel. Wires melted and the cockpit filled with smoke. Why did he unbuckle? Panic? Possibly. Where the hell is Gould's body? Wait a minute. Was he even in the cockpit when the jet crashed?

Shakley grabbed the remote and turned on the TV. He logged into the ship's digital video library, found the files he wanted, pressed play.

In the sky behind the ship, the fast-approaching Hornet pitched and yawed as if flown by a drunk but Shakley knew better. Melted wires had knocked out the autopilot. Gould worked the stick and rudder pedals manually.

Shakley pressed pause. Through his wireframe glasses, quick and observant eyes studied the screen. A lone plane captain stood near the landing area, watching the Hornet approach. Shakley pressed play and heard the amplified voice, "ALL CRASH AND SALVAGE TEAMS REPORT TO EMERGENCY STATIONS IMMEDIATELY. THIS IS NOT A DRILL." It bothered him that the plane captain didn't get out of the way. A landing safety officer stood on the port side aft. Shakley noted a brunette ponytail under the officer's helmet. Wearing a white vest and khaki pants, she waved a pair of colored paddles, signaling Gould to pull up. Shakley saw Gould's crash helmet in the cockpit now. He held the pause button and the crash played in slow motion. The safety officer frantically signaled Gould to pull up. Just as his nose gear was about to touch the deck, the main wheels slammed into the round down on the flight deck's aft-most end. The safety officer dove into the catwalk as a chunk of wreckage flew past her.

Shakley winced.

Catastrophic crashes were routine in his line of work, but he rarely had the opportunity to watch video of this quality. No code could describe the hot ball of admiration swelling in his throat as he watched Gould struggle to control tons of space-age alloy and electronics gear racing forward at over 200 miles per hour. Seconds before dying in a scrape of fire and steel, Gould's jaw showed grim determination. Shakley gulped down the hot gob of emotion clogging his throat, and attempted to dismiss the crash's human element. Codes could never capture this untidy business.

If Gould stayed buckled to his ejection seat, he could have yanked a lanyard and shot himself into the sky. He could have traded death in a fiery crash for a splash in the ocean.

"Sabotage shit," Shakley whispered, "this looks like suicide." He wondered if Gould was dealing with any emotional stress, but he pushed speculation from his mind. "What are the facts?" he asked, attempting to refocus, but another question popped into his mind.

"Where did he go?" Shakley whispered. "Or she? It could be a woman, I suppose." Pressing rewind, Shakley found the plane captain in the brown jersey standing on the foul line, aft of the superstructure. He hit play and saw the person turn toward the camera. He pressed pause and saw a young man in a brown helmet with dark goggles hiding his eyes. A toothy grin pushed apart a pair of baby-fat cheeks. The jet seemed to swoop right in on top of him. Shakley pressed play and the guy glanced back and then turned and looked directly at the camera as the plane crashed a few feet behind him. In slow motion, the Hornet's main landing gear slammed into the round down. The tires blew out and black rubber shreds bounced forward along the deck. A jet fuel mist blurred across the screen. Shakley rewound and watched again. The cockpit canopy flew off, because Gould pulled a lanyard to eject it. One of the main landing gear shocks—a ten-foot-long and one-foot-wide hydraulic cylinder with a blown-out tire at one end—sheared off and flew directly at the smiling plane captain. He didn't even flinch as the shock tumbled end-over-end inches above his head. Orange and black fire erupted around the Hornet. And this kid stood a few feet away smiling at the camera.

Shakley watched the crash a dozen times. He tried to study every pixel as the Hornet hit the deck with tremendous force. Tires erupted, landing gear flattened and snapped like empty pop cans. Panels popped off. The airframe buckled at its center. Both wings flapped downward with incredible force. The skin on the starboard wing cracked and alloy ribs broke through. The engines self-destructed as they sucked in debris. One of the tail cones broke off, bounced on the deck and into the air. Shakley watched in disbelief as the Hornet's tailhook miraculously grabbed one of the arresting cables and dashed forward out of the frame, engulfed in a whoosh of orange fire.

The plane captain with the chubby cheeks disappeared. No wreckage hit him. The blast concussion didn't knock him out of the picture. One second he was standing there and the next he was gone.

The camera stayed focused on the aft section of the landing area while the Hornet continued forward in a crashing blur. Shakley pressed a button and opened a menu where he could switch between six cameras mounted in different places on the flight deck. Three pointed away from the landing area, so he watched the crash from the others. One showed Gould in the cockpit as the jet touched down, but another showed the cockpit empty when the busted fuselage stopped in the landing area. When the jet spun and the fuel exploded, all three shots went completely white, so Shakley concluded that Gould lost control and was thrown from the wreckage.

It was the only logical explanation.

When he wondered about the chubby-cheeked kid standing close to the crash, the phantom sailor theory blinked in his mind.

Phantom sailors are characters in shipboard catastrophe tales that involve mysterious men or women who appear briefly during a cataclysmic event. Phantom sailor stories are rare, and the phantom is always either good or bad.

A good phantom arrives in the heat of a disaster; a sailor nobody knows. The benevolent stranger helps fight a fire or carry a smoke inhalation victim out to a weatherdeck for air. Afterwards people realize nobody knows the person's name.

The bad phantom, on the other hand, bumps an electrician who is working in a high-voltage panel, killing the poor fool in a spray of sparks. A bad phantom kicks over a welder's acetylene tank, setting off explosions and starting fires. When sailors lean too far over the side, a bad phantom bumps them into the sea.

But there are no codes for the work of phantom sailors, so Shakley wrote on his legal pad, "Plane captain, approx. 5-5 190 lbs., standing at the foul line aft, starboard side during Gould's crash. Who is this guy?"

He refined the scenario: Someone sabotaged the plug, causing an electrical failure and sparks under the control panel. A wire bundle melted, filling the cockpit with smoke. And Gould unbuckled. But why? Shakley caught himself, refocused on the facts. It didn't matter why Gould unbuckled from the seat. The simple fact was Gould did unbuckle and that is an easily codified pilot error. Unbuckling degraded Gould's ability to control the aircraft and prevented him from ejecting safely. His main landing gear hit the round down. And when his jet spun hard at an angle, it tossed him from the wreckage, over the side and into the sea.

Shakley sighed contentedly. A combination of sabotage and pilot error codes would neatly complete his investigation.

Then he heard someone knocking at his door.

* * *

106

Shakley opened the door and Keef pushed his way inside.

"Mighty nice room they got you in here, inspector. I'm Mr. Keef. Captain Brandt sent me to, well long story short, I'm your new partner."

If he were on land, Shakley would tell Brandt's man to leave. He'd call the Pentagon and file a complaint. But, being in the middle of the ocean, close to the equator, and having already sensed hostility from Brandt, Shakley decided to play along. He already had his investigation wrapped up, so he looked at Brandt's snoop with mild interest.

"What are your qualifications?" Shakley asked.

Keef sat down and shifted his ass in the chair. His mouth opened. He inhaled. He scratched at a patch of red bumps on his forearm. Finally he said, "Well, ah," and after a pause, he said, "I've been investigating sabotage in the Stinger squadron." Keef scratched his bumps vigorously. "And I also got experience looking for missing bodies."

"You're referring to the pilot," Shakley said.

"No corpse in the wreck—"

"Let me show you the video," Shakley cut Keef off and grabbed the remote.

"I reckon a body don't just disappear—" Keef looked at his arm, where he'd scratched so hard it bled. "What the heck?" he muttered.

"Your first lesson in crash investigations is to not let eyewitnesses fog the data," Shakley spoke in a lecturing tone, and ignored Keef's bleeding. "Of course, if you like sea stories, listen to them after you inspect the wreckage and watch the video. It's rare when the data is so inadequate that you have to rely on eyewitnesses."

Keef smirked at this bald guy's pompous bullshit.

They watched the crash from multiple angles. Shakley paused here and there to explain. "See, the wreckage goes forward out of the frame," Shakley pointed at the screen. "There's no missing-body mystery. Lieutenant Gould unbuckled from his ejection seat, and when he hit the deck, the impact threw him from the wreckage and he went over the side."

Keef didn't notice the mysterious plane captain, and

Shakley didn't complicate the matter by pointing him out.

"Them Stingers fodded a slew of engines and the jet shop thinks somebody's tossing bits of steel down their ventilation ducts."

"So I've heard." Shakley recalled the ranting maintenance chief he'd met in the hangar. He wanted to tell Keef to go away, but he spoke diplomatically instead. "Sabotage may be a factor," he said. "I'll give Brandt a copy of my report before I leave."

"He's set on us working together," Keef said.

"I'll call you if I need anything." Shakley opened the door and ushered Keef out.

As Keef stepped into the passageway, he glanced at the scratched-raw bumps on his arm and decided if they didn't go away after a shower he'd go to sick call and get it checked out.

CHAPTER TWENTY-FIVE – Day 5

"Why don't you want to talk about it?" Captain Brandt sat behind the big desk, swiveling playfully. His blue eyes smiled over that bad-boy smirk.

"There's nothing to talk about," Nikki said, restraining her disgust. She couldn't file sexual harassment charges against him, because the charge would go to him, and even if they went up the chain of command, she dreaded being at the center of the drama that would follow. She blamed herself for falling into the affair before she found out about his dark side.

"You have to sign these papers." She placed the clipboard on his desk and stepped back. She stood at attention and stared directly at the wall behind his desk.

The amused glow in his eyes flickered. He wasn't used to persuading others to do what he wanted. Sure, he could make life miserable for her, just as he'd made it difficult for other girls. He wanted Nikki to come back to his stateroom and do what he knew she wanted to do. Her compliance would allow him to take her beyond her artificial limits. He came out from behind the big desk and sat on the corner nearest her. "Nikki, honey," he started his pitch, "you got frightened. That's natural, baby. Fear is part of the attraction."

* * *

She had screamed when he removed the ball gag.

He tried to force it back into her mouth, but she kicked as if her life depended on it. A minute later, the MAA were banging at the door, but he made them wait while he uncuffed her. She pulled her clothes on and ran out. A crowd had gathered, but he didn't give a shit. He slammed the door, shut off the light and sat in the dark for a while.

All night she laid awake stifling sobs. She didn't want the girls sleeping nearby to hear. Bruises covered her chest where he'd put those clamps. She couldn't imagine what he'd do if she went back for another round of torture. When she thought about his creepy hands touching her, shivers of fear crawled over her skin like bugs.

Slow days passed. A confusing, sinister sensation tingled in her belly when she thought about him.

She'd always had a weakness for rough boys.

It started with athletes in high school. Defensive linemen, point guards, running backs, track stars, third basemen, home run hitters. At first, she liked the popular boys and their quick hands, but later developed an appreciation for the power she had over nerdy boys who were all thumbs. Bold or shy, most managed to lift her shirt and pull down her jeans. A cold beer and a joint always helped. Nothing got her going like being with a boy in a roomy pickup truck cab or best of all, his parents' bedroom when they were out of town.

With Captain Brandt, it was different because he was a man. At first that really turned her on.

She sat in her cubicle doing data entry and the boredom crept in. She found herself thinking about him. The power radiating from his pressed khakis, the golden eagles on his collar points, the curly gold hairs on his brawny, tattooed forearms, his blue eyes and that smirk; it all started seducing her again.

And now, standing in his office, she knew she could escape the temptation by simply turning around and walking out. But then what? Work 12-hour shifts seven days a week, three meals a day and a rerun movie at night. How much boredom could she take before she started fantasizing about him? If nothing else, he provided an escape from the dull days at sea.

* * *

"You know I won't hurt you," he said. "It's like a play and we're the actors."

"Call it what you want," Nikki cut him off. "I'm not into pain."

Brandt pulled the wooden ruler from a desk drawer, and smacked his thigh. "You wouldn't let me spank you with this if I asked permission, would you?" He didn't wait for an answer. "But, if I pull it out in the heat of passion, it makes sense and that shows you can't trust your everyday state of mind to tell you what's gonna feel good when your thighs are burning, Nikki. Trust me, and we'll have so much pleasure together."

All morning she'd sat in her cubicle preparing to resist this. Now she decided to walk out if he didn't sign the papers, but the ruler slapping his thigh distracted her. She looked at the strip of wood, held firmly in his big hand. A crazy kind of heat prickled across the front of her neck because she knew that sting could rock her dull routine.

Like actors in a play, he'd said.

A play with handcuffs and clamps, she painfully recalled, but the ruler whacking his leg held her attention.

"Come on, Nikki, we decide as we go," he coaxed her. "If it gets boring, we add a little action."

"No," she said firmly. "I'm not playing your games anymore." She turned around and walked out of his office.

CHAPTER TWENTY-SIX – Day 5

Air stirred by the helicopter's rotor whipped Bradmore's pant legs, providing some relief from the morning heat. Deckapes chained the helo down and a forklift started moving crates to the aft aircraft elevator, where a team of technicians pried them open with crowbars. Bradmore grabbed the installation manual from one of the crates as horns blew and the elevator lowered.

Getting this unit installed was Captain Fox's number one priority, so Bradmore and his team were determined to make it happen. Welders lit arc torches and started the hot work to attach brackets and erect two 15-foot-tall stanchions ten feet apart on the aft-most area of the fantail. Mechanics bolted a narrow, metal-mesh catwalk with a safety railing between the tops of the two stanchions and Bradmore climbed up to quality check their work.

From his vantage point atop the platform, he saw men and women wrapping up welding gear, hoisting components out of crates and assembling three gray metal boxes. A team of electricians clipped a wire bundle to the overhead to feed the mirage projector with required operating voltage. Another team pulled in fiber to provide remote control of the new gear. Bradmore inspected the flanges atop the stanchions where they'd mount the components.

Everything checked out.

Millions of bubbles spun in turbulent blue vortices out from under the ship. He imagined the massive bronze propellers spinning under the hull. The deck vibrated beneath his boots. His eyes followed the ship's wake, a wide light-blue stripe on the dark surface trailing behind. He remembered the Hayward's Lieutenant saying their wake was like a fingerprint, and they used software to analyze every pixel on a million satellite images to find it.

"We're ready to hoist this unit," a cargo handler shouted.

Bradmore climbed down.

A technician operated an electric winch mounted on cables overhead. It took an hour to hoist three metal boxes, the size of front-loading washing machines and bolt them down. Wires came out one side of each unit and a big glass eye stared out the other. Technicians locked out the high voltage circuit and connected the units to the electrical grid.

Hustling, everyone on the job broke a sweat beneath a merciless sun in a cloudless sky. Fox wanted the mirage projector operational in hours, not days.

Bradmore climbed back up just as the mechanics tightened the last lock-bolts. He plugged his laptop into the control port and waited for the system to boot up. The lasers inside each unit started humming. He remembered spending weeks calibrating the big projector atop the superstructure, synchronizing its millions of lasers, training them to cloak the ship. He had to admit, TenRay technology was PFM—shorthand among electronic warfare experts for Pure Fucking Magic. Bradmore had seen countless electronic gadgets over the years, but to earn the PFM designation, a piece of gear had to perform at a level beyond the known laws of physics, and TenRay technology consistently did just that.

Except, Bradmore reminded himself, for the scary levels of static emitted when they turned it on. And the hum from inside these units indicated that the static level around the ship was about to spike.

Bradmore walked around the narrow service chase to look inside the glass lenses. He knew the TenRay technology in there monitored natural light and shifting color on the water's surface. Simple enough, he figured, with today's color recognition and pattern matching technology. But to project a holograph large enough to cover the ship's two-thousand-foot-long wake—that was TenRay's proprietary secret, the PFM—Bradmore reminded himself as he peered inside each unit through its big glass lens. Clearly, they'd discovered something special in their labs. The thought of working at TenRay intimidated him. Were they black-operators who'd stumbled on something at DARPA or National Labs? Who knew? Stories about engineers making tech breakthroughs at corporations like Verizon and Apple were legendary at the Department of Defense. How many times had an R & D wonk split the corporate sector with their discoveries, patented them, and started their own company?

"TenRay engineers have lightening in a bottle," Fox told him over steak and Lobster, "but they need you to make it work here on the Nimitz."

Bradmore clicked away on his keyboard, booted the operating program, set it to local time, made sure it registered the correct temperature and barometric pressure. The hum out of these units was like nothing he'd ever heard, and he'd heard lots of gear hum. It sounded like money.

Before he powered up the lasers, Bradmore remembered sitting in the back seat of his parent's sedan at a drive-in movie. His dad explained how projectors shined lights through colored film to make the picture on the screen. He bugged his dad until he got out of the car and took him to the front row so he could see for himself. Standing under that gigantic whitewashed wooden screen with hundreds of moths and mosquitoes fluttering in that beam of colored light—that was the first time he experienced genuine awe. For days, he tried to imagine a bulb powerful enough to put moving pictures on a gigantic outdoor screen.

"I'm going to light this thing up," Bradmore shouted to the team, and then he reached inside one of the metal boxes to flip the switch.

"This is just a fancy drive-in movie projector," he whispered, "except it's got an argon-krypton laser and a top-secret Intel chip set."

A solid beam of white light shot from each unit. Amazed and a little nervous, Bradmore stepped back and fought an impulse to shut it down. At some deep level, he knew that projecting so much energy into the atmosphere was dangerous. White light shot through the daylight, nearly to the horizon. It reminded him of a car dealership in San Diego; shining searchlights into the night sky. But here it was noon, and even with tropical sunshine glaring off the water, the three crisp beams of light began to change. One turned blue, the middle one turned a shade of yellow and the other turned green.

"Awesome," someone shouted.

"Wow," another voice echoed.

It sounded like a crowd on the Fourth of July.

This thing is smart, Bradmore realized.

He clicked through screens and watched the light beams dial down to slivers and widen, shining perpendicular to the water. They blended into a single flat, wide beam. The colors adjusted to match the water's shades of blue and green, dappled with white sunshine. Once again, a 9-year-old at the drive in, Bradmore watched in awe as the lasers coalesced in the air, undulating and tossing, cloaking the ship's wake under a mirage that exactly matched the chop on the ocean's broad surface.

CHAPTER TWENTY-SEVEN – Day 6

Brandt already owned Keef; had turned the poor sap into his personal private investigator, and now he toyed with the idea of doing the same to Shakley.

"Give me a few days to look at your crash report," Brandt said. "In the meantime, I have a situation requires your expertise."

"What more can I do?" Shakley asked.

"We've got evidence of sabotage on Stinger engines," Brandt said. "And now you're reporting sabotage on their armament systems."

"Them are serious charges," Keef drawled.

Brandt lit a Parliament and blew out the match with exhaled smoke. "I need you guys to root out the malfeasance in the Stinger squadron."

Shakley's brain scrambled for an excuse to extract himself from this situation, but the pressure mounted with each passing second, and inexplicably he said, "I'd like to stay and help, but—".

"Thanks for volunteering," Brandt said, certain he had Shakley by the short hairs. "Now I don't have to go through the rigmarole of ordering you to stay."

"That won't be necessary," Shakley conceded.

"Great," Brandt proclaimed. He looked at Keef, who sat there scratching a nasty rash on his arm. "You guys are gonna turn the Stingers inside out. Toss their paperwork, computers, living compartments. Do whatever it takes to find out who's sabotaging their aircraft."

"That's not my expertise," Shakley protested.

Brandt slapped a copy of the jet engine report in front of him and said, "Start by reading this."

* * *

A body missing from the wreckage or a stranger appearing in a crash scene video, would normally irritate Shakley. But after a few days on the Nimitz, so many odd characters, like Brandt and Keef and Crenki attached themselves to his investigation, Shakley realized all he could do was keep things from getting out of hand.

He sat in his compartment watching the video of the kid with the toothy grin. He considered the phantom sailor angle, and felt a chill like cold water against his skin. He shivered. He bolted out of his seat and stood there feeling foolish.

He stared at the kid on the TV screen and realized that he was memorizing the good-natured gleam in the young man's eyes, the toothy smile. "Stop," he pleaded, but it was too late. The curse was on him. As long as he was aboard the Nimitz, he was doomed to search for this character.

Self-loathing forced him to shut off the TV. The set went black and he saw a face staring back from the glass screen. He glanced over his shoulder, expecting to see someone lurking there, but he was alone. He squinted and realized it was his own reflection. He wanted to get off the ship, to feel grass between his toes. He went out the door and walked along the passageway, imploring himself to stop pursuing phantom sailors.

* * *

The rash spread along the back of Keef's arms, across his shoulders, down his fat back and into his ass crack. From there it bloomed across his balls and cock, and burrowed in under his overhanging roll of belly fat. Combined with ass-sweat and fart gas, the rash inflamed his hemorrhoid. He couldn't sleep at night, and that put him in a foul mood. At sick call, they gave him a plastic bottle of greasy soap, and he rubbed it everywhere he could reach. It stopped the spread and took the edge off the itch, but he still had red welts where his gut folded over. Chills shivered along his spine and hot flashes made his forehead sweat; convincing him the critters weren't dead. His ears rang. Red veins swelled in the whites of his eyes, and watery ooze pooled on his lower eyelids.

* * *

On the table between Keef and Shakley sat a legal pad with a list of clues printed in Shakley's meticulously neat handwriting.

1. Armament system plug sabotaged on Gould's aircraft.
2. Seven Stinger engines fodded by stainless steel bits.
3. Jenks was plane captain on Gould's flight; Trueblood assaulted in sleep; Chief Crenki (Stinger maintenance chief) threatens subordinates; Commander Aronson (Stinger CO) has a loose grip on discipline.
4. Who sent photo to Gould's wife? Did it cause the crash?

"How does Captain Brandt want us to proceed?" Shakley's voice dripped with sarcasm.

"I'm sick of Brandt riding the hell out of me," Keef said.

"I thought you were pals."

"He's a whirlpool of bad shit," Keef said.

"So, why are you investigating the medical department?" Shakley changed the subject.

Keef shook his head. "Someone's snatching bodies out of the morgue, and I'm stuck on this tub 'til I find out who it is."

"Missing bodies," Shakley said in disbelief.

"You better watch yourself," Keef warned.

"What?" Shakley came up short.

"You might get stuck here like me."

"I think I already am," Shakley said.

"We gotta solve these crimes." Keef glanced at the photo of Lieutenant Gould and the Filipino girl. He thought about the Stinger jet engines, destroyed by mysterious bits of metal. "It's simple," Keef said, as it came to him.

"What?" Shakley asked.

"That cargo plane you flew out here is gonna leave in a few days, and I reckon it'll be the last contact with the real world."

"I don't follow."

"When Fox turns on his invisibility shield," Keef explained, "there's no more care packages from home, no email, no satellite phones, not even a link to the Pentagon."

"What're you getting at?" Shakley asked.

"We solve this case in a couple of days," Keef said, "or we're trapped here."

"Are you suggesting we frame somebody?"

"Course not. We just need to catch a criminal right away."

CHAPTER TWENTY-EIGHT – Day 7

After 0200 the Nimitz steamed with a skeleton crew. Passageways and office spaces fell silent.

Peeping from behind a ladder outside the supply runner's office, Danny Jenks waited for half an hour. Mumbling curses and clawing at his thighs through his pants, he waited for Grady Dutro. And finally, Grady stepped into the passageway and walked aft.

Jenks hung back in shadows cast by steel frames. Grady crossed the galley, walked past the serving line, now dark and quiet. Jenks hid behind a trunk of wires.

Grady bent over and spun a wheel on a round scuttle. He opened it and climbed down through the small opening.

Inside his vest, Jenks clenched the screwdriver's hard plastic handle so tightly his fingers went numb.

Minutes later, the scuttle opened. Grady emerged with a bubble-wrapped aircraft part under his arm. He shut the scuttle and walked outboard into a ladderwell. Jenks stalked his prey. He peeked around corners before rounding them, never letting Grady get more than a few steps ahead.

Grady delivered the part to a maintenance shop and headed back to the supply runner's office.

Jenks followed with determination pulsing through his limbs. He worried about being able to do it quickly, because if Grady got away screaming, people would come running.

Grady walked outboard into an industrial space where only a small red bulb glowed. He pushed back a canvas curtain and opened a door onto a small weatherdeck. Hot night air blew in. Jenks flattened himself behind a steel I-beam and prepared to pounce when Grady came back inside.

He heard the scratch of a disposable lighter and smelled Grady's cigarette.

Jenks imagined punching Grady in the face, knocking him

down, pinning him to the deck, stabbing him in the chest. Now all Grady had to do was walk back through the curtain and die.

A stern voice: "You can't smoke out here!"

"Shit!" Grady bolted through the curtain, orange sparks burst from the cigarette.

"You better run!" the voice again. "I'll write your ass up!"

* * *

The elevator in the base of the superstructure clanged open. Jenks, lurking nearby, heard Grady ask, "Can I catch a ride, sir?"

"Sure, sailor."

"Dammit!" Jenks ran up ladders not knowing where the elevator would stop. He climbed into the cramped maze of passageways behind the bridge. He stalked around corners and waited in the red-lit shadows. He feared running into an ornery officer or an armed marine. Then he saw Grady walking toward him, so he put a hand to his brow. As they passed a door opened, and Jenks saw a woman at a computer studying an aerial picture of the Nimitz. It pricked his curiosity, but a marine stepped out, followed by Captain Fox, and another marine. He followed them down a ladder, his heart racing when he saw Grady walk outboard toward the observation deck. Fox and his marines continued descending.

Hot night air filled Jenks' lungs as he stepped outside. He saw the aft end of the flight deck below, full of aircraft, several with taxi lights flashing, preparing to launch. The sea's black monochrome surface swept past in the moonlight. The roar of jet engines filled his ears. He glanced around the empty observation deck. Grady had to be just ahead where it wrapped around the superstructure. A machine-like voice filled the darkness, "STAND BY, AIRCRAFT LAUNCHING ON CATAPULT TWO."

Jenks heart slammed like a jackhammer under his ribs.

Tobacco smoke wafted around the corner.

Jenks stepped in that direction.

Grady popped his head out and his eyes opened wide.

Jenks leaped around the corner and they stood face to face. He stabbed wildly, the screwdriver's sharp tip struck Grady's collarbone, then his jaw, igniting fear and confusion in both of them.

Grady landed a punch on Jenks' chin.

They stared at each other, stunned.

Then Jenks exploded, whipping his arm wildly, determined to poke the little fucker with his shank.

Grady backed up against the wall, his cries for help drowned by roaring engines.

A demented mix of sobs and laughter burst from Jenks' lips. "You ain't supposed to smoke here, man," he screamed.

Grady fought like a kid who'd never won a playground scuffle. Jenks knocked him down and jumped on, straddling him. He grabbed the front of Grady's shirt with one hand and stabbed with the other.

Right there!

The shank penetrated Grady's neck all the way to the hard plastic handle. A piercing cry escaped Grady's lips, but Jenks jerked the shank like the shifter on a sports car, making a mess insides Grady's neck, drowning his final cry in a bloody gargle.

Jenks didn't hear, behind him, a witness running away. He looked in Grady's eyes and whispered, "You're gonna meet the dead crew now, E-darg." He couldn't tell the exact moment Grady died, and wondered if he was already dead, or maybe just in shock.

He got to his feet, panting hard, his heart hammering a thrill rush of adrenaline in his chest. His boots slipped and stuck in the puddle of blood.

Paranoia closed in like a jail cell and panic jolted his brain. He ran, but six bloody footprints away he froze. He knew they'd bust him if he left the body like this. He wiped the shank on his pants and dropped it on the deck. He pulled the laundry sack and plastic garbage bags from inside his vest.

CHAPTER TWENTY-NINE – Day 7

With eighty men milling around in the Stinger living compartment—some wearing flannel pants, others in shorts or boxers, wife-beater T-shirts, doo-rags, bare feet, flip-flops—it was getting hot. Several pilots and the MAA, under Keef and Shakley's supervision, searched every locker. In every cubicle, an officer went through every article of clothing, every book and every shoe. MAA stood by observing. Probing fingers and prying eyes explored. They looked inside prescription pill vials and sniffed shampoo bottles. They looked through wallets. They searched the digital pictures on every electronic device. They wanted clues to the fodded engines and a digital camera or memory stick containing the original picture sent to Gould's wife.

Up to their elbows in engines, hydraulic systems and weapons all day, the Stingers had returned to their living compartment earlier that evening. A few men watched a movie while others played cards or games on tablet computers. By midnight, they'd all fallen asleep.

The raid came at two in the morning. Officers, chiefs and MAA burst in, turned on lights and shouted for everyone to get out of their bunks.

The Stingers groaned but they understood something evil was operating in their squadron. They willingly opened their lockers. Several said, "I hope you bust somebody. I'm sick of the trouble." Tired, with scraped knuckles, strained backs and sore arms from lugging toolboxes and tiedown chains across the pitching decks all day, they glanced at each other wondering what was being searched for. Who's guilty? Who's gonna get nailed? Big trouble roamed the compartment like a ghost about to wrap its arms around an unlucky sailor. They weren't searching for a few bullets missing from an aircraft's gun—taken for a souvenir. Nothing petty like that. With Lieutenant Gould dead and so many engines fodded, the top brass demanded answers.

* * *

Crenki went straight to Terrance McDaniels' bunk to search for something incriminating. But as he went through McDaniels' gear, the smirk on the kid's face insinuated that someone tipped him off. "You cleaned house," Crenki said, frustration crackling in the nerves behind his forehead. An acidic belch erupted into his esophagus.

"Chief, I keep my locker squared away." McDaniels thought about the cabinet in medical station 12, where Kate let him stash his inventory.

Crenki jammed a hand inside a dress shoe, felt nothing and threw it back into the locker with a bang. "You little—" He had that dog-shit breath from smoking cigarettes.

After so many sabotaged engines, Trueblood getting punched in his sleep and Gould's fatal crash; McDaniels moved his stash. Anyone who didn't see this coming, he figured, deserved brig time just for being stupid.

Frustrated at the prospect of not being able to bust McDaniels, Crenki was making a mess of his clothes when he felt a bulge in the sleeve of McDaniels' peacoat.

"What do we have here?" Crenki's heart raced like a panting rodent.

McDaniels' mouth opened but words failed to come. He saw all his profits snatched up in Crenki's hand.

"You're busted!" Crenki held the sleeve inside out.

"That's my personal savings," McDaniels' voice rose.

Commander Aronson stuck his head into the cubicle and asked, "Find something, chief?"

"McDaniels has contraband sewn into the sleeve of this coat." Crenki tore the lining. A fat roll of fifties and twenties, bound in red rubber bands, dropped from the torn sleeve.

McDaniels snatched it up.

"This man's been selling drugs." Crenki grabbed for the cash. "And these are his profits."

Their fingers tangled on the fat roll of bills.

"Where's that money from?" Aronson asked.

"It's from drug dealing," Crenki insisted. "Look at the fight he's putting up."

"Where'd you get that money?" Aronson asked again.

"It's drug money," Crenki bawled, "or loansharking profits."

"Hold on there, Chief." Aronson placed his hand under theirs. Like a magician untying a knot with a wave of his wand, the bills appeared in Aronson's upturned palm.

"I save every paycheck," McDaniels explained.

Another electric belch erupted into Crenki's esophagus.

With all the Midwestern wholesomeness he could muster, McDaniels said, "This is my college savings, sir."

Crenki opened his mouth to object, but another acidic belch burned his throat so bad he clenched his chest and braced for a heart attack.

Aronson handed the money to McDaniels and noticed wetness around Crenki's eye. "What's the matter, chief?"

Crenki swallowed hard. He opened his eyes wide to keep tears from falling. He coughed something hot and sticky into a cupped hand. His rancid exhale forced McDaniels and Aronson to step back. "I need fresh air," the chief's voice cracked. He glared at McDaniels as he pushed past and left the cubicle.

"This trouble's upsetting him," Aronson said.

"Nobody likes it, sir," McDaniels said.

"They even searched my stateroom."

"No shit," McDaniels said in disbelief.

Aronson thought about the photo sent to Gould's wife while looking at Terrance McDaniels face. This kid wouldn't do something like that, Aronson thought to himself.

McDaniels glanced at his forearm, surprised to see bumps where he'd been absentmindedly scratching.

"Better get that checked," Aronson advised.

* * *

"Whose locker is this?" Keef asked.

"That's Danny Jenks' locker," Trueblood said.

Shouts went up for Jenks but he hadn't returned after work that evening.

"Can we cut the lock without him here?" Rhodes asked.

"Sure, we've got reliable witnesses," Keef said as an MAA stepped over with the bolt cutters and clipped the lock. Keef opened it and suppressed excitement as he looked at the mess before him. Even if this pigsty didn't belong to the culprit, he figured, it was bound to yield something incriminating.

Candle butts, crumpled candy wrappers, porno magazines crammed in with rumpled clothing. A used bar of soap and a twisted tube of Crest without a cap stuck to a gray towel. A metal tray overflowed with coins from many countries, random pills, butterfly knives, a burnt roach clip. A pentagram scraped into the white lacquer.

Rhodes used a pen to lift a charm bracelet from the mess. He held it gingerly and studied the shiny metal charms. Each was a tiny archer with a drawn bow and an arrow ready to fly. Delicate artisanship rendered each figure with a muscular chest and wings on its back. Rhodes' expression turned to shock when he saw horns poking through each figure's hair and little fangs in their mouths.

Keef asked, "Where's Jenks?" But nobody heard the question, because right then an alarm and an announcement boomed throughout the ship.

"SAILOR OVERBOARD ON THE STARBOARD SIDE. LAUNCH THE ALERT HELICOPTER. ALL HANDS REPORT TO SAILOR OVERBOARD STATIONS."

CHAPTER THIRTY – Day 7

A metal door banged.

Heavy boots ran on steel.

"Corpsman!" someone shouted, "I need a corpsman!"

"What's going on?" Commander Sternz ran from her office.

Kate Conrad and Corpsman Gutierrez came out of the records room.

"Someone's been stabbed," the MAA said. "He's bleeding bad!"

"I'll get an emergency kit." Kate took off.

Corpsman Gutierrez ran to grab a stretcher.

"What happened?" Sternz asked.

"There's blood all over the observation deck. They put out a dragnet and caught a guy carrying a bloody laundry bag across the hangar, but he dropped it and ran."

"What condition is the victim in?"

"He's down with multiple stab wounds and bleeding real bad."

Kate ran out of the pharmacy, kit in hand. Gutierrez appeared with a stretcher.

"We'll follow you," Sternz said. "Let's go."

As they ran, the MAA shouted back, "Stuffed him in a sack and left a bloody mess behind. We almost caught him on the hangar, but he dropped the body and ran."

They arrived on scene utterly unprepared. A small crowd stood around an unconscious sailor on bloody, ripped plastic. A mechanic pressed his jersey against the victim's neck and chest.

Kate felt a faint pulse at the wrist. Under the jersey, she found a constellation of puncture wounds and a tattoo of a pentagram above the word DAMMED on the left side of the victim's chest.

* * *

Kate, Gutierrez and an anesthesiologist scrubbed for emergency surgery.

Sternz entered the prep room and said, "They found this on the observation deck." She held out a screwdriver sharpened to a point and covered in dried blood.

Gutierrez tied a drawstring at her waist and Sternz pulled on latex gloves.

A corpsman burst in. "We lost his airway."

* * *

Surgical lamps glowed, life support equipment beeped. In green scrubs, gloves, facemasks and skullcaps the team surrounded the operating table.

As Kate wiped the blood-streaked neck and chest with disinfectant-soaked gauze, the heart rate monitor emitted an urgent tone and flatlines crossed the screen.

A rattling noise erupted from the dead man's mouth.

"His last exhale," the anesthesiologist said as he lifted the oxygen mask.

Someone pressed a button to silence the shrill noise. The ship's steady hum filled the silence.

Behind her surgical mask, Gutierrez grimaced.

Flat lines continued crossing the heart monitor.

Sternz checked for a pulse, but found none.

Suddenly, the dead man grabbed Sternz's wrist. "He's alive," she declared, as she tried to pry his fingers loose.

His jaw open and closed so violently his teeth clacked together. His eyeballs rolled crazily, stopping here and there, as if trying to make contact with those around the table. Broken bits of words slurred off his tongue, "edrew ill mut n ekwa!"

Flatlines crossed the heart monitor.

Sternz broke the dead man's grip on her wrist. "Cardiac resuscitation!" she ordered.

Gutierrez squeezed lubricant onto the paddles.

"—eware of —ed crew mutin on —ekwa," blood ran from

the dead man's nostrils.

Sternz grabbed the paddles and pressed them to the man's chest.

An alarm boomed and an urgent voice announced, "SAILOR OVERBOARD ON THE STARBOARD SIDE. LAUNCH THE ALERT HELICOPTER. ALL HANDS REPORT TO SAILOR OVERBOARD STATIONS. THIS IS NOT A DRILL."

The body bucked from the electric jolt. A gout of blood erupted from his mouth. His eyes blinked and he groaned, but still another flatline beeped across the heart monitor.

Sternz jolted him again.

The body lay still on the operating table.

Everyone looked at each other, wondering what the hell was going on.

And then the man propped himself on his elbows and looked around. He made eye contact with Gutierrez and then Sternz. "Beware of the dead crew." His words were unmistakable. He looked at Kate Conrad and said, "They're going to mutiny on the equator."

"Holy shit," Gutierrez whispered.

The dead man collapsed on his back as another flatline cross the monitor. His head lolled to one side and his tongue hung from his mouth in an exaggerated expression of death.

"Who the hell are the dead crew?" Gutierrez asked.

Kate looked at the crude tattoo on the dead man's chest—a pentagram over the word DAMMED.

"I don't know," Sternz replied, as shaken as the rest.

It started as a patter, rose to a drum roll, and finally the trampling of 10,000 boots reached a crescendo as sailors ran to their overboard stations.

In a few minutes, every person aboard would report in and they'd all know that Danny Jenks was in the water.

CHAPTER THIRTY-ONE – Day 7

Officers sat around the conference room table. Coffee cups and tablet computers scattered about the polished Mahogany.

Captain Fox placed his hand on the shoulder of a young, red-haired lieutenant sitting next to him and said, "Lieutenant Gallagher here will be our prosecuting attorney. But before we get started, I want to make it clear that no matter what the crime, every sailor aboard this ship deserves a fair trial before we find them guilty."

"In order to stick Jenks with multiple life sentences," Gallagher said with a businesslike expression on his freckled face, "we have to put him through the formalities of a general court-martial."

Captain Brandt laughed sharply. "We're gonna throw the book at this kid!"

Commander Aronson's brow furrowed, because Lieutenant Gould was dead and he couldn't duck the blame. An ass chewing didn't worry him because that would heal. Red text worried him. He knew he'd have to fight to prevent a red text reprimand in his record. Red text stopped an officer's career dead in the water.

Commander Shakley drummed his fingers on a neatly bound report, documented with meticulously selected sabotage and pilot error codes. "My testimony will connect Jenks with the sabotage of seven Stinger engines," Shakley said decisively. "I'll also present evidence implicating Jenks in the sabotage of Lieutenant Gould's aircraft."

"I'll meet with each of you to plan your testimony," Gallagher said.

"I want everyone to know," Captain Fox said, "that we will commence another cloaking exercise as soon as this matter is settled and unnecessary personnel—" Fox glanced at Keef and Shakley, "—are flown off the ship. He glared at Aronson, "I expect my entire airwing will be ready to fly."

Everyone understood Captain Fox's message: Pin this mess on Jenks and get back to work.

"I got a list of Jenks' violations cross referenced to the evidence." Keef handed Gallagher a sheet of paper.

The words murder, necrophilia, theft and sabotage leaped out at him. "Thank you, Mr. Keef," Gallagher said.

"This kid's locker was unbelievable," Keef said with animated glee. "He had a dead snake in a shoe and dirty skivvies stuck to—"

"Save it for the witness stand, Keef." Brandt turned his gaze on Aronson.   "I fail to see why you, as the Stinger commanding officer, would allow such a troublemaker to work on the Nimitz's flight deck."

"Well," Aronson replied, "perhaps we should have a psychiatrist testify."

"We haven't got a psychiatrist on board," Brandt said. "Besides, anyone who needs a shrink is unfit to serve in the Navy."

"I examined Jenks briefly after he was locked up," Sternz said, "but I plan to thoroughly evaluate his mental condition—"

"Don't bother! We're not interested in hearing a sob story about how his mother didn't breast feed him." Brandt focused his attention back to Aronson. "I want to know how this criminal was serving as a Stinger all this time."

"According to his aptitude tests, Jenks is a genius," Aronson said. "He was first in his class at avionics training and that's a grueling program."

"He might be a sociopath," Sternz persisted.

"Within a month after joining the squadron he could troubleshoot any bug in the Hornet's electrical system." Aronson said as he planted his big elbows on the table. "Lieutenant Gould himself wrote Jenks outstanding fitness reports. He was such a straight arrow, we sent him to special weapons school in Nevada."

"This kid is nuke loader certified?" Fox asked in disbelief.

"Yes," Aronson said.   "Two years ago he was a model junior petty officer, earned loading crew leader status in record time." Now that he had their attention, Aronson paused and sipped his coffee. "Then one day Lieutenant Gould heard that Jenks had compromised classified information. When Gould and I called Jenks in to ask him about it, he demonstrated outrageous insubordination. I ordered him to calm down. Sometimes these smart types self-destruct if they're accused of anything. Jenks insisted we tell him who made the allegations. Gould explained we were doing a routine follow up, but Jenks waved a finger in my face and demanded I tell him who accused him. He left me no choice, so I put him on restriction and docked his pay. A week later, he was involved in a drunken fistfight. One offense led to another, and he eventually did two weeks in the brig. His career as a weapons handler was over. He went to the line division to carry tiedown chains and wash aircraft. He hasn't been in trouble in over a year."

"He caused a lot of trouble on your watch," Brandt said.

"He might plead insanity," Gallagher said.

"I'll ensure that doesn't happen," Brandt said.

"Regardless of his defense, he'll spend the rest of his life locked up," Gallagher said.

"I want him chopping rocks at Leavenworth until he's ninety-nine years old," Brandt demanded.

"Let's give Gallagher the evidence and wrap this up," Captain Fox insisted.

But Brandt said, "Captain, allow me to ask Aronson another question."

"Very well."

Brandt glared at Aronson. "It sounds to me like you were searching lockers for clues to the problems you're having when you stumbled on enough evidence to convict this kid of every serious crime committed aboard the ship. Can you explain how one person under your command could inflict so much damage and get away with it for so long?"

Aronson calculated his response. He could roll over and play dead, which would mean getting a viciously worded red-ink reprimand in his record and possibly lose command of the Stinger squadron, or he could grab Brandt by the horns and settle it now. Aronson inhaled sharply through his nose, sneered at Brandt and said, "Stop twisting this around to make me look bad. This kid stole a dead body from your morgue, and he's been holding black masses in your anchor chain locker for Christ's sake!" Aronson paused long enough to shift his tone from rage to rational. "Like all of you, I've been investigating, and now that we've caught him, it's clear that Gallagher and Sternz are correct. This kid is ruthless but he's smart enough to have eluded multiple investigations."

Brandt sat back and glared around like a bull that just had his horns ground down. "In spite of sloppy investigative work," he looked at Keef, "we did finally catch this little bastard."

After an awkward silence, Brandt spoke again. "We need to make sure the Pentagon doesn't review this for a while," he looked directly at Lieutenant Gallagher. "You have to nail Jenks so hard on all counts that anyone who glances at this case will see such a big knot they won't want to untie it."

Everyone looked at Gallagher, the redheaded lieutenant. "The key will be to hold Jenks in the ship's brig for as long as possible," he said. "The more time that goes by before he gets back stateside, the less likely anyone will reopen his case."

"I'll make it happen," Brandt said.

"Very well then," Fox said and looked at Gallagher. "My resources are at your disposal."

CHAPTER THIRTY-TWO – Day 8

In the back of the ship's administrative office, Captain Brandt found Lieutenant Jones, a wrinkled old man who claimed to possess a certificate in legal training. Brandt considered it pure luck that no one in the department had ever heard of the old fart. Lieutenant Jones had a full head of black hair and seemed wiry and spry in his neatly pressed uniform. When Jones had little to say, Brandt decided he was the perfect defense attorney for Danny Jenks.

Brandt plopped a copy of the Manual for Courts-Martial on Nikki Thompson's desk and told her to complete all the required forms right away. He scooted behind her desk and leaned over and opened the manual, as if he was going to show her some particular section. When he rubbed his forearm against hers, she stood up and shoved him hard. "Get the fuck away from me," her voice strained.

Fire flared in his eyes as violence sparked between them. "My responsibility as the court recorder," he smirked, "is to ensure that guilty verdicts and a life sentence stick to this son of a bitch like hot glue, and you're going to help me do it."

"Whatever, just keep your hands to yourself."

Nikki tagged all the evidence, which included the letter Gould received from his wife, the photo of Gould fondling a prostitute and a memory stick found in Jenks' locker with the digital original on it. Nikki displayed the devil charm bracelet, a bag of marijuana and a silver Navy ring on the evidence table, along with a glossy color picture of Stanley Comello in his cracker jacks standing at attention before an American flag. Several photos of Grady Dutro, with 27 puncture wounds circled and numbered on his face, neck and chest. The bloodstained screwdriver, sharpened to a point, sat beside a wad of bloody plastic and a laundry bag. Several coil-bound reports, that nobody wanted to read, stacked in a pile.

* * *

Brig guards shaved Jenks' head, shifting his demeanor from drifty-eyed moron to violent criminal. Sleeveless white paper coveralls, revealing a scrawl of demonic tattoos and an infectious looking red rash, left the jury with little room to doubt Jenks' unstable mental condition. A chain hanging between his handcuffs and leg irons jangled on the deck when he scratched himself, which was often. His looks alone practically convinced everyone in the room that Jenks belonged behind bars.

* * *

Gallagher called Commander Aronson to the stand first and asked about Jenks' disciplinary record.

"Danny Jenks impressed everyone in the squadron when he first arrived," Aronson explained, "but then he got in trouble, he spent time in the brig and got busted in rank. He seemed to settle down after I assigned him to work in the line division."

Chief Crenki, heavily sedated on painkillers, lips white from chewing antacid tablets, provided the exact dates and times that each engine was fodded. Gallagher didn't ask about Jenks' character or work habits, but Crenki freely peppered his responses with negative innuendo. Several times Gallagher cut Crenki off and asked that he provide only facts.

Under oath, Terrance McDaniels said Jenks watched his aircraft, number 309, right before it fodded an engine. McDaniels felt like a rat for incriminating a fellow enlisted man, but when he glanced at Jenks, it was clear something had gone terribly wrong in the dude's brain. After testifying, Terrance took his seat and looked at the bumps on his arm. He remembered grabbing Jenks that night in the catwalk and figured that's where he picked up this strange rash.

Petty Officer Trueblood took the stand. Bruises shined like raw meat around his eyes. He told the court: "Over a year ago, I roomed with Jenks when we were stationed ashore for training and I heard him regularly sharing classified information with people who did not have a need to know. He smoked marijuana and stayed awake past taps listening to devil music."

"Please explain how Jenks shared classified information," Gallagher said.

"We joined the Stinger nuclear weapons loading team at the same time, so we got orders to training in Nevada—"

A member of the jury pointed at Jenks and asked, "Does this man have nuclear weapons training?"

Gallagher let the jury stew on the possibility that Jenks, a satanic madman and a murderer, knew how to arm nuclear weapons.

"Can you answer the jury's question?" Gallagher asked.

Trueblood glanced at his boss, Commander Aronson, who gave an affirmative nod.

"Airman Jenks graduated from fire control technician training and nuclear weapons school," Trueblood said. "He knows everything the Navy will teach an enlisted man about weapons, nuclear or otherwise."

"How do you know this?" Gallagher asked.

"Because I went to school in Nevada with Jenks, and they taught us how to load, arm and detonate nuclear weapons. After training, we roomed together. That is until he got busted for compromising classified information."

"Is that why Airman Jenks assaulted you in your sleep?"

"Yeah, I—" Trueblood paused. "They never caught who hit me."

Next Gallagher called Commander Shakley to the witness stand and questioned him about his investigation into the Stinger's fodded engines. Shakley made it clear that the metal fragments found inside the damaged engines had the same metallurgical properties as the devil charms found in Jenks' locker. He held the bracelet, with one end in each hand, so the jury could see it.

Gallagher pointed a pencil at the charms dangling from the bracelet and said to the jury, "Notice the charms are evenly spaced across only half of this bracelet."

The jury members' expressions remained blank.

"At one time this bracelet had fourteen charms, but now it only has seven," he touched the dangling demons with his pencil eraser. He took the bracelet from Shakley and handed it to a member of the jury. "Examine it for yourself and see where seven devil charms have been broken off." Then he snatched the engineer's report and waved it over his head. "Seven charms missing and according to this report seven Stinger engines sabotaged."

Shakley also testified that Jenks had performed preflight checks on the aircraft Gould flew on his ill-fated flight. Shakley linked the broken safety-wire, and the cannon plug with the missing prongs, to Jenks' detailed knowledge of armament systems. He didn't say Gould's death, and the destruction of his aircraft, were Jenks' fault, but Lieutenant Gallagher made the connection for them when he told the jury, "Danny Jenks is a devil worshipping saboteur who tormented Lieutenant Gould and his wife. His actions, directly or indirectly, caused Gould to crash his aircraft and endanger the lives of every person on this ship."

The sailor who witnessed Jenks stabbing Grady Dutro told her story. "I went to the observation deck to watch airplanes take off, but when I got there I saw Daniel Jenks stabbing Grady Dutro. I ran and found the MAA and took them back to the observation deck, but nobody was there, only a sharpened screwdriver in a puddle of blood."

Testimony from a petty officer on the ship's MAA squad explained how they chased Jenks across the hangar, and how he dropped Grady Dutro's body and led them on a wild chase through passages and up and down ladders before he finally jumped overboard.

Gallagher questioned the medical officer, Commander Sternz, about the stab wounds on Grady Dutro's neck and chest. While she provided expert medical testimony, confirming that Jenks stabbed Dutro with the sharpened screwdriver, Gallagher handed the shank and the gruesome picture of Dutro's naked corpse to the jury for their examination.

Next, Gallagher questioned Mr. Keef about his medical department investigation.

"I had no luck on the case," Keef explained, "but Captain Brandt assigned me to assist Mr. Shakley on the crash investigation—"

"This seems rather extraordinary," Gallagher said with mock incredulity. "Charges of murder and sabotage have been brought with overwhelming evidence, and now the jury is to believe that Jenks is also guilty of stealing a corpse from the morgue?"

Keef sucked in his enormous belly and shifted his ass in the chair. "I'm fixin to tell about my investigation and show some evidence. I reckon the Jury can make up their own minds."

"Okay," Gallagher agreed. "Please explain how you connected Jenks to this hideous act."

"Stanley Comello had gotten crushed to death by a jet engine shipping container, and his body went into the morgue—"

Gallagher handed the glossy portrait of Comello to the jury. They passed it around and examined the chubby cheeked young man standing proudly in his dress uniform before the American flag.

* * *

When Shakley saw the picture, a horrible disturbance vexed his thoughts, because he recognized Comello as the phantom sailor he'd seen in the video of Lieutenant Gould's crash.

* * *

"That ring over yonder," Keef pointed to the evidence table, "it was on Comello's finger when they stuck him in the morgue."

Gallagher removed the ring from the plastic bag and handed it to the jury. They examined the blue gem and "Stanley Comello USN" inscribed inside.

"And how does this ring connect Jenks to Comello's missing body?

"I found that there ring in Danny Jenks' locker."

"Are you saying that Danny Jenks stole Stanley Comello's corpse from the morgue and kept his ring as a souvenir?"

"I'll tell you that ring was on Comello's finger in the morgue and the next place it showed up is Danny Jenks' locker."

Before resting the prosecution's case, Gallagher called Sternz back to the witness stand, where she stated that Stanley Comello's body had in fact vanished from the morgue and remained missing and unaccounted for.

Terrance McDaniels couldn't wait to drop that bombshell on Kate.

Shakley wondered how Stanley Comello, a dead man, could possibly have been on the flight deck during Gould's crash. He looked at Jenks and saw arms covered with tattoos and an angry rash; manacles locking his wrists and ankles. Shakley considered the charges: murder, steeling a corpse, sabotage. It made a mad sort of sense that Jenks had snatched Comello's body from the morgue and brought him back to life in a demonic ritual. For a second Shakley believed that Comello had come back from the dead—and now he was a phantom sailor roaming about the ship. But that's impossible, Shakley told himself. The guy in the video had to be someone who looked like Comello. Shakley glared at Keef and wondered if he had planted the ring in Jenks' locker.

* * *

Lieutenant Jones sat perfectly still and didn't utter a peep the entire trial, so nobody knew what to expect when Brandt called him to present Jenks' defense.

Jones stood quickly and took two springy steps forward. His thick black hair looked like a wig the way it slicked back from his emotionless, wrinkled face. He cocked his head at an angle as if he were listening for a sound nobody else could hear.

Seconds ticked by with Jones frozen like that while Captain Brandt looked on feeling embarrassed. I should have checked this guy out better before assigning him to defend Jenks. He's going to cause a mistrial if he doesn't get on the ball. Brandt considered speaking up but wondered what he could say to get this senile coot back on track.

The Jury members shrank back at once, their chair legs scraping noisily against the floor when Lieutenant Jones opened his eyes wide and revealed red veins and watery ooze. He scratched at both elbows and finally, in a creaky rasp, through crooked yellow teeth, he said, "If Danny Jenks utters so much as one syllable he'll incriminate himself." And with that, Jones turned abruptly and walked back to his seat. With a fiendish smirk on his lips, he winked at Captain Brandt.

Gallagher cleared his throat and dove into his closing argument. "With a simple statement I will rest the case of the

United States Navy versus Daniel Jenks on charges of murder, sabotage, Satanism, drug use and theft of a shipmate's corpse from the morgue. And that simple statement is this. We do not need to hear from Danny Jenks because nothing he says could refute the evidence presented against him."

* * *

The chain between Jenks' wrists and ankles jangled on the deck when he stood to hear the verdicts.

"The jury finds Daniel Jenks guilty of the murder of Seaman Grady Dutro," Brandt read, "guilty on seven counts of sabotage for willfully and intentionally damaging jet aircraft, guilty on one count of sabotage for willfully and intentionally damaging the electronics system of a jet aircraft contributing to the death of Lieutenant Gould, guilty of possession of controlled substances and guilty of stealing Airman Stanley Comello's corpse from the morgue."

Jenks yawned as if waking from a nap. His chains rattled as he rubbed his eyes. He glanced around, first at Lieutenant Gallagher and then at the members of the jury. Then he looked straight at Captain Fox.

"What do you have to say for yourself?" Fox asked.

"I didn't steal a body out of your morgue," his tone calm. "Likely it was a member of the notorious dead crew who are walking about your ship as we speak."

Jenks spoke with a calm seriousness that convinced everyone that what he said was true, at least for him. This caught most off guard. If he'd screamed or cursed, he'd have discredited himself, but his sober tone made everyone perk up with curiosity.

But then Jenks shifted his feet, the chains jangled, and broke the illusion.

"That's enough out of you," Fox said.

The guards grabbed Jenks arms and nudged him toward the door.

"Don't rub elbows with the dead crew," Jenks hollered. "Satan will lead a mutiny if you do!"

A guard slapped a big hand over Jenks' mouth, as they

wrestled him out of the compartment.

Shakley wondered about the video of Stanley Comello smiling as Gould's Hornet crashed behind him. Sternz wondered if Jenks had really snatched Stanley Comello's body from the morgue; and what about Donna Grogan and Larry Burns? A pang of guilt quivered in Keef's big gut as he glanced at the silver Navy ring on the evidence table. Nikki Thompson looked at the old man, Lieutenant Jones, and wondered where he'd come from. She'd worked in the ship's administrative office for several months, but had never seen Lieutenant Jones before.

CHAPTER THIRTY-THREE – Day 8

Terrance admired Kate's smooth complexion, her lips and straight white smile. He glanced in her eyes and couldn't wait to see her facial expression change.

"Quit looking at me like that," she said

But he kept right on mooning at her with a big grin. And then he dropped the bomb. He said, "I heard Sternz testify that Stanley Comello's body was missing from the morgue."

"No way!" Her eyes opened wide.

"Sternz said it at Danny Jenks' court martial." He could see the wonder and disbelief charging through her brain. "And a guy named Keef has been investigating the medical department."

"Big guy with a Texas accent?"

"Yup, said he found Stanley Comello's Navy ring inside Jenks' locker."

"That's a lie," she said. "I took that ring off Comello myself."

"Keef said it was on Comello's finger when Jenks took him from the morgue."

"Did they say anything about Donna Grogan or Larry Burns?"

"Just Comello."

"What'd Sternz say exactly?"

"Just that Comello's body was missing from the morgue."

"What else?" she insisted.

"Nothing, but Keef said Jenks used Comello's body for a black mass or something like that."

"How did Jenks get into the morgue?"

"They didn't say," Terrance said.

"A person can't just walk out of the medical department with a body slung over their shoulder," Kate said.

"Jenks carried a dead guy in a laundry bag down from the

observation deck to the hangar," Terrance said.

"Yeah, but that was in the middle of the night," Kate protested. "Comello disappeared from the morgue in the afternoon. Somebody would have seen him."

"Maybe somebody helped him," Terrance countered. "Any shady characters working in the medical department?"

"I pulled that ring off Comello's finger myself," she insisted.

"What happened to it then?"

"I put it in a plastic bag with his wallet, and put it in a big envelope and I wrote his name on it." She tried to remember. "Then the envelope went somewhere," she said hesitantly. "OH MY GOD!" she shouted, "It must have gone to Keef!"

"Maybe he planted it in Jenks' locker," Terrance said.

"You think he framed Jenks?"

"I don't know." Terrance pulled up one of his sleeves and showed her his arm. "These bumps are driving me crazy."

"How'd you get that?" she asked

"From Jenks," he said, scratching hard. "He's a total skeezball."

"Jenks?"

"Yeah," he said with a sense of dread. "He probably got it from messing with dead bodies."

"Gross!" Kate stepped away.

"Thanks," Terrance said. "I have satanic death rot and all you can say is gross?"

CHAPTER THIRTY-FOUR – Day 8

On the TV, four Hornets sat parked in a row. Mechanics and handlers in colored jerseys dotted the scene. Shakley pressed pause and grabbed the glossy picture of Stanley Comello from the table. He held the picture next to the TV. He pointed from the picture to the face on the screen. "Any resemblance?" he asked.

"That fella looks like Stanley Comello," Keef admitted.

"Now watch this." Shakley pressed play and Comello walked over and stood next to one of the Hornets. A pilot and a plane captain walked around it performing preflight checks. Comello smiled directly at the camera before it panned forward.

When it panned back, Comello was gone, the pilot was in the cockpit, and the plane captain was starting the engines.

"This video," Shakley proclaimed, "is from yesterday."

"Dammit!" Keef shook his head.

"Yesterday," Shakley declared.

"We're off this ship," Keef said.

"That Hornet—" Shakley said.

"I am not hearing this," Keef interrupted.

"That Hornet fodded an engine on the launch yesterday."

"And I reckon you took it apart and found a little devil inside," Keef said.

"Not yet—"

"My ass!" Keef yelled. "We're on the last flight off this boat."

Shakley's shoulders slumped.

"This ship is fixin' to go invisible and cross the equator," Keef said. "I don't know about you, but I'm not getting on my hands and knees so a bunch of kids can paddle my ass!"

"That's Comello," Shakley pointed at the TV.

"Who?" Keef asked.

"Stanley Comello," Shakley said.

"Never heard of him," Keef replied.

* * *

Even a pint-sized beaker of refrigerated, mint-flavored Mylanta with two shots of Benadryl stirred in, couldn't extinguish the peptic burning sensation at the base of Crenki's esophagus.

No matter what Sternz said to console him, no matter what pills she gave him, no matter what kind of frothy, numbing concoction she mixed to cool his insides, Crenki worried that he was on the verge of a heart attack. At the back of his mouth, he could taste blood seeping from ulcers in his stomach.

"Navy coffee and cigarettes have ruined my belly and played havoc with my heartbeat," he claimed. "I cough blood and I'm telling you, doc, there's blood in my stool!"

"Normally, I'd give you a physical before sending you off the ship, chief," Sternz explained, "but your orders just came down and the cargo plane is leaving right away."

"Is it safe to fly in my condition?"

"Absolutely," Sternz said as she typed a note in Crenki's record and pressed the enter key.

* * *

Strapped in among the mailbags in the back of the cargo plane, Shakley and Keef nodded as Crenki climbed in and sat in the empty seat across from them.

A few minutes later, the aircraft taxied to the catapult. In a crescendo of roaring engines, the little plane shot off the bow and flew into the sky.

Crenki watched through a tiny window as the ship vanished on the shimmering water below. He strained his eyes, looking for the line where the sun rides from east to west, where lowly pollywogs make the mysterious passage to become Trusty Shellbacks. A dull ache scratched inside Crenki's chest; not his bleeding ulcer though, just a pang of regret. His naval career would always be incomplete. He would always be a lowly wog.

CHAPTER THIRTY-FIVE – Day 9

At 0830 every other morning, Kate Conrad grabbed a medical kit and followed Sternz along the main deck and down several ladders to an iron gate. A brig guard thoroughly examined their ID cards before unlocking the gate and allowing them to enter the brig. In recent weeks, Kate had become impatient with the guards' robot-like examination of her ID, even though she arrived at the brig every other morning at the same exact time. But after seeing firsthand how Jenks made a pincushion out of Grady Dutro, and knowing that they had Jenks locked inside the brig now, she found the guard's meticulous inspection of her ID reassuring.

Rumors circulating around the medical department identified Jenks as the body snatcher. According to one outrageous account, Jenks dismembered and ate the dead, leaving their bones in the bottom of one of the anchor chain lockers. Another rumor described Jenks as an enraged Shellback, possessed by spirits from the deep. Some said Davy Jones and his minions had come aboard and tormented Jenks until he went on a pollywog-killing spree. The approaching equator-crossing ceremony, according to some of the old Shellbacks, would be an especially brutal torture for all the unworthy pollywogs aboard.

The first few times Kate went down to the brig, the big clanking locks in the barred doors and the jangling key rings carried by the muscular marine guards intimidated her. The walls were the same green as chocolate chip mint ice cream; she figured it helped keep the prisoners calm. The cells were tiny and nondescript, each designed for one occupant, with a metal toilet and sink and a narrow bunk that folded down from the wall on chains. Each prisoner had a thin mattress, a black scratchy wool blanket, two flat sheets and a pillow. Most cells had doors with bars while others were solid plates of steel with a peephole and a little pass-through for food, which was sometimes bread and water. The only reading material allowed was the Bluejacket's Manual. Electronic devices were banned.

There were 16 prisoners in the brig. Sternz and Kate examined them all, saving Jenks for last.

* * *

Outside the steel door, held shut by several deadbolts, Sternz asked the guard, "Has this prisoner done anything violent?"

"No, ma'am. He's been on his back, moaning, that's about it." The guard pulled her club from a ring on her belt and made ready to use it. Drubbing her hand with the club, she told Sternz, "He's a murderer and we consider him dangerous."

Sternz glanced at Kate and then looked at the guard. "I want him shackled at wrists and ankles and secured to this fixture." She pointed to a metal ring welded to the bulkhead at eye level.

"I'll need some extra muscle." The guard walked away.

Kate studied the ominous door. Three hinges welded on one side, a peephole at eye-level, and a rectangular pass-through for food.

"He's a disturbed individual," Sternz warned, "capable of deranged and violent behavior."

"Is this the guy who stabbed Grady Dutro?" Kate asked.

"Yes."

Kate was on the verge of saying that she'd heard Jenks had stolen a body from the morgue, but stopped herself and asked, "Is murder his only crime?"

"He vandalized aircraft," Sternz said, while Kate studied her facial expression for unspoken information. "And he had drugs in his locker."

Amazed at her boss's unemotional, robotic precision, Kate almost said she'd heard Jenks stole a body form the morgue. Instead, she said, "This morning I read Jenks' medical record."

"I looked at it myself," Sternz said.

"I counted eleven treatments for gonorrhea."

"Did you look closely at the test results?"

"Just glanced," Kate said.

"The culture testing showed that several times he waited

months to seek treatment, and going that long with gonorrhea causes brain dysfunction and scarring of the heart muscles."

"That probably explains why he's so violent," Kate said.

"Correct," Sternz said.

The brawny woman who had escorted them from cell to cell, and two other guards, came down the passageway with shackles and chains jangling in their hands. Their white T-shirts stretched over broad chests and beefy shoulders.

"Until we get him chained up," one of the guards said, "please move to the end of the passageway."

Kate and Sternz listened as the guards struggled with Jenks inside the cell.

"You think you've got me trapped," Jenks' voice echoed along the narrow passageway, "but this tin box won't hold me!"

"Get the cuffs on him," one of the guards ordered.

Jangling chains, cursing and grunting.

"Okay, let's move him."

As one guard's broad back came through the open cell door another shouted, "He bit me!" Arms and legs thrashed in the doorway. Jenks swung his fists as much as the chains allowed. A drum roll of baton blows beat him until the guards were panting and Jenks lay in a heap.

Kate pulled out heavy duty Latex gloves and handed a pair to Sternz.

*   *   *

Sternz's snipped off Jenks' paper coveralls with a pair of scissors to reveal large blotches of red rash covering his arms, extending across his back and down between his buttocks. All across his torso, the rash obscured the artwork and lettering tattooed on his skin.

Kate cringed. She struggled to make sense of this naked thing. She thought about abused patients in an old-time insane asylum. But this killer didn't fit the helpless patient profile; nevertheless, a subtle sense of pity crept over her unexpectedly.

When Sternz put a hand on Jenks' shoulder, he relaxed. His knees bent as if the chains were weighing him down.

"I want to listen to your heart," Sternz said, as the cold disk of her stethoscope touched his chest. She put her head close to his shoulder. He turned, chains jangling, and stared straight into her eyes. He had the tube of her stethoscope pinched in his fingers, and she flinched back, startled.

The stethoscope yanked from her ears.

Dropping it to the deck, Jenks whispered as if telling a secret, "The tigerfish are swarming."

A guard stepped over, club raised.

Jenks whispered, "They've surrounded the ship."

Sternz waved the guard off. She took a syringe from the medical bag and said, "Stay still while I draw your blood." She swabbed the crook of his arm and stuck the needle into a vein. As blood filled the collection vial, she studied a green and black dragon, its tail wrapped around his bicep. A pentagram above the word DAMMED on the left side of his chest. She recalled the stabbing victim, Grady Dutro, had the same tattoo.

*   *   *

After the guards locked Jenks back in his cell, he whined like a cat with a broken tail trapped in an empty dumpster.

The guards led Sternz and Kate back through a cage door. A logbook sat on a metal podium on a gleaming tiled floor. Sternz entered the time and date, and noted that all prisoners were in satisfactory health. She flipped back several pages, read the entries and noted nothing unusual during the past 48 hours.

"I want you to do two things for me," Sternz told the guard.

"What is it, ma'am?"

"First, I want you to make sure Jenks showers with this." She handed over a plastic bottle of BacteroDerm soap.

"Yes, ma'am," the guard replied.

"Second, I want all the guards to record observations on Jenks' behavior."

"How about we put a pad here by the logbook?" the guard suggested. "And we'll write a note about him after each round."

"That would be great."

"He's not leaving the ship any time soon," the guard said.

"That's precisely why we need to keep a close eye on him," Sternz said. "I don't know if you were informed, but when the MAA tried to apprehend him, he jumped over the side."

"He's dangerous, huh?" the guard asked.

"An observation log will help us figure him out."

"What do you want us to write in it?"

"Descriptions of what he says and does."

"Yes, ma'am."

Before leaving, Sternz said, "He's a convicted murderer, and his mental health is impaired. Everyone dealing with him must use extreme caution, because he might lash out violently when you least expect it."

*   *   *

With the blood sample dropped at the lab, Sternz sat at her desk and reconsidered the case they'd made against Daniel Jenks. Was it decided too quickly? And what about the other missing bodies? Had Jenks stolen Donna Grogan and Larry Burns too? These woeful speculations sparked more questions. How could Jenks have walked out of the morgue with three dead bodies? It's locked and only a few know the combination. He couldn't have done it alone. Who helped him? She felt the too-quick and too-neat convictions unraveling. Did Comello's corpse really have a ring still on its finger as Keef claimed? Fox and Brandt wanted to blame it all on Jenks! Fox especially, because he wanted to get back to his cloaking exercise. Frustration tied her thoughts in knots. But what could she do?

She considered his rash and satanic tattoos, remembered him threatening Captain Fox and the constellation of stab wounds he'd left on Grady Dutro. He's a cold-blooded murderer, she concluded again.

CHAPTER THIRTY-SIX – Day 9

Sailors sat at glowing computers in the dimly lit electronic countermeasure command center.

Captain Fox and Mr. Bradmore stood at the center of the compartment.

"Prepare to commence the cloaking exercise," Fox said.

Bradmore repeated the order loud enough for everyone to hear. Men and women at workstations began reporting out.

"TenRay warming up."

A technician wearing a headset stood near the large touch-sensitive, see-through display lit with a 3-D scale image of the ship. It showed the cloaking system components in their actual locations. The technician touched an icon on the screen, opening a data window that displayed parameter updates.

Fox paused behind the new satellite-tracking technician. Pictures of ships taken from earth-orbiting satellites flashed on her screen above a status bar climbing steadily to 100%.

"What's the capability of this workstation?" Fox asked.

"Well, sir, we know the orbit of every satellite with image capability," the technician explained. "The instant one comes over the horizon we hack it and stand by to feed it the image we want it to see."

"How much testing have you done?"

"We've taken over seven-thousand pictures of the Nimitz from cameras on nine different satellites over the past forty-eight hours, and we've fed them images of fishing trawlers, supertankers, garbage barges, cruise ships, you name it, if it floats I have a picture of it in my database."

"What about simultaneous threats?" Fox asked.

"Yesterday we had three satellites overhead for several hours" the technician said proudly. "We took hundreds of pictures of ourselves and every one of them showed exactly what we projected on the holograph."

"Keep up the good work," Fox said.

"Mr. Bradmore," someone shouted. "The TenRay is ready for total spectrum processing."

Captain Fox and Mr. Bradmore stepped over to the big monitor at the center of the compartment. Bradmore slipped his key into the panel and typed his user-ID and password. On the big 3-D screen, the system components glowed yellow.

Fox inserted his key and typed his credentials. One by one, the cloaking system components and the fiber optic network connecting them turned green.

"TenRay report," Bradmore ordered.

"Processing at full spectrum," a technician shouted.

"Flatpanel array report," Bradmore said.

"Processing at max capacity."

"Video cameras?"

"All cameras streaming live, sir."

"Laser holograph projector?"

"Ship cloaked three-hundred-and-sixty degrees."

"Fantail mirage?"

"Confirm, projecting broadband image astern, sir."

"Sonar report."

"Peak capacity, pinging down nine hundred and twenty-two fathoms to the muddy bottom, sir."

"Captain," Bradmore said, "the Nimitz is invisible."

CHAPTER THIRTY-SEVEN – Day 9

Screams of agony and spit erupted from his cracked lips. Tears ran from his swollen eyes. A million microscopic creatures chewed into the flesh on the backs of his arms and legs. Itchy bumps prickled across his back, down the crack of his ass and onto his white thighs.

A school of tigerfish swam in slow, menacing circles around him. The sleek small ones darted quickly and the cell's florescent light shimmered on their orange and black stripes. A big one slid by with its gills undulating, black rubbery lips pulsating. Its mouth opened and closed rhythmically, revealing jagged teeth.

He relaxed for a moment and one of the damn things nipped the back of his neck. He jerked around to fend it off, but another nibbled his ass. This torture went on for hours.

A brig guard watched through the peephole and then made a note in the logbook: "Prisoner is thrashing on the floor. He didn't touch his bread and water so he must not be hungry."

Flailing about, fighting off tigerfish, raised bruises on Jenks' back and knees. He scratched the chapped skin on his elbows with one hand and clawed his thighs with the other. His breath came in ragged gasps.

A big tigerfish squeezed out of an air vent in the ceiling and hovered menacingly above. The creature circled down; its yellow eyes winking slowly.

He touched its undulating gills as it nuzzled his leg, and his fingertips sank into its thick coat of slime. Something tingled inside his hand.

"What the—" He yanked his hand away.

Its rubbery lips opened, revealing splintered teeth. Its tiger-striped scales quivered as it darted directly at his belly and bit him. He screamed and punched it while running in a panicked little circle. Pain shot through his torso and blood appeared where it bit

153

his stomach. Jenks slammed himself into the bulkhead in an attempt to get it off but it refused to let go. In a rage, he threw himself as hard as he could, repeatedly, into the gray steel wall.

A brig guard heard the commotion and pressed an eye to the peephole. She saw Jenks stumbling in a daze. His wobbly knees folded and he collapsed. The guard walked back to the logbook and wrote, "Heard a loud bang and now Jenks is resting face-down on the floor."

* * *

Hideous laughter echoed off the walls. Jenks heart bolted with anticipation. He got to his knees and bowed his head. Slowly he lifted his gaze, expecting to see Satan, but he saw his lousy defense lawyer, Lieutenant Jones, standing there inside his cell. Waxy grease slicked his black hair back from his brow. Deep wrinkles cut the skin around his eyes. He wore a black tuxedo with tails and gold buttons, a white shirt with a ruffled front and a black bowtie. A pearl-handled sword hung in a scabbard on his belt.

"Am I getting a retrial?" Jenks asked confused.

Jones' lips curled into a brown-toothed smirk. "No," he said, "there won't be another trail, not for you anyway."

"You did a lousy job defending me." Jenks stood up.

"You were guilty," Jones said.

"I didn't steal a corpse from the morgue."

"They pinned that one on you." Jones scratched the back of his arm with a white-gloved hand.

"You got this damn rash too?" Jenks indicated his arms; scratched raw. "It's driving me nuts!"

"Get used to it," Jones advised. "Blasted tropical fever,"

"Tropical what?" Jenks' face crimped in confusion.

"Catch it from sea creatures," Jones said. "You haven't seen any sea creatures, have you?"

"The slime on the tigerfish!" Jenks knew he'd gotten it from Ratcomb.

"It burrows under your skin and breeds."

"Why are you here?" Jenks changed the subject.

"I'm the one you're waiting for."

"Shit. I'm not waiting for you," Jenks sneered and stepped close to Jones, his fists clenched at his sides. "I'm waiting for Satan."

Jones spat to the side without taking his eyes off Jenks, and said, "Satan shit his little red pants when he met me."

"I seriously doubt that," Jenks said.

Jones grinned and said, "There's so much you don't know."

Jenks made a grab at Jones' lapels, but Jones got the jump and clamped his hands around Jenks' neck. He lifted him off the deck and pressed his back against the wall.

Jenks gasped, surprised by the old man's agility and the power in the big thumbs pressing against his windpipe.

"Now that I have your attention," Jones said, "I'll make you an offer."

A blue tint crept into Jenks' face as he struggled to breath. He clutched Jones' wrists and tried to pull the powerful hands off his throat, but only managed to loosen them enough to croak, "I'm not interested."

Jenks' carotid artery pulsed against Jones' palm.

They stared into each other's eyes, and Jones expression softened. "I sure do look nice in this suit!" Jones' eyebrows arched, as if to say, don't you think so? "And I sure do argue eloquently," his voice bubbling with phony enthusiasm. "Fancy clothes and highbrow rhetoric is what I'm all about, can't you tell?"

Jenks lungs ached for air.

"And there's this little matter of my hands around your neck, eh?"

Jenks' tongue slipped out and a rattling noise came from the back of his throat.

"It's really something, ain't it," Jones asked, "how so much of our civilized behavior relies on the way people dress and how they talk?"

Jenks' heels kicked against the wall and his hands, on Jones' wrists, shivered in an uncontrolled convulsion.

"But we know fancy clothes and big words don't add up to shit. Ain't that right?"

Jenks' eyes blinked all crazy.

Jones clenched his teeth and growled, "After you peel the

veneer off our civilized behavior, Danny, what do you have left?"

Tears trickled down Jenks' blue cheeks. Clear snot ran from his nose.

"What's left of your humanity without our fancy clothes and persuasive conversation?" Jones growled and spittle flew from his lips.

White slobber formed at the corners of Jenks' mouth. His heels stopped kicking. His arms hung at his side.

"Where are your God and your devil now?"

Jenks couldn't reply.

"I'll tell you where they are," Jones screamed, "They're in your fucking head!" He squeezed tighter and stared into Jenks' eyes, trying to connect with his last glimmer of life, "So, what is our human race then?"

Jones loosened his grip the slightest bit.

Jenks gulped air and whispered. "I don't know."

Jones' ancient eyes leered at the foolish sailor. He re-tightened his grip, blocking Jenks' airway and cutting off the flow of blood to his brain.

"I'll tell you," Jones whispered. "Humans ... are ... maggots! All you do is eat and fuck, and you, Danny Jenks, have been thoroughly eaten ... and thoroughly fucked!"

With his last ounce of strength, Jenks said. "What do you want?"

"I want to save you, my friend, save you from this doomed ship," Jones said with mock benevolence.

Jenks nodded.

"So, you're joining my dead crew, is that it, Danny? Do I have your oath now?"

Jenks nodded again.

At that, Jones dropped him in a heap.

The pressure inside his skull decreased as he heaved several ragged breathes. He glanced at his lawyer's face, now shoved down at him full of expectation. A shock of waxed black hair flopped across one dark eye.

Jenks wondered why Jones had choked him and asked all those crazy questions. And then it occurred to him that Jones was a low-level demon trying to get him to sell out before his big meeting with Satan.

"Why do you want me?" Jenks stalled.

"There's a particular wog aboard this ship who is passing himself off as a Shellback," Jones explained, "and I am conspiring to punish him."

"What are you talking about?" Jenks was confused.

"King Neptune, on the other hand, has a substantial grievance of his own—"

"King Neptune?" Jenks wondered aloud.

"Yes," Jones said matter-of-factly. "Neptunus Rex, Ruler of the Raging Main and all that, he's hot over this invisibility shield. It's messing with his magical powers or some such—"

"Why do you want me?" Jenks asked, propping himself up on an elbow, circling back to his original question.

"Because you have secret knowledge," Jones' voice popped with excitement. He leaned close to Jenks and whispered, "You can bring this tub to the bottom in grand fashion."

Jenks took a deep breath and went all in. "I demand to see Satan."

Supremely disappointed, Jones stood up straight and shook his head. Gritting his teeth, he inhaled sharply and leaped into the air and drew his knees up to his chest. His tuxedo tails flapped upward, the pearl-handled sword on his belt rattled in its scabbard.

The sight of Jones dressed so splendidly and leaping so high sent a temblor of fear through Jenks.

The heels of Jones' shiny black boots stomped on Jenks' right leg, shattering both bones below the knee.

* * *

A SHRIEK like an injured animal alerted the guard who peeked in and saw the prisoner on his back, moaning, leg bent at an impossible angle.

"Oh, gross," the guard whispered. "Is he pissing himself?"

Moments later, brandishing handcuffs and a straightjacket, three guards cautiously entered the cell.

Jenks leaped to his feet and swung a fist.

The guards stepped back as the lower half of Jenks' right

157

leg crumbled.   The broken end of his shinbone tore through the paper coveralls and scraped against the floor.

A jolt of pure pain shot up his leg and into his hip. It zinged up his spine and struck the base of his skull.

As he collapsed, he saw urine and blood messing his paper coveralls. Blotchy bruises and a red rash covered his tattooed arms. His head swam in dizzy nausea. His eyes simmered in a hot, red soup.

PART IV

CROSSING THE LINE

CHAPTER THIRTY-EIGHT – Day 9

Captain Brandt looked at the certificate hanging on the wall behind his desk. There were no degrees or awards; only this certificate in a wooden frame. Across the top, King Neptune rode the surface of the sea in a chariot pulled by dolphins. Bright orange fish with black stripes, like Bengal Tigers, leaped in the chariot's wake. A jumble of seahorses, mermaids and skeletons in sailor caps and knotted neckerchiefs drifted in the margins. Along the sandy bottom, rotten timbers rose from a shipwreck. Davy Jones stood with a boot atop a treasure chest overflowing with gold coins, his elbow propped on one knee and his chin on his fist. Mermaids and sharks swam all about.

Brandt read the certificate in a low whisper. "Let it be known to all Shellbacks, worthy mariners, sailors, plank owners and to all seamen from all nations, and let it be known to every lowly landlubber, scalawag, pollywog, urchin, vermin and to every denizen of the sea, that Samuel Brandt has crossed the equator and has been duly initiated into the Royal Order of The Deep and thus has the title of Trusty Shellback bestowed upon him by Neptunus Rex, Ruler of the Raging Main.

Brandt grabbed a pen and a yellow sticky note from his desk drawer. He looked at Jones and made a list: tricorn hat, black wig, sword, old-fashioned officer's jacket, tattered pants. He noticed Jones wore no ranks. "That's strange," Brandt whispered,

"I thought he was a captain."

Brandt left his office and walked briskly along the main deck. Men and women stepped out of his way. A few addressed him with sharp calls of, "Good morning, sir."

He ignored them, kept his eyes straight ahead. He turned outboard and went through a door, into the administrative office.

"Attention on deck!" someone shouted when he entered.

Clerks and petty officers sprang to their feet.

"At ease," Brandt growled. He strode around desks crowded with three-ring binders, stacks of paper and computer terminals. He went back into a hive of neck-high cubicles and found Nikki Thompson sitting at her desk curling dumbbells.

"Good morning," Brandt said.

She ignored him until he started coming around behind her desk. Then she dropped her dumbbells, stood up and raised her hands in a protective stance. "Keep your distance, asshole," she whispered.

He stuck his note on her screen. "It's a Davy Jones costume," he said.

"Certainly not for you," she quipped.

"I'm one of the highest ranking Shellbacks on board."

"Just because you say it doesn't make it true," she said.

"Put the items on that list in my office, wog, and maybe I'll put in a good word for you with King Neptune."

CHAPTER THIRTY-NINE – Day 10

They shot Jenks full of sedatives and carried him back to the brig. A plaster cast encased his entire right leg. They put him in a straightjacket, moved a cot into his cell and strapped him down. His eyeballs rolled, he mumbled and yelled and wiggled his fingers and toes.

They put an adult diaper on him, because the straight jacket prevented him from using the toilet.

He emerged from the sedative-induced spell to find a guy sitting on the side of his bunk.

"Who are you?" Jenks mumbled.

"I'm Stanley Comello." His visitor smiled with little-kid enthusiasm.

"You stink, dude."

"I don't smell nothing," Comello replied.

"Like sweat and old jizz." Jenks was sick of this visitor already.

"You gotta join us," Comello said.

"The dead crew?" Jenks groaned.

"You don't join—you're gonna drown."

"Tell Satan I'm ready to see him now." Jenks spat at Comello.

"You shouldn't a done that." Comello wiped his eye and started cracking his knuckles.

"Guard!" Jenks felt vulnerable. "I need a pain killer!"

"Don't you think this is a little strange?" Comello asked, no longer smiling.

"Hey, the dead crew is all good," Jenks said. "I just want to meet the devil before I sign up, ok?"

"You don't get it."

"I just want to meet the man himself," Jenks shot back.

Comello slapped a hand over Jenks' mouth, and Jenks tried

to inhale but all he got was grimy sweat off Comello's palm.

"If you join us, I'll let you breath," Comello said.

Jenks' Adam's apple bobbed urgently and his eyelids fluttered. He nodded yes, and Comello lifted his hand.

"You gonna join?" glee in Comello's voice.

"I know you," Jenks gasped. "They said I took you from the morgue."

"That's right," Comello said.

"Well, what are you doing here?" Jenks stalled. "What's with your shirt, why's it ripped like that?"

"Somebody cut it," Comello glanced at the twine he'd used to sew the rip on the front of his shirt.

"So, how'd you die, anyway?"

"It was an accident," Comello said, running his fingers along a straightjacket strap.

"Prove you're dead," Jenks demanded.

"Sure." Comello stood up and opened the door.

A log of shit slid from Jenks' asshole when he saw Grady Dutro walk in—little round puncture wounds speckling his neck and chest.

"Guard!" Jenks screamed. "I need a pill! My leg really fucking hurts!"

"You've had it wrong this whole time," Grady said, as he slapped a hand over Jenks' mouth. His skin was creepy green. His eyes sunk in their sockets and his lips were cracked. "It ain't about God and the devil, like you said."

Even with Grady's fingers pinching his nose, Jenks smelled something horrible and realized it was the Hershey Kiss in his own adult diaper.

Crimson-red blood seeped from Grady's wounds and trickled along his clammy skin. It dripped on the white straightjacket. He grabbed Jenks' forehead with his free hand and held him so he could look in his eyes while suffocating him, but Jenks opened his mouth and bit the pad of meat below Grady Dutro's thumb.

"You fucker!" Dutro tried to pull away.

Jenks tasted blood.

"Let me go," Dutro shouted.

Even in a straightjacket, Jenks mused, I own this fool.

Dutro pulled but couldn't break Jenks' grip.

"Let him go!" Comello punched Jenks in the nose.

Dutro pressed a boot against Jenks' throat, grabbed his wrist with his free hand and pulled as hard as he could.

Blood splattered across Jenks' cheeks and Dutro screamed as the meat on the palm of his hand ripped away between Jenks' teeth.

"You're my bitch, E-darg," Jenks howled.

Dutro punched Jenks in the nose.

"You are my little bitch!"

*   *   *

Through the peephole, the guard saw blood around the prisoner's mouth. Cautiously, he unlocked the door and stepped in.

Bruises rose around Jenks' eyes. Indecipherable growls spewed from his mouth.

"What's going on in here?" the guard demanded, drawing his club and looking around suspiciously. The stink of rotten fish and feces struck his sinuses. He noticed a bloody wad on the floor and stooped over to poke it with his club. "What the hell, Jenks? Did you bite off the tip of your tongue?"

CHAPTER FORTY – Day 10

The metal door banged open and Darnell Ratcomb stumbled into the examination room. Tears ran down his cheeks as if someone had rubbed a freshly cut onion in his eyes.

"What the hell?" Kate asked. Darnell collapsed, and she caught him under the arms. Corpsman Gutierrez helped lift him onto an examination table. Scabs covered the backs of his arms.

"Put on gloves and a mask," Gutierrez said. "This looks contagious."

Darnell laid back, delirious, his breathing haggard. Kate went straight to the sink and scrubbed her hands and arms.

Commander Sternz entered and put on gloves. She grabbed Darnell's wrist and lifted. She studied the red welts and scaly scabs on the backs of his arms under a bright light. Then she unbuttoned the front of his shirt to reveal the rash spread across his tattooed chest.

"Do you know Danny Jenks?" she asked and saw a flicker of recognition in his eyes.

"Never heard of—" Darnell wheezed.

"Do you know Grady Dutro?" she pressed a fingertip into a tattoo on his chest—a goat's head in a pentagram over the word DAMMED.

"Never heard of him either." Darnell closed his bloodshot eyes. "I don't feel right."

"Quarantine this man." Sternz stormed toward the door. "I want everything in this room sterilized, and both of you shower with BacteroDerm."

*   *   *

Sternz slowed as she drew closer to the morgue. For the first time since helping send Jenks to the brig, she wondered if

164

Grady Dutro's body was still in there.

Dread swirled in her stomach as she glanced at the black painted floor and stepped over to the shiny metal drawers. She pulled a handle and felt the latch open, but instantly she could tell the drawer was too light on its metal rollers. And she was sure this was the drawer they'd put him in.

She slammed the drawer and pulled another open.

Click. Empty. Ice water filled her veins.

Click. Empty! Red rage blanked her mind.

Click! Every drawer was empty!

Suddenly she knew that nobody had stolen bodies from the morgue. She knew they had vanished on their own, but her military bearing and medical training shut down that nonsense.

Her anger turned to suspicion.

"Is Ratcomb the ringleader?" she wondered aloud. "Is Jenks his underling? Do they have help from inside my own department?" She exited the morgue, certain they'd convicted Jenks under the faulty premise that he was working alone.

* * *

Skin cells taken from Ratcomb and Jenks looked red hot. Sternz feared a contagion. Thousands of rash-covered, fever-ravaged sailors would descend on the medical department if she didn't take action. She grabbed the phone but paused before dialing. Jumping Brandt and going directly to Fox meant trouble, but she wanted to avoid Brandt. She knew if she went to Brandt first, a perverted version of her message, at best, would get to Fox. She punched in his extension.

"This is Commander Sternz. I must speak with Captain Fox." She waited for him to come on the line. "Several members of the crew are infected with tropical bacteria," she said. "It's contagious, causes a rash, red eyes and fever. I must dispense BacteroDerm soap to you and your staff . . . yes, the entire crew must shower with it . . . I know we've begun the cloaking exercise . . . Total radio silence . . . Absolutely, Captain—"

A woman came on the line. "He'll see you ten minutes."

CHAPTER FORTY-ONE – Day 10

Terrance awoke in a chair in the library with his legs stretched out and his head leaned back on the wall. Through the steel above, jets rumbled as they launched off the flight deck. The afternoon sorties taking off made him feel left out, because his jet was down in the hangar getting a new engine installed.

He stood up and walked through the stacks, across the reading room and past the circulation desk. The door crashed open and an oddly familiar looking guy entered the library. A glance revealed crusty ooze around his eyes. A pungent fishy stench wafted off him.

Terrance shoved past, walked along the passageway and took two steps down a ladder before charging back to the library.

Greasy mechanics were a common site around the ship, but the grease and the fishy stink on this guy filled the reading room. Terrance walked over and spun the paperback book carousel, pretending to browse the mysteries and thrillers but he couldn't take his eyes off this kid. A dazed look hovered around his face, as if he were in numb shock after a horrible accident. Terrance noticed something unusual about his turtleneck, and he inched around the carousel to get a closer look. He didn't understand why the fabric was oddly bunched. He squinted and could see that it was sewn from collar to waist with twine.

Terrance wondered why anyone would sew a ripped jersey when he could just toss it and get a new one.

A strange sensation prickled through his brain. Synapses fired in an unfamiliar sequence as it occurred to him that this fellow was dead. He told himself it couldn't be. It made no sense. But how could he ignore the fact that the dead guy he'd seen in the picture at Jenks' court martial was standing several feet away from him.

I can't be him, Terrance argued with himself. But it is him.

It looks like him.

Stanley Comello!

The guy missing from the morgue.

Jets rumbled overhead. Terrance had to get back to the line shack. He was supposed to help his mates launch and recover aircraft.

Through his dirty brown sleeves, Comello scratched the back of one arm and then the other.

Terrance decided to ask his name, but when Comello saw Terrance coming towards him, he bolted out of the library.

Terrance followed and saw him go through a watertight door at the end of the passageway. The door slammed and the wheel at its center spun and latched.

Terrance tried to turn the wheel but it wouldn't budge. A jet fired its engines on the catapult overhead. He waited a moment then turned the wheel with all his strength. The door opened. Terrance leaped into the catwalk and realized this was a restricted area; he'd walked right past a sign on the inside of the door warning him not to proceed during flight operations. He saw an A-6 Prowler rocketing at 150 miles per hour—twin engines hurtling the aircraft at full power—directly at him on the steam-powered catapult. The shuttle reached the end of its track, and a tremendous CLANG rang right through Terrance's chest. As the bomber took off from the deck, its tires whizzed bye, mere inches from Terrance's face. His ears rang as if someone had fired a shotgun next to his head.

A man in a green vest ran toward Terrance waving and shouting. Terrance knew he would be in trouble if the man caught him, but he took the time to glance along the catwalk in both directions. Comello was gone. Terrance grabbed the railing, leaned over and looked down. Had Comello jumped over the side? Terrance scanned the ocean. Something caught his eye. Close by the side of the ship, 80 feet below; something black and orange in the water. A fish? Garbage thrown overboard? It flicked and darted into the murky darkness. Was it a fish? He wasn't sure. Maybe sunlight playing on the water.

The catapult operator charged toward him, leaping a coiled fuel hose and yelling, "You're gonna get yourself killed!"

Terrance hurried through the door, ran past the library and

scrambled down ladders to the hangar.

* * *

"Stanley Comello," Terrance whispered as he weaved his way between the support equipment, his ears still ringing. He remembered the photo passed around at Jenks' trial. Comello looked like a 15-year-old kid with smiling chubby cheeks.

"It can't be Comello. He's dead!" Terrance climbed ladders from the hangar to the line shack. Kate's going to flip out when I tell her.

As he heaved a set of chains onto his shoulders, he remembered Jenks talking crazy about dead guys taking over on the equator. "Jenks is nuts," he whispered as he stepped into the catwalk, "and Comello is dead."

From the deckedge speaker a voice boomed, "STAND BY TO LAND AIRCRAFT. FIRST AIRCRAFT AT ONE MILE."

Terrance inhaled salty air mingled with smoky jet exhaust. Leaning against the railing, he gazed down at the sea churning past. It made no sense. That guy, whoever he was, stank like rotten fish. He looked like Frankenstein. His eyes dripped watery goop. His ripped jersey—sewn with twine. And how did he vanish from the catwalk? Terrance gazed at the immense ocean; whitecaps dancing for miles and miles. He wondered how gravity could hold all that water in place. Why didn't it peel off the surface of the earth in one big curling wave and flow into outer space?

And that's when he saw orange and black in the water by the side of the ship again. Was it sunlight, he wondered, or the swish of a fish's tail?

CHAPTER FORTY-TWO – Day 10

Sternz sat on a cushioned wingback chair in Captain Fox's private stateroom. An oil painting of an old battle ship hung on the wood paneled wall behind his small desk. Dark Berber carpet covered the floor. It was the only carpet on the ship.

Fox had his marine guards stand at ease while she explained how to wash with BacteroDerm, and when they had no questions, he posted them in the passageway outside. Fox sat on the edge of his desk and looked at Sternz with raised eyebrows. "You used the word epidemic, commander."

"It's a bit more than that, sir. Allow me to explain."

"Very well," Fox said without emotion.

"Daniel Jenks has a terrible rash covering his torso, bloodshot eyes and a fever. This morning several people came to sick call with similar symptoms, but an hour ago, when a man named Darnell Ratcomb staggered into sickbay, overcome by the same symptoms, I realized we could have an epidemic on our hands." She paused for a moment.

"You said there was something else."

"Ratcomb has the same tattoo as Jenks and Dutro," Sternz continued, "a pentagram and the word dammed, a symbol for Satanism. I became concerned that those three and possibly others are involved in devil worship and stealing—" Sternz almost said bodies, but chose her words carefully. "I believe they worked together to take Stanley Comello's body from the morgue."

"Interesting," Fox put his hand to his chin and thought for a few seconds. "Can we discuss the possible epidemic?"

"Every person aboard must shower with BacteroDerm soap," Sternz replied. "Those who exhibit fever and rash must be quarantined."

"Will anyone need to be flown off the ship?"

"If we have more than a couple hundred quarantined, yes,"

Sternz said, knowing Fox wanted to keep the ship cloaked.

"I'll have someone from logistics contact you to develop a contingency plan. In the meantime, do whatever it takes to stamp out these bacteria," Fox said. "Now what about these devil worshipers?"

"Well," Sternz paused, concerned about how to word it.

"Speak your mind," Fox said.

"At his court martial Jenks said a dead crew would cause trouble on the equator," Sternz willed herself to relax. "And Dutro muttered something about a dead crew."

"What do you make of it?" Fox asked.

"There's a gang planning trouble on the equator."

"Commander, how many times have you crossed the equator?" Fox asked.

"Once as a wog and twice as a Shellback, so I'm aware of the hype among the crew as we near the equator. However, I am concerned about gang activity. Security could be an issue when we cross the line." Now, after voicing her suspicions, she saw the humor in it. Chuckling, she said, "I know this must sound crazy—devil worshipping sailors mutiny on the equator."

"It does sound like a rumor one expects to hear in the enlisted galley," Fox said.

Sternz worried that she was being an alarmist; first by jumping Brandt in the chain of command and now by wasting Fox's time with her speculations.

"I've heard plenty of these tales," Fox said, surprising her. "Many from outstanding officers like you."

Sternz sighed.

"Years ago as a lieutenant," he said with a nostalgic tone, "I set sail out of Norfolk, on a troop transporter with eight-hundred young marines, all wogs, aboard. They put out the word that they would refuse to pass on their hands and knees before King Neptune if the ship crossed the equator, and we had less than a hundred Shellbacks to challenge them. As we neared the equator, those brazen wogs took over the galley. They banged on pots and pans. They went marauding about the ship. We were on the verge of a riot. I was standing beside the wardroom table when several senior officers tried to convince the captain to call the whole thing off. But he was an old Shellback—cool as ice. 'Lowly wogs will not run this ship,' he said firmly. 'We will cross the line and every wog will be whipped for insubordination.' And that was that, so with great trepidation, we Shellbacks divided into gangs, and we dressed like pirates, and we each got a length of fire hose to whip the pollywogs, and we charged into their living quarters and the galley where they were holed up."

Fox glanced around with a dramatic air as if making sure no one was eavesdropping on his secret. "When we showed the courage to face those unruly wogs, all of a sudden there were Shellbacks among us who I'd never seen before, savage pirates with scruffy beards and red eyes and liquor on their breaths."

"Really?" Sternz asked, hardly able to believe he was telling such a tall tale.

"Yes, and I'm convinced they were true members of the Royal Order of the Deep, come from the brine of the sea to ensure those wogs got the whipping they deserved." Fox had a gleam in his eye. He chuckled. "What do you make of that, Sternz?"

She wanted to bring him back to the present. There were bodies missing from the morgue, a murdered sailor, a psychopath in the brig, a widening ring of Satanists and a contagious rash. She wanted him to take extra security measures, but he was full of reverie and sea stories.

CHAPTER FORTY-THREE – Day 10

Kate ran a finger along the spines of books and read their titles. She knit her brows and pretended she couldn't find the book she was looking for. She walked out of one aisle and entered the next.

According to their hook-up plan, he would wink and she'd wink back. Without a word, they'd leave the library and take separate routes to medical station 12. But Terrance didn't wink. He walked directly at her. She squeezed to one side between the shelves. He clutched her arm and whispered, "You're not gonna believe what happened."

"Tell me when we get there," she whispered and walked hastily out of the stacks.

A few minutes later, in medical station 12, she flicked on the lights. After a moment, he undogged the door from outside and stepped in.

"You're not supposed to talk," she complained.

"Sorry, but—"

"It turns me on when we meet without talking," she said.

He pulled her close. "You're not gonna believe who I saw."

"Who?" She pushed away.

"Stanley Comello."

"Whatever."

"In the library," he insisted.

"He's dead!"

"Then it was his evil twin."

"Cut the crap, Terrance."

"He looked exactly like Comello."

"You saw a dead man in the library?"

"Yes and he was stinky and creepy."

"Are you stressed out?" She turned around and leaned back on his chest, "I am."

He massaged her shoulders. "What's got you stressed?" he asked, realizing she'd switched the conversation.

"Comello and Dutro died in front of me. Duh. And now we're fighting a rash," she said. "And I have to visit Jenks in the brig every other day."

"Oh, baby," he said, "I'm sorry."

"And I'm worried about crossing the equator."

He sat on one of the liferaft drums, still stowed in the medical station because deck department welders hadn't gotten around to installing them outside in the flight deck catwalk yet. She stood between his knees, and he rubbed out the tension in her neck and shoulders. "Just make sure you have a pair of kneepads," he said.

"Kneepads?" She tilted her head as he worked on a tight spot.

"You'll be on your hands and knees all day."

"It's all in fun, right?"

"Every Shellback gets a two-foot length of fire hose," he said, "so you'll be getting spanked all day."

She spun around and put her hands on his thick neck, playfully choking him. "Tell me what's going to happen!"

Her eyes made him forgot what they were talking about. He leaned in to kiss her.

"Stop!" She throttled him playfully. "What's going to happen on the equator?"

"I can't tell you," he blurted.

"Why?"

"Because, you're a wog."

"Tell me." She choked him harder.

"Okay, okay." He pulled her hands away, spun her around, continued massaging. "They'll wake you up early and put shaving cream and shampoo all over you. And that's when you better put your kneepads on."

"I know that part," she said impatiently. "Tell me what's really going to happen?"

"A doctor's gonna rinse your mouth with an enema bag full of vinegar and green food coloring."

"Gross!"

"You'll have to kiss the fat baby's belly and then you'll have to—"

"Wait, wait. Hold on," she stopped him. "The fat baby?"

"They'll have several really fat people sitting around shirtless with buckets of slop between their legs, and you have to crawl up and they'll take a handful of slop and smear it all over their belly, and they'll grab you by your ears and mash your face against their belly."

"Nasty!"

"Then they'll make you kiss King Neptune's feet."

"I'm not kissing anybody's feet," she declared.

"Yeah, you will, and you'll kiss the feet of the guys in his harem."

"Guys in a harem?" she asked, confused.

"They're in drag."

"I will not kiss a cross dresser's feet!"

"If you don't, a bull-dyke will whip your ass."

"Stop lying," she said.

"The night before, they'll pack the hangar with thousands of Shellbacks all dressed like pirates and mermaids, and a bunch of wogs on the runway in drag like they're in a beauty pageant."

"Are you making this up?"

"No," he assured her. "The male wogs who win the pageant will be in Neptune's harem."

"Seriously?" She turned to face him.

"It's all in fun," he said, admiring her eyes again, "just remember your kneepads."

This time when he leaned in to kiss her, she kissed him back.

* * *

After they put their clothes back on, they sat atop the liferaft drums, face to face, with their knees together. The overhead fluorescents were off, and a small battle lantern cast their shadows in its eerie red glow.

"You should see Jenks," Kate whispered with genuine loathing. "Horrible tattoos and a rash, he mutters about the devil

174

and—"

"The dead crew," Terrance said.

"How'd you know?" she asked.

"He said some nonsense about his friends starting trouble on the equator."

"Dutro said the same thing," Kate said. "He was dead, or almost dead, but he said the dead crew would mutiny on the equator."

"Did you cut Comello's jersey off like this?" Terrance made a scissor motion from his neck to his waist.

"Yeah, exactly like that, why?"

"The Comello-looking guy," Terrance said, "was wearing a ripped jersey like that, but it was sewn with a piece of string."

They fell silent, dumbstruck by the weirdness of it.

"Maybe someone helped Jenks steal Comello's body," Kate said.

"Yeah, and they did voodoo on him!" Terrance giggled. "And now he's like a zombie."

"What if the bodies missing from the morgue are the dead crew and they're gonna mutiny on the equator?"

"Nice," he said. "Zombie sailors mutiny on the equator!"

They laughed an unsettled sort of laugh.

"Jenks broke his leg," Kate said, "and now he's in a straightjacket."

"How'd he break his leg?"

"I don't know," she said. "And he bit off the tip of his tongue."

"Bit the tip off his tongue?"

"He's a lost soul," Kate said, "like the most insane bad-guy you could ever imagine."

CHAPTER FORTY-FOUR – Day 11

The guard tightened the straightjacket while Jenks stared at the ceiling where a tigerfish squeezed through the ventilation duct without making a sound. Jenks twitched against the straps; worry darkened his bruised eyes.

"How you feeling, Jenks?"

The tigerfish swam in slow, menacing circles. Jenks wondered if the guard could see the shadows the big fish made when it swam in front of the light.

"I said, how you feeling, Jenks?" The guard asked again.

Jenks stared so intently past him the guard looked up but didn't see anything.

"Oh, fuck you then, Jenks." The guard walked out and slammed the door.

* * *

As soon as the door shut, keys jangled outside and it opened again. Lieutenant Jones stepped in. He wore a tuxedo with a sword in a scabbard on his belt. He scratched furiously at his elbow.

"Ask that bitch doctor for her special soap," Jenks said. "It cools the itch."

The tigerfish circled in front of the light, throwing shadows across Jenks' face.

"This is your last chance." Jones crossed his arms. "If you join the dead crew, you won't have to die when this ship goes down."

The big fish slid to a stop and hovered above Jenks' face. Its yellow eyes blinked slowly over large emotionless pupils. Its mouth opened and closed, showing off crooked, bony teeth.

"What do you want?" Jenks blubbered as fear got the best of him.

"For you to join the dead crew," Jones said earnestly. "Your knowledge of newfangled weapons is exactly what we need."

"I'll join, I promise," Jenks stammered as the fish fluttered its wispy side fins, sliding closer to his face, "I'll do whatever you want, right after you introduce me to Satan!"

"Christ on a crutch!" Jones shook his head. "You still don't understand."

"I just want to meet the devil," Jenks whined. "He's the leader of the dead crew, right?"

"No," Jones mocked in a whiny voice, "he's not the leader of the dead crew."

The fish's tail drifted upward and its face pointed straight down. Its fleshy lips pressed against Jenks' face. Its side fins fluttered and its gills undulated. It gulped Jenks' face and most of his head into its mouth. It gulped again and this time Jenks' head rose off the pillow and his neck bent forward. The fish torqued its body and swished its tail and drove itself down while sucking in Jenks' entire head. It swam backwards, tugging Jenks' upper body off the bed. It gulped a third time and sealed its thick rubbery lips around his shoulders. The restraining straps stretched to their limit as the fish pulled Jenks neck at a painful angle.

His screams were stifled. His bound arms and legs thrashed what little they could.

The tigerfish bit down hard, driving its sharp teeth through the soft parts of Jenks' neck.

*   *   *

Sunbeams shined through the warm blue water and sparkled on seashells strewn across the white sandy bottom. Jenks wondered if he was dreaming about the time he and Ratcomb went snorkeling in Hanauma Bay on Oahu. He looked toward the surface and saw that he was deep under water, which was weird because he wasn't wearing scuba gear, not even a snorkel, and he had no urge to breathe. He kicked his feet, reached out his arms and pulled through the water with ease. Gliding by below, a glossy pearl rested on a pillow of pink meat inside a gigantic clamshell. He swam with a school of silver fish in a barely perceptible current.

He skimmed above kelp swaying like green kites blowing on a breeze. A delicate creature slithered through the green strands below. Long blonde hair flowed over slender white shoulders. Curious, Jenks swam down into the slippery tangle.

"Wait for me," his words unintelligible.

He glimpsed her again, deeper.

"Who are you?" He kicked and tried to catch her.

Darkness filled the depths and he turned this way and that, realizing he'd lost her. Strands of kelp tangled around his arms. He craned his neck, looking for the surface, but long undulating tubers and slippery green leaves, shifting on the currents, blocked his view.

Then she appeared behind him, grabbing his shoulders.

He turned to face her, captivated by her brilliant red lips and blue eyes shimmering in the liquid light. Thick, wavy blonde hair floated buoyantly in the water all around her radiant face.

Hugging him around the shoulders, she pulled him close, and crushed her breasts against him. Her magic blue eyes and the promise of kissing her stole his attention. His face flushed with desire. She pressed her flat, hard belly against him. His erection swelled urgently, like a wet dream quickly climbing to a climax. He knew he'd never get the drawstring on his trunks unknotted in time, so he held her close, looked into her eyes and surrendered to a brief cataclysm of delight.

Tumbling over the crest of a wave, they rolled in the turbulent water with white foam spurting all about. Coarse sand and broken seashells churned in the shallows. He coughed on a salty mouthful. It stung inside his nose. He glimpsed a sandy beach and palm trees as another wave broke over them. Her arms wrapped around his shoulders. The undertow tried tugging her back out to sea, but he scooped her in his arms and trudged toward shore with waves crashing over them.

Silver flashed beneath the surf.

His fingertips pressed against interlocking scales embedded like armored snakeskin on her ass, and he screamed as he dropped her in the knee-deep surf. He leaped away but stopped and marveled at her.

Half woman—half fish.

Thick ropes of blond hair framed her face and cascaded

down in tangled wet curls over her dainty shoulders. Her delicate arms folded across her chest. Tapered fingers with pearly-white nails barely concealed her voluptuous bosom. Under the water, she had a woman's wide hips, but from just below her navel silver scales, thick and tough and speckled aquamarine and silver, covered her down to the tip of her long serpent tail.

He couldn't tear himself away.

Her eyes cast a longing gaze at him and her mouth turned down in a pout, hurt by his reaction to her body. Her tail slithered and curled beneath her and her torso rose out of the surf. As she moved closer, her hands reached tentatively and gently touched his hips. She slid close, pressed her cheek against his belly, and gazed up at him.

A big wave crashed and sent them tumbling.

* * *

He awoke on his back in a puddle on the floor. Disappointment twisted his guts. At a glance, he recognized his jail cell and was startled to see the straightjacket straps hanging loose over the sides of the mattress. His hair was soaked and salt burned the back of his mouth. Confusion turned to a tangled mess of guilty pleasure at the sight of her writhing out from under his bunk, and sliding snake-like across the deck toward him.

"Danny Jenks," her voice a chime inside a glass sphere. A silver stud sparkled on the tip of her tongue. "I hope," she giggled, "I don't get you in trouble."

He crab crawled away, dragging his cast, but his back hit the bulkhead and she kept coming.

"We'll get along fine, Danny." A mysterious chime rang in her voice, like crystal champagne flutes touching in a toast. Her silvery tail coiled silently, and then in one slithery motion she slid close to him. Her fragrant breath filled his nostrils.

His quivering hand touched her scaly hip and jerked away. He flinched and banged his head on the steel wall. Angry, he shoved her, but his fingers tangled in her wet hair and her big breasts filled his hands.

Their eyes met—his wide, hers a teasing gleam.

Her bosom, overflowing his hands, made stress and doubt fall away. Something full of potential swelled and trembled inside him.

"What's your name?" he asked.

"Naomi."

"How old are you?"

She giggled.

"How did you get to be a mermaid?"

Her tail slithered between his legs, the wet fin on the end fanning out and flapping against his back.

"A long time ago we sailed on a clipper from Singapore to Australia," Naomi said, "we were going to live in Sydney, but pirates attacked." Her blue eyes mesmerized him. "My husband fought gallantly, but that gang of brutes beat him down." She combed her hair back with long tapered fingers. "They tied me up in the captain's bedchamber," she whispered, "and you can't imagine what those lusty buccaneers did to me, Danny."

He watched for the silver stud in her tongue, wondering how it would feel if she French kissed him.

"When they were finished they tossed me over the side." She feigned fear. "Sharks nuzzled me with their snouts, trying to decide where to bite first. The water boiled with their thrashing tails. I cried out for the pirates to take me back on board, but they sailed away. I thought I'd be devoured, but I said prayers I used to know and the mermaids rescued me."

As he lay in this creature's arms, Jenks reconsidered his notions about God and the devil locked in combat.

"Beneath the waves there's a world of natural wonders," Naomi told him. "A realm of pirates and sailors drowned at sea. There's scuba divers who ran out of air and swimmers who lost their way, drowned surfers and children swept from the beach." Naomi's blue eyes opened wide, and the stud clicked on her teeth when she spoke. "And creatures, Danny, glorious and horrible creatures in Neptune's realm under the waves."

He closed his eyes, puckered his lips and leaned in, but she turned her cheek to him and giggled.

He felt embarrassed but didn't care because he wanted to be a fool for her. She had freed him from the straightjacket and he knew she could free him from this cell too.

Sure, he could comprehend pirates and dead sailors, fish striped like tigers and Naomi with her scaly tail and curly hair. If the devil is aboard this ship, he reasoned, why haven't I seen him? A fiery hell suddenly seemed a lot less appealing than realms beneath the waves.

She made him give up on the devil and rituals and hell. It didn't matter that she had a tail. He leaned in to kiss her again.

She arched her back, and pressed her boobs against him.

"You're a lusty buccaneer too, Danny Jenks," she said, wiggling her tail and turning her head, allowing him to kiss her cheek. "What will it take to get you to join the dead crew?"

CHAPTER FORTY-FIVE – Day 11

Over Sternz's shoulder, Kate read the Jenks' observation logbook.

0100: Prisoner shouted: "The dead crew has a plan for me but I won't join until I meet the devil."
0300: He's humping the air and calling for Naomi.
0500: Whispering and seems like he ain't alone in there.
0700: When I tightened the straps, he smiled and told me Naomi took care of his boner.
0900: Jenks said: "It's a powerful weapon and you want to short circuit the arming sequence?"

Sternz entered Jenks' cell and found the straps loose. She studied the serene smile on his face. A musky odor rose from moist spots around the edges of his diaper. She said to the guards, "Shackle him in the passageway," and told Kate, "Prepare a sponge bath. He's filthy."

Jenks remained docile while they unstrapped him, lifted him off the cot and chained him in the passageway.

Kate snipped off his paper coveralls with surgical scissors. BacteroDerm had reduced his rash, now only discolored blotches on the backs of his arms and legs. She held her breath while removing his loaded diaper.

Sternz put a finger under Jenks' chin and studied his face. Bruised purple rings surrounded his eyes. She looked at the stubble on his jaw, examined his teeth and looked in his eyes. Something rodent-like lurked in the angles of his skull. She wondered what had taken the fight out of him.

After Kate sponged his back and legs, taking care not to get his cast wet, their eyes met and some weird energy flowed on his gaze into her.

"Who have you been talking to?" Sternz asked.

The guard's ears perked up.

Jenks sighed as if ending a long contemplation.

"Who is Naomi?" Sternz asked casually, not wanting to agitate him. She wondered if he would trust her.

Kate ran the warm, wet sponge across Jenks' back, over his tattoos.

*   *   *

After so many months at sea, Kate barely noticed the ship constantly rising and falling on ocean swells. But the water in the wash bucket tipped so far it almost overflowed. The angle made no sense, until she thought about it, because she could feel her legs tensing against the deck's angle as the ship climbed a steep swell. The water in the bucket slowly sloshed from one side to the other, and the muscles in her feet and ankles adjusted as the ship rolled over the top of another wave's crest.

"Who have you been talking to?" Sternz asked again.

A chain attached to Jenks' handcuffs looped through a ring on the bulkhead. This allowed his hands to flop down across his chest. His gaze changed from an empty stare to vague amusement.

"Naomi," he answered in a tranquil voice. "She's gonna take me with her, after—" Jenks giggled.

Sternz wondered what it had to do with the log entry about arming a powerful weapon. "Who's Naomi?" Sternz asked.

"She's a mermai—" Jenks stopped. His hands went to her neck, his thumbs squeezing tight on her throat.

The guard had his back turned.

Kate grabbed his wrist and pulled. "Let her go," she shouted.

The guard got his club out and whacked Jenks on the back a few times but he wouldn't let go.

Sternz clutched at his wrists.

The guard put his club across Jenks throat and yanked back with both hands.

Jenks kept his fingers clamped tight.

Another guard jammed his keys into the lock in the cage

door at the end of the passageway. He threw the door open, ran over and pummeled Jenks' face with his black wooden baton.

Jenks sustained several solid blows on his forehead and across his cheek before he raised his hands to protect himself.

Two more guards arrived. They unchained him from the hoop on the bulkhead, threw him on his cot and began strapping him into the straightjacket.

Kate put a hand on Sternz's shoulder and noticed a splatter of blood on the floor. There was a tooth, roots and all.

CHAPTER FORTY-SIX – Day 11

Terrance McDaniels knocked on Commander Aronson's door. When it opened, Aronson stood there in boxers with shaving cream on his jaw and upper lip. The man had a wide, hairless chest and sloped shoulders. He had skinny legs and knobby knees. His feet were enormous, with toes scrunched on top of each other. Terrance smirked at the ducks on Aronson's boxers.

"I'm not doing business with you anymore," Aronson whispered, before Terrance could say anything.

"Actually, sir, I need to talk to you about Jenks. I don't think he was working alone. A friend of mine in the medical department says there's more than one body missing from the morgue." Words dashed from Terrance's mouth like track runners bolting at the bang of a starting gun.

"I'm late for a meeting with the air group commander." Aronson started closing the door.

Terrance panicked and started ranting. "Jenks couldn't steal a body by himself and another thing is how they heaped all those convictions on him."

Aronson put his authoritative stare on Terrance, but it didn't work because he looked goofy in duck-print boxers and shaving cream.

"I need to talk to you," Terrance said.

A female captain in pressed khakis walked by and grinned at Aronson. After she passed, he stuck his head out and looked quickly up and down the passageway.

"Get in here." He yanked Terrance into the stateroom by the arm. He went back to shaving in the mirror above the tiny sink. His pressed khakis laid out across the bunk. A bottle of BacteroDerm sat on the shelf above the sink.

Aronson thought maybe Terrance needed consoling after seeing Jenks convicted, but decided to hell with the father-son soft talk. Jenks murdered a shipmate and stuffed him in a laundry sack, for crying out loud.

"Sir, I've been thinking—"

"One second."

Terrance realized that Aronson was not going to take him seriously. The guy in duck print boxers, Terrance reminded himself, earns a paycheck dropping bombs on people. Just because he bought a few packs of cigarettes, doesn't mean he's my friend.

As Terrance watched Aronson rinse and dry his face, and slap on aftershave, he felt the ship climbing a steep swell. Without thinking about it, Terrance put a hand on the bulkhead.

Aronson lifted a leg to put on his pants, lost his balance and sat down hard on the corner of his bunk to avoid falling on his ass. He put on his shoes and thought about how he was going to drop Terrance McDaniels' petty concerns like a rock to the bottom of the ocean. He tied his laces in tight, conclusive little bows.

"Sir, I thought—" Terrance attempted.

"Bear with me," Aronson cut him off and pulled a T-shirt over his head.

"I'm worried about this trouble with Jenks," Terrance said.

Aronson had narrowly escaped the career-killing red ink in his fitness report over this mess with Jenks. Besides, he reminded himself, this case has so many captain-sized knots tied around it a congressional subcommittee won't be able to untangle it. As he slipped on his shirt, he decided that McDaniels would be gone in less than a minute.

"You see," Terrance said, mistaking Aronson's silence for permission to speak, "my friend in the medical department said several bodies were missing from the morgue. And that means—"

"McDaniels, if you didn't understand the legalese at your friend's court martial—"

"He's not my friend," Terrance snapped.

"He's a dangerous criminal," Aronson growled, then more calmly, "He got caught and prosecuted and now he's in the slammer for life."

"He wasn't working alone," Terrance said.

Aronson buttoned his shirt, tucked it in and fastened his pants. While buckling his belt, he thought about how he was going to explain another fodded engine to the air group commander.

Aronson opened the door, ushered Terrance out. "Appreciate the concern, McDaniels," he said. "If inputs are needed, I'll be sure to consult you." He closed the door and jiggled the knob to ensure it locked.

"Sir, you don't understand."

Though only an inch taller, Aronson stared down at Terrance with cold superiority in his eyes. No longer comical in boxers and shaving cream, Aronson, now in full uniform, projected an attitude bristling with annoyance. "On the contrary, McDaniels, I understand the situation perfectly. You seem confused, and I suspect the exposure to these grisly events has caused you to manifest a debilitating amount of stress. I'm even questioning your ability to work in the hazardous environment on the flight deck."

"This is not interfering with my work."

"So, everything is fine then?"

Stunned at the threat of being sent to work in the galley or the laundry, Terrance replied, "Yes, sir. Everything's fine."

"I'm glad I could help you solve your little problem." Aronson turned sharply and walked away.

The ship descended into a deep trough on the rough ocean, and Terrance put a hand on the bulkhead to steady himself. The slapdown made him want to catch some fresh air, so he went to the hangar and stood near one of the aircraft elevators.

A hot, sticky breeze blasted across the ocean's rolling surface. It slapped his face and burned his lungs. On the horizon, orange and black clouds brewed up a storm. Curtains of rain poured down and lightning crackled across the bruised sky.

CHAPTER FORTY-SEVEN – Day 11

Jenks lay on his bunk pretending to thrash against the straps. He grunted and groaned to make it look good, but under his breath he mumbled, "Come on, guard. Come in here and die."

The guard unlocked the cell door and stepped in. He glanced at Jenks and his brow wrinkled, perplexed. A quizzical look twisted the guard's face. He bent over to get a look at the straps and realized something was amiss.

Jenks' arm shot up, his hand clutching a metal bunk leg. It sounded like bowling balls clunking together. The guard stumbled and Jenks delivered two more hard whacks on the man's skull.

Blood flowed across the deck.

Jenks hobbled from the cell with the guard's key ring jangling in his hand.

*   *   *

The bell stopped ringing, a squeal of feedback and then a computer-generated female voice announced: "AWAY THE MARINE SECURITY TASK FORCE. AWAY THE FLYING SQUAD. THIS IS NOT A DRILL. SECURITY BREACH, AFT WEAPONS MAGAZINE."

Kate Conrad shouted at people to get out of her way. She accelerated easily, running downhill as the ship rose on the face of a steeply pitching sea. Near the aft weapons magazine the ship rolled under her feet and descended the wave's steep back, causing her to slow as she began running up hill.

In the main galley, she found the squad gathered around Fire Marshall O'Malley. He stood at the center of the team and took control of the situation. "There's a security breach in the mag' below us," he said.

Kate, jacked on adrenaline, found his handsome mug and

buff shoulders reassuring.

"Stand by," he ordered. "I'll keep you posted."

Kate took a seat at one of the tables and waited. Her body shifted forward and back every few seconds as the ship tossed on big ocean swells. They'd entered a storm, and she wanted to go out on a weatherdeck to see the waves for herself.

She glanced at a hatch in the deck leading down to the magazine. There were vaults down there where they stored bombs, rockets, missiles and nuclear weapons.

To Kate's surprise, she saw Commander Sternz talking to O'Malley. Then Sternz went down the hatch into the magazine. Kate wondered why Sternz was on scene. If there's a medical emergency, she thought, I should be down there too.

She waited, impatiently.

A few minutes later, Sternz climbed up through the hatch.

Kate walked over.

Worried lines crossed Sternz's brow, and a dazed look betrayed her normally stoic demeanor. She clutched Kate's arm. "Jenks escaped from the brig," she whispered.

Their eyes met but didn't connect, and Kate saw a rattled woman—not her commander.

Sternz trembled and her eyes flitting about, unable to focus. "He tried to break into the nuclear weapon's vault," she said as if trying to understand it herself.

Right then a marine emerged from the hatch pulling a stretcher laden with a body under a white sheet.

"They shot him," Sternz stammered. "He's dead."

Stunned, Kate grabbed the stretcher and helped carry Jenks to the morgue.

*   *   *

"I need to talk to you, ma'am."

Sternz took Kate into her office. "What is it?" Sternz collapsed in the chair behind her desk.

Kate said, "Bodies are missing from the morgue and I think it has something to do with Jenks and Dutro and Ratcomb."

Sternz kept coming back to the same conclusion herself, and

she guessed it was obvious to Conrad, who had been close to the situation.

Thinking she might finally get some answers, Kate said, "The rash and the missing bodies are linked to these guys, but with Jenks in the brig, Dutro dead and Ratcomb quarantined, it doesn't make sense. Like, how did Jenks break his leg? How did he get out of a straightjacket and escape from the brig?"

Sternz came out from behind her desk and put a hand on Kate's shoulder. "There's an investigation underway."

"Investigating what?"

Sternz snapped back to her cold self, assuming a rigid posture, eyes sharp. "You seem stressed," she said.

"Grogan, Burns and Comello are missing," Kate said, "and now Jenks is dead. I just want to know what's going on."

"What's going on," Sternz mimicked Kate, "is an investigation. That's what's going on."

"There's a rumor Jenks stole bodies from the morgue," Kate raised her voice.

"Maybe he wasn't working alone," Sternz said, wondering if Conrad knew Dutro's body was gone. She leaned in close and spoke with cool confidentiality. "You're a good worker, Conrad. I hope you're not implicated in any of this."

Kate's jaw dropped in surprise.

"I'm sure there'll be more convictions," Sternz said.

"I haven't done anything wrong," Kate said.

"You're close to the circumstances," Sternz said.

Kate saw some weird machinery clicking and whirring behind Sternz's brow, but couldn't understand it.

"Let's just say you're a person of interest."

This perverted logic made Kate want to back out of Sternz's office as quickly as possible. "I'm just worried about the bad things going on."

"I understand you don't like what I have to say." Sternz opened the door.

"I haven't done anything wrong." Kate walked out.

"I'll always have an open door policy," Sternz said as she shut the door in Kate's face.

CHAPTER FORTY-EIGHT – Day 12

Before women served aboard battleships, equator-crossing ceremonies had degenerated into half-day hazing rituals—something along the lines of a brutal fraternity initiation—followed by a steak and lobster lunch and afternoon naps.

Costumes became more outrageous as larger numbers of women crossed the line. Yards of colorful fabric, buckets of sequins and boxes of cheap crazy-colored wigs were stowed away before ships left stateside. Lady Shellbacks took on greater responsibilities for festivity planning. And when the gay and transgender sailors started serving openly in the Navy, the sexual aspects of the event came completely out of the closet. Crossing the line transformed into a Mardi Gras costume party with an ancient-mariner theme.

* * *

All afternoon aircraft handlers cleared most of the jets off the hangar, moved them to the flight deck and fastened them down with extra chains. This created a wide-open space in the hangar for the beauty contest.

That evening, strong winds whipped up high seas, and rogue waves crashed against the ship. A big comber splashed water into the hangar and several boatswains with squeegees and mops were sent to clean things up. In a big puddle, sloshing across the hangar, they found a curious orange fish with black stripes. It was slimy and ferocious with sharp snapping teeth.

Captain Fox ordered all exterior doors shut to prevent waves from washing anyone over the side.

That night, all the Shellbacks crammed into the hangar to hoot and holler and watch contestants vie for a spot in King Neptune's harem.

* * *

A mashup of classic rock anthems, disco beats and bravado rap blasted from amplifiers stacked on both sides of the center stage. Androgynous beings, girliemen and bullywomen, strutted on the beauty pageant runway, while thousands of excited men and women, dressed like pirates, mermaids, sea hags, serpents and sharks, all gyrated to the music while hooting and whistling. Quite a few sailors put a black patch over one eye. From many a sleeve poked a metal hook. It was impossible to distinguish who was who because the costumes and make-up obliterated the structure normally imposed by uniforms. On the equator, nobody wore uniforms; there were only Shellbacks and pollywogs.

Many women had their legs wrapped in tight sequined green stockings, tailored to look like a mermaid. They wore strands of kelp and seaweed woven into their hair, and barrettes adorned with seashells and starfish. Many men wore cut off shorts or outrageous baggy pants, skintight shirts with the collars and sleeves cut off. Glittery makeup designs, fake scars, drawn-on beards and mustaches, outrageous amounts of eyeliner and brilliant colored lips flashed through the crowd. Everyone, it seemed, sported wild tattoos, some real and some fake, decorating exposed skin with skulls, hearts punctured with arrows, battleships blasting cannons, sea creatures and pirates—lots of pirates. Many revelers waved swords and trident forks, craftily fashioned from strips of wood, cardboard and aluminum foil. The raving crowd pulsated to the musical beats blasting through the hangar.

All at once, a roar erupted as a pretty man wearing a bikini came strutting down the runway. He wore a wig fashioned from a new white mop. Lusty whistles and catcalls erupted from the crowd. His bikini top stretched over two missile nose cones. As he spun at the end of the runway, the full length of his cock sprang loose from his bikini bottom. The crowd went crazy. He flashed a piece of cardboard with, "Neptune's Girl" printed on it. While strutting back he made a clumsy attempt to tuck his junk back in. He flipped the cardboard over and flashed the message on the other side: "Vote for Me!"

*   *   *

Master at arms patrolled the throng's perimeter, occasionally pulled sailors out and told them to calm down. A rowdy bunch of snipes from the deck division, reeking of alcohol and weed, started a fistfight and were herded below for Breathalyzer tests and urinalysis.

*   *   *

Terrance had crossed the equator on an earlier cruise aboard the Nimitz, so he'd seen this mayhem before. Kate, on the other hand, couldn't believe her eyes.

Thousands of men and women, usually hard working and alienated from each other, had completely cut loose. After months at sea they needed to blow off steam. The silos between their departments and the barriers between their ranks vanished under an explosion of costumes, make up, loud music and sexual hijinks. A conga line snaked its way through the crowd. Mosh pits formed spontaneously, with people crashing into each other. Dirty dancing couples bumped and groped. Every few minutes, someone leaped onto the runway, dove off and surfed away on the crowd.

Kate wanted to join the fun, but she and Terrance had something important to do. If they were going to see Stanley Comello, they'd agreed, it would be here at the pageant.

*   *   *

The sight of so many people dressed in costumes, dancing and whooping it up, made Terrance remember when he had crossed the line. He'd been in awe of the pirates, mermaids, sea-creatures, and especially the gender-bending cross-dressers. On this night—the night before they officially crossed the equator—everyone would have fun, but tomorrow when they crossed the line, things were going to get scary. Shellbacks would be paddling pollywogs with wet lengths of fire hose, and rubbing handfuls of rotten food in every lowly wog's hair. Wogs would be forced to climb into a tub of putrid garbage and roll around, and then they'd be sprayed off with a fire hose. But tonight Terrance looked at the crowd with a dash of relief, because he'd been through it and survived. But, even though he was a Shellback, with every right to enjoy the pageant, a drop of fear poisoned his belly. So many wildly dressed people crammed into the hangar—it was too outrageous, he feared.

"Some of these people look like they just swam up from a shipwreck," he told Kate.

"I had no idea there'd be costumes like this," she said, wide-eyed, as a pack of sailors walked by with bulldog masks tight on their faces.

Many of the merry makers had hair too long and too thick. Water dripped off their ragged, outdated uniforms, accumulating in puddles around them. The dog-faced sailors barked and growled and ran about nipping at their mates as if they really were dogs, finally let off their leashes.

Ripping guitar riffs and sonic bass beats roared through the hangar and hoots and hollers and hand clapping rose from the crowd. On the runway, a line of men in women's nightgowns, panties, bras, makeshift wigs and high heels strutted along. Their hairy chests and legs, and their awkward gaits betraying their gender.

At evenly spaced intervals along the runway, women wearing knee-high black leather boots, shorty-shorts and tight tank tops were posted as bodyguards and bouncers. Their greased muscles, slicked back hair and black phallic batons lent a threatening authenticity to their militant-lesbian look. A steady roar of approval rose from the crowd, where many clapped their hands above their heads in unison with a party rock anthem blasting from a stack of amplifiers.

"Look!" Terrance said to Kate. "Is that him?"

"Where?" She peered into the sea of waving arms.

"It's Comello," he shouted, grabbing her arm, pulling her through the mob.

Kate caught a distinct whiff of booze and turned her head just in time to look into the wide-open mouth of a howling dude who hadn't shaved in several days. She pushed through the gyrating crowd, the unreality of the situation unfolding around her.

"He was right here," Terrance shouted, "still wearing that ripped jersey."

"It's too crowded," Kate said. "Let me get on your shoulders."

He kneeled down and she climbed on.

"Do you see him?" He wobbled about trying not to topple over.

Suddenly, a body builder in an elaborately feathered Indian headdress, bright green baggy basketball shorts and combat boots crashed through the crowd with a mermaid hoisted across his brawny shoulders.

A hand clutching a wooden sword shot up from the crowd and delivered several hard spanks on the mermaid's ass, and others wielding swords and tridents joined in.

The mermaid shrieked and kicked her tail.

"I see him," Kate shouted and spun excitedly to one side, yanking Terrance's head around just as the mermaid kicked Kate in the ribs and sent her tumbling backwards.

Through the crowd, Terrance caught a glimpse of those baby-fat cheeks.

Kate reeled hard and Terrance stumbled and sent her falling backwards off his shoulders. Hands rose from the crowd and caught her, but Terrance got shoved after stepping on someone's foot, and Kate went down into a tangle of bodies.

The mermaid on the Indian chief's shoulders kicked a pirate in the back of the head, knocking his glasses off. Then the mermaid kicked some chick in the face so hard her nose bled.

A muscular dude in mirrored Ray-Bans, a dollar-store black wig, and an overstuffed silver Speedo, decided he'd had enough of the kicking mermaid, so he grabbed her tail with both hands and began yanking this way and that.

An unsuspecting sailor caught an elbow in the jaw.

A poorly aimed punch hit a bystander in the neck.

Kate landed on her back and someone stepped on her arm. She screamed.

Terrance shoved people out of the way and pulled her to her feet. "If we get split up," he said, "meet in the library."

The MAA weighed into the melee swinging batons and

cracking sailors across their backs. A shot of pepper spray stunned the riotous bunch. Several sailors took defensive stances and threw punches at anyone who came near. People stumbled, got trampled by those fleeing the pepper-spray. Attempting to escape the crush, individuals climbed onto the runway. Several baton-wielding dykes beat them back while others pulled people from danger. Within minutes, too many were standing on the runway and the structure collapsed with a CRACK and a BANG.

A hip-hop hit with a monster bass beat blasted from the stack of amplifiers as the riot spread.

Stanley Comello ran and Terrance chased him.

CHAPTER FORTY-NINE – Day 12

Captain Fox laid the wig, with a white beard attached at the sideburns, over his wingback chair. A white robe hung on a hook on the back of the stateroom's door, and his trident, fashioned from a broomstick, a wire hanger and tin foil, leaned in the corner. He placed the crown, made by a metal smith in one of the ship's machine shops, atop his head, and studied himself in the mirror. Staring back, he saw a pale comparison of the real King Neptune. Of course, he'd never seen the Ruler of the Raging Main, but he'd imagined him many times. When he observed a storm-tossed sea or relaxed during a rare moment while gazing at the ocean, Fox had conjured, in his seafaring imagination, visions of Neptunus Rex. He envisioned a supreme being, part immovable coral reef and part crashing tsunami—nature's wrath incarnate. There in the mirror, he saw only himself with a tin ornament atop his head. "Doesn't capture the power," he whispered, somehow sure Neptune's brow shined with an awesome light.

He called the command center.

"Fox here, give me a report."

"We're cloaked three-sixty," the watch officer answered. "A Chinese sub inside eighty miles, picked it up twenty minutes ago."

"How did we handle it?"

"The first time it pinged us, we projected a small diesel engine fishing boat."

"Good," Fox said.

"We've been fading ourselves off their sonar to the southwest. There's lots of surface static, rain started two hours ago, lightning fifteen minutes ago, seas are averaging thirty-five feet."

"How's the sub behaving?"

"Bearing northwest at twenty-two knots, two-hundred meters down."

"Any lightening hit us?"

"Six strikes on the flat panel array," the watch reported. "We might be generating this storm with our own static."

"Has anyone gone aloft to take a direct reading?"

"Bradmore has a team up there now."

"Here's what I want done. Are you ready to take orders?"

"Yes, sir."

"Whether it's our static pulling down this lightning or not, I want the mirage projector on at all times. If we shut it off, the Hayward might locate us. Electrical storms level off at about eight strikes an hour and that won't cause any problems. We can take fifteen. Notify me immediately if we exceed ten an hour for two consecutive hours. Is that clear?"

"Yes, sir. Anything else?"

"Yes. I want meteorology to provide a detailed report to the command center every fifteen minutes. We need to know if it's our static pulling down this heavy weather or a typhoon starting to blow."

"Very well, sir."

He hung up.

Beneath his feet, the ship rolled on long, powerful swells. Their erratic spacing concerned him. He set the crown on the chair with the rest of his costume. He shut off the lights, climbed into his bunk and fell asleep.

With a whistling snore blowing from his nose, Captain Fox slept heavily and dreamed.

*   *   *

In a big oval mirror with an ornate golden frame, Fox examined his reflection and felt amorous toward the regal being looking back at him. With great satisfaction, he realized he truly was King Neptune. A dazzling gold crown, sparkling with brilliant jewels, encircled his massive brow. A full head of flowing white hair cascaded down in looping curls over his bare, broad shoulders. Bushy side burns covered his cheeks, and a thick white beard jutted from his chin. From his forehead down across his handsome nose and cheeks to his bulging shoulders and his muscled chest, his skin shone with a radiant brown tan. Deep furrows across his forehead and crow's feet at the corners of his eyes gave him a mature but slightly dangerous look. Even with this favorable self-impression, Fox had a vague suspicion that there was a flaw in his new and invigorated visage. So, he examined his reflection in the mirror closely and searched for something that wasn't quite right. His crown and hair were certainly masculine and dignified. The bridge of his nose formed a decisive line down the center of his handsome face. His trimmed white mustache curled perfectly above his moist red lips, and when he smiled, the shine off his gleaming teeth rivaled the brilliance radiating from the crown atop his head. He turned his oversized cranium on his powerful neck and caught glimpses of his chiseled profile. He stepped close to the mirror and studied his reflection, but he couldn't figure out what was wrong. And then the weirdness of it startled him as he noticed, with ill unease, that he could see his wiry white brows, his eyelids and their delicate lashes, but he could not see his own eyes. He blinked several times and rubbed his eyes with his blunt fingers, and all the while, wondered why the eyes in his reflection were invisible.

Then, to Fox's surprise, the man in the mirror reached through the ornate golden frame, and his massive hand grabbed Fox's shoulder in a crushing grip. It shook him violently, and shouted, "Wake up!"

Fox blinked and squinted and rubbed his eyes with his fists as he had upon waking from dreams as a child. Grains of sharp crystal sand had crusted in the corners of his eyes while he slept and they scratched his eyelids as he rubbed them away.

He was back in his stateroom aboard the Nimitz, or at least he thought that's where he was.

An old man, wearing an immaculate starched white jacket with a high collar, sat ramrod straight in the wingback chair beside Fox's bed. Five gold stars shined on the old man's shoulder boards. Crushed pearls and colorful gems sparkled on a crown sitting atop his silver-gray hair. The old man reached over and clamped one of his massive hands tight on Fox's shoulder and shook him violently.

"Captain Fox," the old man shouted.

"What do you want?" Fox asked, his voice a barely audible squeak.

"I am Neptunus Rex," the man's voice boomed like thunder rumbling across the sky.

Fox tussled against the sheets, coiled like ropes around him. The harder he fought, it seemed, the tighter his arms became bound in the evil bed linens.

"What's the meaning of this?" Fox demanded, looking at his visitor whose face shone with a pearly white brilliance.

Water gurgled up through his mattress, soaking the backs of his legs and his sheets and blankets and spilling over the sides of his bed and flooding the compartment. He watched his pillow float away as a flood rose rapidly around him.

Disoriented, Fox watched Neptune grow and swell. Agog, Fox got lost in the rough texture of Neptune's hair and the expanse of his face. He imagined himself as a microbe without a soul, a thing with no intelligence, dumbstruck in the face of a supernatural being. His stateroom melted away, and he was up to his neck in water, treading with his arms and legs, pumping his limbs, struggling to stay afloat. Neptune loomed over him, a bare-chested giant rising out of the water. Bolts of lightning cracked across the darkness and black-bottomed clouds swirled over Neptune's massive head. In the pores of his skin, Fox saw trilobites scurrying on ragged claws across the floor of a silent sea. Thunder rumbled from Neptune's throat and foaming white waves crashed through his teeth. Saltwater splashed over Fox's head and dragged him down to the sunless depths where sharks circled menacingly in the murk.

Fox pumped his arms and legs and swam for the surface where he treaded water desperately trying to catch a breath. Salt stung his eyes. He salivated uncontrollably. Moonlight glowed from an obscure angle, illuminating the water for miles around. The Nimitz was gone. A swift current, like a raging river, pulled him along. For a while, he swam against the powerful current, but fear crept into his guts as he gradually realized he could not escape. After a while, overcome by exhaustion, he eked out a doggy paddle with his shivering hands.

Like a toy boat, alone in the ocean, he swept along in the dim gray glow with only the crashing waves and a hush of wind in the night sky. Gradually the angle of the water increased, and little by little, it drew him onto the face of a racing wave. Up he went, rising on a colossal tsunami, higher and higher on the wave's treacherous face.

The wind rose to a roaring crescendo as he neared the foaming apex. It banged him about with the crashing clamor of a freight train. A scream drowned in his throat under mouthfuls of foamy saltwater.

Fox's legs tumbled over his head and his arms flailed; his hands unable to grasp anything. Water churned all around, tossing him to the crest of the wave and then over the top, where he plummeted as if he'd jumped off a tall building. He flew through space, between a black maw about to swallow him and tons of angry water set to crash on top of him. One coherent thought filled his mind when he saw the rocks, black and jagged. He knew they'd been beaten by waves and pulled by powerful tides, but hadn't budged since the beginning of time.

A second before impact, Captain Fox died of fright. And the great wave of seawater, with its salty abrasive scrubbing power, washed away every molecule of his being, and no stain remained where he became invisible.

"In accordance with ancient tradition," Neptune said, "I relieve you of your command. I will navigate this ship across the equator and preside at the initiation of all your lowly pollywogs. Now, sleep like a sailor drowned at sea, Mr. Fox. Sleep soundly."

CHAPTER FIFTY – Day 12

Brandt laid out the Davy Jones costume on the chair in his stateroom. He studied his fake sword, old-style tricorn hat, ruffled shirt, old-fashioned officer's jacket and black wig. Nikki had done a reasonably good job gathering his costume. He stripped down to socks and boxers to go to sleep but decided to put on the costume to see how it looked. The scraggly wig looked fake, but he put on the tricorn hat over it and saw a glimmer of seafaring ferocity in his reflection. Maybe it was his tattoos, or the ruffled shirt, and the way a few clumps of the wig hung around his scowling face below the jutting, bent brim of the hat. Was there some ancient mariner energy there? Either way, he hoped it was enough to pull this off. I'm certainly not going through wog day on my hands and knees, he decided for the thousandth time. He stripped off the costume and laid each piece across the back of his chair. He set his alarm for 0430, climbed into his bunk, rolled over and fell asleep.

Later, he awoke in the dark with a wet hand shaking his shoulder. "Who's there?" he demanded.

"You've arrived on the equator, wog," a raspy voice in the darkness.

Brandt fumbled for the light and blinked as his eyes adjusted to the brightness.

He swung his legs out and his feet splashed in a cold puddle. "What the hell is this?"

He unlocked the door and looked down the empty passageway. Bumping dance music echoed up the ladder from the celebration in the hangar. The ship strained as she rolled over a rough sea. He slammed the door and locked it. As he pressed the speed dial button for the administration office, he put the phone to his ear and glanced at the glowing red numbers on his digital clock. 11:33.

"This is Captain Brandt. Who was sent to wake me?"

"Hold the line, Captain." Brandt heard music coming through the phone even louder than he'd heard it in the passageway outside his stateroom. "Anyone send a wakeup call to Brandt?"

"Not me," someone said.

"Hell no," came another reply.

"Nobody from here, sir."

Feeling foolish, Brandt changed the subject. "Sounds like a party's going on."

"The music, sir?"

"Yes, quite a ruckus," he said. "It's twenty-three-thirty; it should have been over by now."

"Too much fun at the beauty pageant, I guess it got a little carried away."

Brandt called the medical department but nobody answered. He called the bridge and damage control central trying to find out who woke him. As he talked to people in different locations around the ship, he heard loud music and carrying on in the background. All reported no wakeup call sent for him.

He lit a cigarette and sat on the edge of his bunk wondering who was playing tricks. He tapped a bare foot on the wet deck and knew he wasn't dreaming. There'd been someone in his stateroom. How else had the water gotten there? His anger swelled as the ship rose sharply. He knew they were onto him. Panic frittered along the dark edge of his mind. "They know I'm a wog." He exhaled smoke.

He called the MAA and told the woman who answered the phone, "That damn party is spreading all over the ship."

"Well, sir, there were more spectators than we expected, but we're trying to shut it down now."

The right thing to do was to broadcast an announcement declaring the party over, ordering everyone not on duty back to their living quarters. But he tapped his foot on the wet floor and hesitated, because he suspected there was a group of officers out there, probably right around the corner at the end of the passageway. He imagined them snickering and preparing to burst into his stateroom to begin initiating him any minute.

We're on the equator, he reminded himself.

Shellbacks have taken over!

"I'm fucked sideways," he muttered.

"Excuse me?" the MAA asked.

"Shut down the party," Brandt snapped. "If it's not under control in thirty minutes, call me. I'll make a shipwide announcement and put a stop to all this grab-ass."

"Yes, sir."

Brandt snuffed his cigarette, climbed into his bunk, shut off the light and rolled over.

"I said get up, wog," a voice in the dark demanded, and a cold wet hand shook his shoulder. "You've reached the line!"

Dumbfounded, he fumbled for the light, and there was Lieutenant Jones, sitting in his chair. Jones wore an outrageous orange, crushed-velvet tuxedo with black piping on the pant legs.

"You son of bitch!" Brandt stood up and put a hand on Jones' shoulder. Water dripped from Jones' thick, black hair. Brandt said, "You're soaked and you're getting my costume wet."

Rowdy shouting erupted in the passageway.

Jones leaped over and unlocked the door.

Brandt pounced on his back, shouting, "No you don't!"

But it was too late. The door burst open and a gang of wildly attired Shellbacks and drunken buccaneers poured in. They knocked Brandt down, but he jumped up and fought back. He jabbed a man in the eye, and punched a woman in the mouth, but a pair of strong arms wrapped around his chest. Too many hands to fight grabbed his arms and legs. Hands choked him around the neck, wrestled him down and pinned him to the deck. Someone pressed a knee in the small of his back. Another son of a bitch twisted his ears. A sudden kick to the ribs knocked the air from his lungs. They wound a thick rope tightly around his chest and arms. Handcuffs closed on his wrists behind his back. A hand smacked his face and a woman with a cockney accent, said, "Won't lash out like that again will you, Davy Jones?"

"Davey Jones," a voice mocked.

Roaring laughter filled the compartment.

A fat man sat on Brandt's back, pinning him helplessly, preventing him from catching his breath. Sharp pain radiated where he'd taken a kick in the ribs.

In the scuffle, Brandt's underpants had twisted around

sideways, giving him a painful wedgie.

Hatred boiled in his belly. He'd line them up at captain's mast and sentence them to brig time on bread and water. But something wasn't right. The unreality of the situation forced him to stifle his anger and reevaluate.

Brandt forced himself to calm down and examine these hoodlums. Their clothing all mismatched articles of mariner garb from a multitude of navies. They spoke languages with accents he couldn't understand. A rough looking bitch caught his eye and he wondered at the sight of her greasy black hair under a filthy wool cap. And there was a tanned, shirtless boy with dark hair and almond eyes. Brandt knew there were no kids aboard the ship. And there was a woman with a beard and tattoos on her face! A stooped old man with brown spots covering his tissue-paper skin held a long sword that made Brandt think of an old-time weapon—a cutlass or a rapier— whatever the hell that was. A short guy with missing teeth and rolls of fat stretching his tattered shirt, had bandoleers full of bullets crisscrossing his chest and pistols hanging in holsters at his hips.

Brandt struggled to make sense of it. Were these pirates? Actual fucking pirates! Were they taking over the ship? How did they get aboard? Is Jones the ringleader? As Brandt grappled with the notion of Jones leading a mutiny, he licked his lips and tasted his own blood, triggering another wave of rage.

"I'll get revenge on you bastards," he howled.

Another boot kicked his ribs. His vision flickered.

* * *

Coming out of the blackness, Brandt leaped to his feet and lunged for the door, intent on crashing through to the passageway, but a stocky woman in tattered pants and a leather vest cracked him on the back of the head with a sock full of coins. His vision blackened as he collapsed again.

Awhile later, when he regained consciousness, he discovered the brawny woman scowling at him, her arms crossed defensively on her chest. His vision focused, and he saw two pistols, one tattooed on each of her forearms.

Brandt leaped to his feet and tried to head butt Jones. But before connecting, he went down under a flurry of punches. His nose bled. Bruises bloomed around his eyes.

* * *

Jones stepped to the center of the crowded compartment, resplendent in his orange crushed-velvet jacket with tails and narrow lapels over a ruffled, white shirt and matching orange pants. He wore white silk socks and black leather shoes with shiny silver buckles. A jewel-handled dagger stuck from the black leather belt at his waist. He spoke in long flourishing sentences and used exaggerated, almost comical, gestures, as he ordered the others about. He called two men and three women and swore them into a jury. They sat side by side on Brandt's bunk and forced Brandt to lie beneath their feet. A woman with red, gold and green reggae beads braided into her dreads removed a scroll from inside her vest and handed it to Jones.

He broke the wax seal and unrolled it. He read aloud, "The Royal Order of the Deep hereby charges Samuel Brandt of the USS Nimitz with crimes against the Realm." Jones cleared his throat. "Impersonation of a Shellback, when in fact you are a lowly wog." The crowd hissed. Jones rolled the parchment down. "You plotted to impersonate me, the most Honorable Davy Jones, during this equator crossing ceremony." The crowd grumbled. Someone threw the Davy Jones costume in Brandt's face. "And," Jones continued, "you are charged with disparaging the reputation of many hearty shellbacks."

"You'll pay for this," Brandt shouted.

"This man is guilty," a member of the jury declared as she reached down and socked Brandt in the ear.

"How do you plead?" Jones asked.

"I admit nothing," Brandt shouted.

Another kick in the ribs so hard he coughed blood into the back of his mouth.

CHAPTER FIFTY-ONE – Day 12

Inside a wire-mesh cage at the bottom of a ladder, beneath the galley, a marine stood watch. Behind her in three massive vaults everything from bullets to 1500-pound bunker busters, air to air missiles and nuclear weapons were stored. Everything in the ship's world-ending arsenal sat strapped in neat rows on metal racks behind locked doors.

Music boomed from the cavernous hangar two decks above. It echoed through ladderwells and passageways and grated on the ears of the marine guard standing in her wire mesh cage. At the top of the ladder a few feet in front of her, sailors ran wild in the galley, laughing and yelling.

Tonight the ship tossed so hard on the pitching sea, the guard checked to make sure the brake levers on the forklifts were set. She walked across the checkered tiles, past two elevator shafts, closed off by retractable grates. She walked along the row of stainless steel vault doors, each with a dial the size of a tea saucer embedded in its center. Around each dial's face, numbers etched from zero to 99. Each door a slab of steel, ten feet high, six feet wide, and six inches thick, a precision-made machine on hydraulic hinges. Inside the vaults, strapped to storage racks, hundreds of rockets, bombs and missiles rested in climate-controlled darkness.

She glanced at the dial on the first door and noted that it pointed to the zero position, as it should. She checked the gauge on the Halon fire-suppression system next to the door and it showed a full charge. She'd learned in training that Halon gas extinguishes a fire by neutralizing oxygen without damaging electrical equipment, which makes it the perfect firefighting agent for weapon storage areas; the downside was that anyone inside a compartment filled with Halon suffocated to death.

She paused at the last door in the row. Her eyes lingered on the yellow and black nuclear symbol, and she wondered what would happen if one of the weapons in there went off. She imagined the entire ship melting under a mushroom cloud. What kind of gadget is inside a nuclear bomb, she wondered. She'd seen nukes many times. They were sleek white tubes, five or six feet long, a pointy nose and fins like a shark's tail on the end. They didn't look any different from other rockets and missiles, but she'd seen enough safety training videos to know they were different.

Then she noticed the dial on the nuclear vault pointing to the number one, and her hand went to the butt of her pistol. She quickly scanned the area as her mind flashed back to the previous night. She glanced down at the bloodstained yellow tiles. Two marines, scrubbing with hot soapy water and bristle brushes, had been unable to remove the stain. Ten tiles, she counted, had to be scraped off the deck and replaced.

She moved the dial on the vault door one click. "There," she said, aligning the etched arrow with the zero perfectly.

* * *

A hundred times, she'd stood watch at this station, the only entrance to the weapon's vault, and never had an unauthorized person come down the ladder from above.

But last night was different, she told herself as she replayed the memory in her head.

She'd been walking exactly where she walked now when he came down the ladder, sliding on his backside because of the big cast on his leg. He wore paper coveralls. Red welts and tattoos all over his arms. He had two black eyes and he waved a metal pipe over his head as he charged.

"Stop!" she shouted, but he kept coming.

She stepped back and drew her pistol.

"Stop or I'll shoot," she shouted, wondering where this lunatic had come from.

He swung the pipe.

She ducked.

He hobbled to the nuclear vault and turned the dial.

"Put your hands above your head!" she ordered.

He ignored her.

If he knows the combination, she realized, he'd be inside the vault in seconds. She shoved him away, tried to make eye

208

contact, but he swung the pipe again. She imagined him inside the vault banging on the nukes.

"Put your hands over your head," she yelled again, "or I will shoot you."

He ignored her, continued spinning the dial in one direction then back in the other as if he knew the combo. She didn't know it but knew it had four numbers. If this lunatic knows it, she figured, he'll have that door open in a second.

"Step back and put your hands up!" She took aim.

He kept spinning.

She pulled the trigger.

The bullet entered his torso a few inches below his left armpit and spun him around.

She was amazed when he didn't collapse.

He stepped toward her and she shot him again, through the middle of the chest.

Her ears rang and the acrid odor of spent gunpowder burned her nostrils. And then the strangest thing happened. He looked at the hole in his chest and looked at her and he smiled, as if he was grateful to her. Then he collapsed and she ran to sound the alarm.

*　*　*

"Crazy shit," she told herself.

She wrote an entry in the logbook: "2330: ALL SECURE."

The ship lurched steeply, rising on a powerful swell, and she heard a faint pop and a muffled screech. She ran to the nearest vault door, pressed her ear to it and listened as the ship rose and fell with increasing intensity. But the vault remained silent.

The music coming from the hangar two decks above was getting louder as the night wore on, and now people were in the galley, directly above, laughing and roughhousing. She walked to the base of the ladder and shouted, "Move your rowdy nonsense away from my magazine!"

Stepping back into her guard station, feeling cocky, she mumbled, "Shit, I might shoot somebody, like I did last night."

She wondered how that kid Jenks escaped from the brig. She'd stood countless watches but never had a reason to draw her weapon, never mind actually shoot someone until last night.

* * *

Fifteen minutes later, she checked the vaults and Halon gauges again.

"Strange," she squinted at the dial on the nuke vault, where the etched arrow pointed to the number seven. "I put it on zero," she whispered, wondering if the ship's swaying had moved it. Never seen it move like that, she thought, but the ship never swayed this hard before either.

Her palm went to the butt of her pistol as she turned slowly, expecting to see a silent intruder.

But, nobody was there.

Unsure of what to do, she decided not to call away another security breach. She spun the dial back to zero, felt it click with mechanical precision on each digit. While walking back to her guard station, she realized with an unpleasant certainty, that the swaying of the ship hadn't caused the dial to move.

What had, she wondered as she wrote "2345: ALL SECURE" in the logbook.

* * *

At midnight, the dial pointed to 11.

She ran to the guard station and picked up the phone. "Something strange is going on," she told the watch. "The dial on the nuclear weapons vault keeps moving off the zero, but nobody is down here except me."

"Are you reporting a security breach?" the watch asked.

"This magazine needs to be inspected."

"To initiate an inspection," the watch explained, "I gotta sound the alarm."

"I hate to cry wolf," she said, "but there's something fishy going on down here." She imagined the mayhem she'd create by calling a security breach in the middle of the festivities on the hangar. "Yeah," she said, "go ahead and sound the alarm."

CHAPTER FIFTY-TWO – Day 12

Terrance McDaniels chased the Comello lookalike up ladders and forward through a passageway where he found himself in the middle of a gang of rowdy Shellbacks pounding their fists on stateroom doors and stamping the deck with their heavy boots.

Recklessly, Terrance chased the gang around a corner and almost ran up their backs. One man turned around and froze Terrance with a glittering stare. A gray-black beard sprouted so thickly from the man's face, Terrance saw only a pair of bloodshot eyes leering at him from a mass of facial hair.

Terrance lowered his stance and prepared to defend himself.

The man's scruffy scowl softened as he pressed a bottle into Terrance's gut. Without hesitation, Terrance snatched it and guzzled what tasted like spiced rum. The heat of it made the inside of his cheeks sweat. "Thanks, shipmate," Terrance said as he handed it back.

The man chugged again and shoved it back at him. "This'll be a great trial, mate?" The man's rotten breath came over brown stubs that had once been teeth.

"It sure will." Terrance took another swig. He hadn't had a drink in months, since the Philippines, so the concoction went straight to his head, making him woozy.

A door opened and Terrance followed the crowd into a stateroom.

* * *

At first, he couldn't see through the mob of men and women jammed into the tiny space. Their old-time hats and greasy wet hair above surly faces seemed to fill his eyes. What did I just drink, he wondered, as he caught a glimpse of Lieutenant Jones in a ridiculous orange suit, reading from a rolled-up parchment.

"Wow," Terrance whispered when he saw Captain Brandt, beaten down and bound with a thick, old rope.

Another swig from the bottle brought on a rush that sloshed from side to side in his skull. He leaned into the crowd as the ship dropped beneath them like a roller coaster car.

Each time the pirate pushed the jug into his gut; Terrance swigged more and worried less. He joined in laughing as they ridiculed Captain Brandt. He wondered if he'd really seen Comello in the crowded hangar, and who were these hoodlums—most of them soaking wet and stinking like dead fish, carrying swords and knives and drinking liquor. Wondering if he should run to the MAA and raise an alarm, he decided that would be a mistake, especially now with alcohol on his breath.

Right then a bell rang an urgent call throughout the ship. A squeal of feedback, and then a calm computer-generated female voice announced "AWAY THE MARINE SECURITY TASK FORCE. AWAY THE FLYING SQUAD. THIS IS NOT A DRILL. SECURITY BREACH, AFT WEAPONS MAGAZINE."

* * *

Kate lost Terrance in the ruckus so she ran to the library.

She sat in the back of the stacks and watched thousands of books slide an inch over the edges of their shelves, and then the ship rolled the other way and they slid back. The librarians strung bungee cords to prevent books from falling off and they were working pretty well, but tonight the sea ran rough and every few minutes a book or two, usually a thick hardback, leaped over a rubber cord and tumble to the deck. She walked over and picked up a book that had fallen. As she slid it back into its spot, a librarian wearing black plastic-framed glasses entered the row carrying a box of clattering metal rods.

"I've never done this before." He dropped the box.

"What's that?" Kate asked.

"Battening down the hatches." He pulled a rod from the box and fixed it against the books along one of the shelves.

Kate saw right away how he attached the metal rod to little brackets on each shelf and then removed the bungee cord and tossed it into the box.

"Here, I'll help you," Kate said as she pulled a rod from the box and snapped it in place, securing another shelf loaded with books.

"All hands on deck," the librarian said.

"I wish they'd steer out of this storm," she said.

She braced herself against the bookshelf as the ship began nosing over. Her entire body clenched as the compartment seemed to turn over on its side. Thousands of books slid partway off their shelves—the weight of a million words shoved by a violent ocean, straining against elastic bands. She felt the weight of the entire stack threatening to topple over and crush her if the ship tilted another inch.

"We better get out of here," the librarian said, as hundreds of books tumbled over the elastic cords and crashed all around, several knocking them on their heads and shoulders.

Right then the alarm bell rang, and the ship pitched back to almost level.

Kate quickly snapped another metal rods in place.

"I wish I could stick around and help," she told the librarian, "but I have to respond to this alarm."

"Be safe," he said.

Kate bounded over books scattered on the floor and headed out of the library. In the passageway, she was surprised to hear for the second night in a row, "SECURITY BREACH IN THE AFT WEAPONS MAGAZINE."

*   *   *

The ship leaned so far over it caused cabinets and drawers to spew their contents. Fire extinguishers, spanner wrenches, pots and pans and toolboxes—anything not securely stowed—broke loose and rattled about on the deck.

Kate grabbed both railings as the ladder pitched forward and jerked sideways like a rodeo bull. She tightened her grip and hooked one foot under a rung as she recalled stories about sailors on smaller boats attempting to climb down ladders on rough seas, only to be bucked off and thrown to the deck where they suffered a broken wrist or a concussion.

She wondered why they were calling her to the aft magazine again, especially after Jenks had been shot dead there the previous night.

Music and crowd noise came up from the hangar, and she wondered why the MAA hadn't shut down the party by now, especially after hitting the crowd with pepper spray and the runway collapsed.

A standoff between roughnecks in pirate costumes and MAA with their clubs drawn blocked the main deck passageway.

"Make a hole!" Kate shouted, but nobody stepped aside.

A burly MAA held one reveler in a headlock while another MAA tried to cuff him. Two more MAA had their Tasers drawn, holding the anxious gang at bay.

"Flying Squad," Kate shouted, "coming through!"

"Move aside," one of the MAA shouted, waving his Taser.

The fellow in the headlock gave his captor kidney punches and kicked at the woman trying to put the cuffs on him.

As Kate barged into the crowd, she counted a dozen of them and they were dressed more frighteningly than anyone she'd seen earlier at the rally. Several held swords and knives.

An old-timer in officer's regalia, including a black tricorn hat, a tattered blue jacket with faded gold trim and a full rack of worn-looking medals, stared at her with flared nostrils and lust in his eyes. Another man's scraggly beard hung from ruddy cheeks; the whites of his eyes set off by heavy black mascara. She pushed through and saw a thick bunch of dreadlocks hanging lopsided from a woman's head, crawling with silver insects. A length of wire wove through multiple piercings in one guy's ear and metal tacks poked out through the sides of his nostrils.

"Excuse me," Kate said as she shoved through arms with elaborate full-sleeve tattoos. Many of the faces sneered at the MAA as if itching for a fight. Nobody on either side was backing down.

A man with dark eyes, deep in wrinkled sockets, his withered cheeks stretched over bulging cheekbones, grabbed Kate and pulled her close. Face to face, his thin gray lips opened over toothless gums. On feculent breath, he whispered, "Have you come to play with the dead crew, missy?"

"Let me go!" she yelled and broke free. The entire gang erupted in laughter. She stumbled backward. A hand groped her ass. She spun away and ran.

She shot a glance over her shoulder just as one of the shirtless derelicts threw a punch at an MAA who fired his Taser. The fool collapsed in a fit. His mates hooted like a bunch of schoolchildren who'd never seen a stun gun.

As she ran, Dutro's warning about a mutiny on the equator skittered across her mind.

A moment later, she arrived in the galley and saw her Flying Squad mates with painted faces, kooky wigs, pirate hats and plastic swords. A hip-hop hit with a throbbing bass beat pulsed in the hangar above and her worries about the gang scuffling with the MAA dissipated.

O'Malley stood at the center of the team with his reassuring linebacker shoulders and chop-top crewcut. He held a clipboard and shouted, "There's no problem, nothing like last night. The guard just wanted someone to check the lock on the nuke vault, so we're standing by."

Kate took a seat and waited. She thought about how the ship usually rolled fore and aft—up the face of an ocean swell, over the top and down the other side—but not tonight. A growing unease sloshed in her belly. The bright blue deck in the dining area heaved and pitched at an odd angle as the ship slid sideways across an unpredictable swell.

She wanted to run back to the library and meet Terrance and find out what had happened, but a dreadful awareness filled her. Curiosity about everything happening—missing bodies, the rash, warnings of mutiny, seeing Comello, Jenks getting shot, and now for the second night in a row, on the very night the ship arrives on the equator, a security breach called away to the weapons magazine—and it all connected. A sinister energy fired through the synapses in her brain, connecting seemingly unrelated events. Static crackled all around her. Her clothes charged with prickles of electricity like a cheap synthetic blanket just out of the dryer. A tingling sensation crossed her scalp, a low voltage current charging the roots of her hair. The follicles on the back of her neck stood up as if she'd swallowed a hot pepper. She bolted from the chair because she realized that Danny Jenks was dead and his body would certainly be missing from the morgue!

She imagined Jenks' corpse walking along the main deck passageway, limping, dragging his cast, poop leaking from his diaper. She almost giggled, but no, she thought, and then easily imagined Jenks as a pirate with a sword, running with that gang she'd seen challenging the MAA.

The deck heaved beneath her, and she reached to grab a pipe running along the bulkhead, but as she did, an electric spark shot from the pipe into her fingers.

"What the fuck?" She yanked her hand away!

She had to do something and thought about her boss, but knew Sternz wouldn't be any help in this situation.

She walked quickly to the hatch and went down the ladder into the weapons handling area looking for Fire Marshall O'Malley.

* * *

The nuclear weapons vault swung open just as Kate stepped alongside O'Malley and the Marine security task force. Inside the vault, overhead fluorescents illuminated row upon row of sleek bombs strapped on metal racks. As O'Malley and the marines entered, Kate glanced at the nuclear hazard symbol on the door and followed them in.

The others moved ahead, but Kate stopped and looked at one of the bombs—a glossy white cylinder about five feet long with a pointy nose and a blunt finned tail. It was as big around as a volleyball. She reached out to touch the weapon but jumped back as a tiny spark of static zipped from the bomb and jolted her hand. The whole ship, she realized, was charging with static. The situation had a surreal aura because even down here in this high security area, she heard the rowdy shouts of a crazed crowd singing along with the strumming and thumping of a classic rock hit. Why hadn't someone shut down that party?

A loud BANG and the SCREECH of bending metal.

Kate whipped around, expecting to see a bulkhead busted open and seawater pouring in.

She ran through the aisles, following the sound of a man

screaming. She turned a corner and came to a storage rack that had toppled over. A missile had slid out and was rolling loose, clattering on the deck. A marine lay beneath the twisted metal.

"Get this off me," he shouted.

O'Malley, Kate and another marine grabbed the rack and lifted. With awkward footing on the pitching deck, they could only lift the heavy rack an inch. Kate let go and the others held, as she dragged the marine clear.

"This shit didn't come loose on its own!" one of the marines hollered and waved his pistol in the air. "I'll shoot the son of a bitch who's in here!"

"Put that gun away," O'Malley shouted, and told Kate, "Get a stretcher!" He pointed at the injured marine, who was lifting his pant leg to show them a broken shard of white shinbone.

"I'll be God dammed!" The marine continued waving his pistol. "There's someone in here!"

"Holster that pistol and secure these weapons!" O'Malley put a hand on the marine's shoulder.

"What's gonna break loose next?" the marine ignored O'Malley.

"I said, holster that weapon, marine!" A red glow seethed on O'Malley's perspiring face. "If you're concerned someone is loose in here, we'll seal this vault and fill it with Halon gas."

CHAPTER FIFTY-THREE – Day 13

A stout man with a square face and a trimmed beard accused Brandt of licking urine drippings off toilet seats and collecting pubic hairs from shower drains. A skinny old man in a flattened skipper's cap swore he saw Brandt prancing around in women's undergarments. A boy, no older than 12, told the court in a precocious sing-song that Brandt always sat down like a girl to make pee and he always neglected to wipe himself after squeezing out a turd. The bearded woman came before the court and, with a straight face, charged Brandt with pulling the sheets over his own head and inhaling deeply after farting in bed.

They looted Brandt's closet and drawers, tossed his clothing and toiletries about.

A chubby pirate with a hairy back had everyone hooting as he danced around modeling Brandt's cock-thong. His fat rolls jiggled as he leaped and pirouetted for show.

Brandt insisted that he was obligated to respond to the security breach alarm, but waves of raucous jeering shouted him down. Refusing to yield, Brandt continued to harangue them until someone found the ball gag in his bondage toy chest. Upon seeing the restraint, Jones ordered it affixed to Brandt's mouth. Renewed waves of laughter broke from the crowd as Brandt struggled helplessly against the bearded woman attaching the apparatus to his face.

The surly pirates crammed into the stateroom smoked and drank, cursed and made threats. Brandt slouched in a heap, under the weight of so many cold stares.

"Now that you've heard the evidence against you," Jones asked, "do you have anything to say in self-defense?"

The compartment went quiet, except for the wheezing of an old timer. A barefoot, shirtless kid in bellbottoms grabbed the straps on Brandt's mask and asked, "Should I remove it?"

An argument erupted between those who objected and others who wanted to hear what Brandt had to say.

Terrance stared in disbelief at the shirtless kid who stood poised to remove the gag. Red pockmarks speckled his face, neck and chest; some scabbed over but many oozed blood and trickled puss across his gray-blue skin. Dutro, Terrance thought as he studied the deathly face. Trying to clear the drunken confusion swirling in his mind, Terrance blinked hard several times and shook his head. Is my mind playing tracks on me, he wondered. Either that or Dutro has joined the dead crew!

The door banged open and a marine burst in. Someone shouted, "He's got a gun!"

A tussle ensued and the marine's pistol went off.

Everyone froze as the BANG and the odor of burnt gunpowder filled the tiny space.

Terrance looked at the pistol in the marine's hand, its barrel smoking, and followed where it pointed. To his utter amazement, he saw a smoking hole on the right breast of Jones' tuxedo jacket.

Jones looked at the hole, fluttered his hand to dissipate the smoke. An impatient look twisted his face as he growled, "Please subdue this man!"

The entire crowd piled onto the marine, and beat him down with reckless violence.

Terrance ended up half-buried beneath a tangle of arms and legs where he heard, punctuating the riotous shouts, the pistol pop off two more rounds. Truly afraid for the first time since entering the compartment, his liquor-soggy brain considered leaving, but before he could decide, the crowd bound the marine and forced him to sit beside Brandt. The trail continued.

Dutro, or his look-alike, tore the gag from Brandt's mouth and a hush fell over the crowd. He stretched his jaw and leered at the kangaroo court. He considered admitting the truth—that he was a wog—but knew that confessing anything to these tyrants would only worsen his situation. When Brandt refused to speak, Jones ordered him gagged again, and Brandt fought helplessly as they forced the ball into his mouth and fastened the Velcro straps.

"The prosecution calls another witness," Jones announced.

A young man in a filthy brown jersey, ripped from collar to

hem and hastily sewn with a length of twine, stepped to the middle of the compartment. A smile spread his chubby cheeks.

Jones asked, "Are you a Shellback?"

"You bet I am," the kid said with mischievous enthusiasm.

"Har-be-gar!" an old salt shouted, "there's a Trusty Shellback!"

Terrance looked on, amazed.

CHAPTER FIFTY-FOUR – Day 13

"Fractured right femur," Kate hastily told the doctor on duty, as they set the marine on an examination table.

She ran to the morgue and punched in the combo on the ten-key pad. Once inside, she flicked on the lights.

Click. She yanked the first drawer open. Cold air washed over her. "Empty!" she mumbled, and slammed it shut.

Click. She pulled the next handle. "Empty!" She slammed it shut.

Click. She jumped back, a shriek of fear stuck in her throat.

Jenks' cast lay there in one piece.

She considered confronting Sternz and then thought about getting a scalpel and going into the quarantine ward. She'd press it to Darnell Ratcomb's throat and demand he tell her the truth about Jenks, the truth about bodies missing from the morgue and the truth about the dead crew. Instead, she ran to the library.

Passageways normally lit were dark. She passed a compartment where sailors were down on their hands and knees, and enraged Shellbacks were whipping and stomping them without mercy. Screams of pain and crazed peals of laughter, like the inside of a Halloween haunted house, echoed along the cramped metal passageways. Kate watched in disbelief as six inches of water came sloshing directly at her along the main deck passageway. It flowed over her boots and splashed onto her pants. She figured it came from an open spigot, a clogged sink or an overflowing toilet—probably all of the above.

She climbed ladders, ran along a short passage and burst into the library. Entire shelves had fallen over, books strewn across the floor. She found Terrance dozing in a chair at the back of what was left of the stacks.

"Where have you been?" Kate shook him and caught a whiff of his breath. "You're drunk!"

"You won't believe it," he slurred.

*   *   *

On the way to medical station 12, they couldn't walk in a straight line for more than a few steps. The ship lurched this way and that, rising then sliding sideways and down, forcing them to clutch fixtures and pipes, anything fast to the ship.

They heeled so hard Terrance thought it might keep right on going and roll all the way over. A fire extinguisher crashed across the deck in front of them. Terrence couldn't believe the mayhem breaking loose.

Clearly, a lunatic had a hand on the ship's wheel.

It sounded like an elephant trumpeting below decks. A tremendous SCREECH of steel plates under pressure as the ship twisted and rolled on the insane sea.

They crashed through the door into their little hideaway, and Terrance went straight to one of the metal liferaft drums. He slapped his hand on top and said, "I'm jumping over the side."

"Don't tempt me," Kate said. "You won't believe what I saw!"

"What?"

"Jenks is missing, but his cast is still there, it's whole, like his body vanished and left it behind."

"I believe it," Terrance said, unimpressed after what he'd seen. He wrapped his arms around one of the drums. With a grunt, he lifted and took an awkward step just as the ship started another steep roll over. Stumbling through the door, Terrance dropped the drum in the passageway. It crashed and rolled toward the door leading outside onto the catwalk. The lid popped off and they saw the bright yellow raft rolled up inside.

"I'm jumping," he declared.

"We have to tell someone," Kate implored.

"I told Aronson but he didn't want to hear it."

"If we jump we'll be committing desertion!" Kate said.

Terrance turned the drum upside down and shook it. A tightly rolled cylinder of heavy-duty, yellow rubber, with a black rope coiled around it, slid out.

Kate grabbed Terrance's arm and spun him around.

He dropped the drum with a clatter and buried his face in her hair. "Let's go for a swim!" he said, his breath reeking of rum.

"That's desertion!" she objected.

"Jenks is missing from the morgue," he said, "and who do you think's in the magazine?"

"I'm not deserting!"

"It's the dead crew!" he shouted. "Jenks has joined them, and they're putting Brandt on trial and they're in the nuclear weapons magazine!" He threw the door open and a torrent of rain blasted in. He grabbed the raft and lugged it onto the catwalk.

"They're taking control of the ship," he yelled above the roar of rain splattering on steel.

Lightning cracked across the black sky, illuminating watery valleys and steep, foam-topped waves. A thunderclap silenced the howling wind and crashing rain.

"Stop!" she screamed.

"He knows how to arm a nuke," Terrance said, his face soaked, his voice intense with alarm, "and he's in that magazine!"

The ship lurched suddenly and tossed her out through the hatch and into his arms. He dropped the raft and caught her.

Rain soaked them to the skin.

The tortured elephant trumpeted again—the sound of the ship in agony as her keel twisted under impossible pressure.

"Are you jumping?" he asked.

"No!" Kate looked away.

The ship came about level and started to heel over the other way. Kate turned to leave and Terrance gently grabbed her arm. Their eyes met.

"You know who the dead crew are don't you?" he asked.

"I do." She turned her back on him.

"I'm jumping," he said, feeling alone in the world.

She walked away.

"I'm gonna jump," he shouted after her.

She vanished down a ladder.

"I'm jumping—" he shouted less forcefully, and then whispered, "—soon."

* * *

Clambering down impossible ladder angles, making her way back to the magazine, Kate heard screams echoing from below.

When she reached the main deck, she made her way aft, like a pinball, bouncing from one side of the wide passageway to the other. Six inches of water sloshed fore and aft and side-to-side.

A pack of marauding pirates ran at her. A barking dog made her ears perk up. She wondered how they could possibly have a dog with them. She stepped to one side as they charged past, waving fire-hose whips over their heads. It was a huge crowd—30 or 40 outrageously dressed and foul smelling men and women running mad—herding a pack of a hundred pollywogs along on their hands and knees. A riot of screaming and shouting, barking and banging on the bulkheads as the gang clambered past.

A burly woman with tangled black hair and dark blue teardrops tattooed at the corners of her eyes pinned an evil stare on Kate. She grabbed Kate's shirt and yanked hard enough to rip the fabric.

Kate pulled away.

The woman held tight.

Two men in scary-real dog masks crowded behind her, twitching their heads from side to side, keeping a lookout.

The liquor-stink on the woman's breath almost made Kate wretch. The woman's eyes rolled around as she struggled to focus on Kate's face.

"You look like a wog to me, pretty girl!"

"Let me go!" Kate demanded.

"Down on your knees!" The wench pulled a curved knife from her belt and poked it in Kate's belly, backing her against the bulkhead.

"This ship is on the line, wog!" the woman screeched. Spittle flew off her lips and spattered on Kate's face.

Kate lunged aside but the woman brought the blade to her throat.

"You want to die right now?" she slurred.

One of the dog-faced men cracked Kate across the face with his length of fire hose. "On the deck, wog!" he snarled.

224

Kate slowly bent her knees, but the other dogman lashed her across the other side of her face. "Move it, wog," he shouted.

Tears burst from her eyes as she joined the herd of crawling wogs. The second her knees touched the hard steel, she remembered Terrance telling her to get kneepads.

At the first opportunity, she jumped to her feet and ran.

"Get back here," the woman screamed.

Kate ran into a ladderwell and sprang to the top in three bounds. In the hangar, she scrambled around jets and support equipment. She crouched, cowering behind a wooden crate in the shadows, and considered running back to join Terrance on his leap into the sea.

* * *

Rain fell with the ferocity of a waterfall splattering on black rocks. Soaked to the skin, high in the catwalk, Terrance coiled the black rope around the raft. He knelt on the pitching metal grate and considered the red handle, embossed with the words PULL TO INFLATE, poking from the rolled layers of yellow rubber. He considered pulling it and leaping overboard. He saw himself hitting the surface and plunging under. He'd have to swim after the raft and, if he could find it, pull himself aboard.

He simply couldn't imagine floating away alone.

"Damn it Kate!" he lamented as rain dribbled off his nose.

He crammed the raft behind a fuel pipe and went into the medical station to wait for her to return.

He sat on the deck and tried to figure out how he was going to get himself and the raft down to the water, 80-feet below, and somehow inflate it and climb in.

The problem teased his drunken brain.

He wondered what would happen if he inflated it and threw it over and tried to swim after it, but it was too easy to imagine the wind sweeping it away across the waves.

He considered clutching it in both arms until he hit the water, but imagined it smashing his chin and breaking his neck.

Stumped again, he thought about lugging the raft to the fantail and jumping off from there, but he worried about the MAA busting him or having it snatched away by pirates.

Rum-buzzed, he struggled to focus. He hoped Kate would return soon. The ship swayed hard, angled so steeply he slumped onto his back. He considered tying the rope through his belt loops, but his thoughts flickered and he dozed off.

* * *

Underwater, he clutched the rope with both hands and could see the rolled-up raft down there dragging him like an anchor toward the bottom. It made no sense because he knew the raft would float, but there it was dragging him into turbid darkness. His lungs ached, and he knew he had to yank that red handle. He pulled the rope hand over hand. If he didn't reach that handle soon he'd be out of breath and he'd drown, so he pulled with all his might. Water rushed past him but he held tight to the rope and pulled and there it was, the red handle sticking from that rolled-up plug of rubber. With a strenuous effort, he grabbed it and tugged but nothing happened.

He tugged but still nothing, so he yanked his hardest!

And the raft started swelling and unrolling as air filled it.

"Kate!" he hollered as the raft shot past him and started pulling him toward the surface. "Kate," his words gargling under water, "I figured it out! I figured it out!"

* * *

O'Malley stared at the Halon gauge and said, "As soon as the gas is cleared out, we're reentering that mag'."

Kate stumbled down the ladder into the weapon's area. Ragged and out of breath, she wondered if anyone here knew that chaos had taken over the ship. She stood behind O'Malley and listened as he spoke into a telephone.

"If you can't locate Fox, then get Brandt on the line!" O'Malley said impatiently. He could extinguish fires, stop flooding, control all manner of catastrophic accidents and prevent the ship from sinking, but when it came to getting proper clearance, he couldn't tolerate bureaucracy. "What do you mean you can't locate

Brandt?" his voice charged with frustration. He lowered the receiver and yelled, "Is Captain Brandt here?" He pointed at a boatswain standing nearby, and said, "See if Captain Brandt is up in the galley. On the double!" O'Malley spoke into the phone again. "I'll get back to you." He hung up. "Where the hell are the captains of this ship?"

"I've gotta talk to you," Kate said.

"Looks like you got in a fistfight, Conrad," he said.

A sailor wearing a silver firefighting suit walked over, pulled off an oxygen mask and said, "All the Halon gas is pumped out and we're ready to go back in."

"I gotta talk to you, O'Malley," Kate said.

"Stand by, Conrad," he replied.

Kate followed O'Malley and the marines into the nuclear weapons vault. They walked back between the rows of sleek weapons strapped on metal racks.

"Oh my God," someone shouted, "get over here!"

They zigzagged through the racks, deep into the vault.

"Sweet Jesus," a marine muttered.

"What devil's work is this?" O'Malley blurted.

Kate peeked around O'Malley and saw one of the nukes in a flashlight's beam. An access panel on the side was pried open and a bundle of colored wires, several cut, dangled there.

"Whoever did this is dead from breathing Halon!" O'Malley said grimly. He shouted, "Search under these weapons for a dead body. And get an explosives expert down here RIGHT NOW to make sure this thing doesn't blow up!"

Kate ran out of the magazine thinking about what she'd seen in the logbook after a guard heard Jenks say something about short-circuiting a powerful weapon.

CHAPTER FIFTY-FIVE – Day 13

Trueblood lay across a kiddie-playground seesaw with his back against the steel pole that connected the seats. It teetered upward, tossing his smiling face high into a brilliant blue sky. Branches heavy with summer-green leaves filled his eyes, as the swaying contraption held him aloft for a long moment.

Below somewhere, kids squealed with delight as they ran wild on the playground. A dog barked somewhere far away.

Predictably, the seesaw pitched down and his head sank while his legs rose in the air. The big smile stretched his lips even as he worried about rolling completely ass over teakettle.

Slowly at first and then all at once it pitched the other way and his head shot into the sky again.

Each time he teetered, he waited for the jolt of the seesaw hitting the ground, but it never came. So, he rode up and down, steeper and deeper—the entire crazy contraption squealing and straining, like steel bending under terrific pressure.

Unexpectedly it tossed him sideways into a steep pitch, and an overpowering sensation made him hold on.

Snapping awake with one hand pressed against the bunk above him, Trueblood clutched a handful of blanket.

"Hit him again," a wet snarl outside the flimsy curtain.

Bare-knuckles punched flesh over bones.

"Get your paws off me," someone demanded. "I'm a Shellback!"

Boots scuffled and hands grappled, tearing fabric in a desperate struggle.

Shocked awake, Trueblood realized that only his thin blue curtain separated him from the riot going on in the Stinger living compartment.

The ship leaned over hard and someone slammed up against his bunk, an elbow poked between the curtain panels.

He glanced at his clock. 4:05.

A whip cracked on flesh.

"Oww, you fucker!"

Snarling. Growling. A dog barked.

He figured the ship had arrived on the equator, and the Stinger Shellbacks, too impatient to wait, had begun initiating wogs.

Trueblood's eyes popped open. He smiled and thought—a dog bark!

And another bark and this time a snarl.

He'd never seen a dog onboard but there were levels he'd never been to down below. Maybe the MAA had drug-sniffing dogs.

His bunk tipped so hard the thin mattress slid forward. He'd never been on seas this rough. He wanted to go out in the catwalk and feel the gale on his face. He'd grab the railing and watch the rolling combers, bigger than foothills, pitching the sea into whitecaps. He imagined foam, like frilly lace on the water, and realized it might be too dangerous to initiate the wogs with the seas rolling so high. The risk of someone washing overboard would be too great. He figured they'd postpone wog day until the storm passed.

He moved a hand to the edge of his curtain, about to peek out, but two hands grabbed his arm and yanked him bodily out of his bunk. He sprawled headfirst into a scramble of men already on their hands and knees like pigs in a crowded pen.

"I'm a Shellback!" Trueblood leaped to his feet ready to fight, but felt vulnerable in plaid boxers and white ankle socks.

He stared in shock, unable to comprehend the stranger's face. Protruding snout and grotesque skin flaps dangled around its cheeks. Trueblood's mind flashed on a bulldog his uncle had when he was a kid. He remembered how docile it was when he slid his finger into the saliva-wet folds hanging sloppily around its mouth. This stranger had that same bulldog's face with beady, black eyes and a saggy snout. The nasty mouth, full of sharp, crooked teeth.

He glanced around and saw dogmen everywhere. A gang of them, throwing punches, whipping Stingers, barking, snarling. The living compartment was under siege.

Dogmen. Trueblood struggled to comprehend this waking

nightmare.

The sudden lash of a belt on his bare back made him look quickly behind, where he saw another dogman, its face a sagging mess. It growled viciously—snapping teeth inside a wet, pink mouth.

A sucker-punch in the gut doubled Trueblood over.

Panic and trouble rang in his mind. Wog day wasn't supposed to be like this. It was all in fun. No one was supposed to get hurt.

Another whip-crack across his back, and the dogman behind him snarled, "Down on the deck!"

Another punch in the gut forced him to his hands and knees, down among the Stingers already beaten into submission.

Trueblood turned to get a look at these villains, but a strap lashed the side of his face. "Keep your head down!"

A welt rose on his cheek. Tears welled in his eyes.

"Who are these guys?" someone asked.

"I don't know," fear quaking in the reply.

The ship's constant rolling brought the green slime of seasickness creeping up from his stomach. Were these just some rowdy sailors, he wondered, wearing masks and raising hell. He spit, trying to get the seasick taste out of his mouth.

He risked another lash when he glanced at them, trying to figure out how he could fight back.

Too many to count, they were all over the compartment, in the cubicles and along the narrow center passageway. Some whipped the men already down. Small gangs went from bunk to bunk pulling men out, whipping and punching them mercilessly. They wore identical black wool jackets, gray pants and black boots. Each held a thick, black strap. They bounded about the compartment, beating down anyone who protested. Their voices, a garbled mix of barks and growls. Their only utterance: "Down on the deck!"

He stole a glance at the door, estimated it was four strides and made up his mind. Lowering his head, he paid close attention to the ship's rocking motion, waiting until he felt it leaning at an angle that would give him a downhill run.

Trueblood jumped up, planted a foot squarely on the back

of the man ahead of him and lunged toward the door.

A whip lashed his shoulders.

A dogman lunged and wrapped an arm around his waist, but he punched its slobbering snout.

It yelped and released him.

With a burst of confidence, he grabbed the doorknob and heard a rallying cry behind him.   As he bolted from the compartment, he glanced back and saw that his bravery had triggered a revolt.

Men were jumping to their feet and fighting back.

He took two steps towards the Stinger ready room, thinking he'd alert the officers, but the ship pitched hard over, slamming him against the bulkhead. He stumbled. His knees crashed on the steel. Pain jolted through his legs.

The door behind him banged open and two dogmen tumbled into the passageway. One cracked a whip on his back. The other pounced on him. He punched the beast's soft snout and it recoiled, howling.

He ran forward but saw more dogmen coming at him, so he dashed through a door.

"Shit!" he said. "I'm trapped!"

He ran to the back of the compartment and slipped into a stall and latched the door. He lowered the toilet seat and stepped onto it. He squatted, attempting to hide.

He grabbed the shit-paper roller and braced himself against the wall. Looking down, he noticed the water in the bowl tilting past 45-degrees.

CHAPTER FIFTY-SIX – Day 13

"Wake up, Terrance!" Kate shook his shoulder.

Bursting from darkness, inhaling a huge breath, he came awake.

Joy filled his heart when he saw her.

"I figured it out," he blurted.

"Figured out what?"

He kissed her and grabbed her hand.

Outside, rain soaked their hair and clothes again. The ship's superstructure, bristling with antennas and tall metal towers, blinked in silhouette each time a lightning bolt zigzagged across the sky. Wind shrieked and thunder boomed in their ears. Far below, the ocean growled like a hungry beast.

Terrance uncoiled the rope from around the rolled-up raft. The high-tech material felt tough enough to withstand a shark bite. He fed the rope through two of Kate's belt loops, and then through two of his own before tying it off around his waist.

They climbed over the railing and clung there timidly. He grabbed the rail with one hand and wrapped his free arm around the raft. Kate clutched a handful of his jersey in one hand and the rail in the other.

They couldn't see the water, but they could hear it churning far below.

Crooked bolts of lightning zigzagged across the sky. In an instant, they rejoined and struck the Nimitz's superstructure, sending white sparks showering across the bridge windows.

The flash illuminated rain pouring from black clouds and typhoon winds ripping the tops off tumultuous waves.

"Do you feel it?" she shouted, as a shock sparked into her hand.

"Yes," he replied. "Jump on three."

"I'm ready!" she tried to sound confident.

232

"One, two, three."

Wracked with doubt, he closed his eyes and took a half step into the howling darkness.

She let go and stepped into the void, clutching his sleeve for all her life.

Half way down, a swirling deluge all about them, and the massive ship passing at their backs, he let go of the raft. A second later, it slapped the surface and they plunged underneath.

*   *   *

The water's warmth surprised Kate, but the sound of the ship slicing through the night-sea close beside her, sent her kicking for the surface.

When Terrance saw the hull's black shadow slide over, he panicked and clawed his way back up to the air.

She gasped a huge breath and coughed on the salt burning the back of her throat. In horror, she saw the raft bobbing on the water close to the side of the ship.

He looked up at the big opening of the hangar bay sliding past and regretted his decision to jump overboard. He felt like a tiny fleck of life with a ton of water crushing his chest and a mile-deep ocean tugging at his boots. He wished with all his heart he could be standing up there looking down and not in the water failing in a fool's attempt to swim.

"Pull the rope," she shouted, but the ship forged ahead like a steel plow, pushing tons of water into a curling white wave over their heads.

She screamed and he froze in fear as the foamy spume, driving ahead of the Nimitz's steep side, crashed over their heads.

The ship slammed into them with ruthless power, crushing them mercilessly under the airless water. Their fingers scraped the slimy, barnacle-covered underbelly. They held their breaths in the turbulent darkness and knew they were about to die. Dead ahead the gigantic propellers were slicing the water with the malicious precision of industrial food processors.

She scraped along under the hull and her fingernails broke as she scratched the barnacle covered steel. The term keelhauled occurred to her. She recalled the ship had four 20-foot-wide bronze propellers and two 55-ton rudders. Fear of certain death seized her as one of the big props came into view.

Terrance flailed about, grabbing for Kate, certain the prop would maul them into bloody chunks.

She dug her fingers into the slime on the hull. A primal scream erupted from her throat. Her fingertips bleeding as they scratched the impenetrable keel. And then her back banged against a contour in the hull, and she bounced off, realizing it was the housing for one of the propeller shafts.

A rush of water pushed him out and he veered off and whisked by. The prop passed mere inches in front of his face. A power-tool WHIRRRRR of metal blades slicing water sizzled in his ears.

She grabbed for him as the big propeller passed. She blinked and saw the blades spinning off a frenzy of bubbles. And they passed on one side of the prop and the raft passed on the other.

Before they could experience even a moment of relief, the rope yanked hard at their hips. They banged together. And the full thrust of the ship drove ahead, pulling them with incredible force.

The rope tangled around the propeller.

A swirling wash of bubbles knocked them together. Kate grabbed for a place to hold on but caught nothing. Terrance saw the prop spinning in front of him, pulling them closer and threatening to chop them to bits with each rotation.

Suddenly the rope snapped, and they WHOOSHED through the gray murk, past the rudder.

They popped up in the wake, gasping inside a slather of sea foam that covered them and filled their mouths.

Terrance grabbed the rope and pulled but it came too easily. He looked around and hoped the prop hadn't shredded the raft to flotsam.

"There," Kate shouted, pointing.

They swam furiously, but the rope tied between their belt loops made it almost impossible.

"Work together," she shouted.

They toiled against one another in the tossing sea, and they finally got their hands on it. Terrance scrambled over the twisted rubber and found the red handle. He pulled it and the raft began to inflate.

Kate grabbed a lug handle and turned just in time to see the Nimitz floating away down a mountainside of water. "Look," she yelled, but the ship vanished behind the holograph.

They clung to the raft as a malicious wind ripped the tops off rabid waves and slapped them in the face with sizzling foam. They pulled themselves in and bounced around as it rode the choppy swells. Inflated ribs covered the oval floor, big enough for ten people. Supply pouches attached inside, along with life jackets, which they pulled on and buckled. The raft almost capsized each time it lurched over a steep swell. Kate tied a bit of rope from her vest to a handle on the side of the raft. Terrance did the same.

Rain poured down and lightning ripped the sky.

"Did you see the ship disappear?"

"No," he replied.

They clambered to their knees and held on. She gripping one side and him the other.

"See anything?" he shouted.

Water blasted their faces like a shower.

"No."

"Look at that," he shouted.

She scrambled over and saw lightning bolts a short way off. "The Nimitz is inside an electrical storm," she said.

A wave tossed the raft onto its surging crest. It sent them tumbling over and flipping upside down. They flew through the air and splashed into the sea. Tons of foaming water crashed on their backs, and drove them down into the airless depths.

They popped up, tangled in the ropes as another wave poured water atop their heads.

The raft was upside down and attempts to right it were futile. They held on and fought to keep their heads up. Gusts of wind smacked their faces. Each wave climbed higher and curled over steeper. The wind ripped so much water off the tops of the waves they couldn't tell where the sky ended and the surface of the sea began.

*   *   *

The dunking went on for hours, but they clung to the raft and rode out the storm, fighting delirious exhaustion all night.

Towards dawn, the low black clouds turned a dreary gray. The storm blew itself out as wind and rain settled in a prevailing direction. They managed to climb into the raft and bail out most of the water. Horrible seasickness had them vomiting until their stomachs were empty, and then for hours they shivered as they sat with their backs against the sides of the raft, their arms outstretched, clinging to the handles. All the while, their eyes wide open as wind whipped their faces, clutched by fear that the next rolling mountain would flip the raft and toss them back in the water.

"A ship," Kate shouted.

Terrance saw only gray haze.

She pointed, but the wave collapsed, dropping them into a wet valley between the rollers.

The next wave tossed them up and he saw it. "The Nimitz," he shouted.

"No, it's a cargo ship."

He could barely distinguish, through the spray, a red and black line of paint on the big ship's keel. He realized he'd been mistaken. It wasn't the Nimitz.

A moment later, another wave tossed them up, and they saw far off on the horizon, a sleek white pleasure cruise ship with lights, like camera flashes popping in the sky all around it.

They dropped into the rinse cycle between the swells before another comber lifted them toward the gray sky. They saw the Nimitz far off, under a pyramid of flickering colored lights. And they knew it had been the Nimitz all along, and what they'd seen earlier was the malfunctioning cloaking system.

Awhile later, they saw the Nimitz for the last time. Far off near the horizon, it rode low in the water, rolling on her side as waves washed over her, seeming to pull her into the depths.

CHAPTER FIFTY-SEVEN – Day 13

The metal door banged open.

Dogmen entered, sniffing.

"He came in here," one growled.

Nothing made sense.   What the fuck is going on? Trueblood's thoughts scrambled. Am I dreaming? He spun the roll of shit paper on its spindle and tore off several squares. His feet cramped from standing on the toilet seat. He considered his chances against dogmen armed with leather straps, when all he had was a few squares of shit paper. I'm not dreaming, he realized as he crumpled the paper and tossed it into the bowl. He looked down at the small, white octagonal tiles with black grout lines between them and saw a dogman's boot.

It grabbed the top of the door and shook it hard.

Trueblood watched the latch jiggle and hoped it would hold.

The PA system crackled and a voice boomed, "STAND BY FOR AN ANNOUNCEMENT FROM KING NEPTUNE."

The dogmen outside the stall howled with delight as a long shriek of feedback climbed higher and higher to a painful, ear-spitting decibel. Sparks flew from speakers throughout the ship. Then a woman's hysterical squeals of laughter echoed everywhere. In anguished gasps, she tried to catch her breath. Her laughter and crying went on for so long, Trueblood knew she was being tortured by tickling. Trueblood imagined the woman on the ship's bridge, pissing herself as she shrieked in agitation. Some sick fuck was holding the microphone to her mouth while several others tickled her. "Stop," she pleaded and laughed uncontrollably. "Stop! I beg you!" Unable to catch her breath, in a peal of hilarious agony. "Please, stop! PLEEEEEESE!"

A hard smack across the woman's mouth and a gruff, "Shut up, wench!"

She cried in shock.

Outside the stall, the dogmen howled for joy at the sound of her being beaten.

Then a man hacked and cleared a hawker from his throat.

"THIS IS KING NEPTUNE," His Majesty's deep voice boomed with authority. "MY DEAD CREW AND I CAME ABOARD THIS VESSEL DURING THE NIGHT AND WE FORCEFULLY RELIEVED CAPTAIN FOX OF HIS COMMAND! WE HAVE TAKEN OVER THIS SHIP'S HELM AND HOISTED OUR JOLLY ROGER ON THE MAST! WE ARE NOW STEAMING EAST TO WEST ALONG THE GOLDEN LINE."

The dogmen outside the stall barked with delight. Shouts and riotous cheers echoed through the ladderwells and along passageways. They echoed from the ship's loudspeaker system, as the mutinous gang on the bridge rallied behind their leader. A chill shivered down Trueblood's spine, and the skin on the backs of his arms and legs turned to gooseflesh.

"I AM SORELY OFFENDED," Neptune continued, "BY YOUR FOOLISH CAPTAIN'S DECISION TO STEER THIS SHIP, WITH ITS FEEBLE INVISIBILITY SHIELD, AND A CREW OF DETESTABLE FILTHY POLLYWOGS, INTO MY FORBIDDEN DOMAIN!" Neptune's voice rose with his tyrannical rant. "AS THE COMMANDER OF THE OCEANS, I DECREE THAT ALL SHELLBACKS AND ALL POLLYWOGS ABOARD THIS SHIP WILL BE BROUGHT TO THE BRINY DEEPS AND MADE TO JOIN MY DEAD CREW IN OUR REALM BENEATH THE WAVES."

A bang and a squeal of feedback, as if he'd slammed down the microphone, ended Neptune's announcement.

Then deep belly laughs of a pirate who'd snatched the microphone. He laughed brazenly, causing a cold shadow of fear to pass through the heart of every soul aboard the Nimitz.

The dogmen outside Trueblood's stall began howling mournfully. Their primal growls, long and troublesome, warned of impending doom.

*   *   *

From down deep in the bowels of the ship, a dreadful HUM vibrated upward through all the interconnected steel plates and pipes. The torturous screech of bending metal scraped at Trueblood's ears. Thin blue sparks, like neon threads, crackled in the air around him. Water in the toilet under his feet bubbled and vaporized. Steam rose around his ankles. A loud CRACK filled him with an appalling sense of loss. The stall's shiny stainless steel walls shook.

The stall rose like an elevator racing toward the top of a skyscraper. A gust of air burst in under the stall and his ears popped. The entire compartment hurtled straight up at tremendous speed. Looking down he saw orange firelight shine through the grout-lines between the tiles. The porcelain commode cracked and crumbled away, and Trueblood clung to the toilet seat with both hands. Scorching heat sent horrific pain raking across his skin. His boxers and ankle sox disintegrated into dust and dissolved on his liquefying skin. The stall door swung outward, broke off its hinges and flew away.

Looking down, Trueblood saw fighter jets, and burning bodies and the ship's superstructure all tumbling away inside a tower of fire that pushed him high into the sky. For miles around, the ocean spread toward the horizon, but directly below, he saw the Nimitz, her outer skin bent like a smashed pop can, her keel broken, her interior spaces breached by the sea, and she was dissolving inside a white-hot light that made him think of a Hubble telescope photo that showed the birth of star.

His finger bones clung to the toilet seat as he flew toward heaven. In his final moment, Trueblood wondered if there was a story like this in the Bible and if there wasn't, well, there would be someday.

CHAPTER FIFTY-EIGHT – Day 13

Immaculate white light flashed across the sky.

A shockwave rumbled through the air.

Tremors shook the depths of the sea.

A loud BANG cracked the heavens.

A column of fire pushed a mushroom cloud of smoke upward and burned a mile-wide hole through the gray clouds, opening a portal into a blue sky full of sunlight. A tremendous gust of hot wind flattened the waves. A crackling fireball radiated outward, vaporizing every raindrop for miles around.

Kneeling in the raft, Kate watched the tower of fire and smoke rise into the sky and saw a disturbance rippling through the air, quickly coming closer. A wall of white-hot light flashed past her. It burned the tip of her nose, and her cheeks. Crackling around her ears and against her scalp, it started burning her skin in earnest, like fire. "I'm going under," she said and jumped from the raft.

Underwater, she felt a rumble, like an earthquake vibrating through the depths. The phrase God's hammer popped into her mind, and she knew Jenks did it.

He blew up the ship!

She unclipped the life jacket and let herself sink. She exhaled and watched the bubbles rising from her mouth toward the steaming surface as she sank further below.

In the same instant, Terrance saw the entire ocean dent itself into a deep, wide bowl. A giant ripple radiated outward on the water. It lifted the raft high into the air, as if he were suddenly in the cheap seats on the rim of an impossibly large stadium. And down there, miles away on the fifty-yard line, a nuclear explosion, exactly like he'd seen in so many Navy training videos.

Tiny blue sparks crackled from squiggly lines etched on the air inches before his eyes. He knew they were molecules breaking apart, leaving trails of microscopic fire. They flickered and penetrated down into the water. Whatever had come out of that bomb was tearing at the fabric of reality. He wondered if he ever had kids would they look like mutants. He thought the water might shield him from the radiation, but it trembled all around as if about to boil. Images of lesions and hair falling out in clumps flashed through his mind.

But a more pressing matter occurred to him. What would happen in a few seconds when the water flowed back to its natural shape, which wasn't a ten-mile wide stadium? He hoped it wouldn't suck him down any closer to the main event, a ten-megaton white-hot arc-welder's torch vaporizing the Nimitz and a billion gallons of salt water. It spewed a column of smoke into the blue circle of sky where the storm had been.

Someone will be in a world of trouble when the Pentagon finds out about this, Terrance mused, as he unclipped his life jacket and dove from the raft. He swam down as far as he could and held his breath until his lungs ached.

A minute later, he surfaced to catch a breath and saw an orange ring radiating across the sky. He looked around for Kate, and called her name, but didn't see her, so he plunged under again. When his breath ran out, he swam for the surface and saw the raft.

"Terrance! Terrance," Kate called.

"I'm here," he shouted.

Her face appeared above him.

"Get in the raft!" She helped pull him in.

A hot wind buffeted all around, and a metallic ashy taste filled their mouths.

She had a supply pouch open, and he quickly sorted out a set of tent poles and an odd shaped sheet of metallic fabric.

They snapped the poles together and fitted them into pockets sewn around the sides.

A billowing black cloud of radioactive water vapor and dust, from what had been the Nimitz, stretched away toward the horizon. Air currents seemed to be carrying the main bulk of it away, but a dirty orange ring of burnt air circled the entire scene high over their heads.

They dragged the fabric across the tent poles, pulled it this way and that to make it fit. They flipped the fabric over thinking it was upside down, and then flipped it over again when they realized they'd had it right the first time. Several elastic bands stretched to secure the dome in place, and a chunky Ziploc zipper sealed them inside a bubble-like enclosure.

Kate dug into another supply pouch sewn inside the raft. She pulled out a laminated card and read it. Then she rummaged in the package again, pulled out a yellow plastic bag with a radiation symbol on it and said, "We need to strip and put our contaminated clothes in here." She tossed the bag at Terrance who unlaced his boots, yanked them off and tossed them in. Their wet clothes quickly followed.

"Now we need to rub this all over our skin," she said, as she tossed him a tube of medicine.

He squeezed a big gob of white cream into Kate's hand. It smelled like mouthwash. She smeared it on her neck and arms. Terrance did the same. And they helped each other rub it on. They wiped off with gauze from the first aid kit and tossed the used wads into the radioactive waste bag.

Kate grabbed a pair of scissors and told Terrance, "Go ahead, clip it." She tossed her head back and let her hair hang down.

"You sure?"

"Yes," she said. "I'm not taking any chances."

He grabbed big chunks of her hair and clipped them off, tossing them into the bag.

Even with her blonde locks cut at odd angles and white cream unevenly smeared over her face, he thought she looked beautiful.

It impressed him that she kept her head and took control of the situation, even in a nuclear blast. God, he hoped they could make it work when all this was over.

Kate made Terrance swallow several pills.

"What are these?" he asked.

"Potassium Iodide."

"What for?"

"Prevents your thyroid from absorbing radioactivity."

They wrapped themselves in shiny silver blankets and leaned back on the sides of the raft.

* * *

Now the sea ran calm, murmuring against the raft. The dome tent glowed with daylight, shading them from the scorching rays.

"Somebody was in the nuclear magazine messing with a bomb," Kate said as she dug around in one of the pouches.

"Jenks?" he asked.

"Probably." She twisted the top off a water bottle and took a sip.

"Did you get a shock from anything on the ship?" she asked.

"I felt static."

"Well, I got a shock off a pipe in the galley and from a metal rack with one of the bombs on it."

"You know we're screwed," Terrance said.

"Because nobody is gonna believe us!"

"Yeah."

"Our only choice is to tell the truth," Kate said, and took a long swallow of water.

"Yup, when we reached the equator," Terrance said, "dead people started a mutiny."

"Nobody will believe it," Kate said.

"We'll say Jenks stole Comello's body from the morgue and he murdered Dutro and he escaped from the brig," Terrance rambled. "Then he broke into the magazine and blew up the ship!"

"But Jenks was dead," Kate objected.

"Then how do you explain his cast in the morgue drawer?"

* * *

In Kate's nightmare, black waves the size of buildings crashed on top of her head. Salty water smacked her face and filled her mouth. She clawed helplessly, trying not to drown in the roiling trough between the waves, and then the surging sea tossed her high into the rain-filled night where the wind exploded in her ears and howled at cyclone strength. Lightening cracked across the sky and

243

for a second she could see the wind ripping the white tops off the waves.

A flash appeared on the horizon, and a BOOM blotted out the storm. A massive column of fire rose into the sky. And the wave collapsed, sucking her down into the cauldron.

The dream repeated with slight variations. But every time, she nearly drowned, an explosion split the sky, a fireball burned a hole in the clouds and she choked on water that tasted like sulfur.

In the raft, Kate rolled from her back to her side and onto her back again as she wrestled with the nightmare.

Waves tossed her into the air, just in time to see the brilliant flash. An explosion cracked the stormy sky. In the wind, she heard sailors calling out for help. She ran down the main deck passageway.

In her sleep, she mumbled, "Gangway! Flying Squad!"

Her thrashing woke him.

He shook her gently.

Something barked and snarled from deep in the ocean.

A bright flash and a tremendous explosion.

A clanging bell and a machinelike female voice calling her name as she tried to run.

A squeal of feedback cut the darkness.

A red glow burned her eyes.

An amplified voice boomed across the waves, "Ahoy, in the liferaft!"

"What's that?" Terrance leaped to his knees.

"Ahoy, in the liferaft!" the voice booming again.

"Are we being rescued?" Kate mumbled still half asleep.

Terrance opened the top of the raft and popped his head out. Shielding his eyes from a white search light, he saw a motorized whaleboat bumping against the raft.

Kate popped her head out too.

A sailor in a chemical warfare suit pointed a shotgun at them. Another held a bullhorn. Another pointed a pistol.

"What ship are you from?" a muffled voice demanded from behind one of the bubble facemasks.

"The Nimitz," Kate shouted.

"How many are you?"

"Two," Terrance said.

"Only two?"

"Climb aboard then."

Kate tried to climb with one arm while holding the space blanket around her naked body. She banged her shin on the side of the boat and slipped, almost fell in the water.

To hell with modesty, she thought as she crumpled the blanket, threw it into the boat and climbed with hands grabbing and pulling her aboard.

Terrance did the same.

The boat's engine filled the air with burnt diesel fumes.

Kate grabbed her space blanket and covered herself as best she could. She and Terrance sat on a bench in the bow of the boat, but had to move to the back, because their rescuers where dragging their raft aboard and stabbing it with knives. They kept stabbing until all the air came out and then they rolled it and stuffed it into a yellow plastic bag emblazoned with a red radiation hazard symbol. But the raft was too big to fit in one bag, so they unrolled it and slashed it with their knives. The raft filled four radiation waste bags sealed with elaborate folds and zip ties. Kate noticed the bags were yellow and see through, which made sense, because as a first responder, she'd want to know at a glance what was inside.

The boat's pilot told everyone to hold on as he pushed the throttle forward. The bow rose out of the water and they motored fast through the darkness.

A ship materialized out of the night; satellite dishes spinning atop the USS Hayward.

PART V

THE LANDLUBBERS

CHAPTER FIFTY-NINE – Day 14

She sat on a cot welded to the deck in a tiny compartment.

A fluorescent bulb shined behind wire mesh in the ceiling.

Kate shivered, realizing it looked like Jenks' cell on the Nimitz. Keys jangled outside. The door swung open on well-oiled hinges. In the passageway, a sailor with a club in a hoop on his belt. Two people in chemical warfare suits crowded in.

Hair chopped at odd angles after radiation exposure, clutching a shiny space-blanket around her naked body, locked in a cell while people in space suites examined her, their faces hidden by the glare of an overhead light reflecting off their domed masks. Kate felt trapped inside a science-fiction movie.

One of her captors unfolded a now-familiar yellow radiation waste bag, while the other pointed at her and said in a voice that echoed behind the face shield, "Put that blanket in here."

Kate complied and stood naked as they ran a Geiger counter over her. Crackling sounds from the handheld device.

"How bad is it?" she asked.

"Not too bad, actually."

Her little cell pitched forward and back as the ship charged over the sea.

They gave her a robe and led her down the passageway. With a tube of the same medicated goop she and Terrance used on the raft, Kate showered and scrubbed herself from head to toe twice.

After she rinsed, they gave her a bristle brush to scrub the shower stall.

Back in her cell, they checked her blood pressure. With a small flashlight, they looked in her mouth, nostrils, ears and made sure her pupils still dilated properly. They drew blood and took urine and stool samples.

"Where's Terrance?" she asked.

No answer.

Later, another chemical warfare suit entered and asked her name, rank and serial number.

Kate told him.

"I want a written statement explaining how you came to be floating in a Nimitz liferaft," the visitor said.

"I jumped overboard," she said.

"Put it in writing." He set a clipboard with a yellow pad and a pen beside her.

She approached it like a school assignment, considered her introductory paragraph and an outline, but then she wrote the words, "We pulled Donna Grogan's broken body from a puddle of maple syrup at the bottom of an elevator shaft, and several hours later she went missing from the morgue." And from there the ink flowed steadily. She didn't worry about spelling or grammar or run-on sentences. She paused here and there, thought about the right way to phrase something but remembered what they agreed to. Just tell the truth.

When she put the clipboard down, a pit of guilt opened in her stomach. Then tears flowed and sobs wracked her ribs and shoulders. She lay on the bunk and pressed her face into the pillow and bawled like a baby.

They gave her pancakes and bacon on a paper plate and a plastic cup of orange juice.

The Hayward shuddered as it raced across the ocean, its sleek narrow keel cutting through the waves, rolling fore and aft much steeper than the Nimitz ever had. They were in a hurry, she figured, because there were powerful people who were pissed off about the Nimitz blowing up.

She awoke to the sound of a shrill whistle blowing several notes and a man's voice calling away the anchor detail.

*   *   *

He did push-ups and sit-ups to burn nervous energy and then fell asleep. When they brought pancakes and bacon, he asked about Kate, but they wouldn't tell him anything so he ate, exercised again and slept some more.

An hour after they called away the anchor detail, the door banged open and two armed guards stepped in. They gave him a pair of pants and a shirt. As he dressed, he asked, "How about shoes?"

"You don't need 'em," one guard said.

They took him through a narrow, low-ceilinged passageway. Gigantic wrenches in metal brackets on the gray bulkhead. At the top of a ladder, one of the guards handed him a lifejacket and a crash helmet and waited while he put them on. They went out a door into brilliant white daylight. He squinted and felt the nonskid surface of a helipad under his bare feet. Ships floating at anchor in a crowded harbor surrounded by skyscrapers and steep hills. His heart raced with excitement as he recognized Victoria Harbor and the Hong Kong skyline. Sudden fear overcame him as one of the guards pulled his arms behind his back and clamped handcuffs on his wrists.

A small civilian helicopter swooped in and landed.

The guards grabbed handfuls of his lifejacket and shoved him into a seat behind the pilot. A man in a dark blue suit with a white shirt and a classy red tie sat beside him. The man glanced down. Terrance followed his eyes and saw a chrome-plated pistol in the man's hand.

"You won't need that," Terrance said.

"Let's hope not," the man replied.

CHAPTER SIXTY – Day 15

A city skyline filled her eyes. She'd never seen this place before. Ferries and hydrofoils, jet skis and junk ships with their sails full of wind, all whisking about on a crowded harbor. Cruise liners and supertankers rolled at anchor in the gray chop. After months at sea, the sight of piers lined with cargo cranes and the waterfront crammed with gleaming skyscrapers and streets swarming with pedestrians and cars, overwhelmed her. Kate felt excited and irritated all at once.

They flew over tall buildings and a sprawling industrial area where gigantic metal storage tanks and train tracks gave way to a jungle beat back by suburban tract homes, highways and corporate office buildings surrounded by parking lots and golf courses. The pilot spoke into a headset, probably Chinese, Kate guessed, and a minute later the helicopter descended to the roof of a three-story brick building surrounded by rolling green lawns, manicured gardens and neatly pruned trees. A high brick wall encircled the place. They helped her down from the chopper, and the man in the suit guided her through a doorway and down a flight of stairs.

They took off the handcuffs and let her remove the crash helmet and life vest. They put her in a carpeted room with a table and chairs. She felt mesmerized by the wood grain pattern in the tabletop and the plush feeling of padded carpet under her bare feet—things she hadn't experienced in months. She walked to the open window and stood there amazed at the sight of leafy trees and fuzzy bushes. The smell of earth and grass enchanted her senses. Several birds swooped past, playfully chasing each other. Insects buzzed deep in the foliage. A slate path wound through raised beds bursting with flowers. After months of sensory deprivation and claustrophobia, the scene overwhelmed her. Her knees wobbled and she stumbled back from the window as a surge, like the ship swaying beneath her, turned her legs to mush. She bumped against the table and plopped into one of the cushioned chairs.

She closed her eyes and inhaled through her nose, then pursed her lips and exhaled slowly, attempting to calm down. She couldn't remember the last time she sat on something so soft.

*   *   *

The man in the suit entered the room. As he removed his jacket and hung it over the back of the chair, Terrance noticed the empty leather holster.

"I'm Shertzer," he said as he sat down. His short, wiry brown hair looked like he went for a trim every week. An overconfident cockiness oozed from his steely grin and hard dark eyes.

"I'm not dangerous." Terrance put his hands on the table, palms up.

"Good to know," Shertzer quipped.

"Where's Kate?"

"Tell me your story," Shertzer said flatly.

"Have you ever served on a warship for an extended deployment at sea?" Terrance asked.

"No."

"Then it's gonna be difficult for you to understand."

"Try me."

It was easy enough telling Shertzer about the cloaking exercise, describing how Stinger jets were sabotaged and bodies went missing from the morgue. But when he told about Jenks killing Dutro, Jenks on trial, Jenks escaping the brig, a weird vertigo closed in. The ceiling in the room seemed to be lowering so slowly he couldn't actually see it moving, but it sure as hell felt like the whole room was getting smaller every second. It took all his concentration to tell his story and not bend his neck to avoid the ceiling coming down on top of his head. He began to question his own sanity. He wondered how his story could possibly be true. He casually reached across the table and touched Shertzer's arm, and was relieved when Shertzer didn't vanish in a puff of smoke.

"I don't care if you believe me," Terrance said. "Kate warned her commanding officer and so did I, but they wouldn't listen." Terrance stood up and stepped toward the window. "They threatened us when we tried to tell them something was wrong."

"Be more specific," Shertzer said.

Terrance looked outside at the lush garden and breathed deeply through his nose, but his chest felt tight and sweat formed on his brow. "Things on that ship were totally out of hand," he said.

"For example?"

"Jenks obviously wasn't working alone." Terrance sounded desperate, as if he didn't believe his own story. "Since Kate worked in medical and I worked with Jenks we talked about what we knew."

"What did you know?"

"It's a big ship, there was a lot of weird shit going on, like it was invisible and bodies kept disappearing from the morgue, and then Jenks like, gets framed for it, but these other guys, Dutro and Ratcomb, were involved and maybe others. They were doing something evil, like a black mass. They might of stole bodies from the morgue and did some kind of voodoo on them, and they came back to life. Fuck, I don't know!" Perspiration shined on Terrance's forehead and a queasy nausea crept up the back of his throat. He clutched the edge of the window as if holding onto an amusement park ride.

Christ, I hope I don't vomit, he thought as he rubbed his eyes.

"What's the problem?" Shertzer whispered.

"I was at sea for over a hundred days and then when I saw dead guys putting the executive officer on trial I jumped overboard and watched the ship sink under a nuclear blast!" Terrance sighed. "You think that might stress a guy out?"

"I suppose," Shertzer allowed.

"Maybe Jenks was a pawn," Terrance continued a bit calmer. "I'm telling you, I saw Stanley Comello in the ship's library, then again on the hanger during a beauty pageant the night we arrived on the equator. He looked like shit, like Frankenstein, dead and brought back to life. His eyes were bleeding. He had a rash. I'm not kidding. Comello was dead! Kate can verify it. They convicted Jenks of stealing his body from the morgue, and I saw him, I'm telling you, I saw him."

"A dead man," Shertzer asked, "walking around the ship?"

"Yes! And the crazy part is I followed him to an officer's stateroom where a bunch of pirates, actual fucking pirates, were putting the executive officer, Captain Brandt, on trial because they said he was a wog impersonating a Shellback, worse than that, he was impersonating Davy Jones."

Relief washed over Terrance, because he was finally able to tell someone what had happened, someone who wasn't on the ship, but he glanced at Shertzer and saw the disbelief in his eyes. He dreaded having to tell this outrageous story, because it stank like bullshit and made him look like a psycho. Doubt punched him in the stomach, but he had no choice but to tell it all to Shertzer, even though he was obviously some kind of spook, a secret agent, probably a former Army Ranger turned CIA.

He took a deep breath and reminded himself that there was no way he and Kate could fabricate a story that would withstand an investigation. As they'd agreed, he told the truth, as wacky as it sounded. The truth was the only thing that would hold up under the grilling they were going to get.

Terrance went all in.

"I think when they turned on the cloaking system and we got close to the equator, something happened."

"Like what?" Shertzer asked with subdued curiosity.

"Like we went into another dimension where dead people came back to life and King Neptune and his minions pirated the ship. Look, I know it sounds crazy, but that's what happened."

"Seriously?" Shertzer asked.

"There are people who can verify it," Terrance said.

"Who?"

"Three guys who flew off the ship after Jenks' trial. One is Chief Crenki, the Stinger maintenance chief until his ulcer popped. Keef is a heavyset guy with the NCIS, and Shakley is a crash investigator."

"Tell me about this," Shertzer said, as he dropped a fat roll of cash on the table between them. It bounced on thick red rubber bands and rolled off the table.

For an instant, his heart hurt as if Shertzer had poured boiling water on his chest. Hot tears leaped from his eyes and sobs burst from his throat. All the Stingers and everybody else he made money from were dead. He buried his face in his hands as several wrenching sobs shook his entire body.

He wiped tears off his face with his fingers, snorted snot back into his nose, and said, "My dad borrowed money against our farm and couldn't pay it back. It stressed him out so bad it gave him a heart attack. He died and left us with nothing. My mom and my brother and me moved into a tiny apartment and went on food stamps. We were so broke my only choice was to join the Navy. My brother sent me cigarettes and chewing tobacco and I sold them on the ship." Terrance wiped the last of his tears off his cheeks with his fingers. "I swore I'd never be broke again."

CHAPTER SIXTY-ONE – Day 19

A smartphone newscast broke the story that the US Navy had detonated a nuclear weapon off the coast of Borneo. But pictures of people in chem warfare suits on a beach on the Java Sea and angry quotes from an Indonesian politician didn't capture viewers. With no video, no body count and no wreckage, there was no news.

Two days later, the captain of an Australian oil tanker dropped anchor in Perth and went to the local TV station with a grainy video of a mushroom cloud rising into a gray sky and burning a huge hole through the clouds. He told viewers around the world that he was 75 miles south of the Indonesian coastal town of Bangkala in the Flores Sea during a violent storm when he saw a magnificent flash of light, heard a tremendous explosion, grabbed his phone and recorded the video. The broadcast cut to his tanker looming over the pier, and then to a close-up of a local geologist holding a crackling Geiger counter as he ran the instrument over the ship's exterior railings.

* * *

Political leaders across Southeast Asia demanded an explanation.

Reporters armed with microphones and cameras got in the faces of Washington politicians and Pentagon officials.

Someone in DC leaked a report on the Nimitz catastrophe.

The media trumpeted: Storm-Nuke Combo Sink Super Ship; Doomsday Device Kills Thousands; Navy's Worst Catastrophe Ever; 5,000 Sailors Perish at Sea.

* * *

Shertzer already had Kate and Terrance in a mansion on a walled estate in the Virginia hills. Every day they begged for information about each other, but Shertzer told them nothing, not even that they were in rooms on the opposite ends of the same underground hallway.

The walls in Kate's cell were impenetrable, a high-tech white compound. Scraping with her fingernail, a fork and a broken piece of a dinner plate didn't leave a scratch. Ten minutes of kicking made her toes sore and brought a guard to her door. They told her to calm down, or they would drug her again.

But after countless hours of interrogations, she stuck to her story about missing bodies, a devil-worshipping nutcase and a dismantled nuclear missile.

They tried truth serum, a lie detector and aggressive questioning under bright lights. A buff chick with a sleeve of tattoos on her right arm beat Kate on the back with a rubber baton. Through it all, she repeated the same story she'd written aboard the Hayward.

*   *   *

Shertzer always wore a fine, dark blue suit, sometimes without the jacket, but always a crisp white shirt, a tie and black shoes with a high gloss shine.

Terrance was doing sit-ups when Shertzer entered, asking, "What's it going to take to get you to modify your story?"

"Sixteen … it's the … seventeen, truth … eighteen."

Shertzer waited.

Terrance hit 20 and slowly stood up. "I was doing sets of fifty until your goons worked me over."

Shertzer smirked but remained silent.

"I know you've talked to Crenki, Keef and Shakley by now," Terrance said. "They told you about Jenks, right?"

Shertzer still pokerfaced.

"You believe us, don't you?" Terrance said confidently. "It's all true about the invisibility shield, missing bodies and Jenks. But it won't look good in the news, will it?"

Shertzer didn't answer.

"I'll tell you what," Terrance stepped close to him and whispered, "if you let me and Kate leave the Navy and we can have some kind of normal life, like we go to college and the Navy pays for it, I'll sign anything you want."

* * *

Without seeing the sun or stars, Kate couldn't be sure, but she figured it was two days since she saw Shertzer last and now he was back in her cell with that smirk on his face. "So, all you want is to be with McDaniels?" he asked.

"And we can have some kind of normal life," Kate stipulated.

"Your options are limited," Shertzer said. "One, you spend the rest of your life in a military prison being forced to take your medicine. Two, we disintegrate you and scatter the ashes. Or, three, you and Mr. McDaniels forget your story about Davy Jones and the walking dead and you—"

"You gotta let met talk to Terrance before I agree to anything," she protested.

"Either way, the story you've been telling never happened."

Her expression was noncommittal.

"I'll prepare a statement for you to memorize and sign, is that clear?"

She considering it for about a second, and said, "Let me see Terrance and then we'll talk about it."

CHAPTER SIXTY-TWO – Day 20

The president sat behind her desk in the oval office listening to the team of experts she'd assembled to help her sort through this mess. Her chief of staff, a Navy admiral and Mr. Shertzer, her fixer at the CIA, sat in chairs before her.

"This disaster has been at the top of the news cycle for over three days and all I've said to the media is, 'This serious matter is under investigation.' And now, gentlemen, I must have an informed and decisive statement," the president demanded. "I must handle the media and calm the public." The president stood up and dropped the report on her desk. "If I'm reading this correctly," she said to the admiral, "the Nimitz may still be out there behind its cloaking system."

"Ma'am, your assumption is highly unlikely." The Admiral paused, thought for a moment and proceeded confidently. "Since the blast occurred, we have been broadcasting messages from every available source, telling the Nimitz to abort the cloaking mission. If she were out there, we'd know it."

"What are you saying, admiral?" the president demanded.

"The Nimitz and her crew are gone, vaporized, and as much as I hate to admit it, the story these kids are telling is as close to the truth as we'll ever get."

"Will you put that on Navy letterhead and sign it?"

"Absolutely, ma'am, for you and the joint chiefs' eyes only," the admiral replied, at once confident and then uncertain at being boxed in so tightly.

"Very well then." The president turned to her chief of staff. "How should we proceed?"

"Ma'am," he began, "we've conducted focus groups and opinion polls in which we asked subjects to choose from five different scenarios. We correlated the results and formulated a storyline that earned a seventy-seven percent approval rating."

"Those are good numbers," the president said with her particular brand of infectious enthusiasm.

"Based on the data," the chief of staff continued, "we recommend that you call a press conference. Your statement is simple and goes as follows. The disaster aboard the USS Nimitz occurred while an explosive ordinance team conducted a drill with a nuclear weapon. The Navy's investigation indicates that a faulty electrical circuit caused the weapon to detonate."

A shade of skepticism crossed the president's face.

"Mrs. President, when we formulated this response," her chief of staff reassured her, "we looked closely at the space shuttle Challenger explosion back in eighty-six. President Reagan could have ordered the public execution of NASA's top brass and the public would have cheered him on."

"He was an amazing man," the president said.

"If you recall, the shuttle exploded with a schoolteacher on board, and it happened on live television with every kid in America watching. By attributing the disaster to a technical failure, Reagan ducked and enabled everyone involved to duck with him. The political lesson learned," the chief of staff explained, "is the American people know that high tech military operations are dangerous. They are willing to accept large numbers of dead military personnel. In fact, at a deep psychological level most people crave this type of disaster—"

"Crave it?" the president asked.

"Yes," her chief of staff continued. "Life is boring and monotonous for common citizens, but a big disaster provides them with much needed catharsis."

The president's look spoke favorably for this option.

"Two days after the news conference," the chief of staff continued, "you will take a swipe at the previous administration, because they drastically reduced military spending. The upswing is that you'll be able to increase military spending and look strong doing it."

"Sounds great," the president said. "What about the survivors?"

"Mr. Shertzer has something special in mind for them," the chief of staff replied.

"At a key moment during the press conference," Shertzer said, "one of the reporters will ask about survivors and your response to this question will unify the nation. Think of it. Right now, everyone wants a scapegoat, and we could sacrifice some Navy brass on the altar of public opinion," Shertzer patted the admiral on the back. "But you can do so much better than that, Mrs. President." Shertzer paused for a moment of dramatic suspense. "Don't give the American people a scapegoat when you can give them two national heroes!"

"Will these two survivors play along?" the president asked.

"They've already agreed to our plan," Shertzer assured her.

"Can they go in front of the press?" the president asked.

"Absolutely," Shertzer said. "They're an attractive couple."

"Is there a love interest?"

"Yes." Shertzer smiled.

"Outstanding," the president exclaimed.

The admiral spoke up. "Corpsman Kate Conrad is a former California volleyball champ and Airman Terrance McDaniels is the handsome son of a Nebraska corn grower. They survived the nuclear blast because they were making love inside the Navy's most advanced, high-tech liferaft."

"Lovers in a liferaft," the president said with unabashed enthusiasm. "People will gobble this up like hot dogs and apple pie!"

"At the press conference you must clarify the difference between a large intercontinental ballistic missile and this weapon," the admiral explained, "which is a tactical nuclear device."

"Hold that thought, admiral," the president cut him off as she stepped to the center of the room, a smile lighting her face. "This will be one of the defining moments of my presidency. I'll galvanize the nation!"

"Yes you can," Shertzer said.

"We need a massive branding operation." The president looked at her chief of staff.

"We've got an agency all over it," he assured her.

She crossed her arms, lowered her head, put her hand on her chin and paced across the oval office, suddenly apprehensive about releasing the survivors to the public. She considered what might happen if they cracked under the media attention. What if they go off message? But, she decided, that didn't matter because the 'lovebirds in a liferaft' spin had enough positive poll potential to compensate for any downside scandal. The public will fall in love with them and their incredible true story, and if they ever tried to cash in on a confessional talk show or a controversial book, they would sully themselves, not her.

"Polish it," the president told Shertzer, "make it sensational, downright heroic! Incredible hardship, lives at risk, and all that horseshit. Make them memorize it and rehearse it under bright lights." She turned to the admiral. "What have we been feeding the media on our search for survivors?"

"Fly-over footage of battleships crisscrossing open water and troops in chemical warfare suits combing a deserted beach, all with a voiceover, making it look like a massive search is underway," the admiral replied. The president squinted. "There is a massive search underway," he assured her. "But that footage is classified."

"Okay, here's how I want to handle it," the president started snapping orders. "Chief of staff; change tack on the terrorist angle, start mentioning the previous administration's military cuts and inferior parts used in nuclear weapons."

"Yes, ma'am."

"In twenty-four hours," she said, "I want everyone pointing the finger of blame, but don't leak enough details, I want it so nobody knows who to point their finger at. We want a frenzy of finger pointing! Got it?"

The three men chirped a chorus of, "Yes, ma'am," as they observed the president's brilliance in action.

"I want the American people to see the government as a nine-headed hydra, and then tomorrow evening I will cut in on every channel, right when people are most irritated. I will explain the faulty electronics part on the tactical nuclear device. Admiral, I want specifics on our new high-tech liferaft and how the Navy is continuing to search for survivors. Two days later we'll blitz the airwaves with live video of the rescue, and then those lovebirds and I will be all over the news."

CHAPTER SIXTY-THREE – Day 21

A few miles south of Washington DC on Highway 95, a Virginia State Police cruiser sped along at 70 MPH with its siren wailing and lights flashing. It cut a path through evening traffic for a black Suburban following close on its bumper. In the back seat, behind tinted windows, Kate and Terrance sat sipping bottled water and watching Fox news on a flip-down screen.

A news anchor recapped the president's message, which Kate and Terrance had missed. It was impossible to tell from the anchor's rhetoric what the president had actually said, but they pieced it together, mostly from reading the text scrolling across the bottom of the screen. Apparently, the president had spoken from the oval office. She said the disaster aboard the USS Nimitz occurred while an explosive ordinance team conducted a drill with a nuclear weapon. The Navy's investigation indicated that a faulty electrical circuit caused the weapon to detonate, and the ship had sunk in the Java Sea near Indonesia. Search and rescue teams hadn't found any survivors, but the search continued.

Outside the Suburban's dark windows, trees and corporate office parks whizzed past in the fading daylight.

Shertzer reached back from the front passenger seat, clicked shut the miniature TV screen. He handed them each a packet with TOP-SECRET stamped in red on the cover.

"Time for you to get on message," he said.

As the vehicle zipped along, they read Shertzer's fabricated account of their ordeal.

They were aboard the Nimitz, making love inside a high-tech liferaft when a tremendous explosion went off. They came to in a jumble of survival gear inside the damaged raft. They survived a violent storm and drifted for days on the open sea.

"We sign this and then what?" Terrance asked.

"We're heading over to do makeup and shoot video on a

green screen," Shertzer explained. "You survived a nuclear blast and a week adrift. I don't even know what that means! Weight loss? Bandages? We'll let the PR people do their thing. Then you'll meet the president. It'll be a media event."

"Meeting the president is cool," Kate said, "but do you have any idea how much it costs to go to medical school?"

"We'll work that out," Shertzer said. "The president wants to pin medals on you."

"I don't know about being on TV," Terrance said.

"You'll be an international sensation," Shertzer declared, "X-Box is already prototyping your game."

"I'll go along with this story," Terrance said, "but I don't know about being on TV."

"Don't worry," Shertzer spoke confidently. "The president's press handlers are the best in the business."

"This is all lies," Kate said, waving the papers at him.

"So is everything out of Washington," Shertzer said. "We'll put you on talk shows and release lots of photos. There'll be sound bites, paparazzi, T-shirts—full media saturation with lots of swag and bling and flag waving."

"People won't believe this," Terrance protested.

"Yes they will." Shertzer stopped abruptly and scratched his elbow. "They'll drink it like sugar water, but they'll be bored with it after two weeks. We're already designing another media event to bump you out of the news cycle. We'll report that all the attention is negatively impacting your relationship and that'll make all but the biggest weirdoes back off."

"Weirdoes?" Terrance asked.

"Then we'll put a doctor on the news who'll say you have to spend a couple weeks in the hospital."

Kate and Terrance exchanged a concerned glance.

"Hospital?" Kate asked.

"Lingering effects of radiation," Shertzer explained.

"You're not locking us up again," Terrance said.

"No," Shertzer assured them. "You don't even have to go to a hospital, just wear sunglasses and lay low," he explained. "Then you two fade into history—national heroes."

Acknowledgements

Thank you to family, friends and fellow writers who read early revisions of Sailors Take Warning and graciously provided suggestions for improvement: Tira Plumondore, Joan Rogers, Magdalen Power, James Bernard Frost, Erick Fleck, Edward Morris, Terra Chapek, David Marshall, George Fleck and Amanda Glover. To all the good people at World Cup Coffee in Portland, Oregon and St. Mark's Coffee House in Denver, Colorado; thanks for the caffeine. Last but not least, I owe a special debt of gratitude to all the men and women with whom I served in the US Navy.

Turn the page for a sneak preview of:

SAILOR'S DELIGHT

A novel

By Malcolm Torres

Available on **www.amazon.com** in 2014

Prologue

The Northern Pacific Ocean ran rough beneath a blue sky. Gusty winds tore the tops off the whitecaps and splashed spray in the troughs between the waves. Big brass propellers churned beneath the great gray ship and pushed her bow forward, cutting a tattered wake on the gray-blue water.

Several plane captains—sometimes referred to as turd shirts because they wore brown helmets, brown jerseys and brown flotation vests—clambered from a watertight door in the hull and tromped along a catwalk of welded metal grates and railings. They carried tie-down chains slung over their shoulders. In a few minutes, their A-7 Corsair jets would land and the plane captains would scramble across the deck, weave between blasts of engine exhaust and spinning propellers and secure their aircraft to the deck. For the moment, though, they hung their chains on the deck-edge scupper and stood in the catwalk waiting for their jets to land.

Dual engines whistling like bottle rockets, several F-14 Tomcat fighters had landed. With big propellers, spinning so fast you couldn't see them; an E-2 Hawkeye had landed. A-6 Intruders, engines rumbling like thunder in a bowling alley, had landed. And now an A-7 Corsair roared down out of the sky with its tail hook extended, accelerating toward the arresting cables in the landing area.

A man's voice, crisp with amplified intelligence, suddenly squelched the thunderous roar. It spoke from deck-edge loud speakers mounted in the catwalks all around the flight deck. "CORSAIR NEXT! STAND BY TO LAND AIRCRAFT!"

Christopher Marlow helped Larry Tynan heave three chains onto each shoulder, just as the Hawkeye, a big aircraft with enormous propellers on each wing, backed into its parking spot on the deck directly above them. The hurricane gale thrown back by the Hawkeye's whirling propellers pressed Larry's goggles flat on his face. Steven Oaks, Angelo and Martin Weary were there gripping their greasy knuckles white on the scupper, holding fast as the air blew back on them. The tremendous

1

HURRRRRR and WHIRRRRRR of the Hawkeye's propellers whet the senses. Just a few feet away it rolled slowly, precariously backward several inches with each burst of power applied to its engines by the pilot in the cockpit at the throttles. The fuselage and the folded-back wings weighed heavily on the Hawkeye's stout hydraulic landing gear and its black rubber tires. A flight deck director, in a gold jersey, helmet and goggles, gave hand signals to the pilot, kept the Hawkeye going backward until its tires were just a few feet from the scupper. Blasting stronger than a gale wind, air came off the Hawkeye's starboard side propeller and hit the young deckhands hard in their smooth young faces.

When Larry Tynan's A-7 Corsair touched down in the landing area, Christopher Marlow helped Larry put three chains over each shoulder. Larry smiled a thank you because talking on deck is useless. He turned around and stepped up the ladder onto the flight deck. One of Larry's chains got stuck on the scupper and he halted. He looked back, frustrated. The chains always were too heavy for Larry. Although he had big shoulders and staunch legs, a layer of baby fat trimmed his limbs and torso. For one second Larry's blue eyes, framed in black rubber goggles, cried for help.

He knelt as Christopher Marlow unhooked the chain from the scupper and then threw himself forward.

In his frustration, Larry forgot himself. He'd received a real sweet letter from his girlfriend back in Detroit, and since he was going to be out of the country for nine or ten months she was going to date some other guy for a while. And that thought stuck in his mind when that link got stuck on the scupper.

Larry threw himself forward with the palm of his baby-fat hand on the front of his helmet and his other arm across his chest, holding the chains and turnbuckles, but instead of walking outboard from the Hawkeye's landing gear Larry lurched forward next to the fuselage and the propeller caught him as it arced around.

When the prop is spinning, it's a blur, invisible. It might've only knocked Larry's arm off but the chains tangled on the prop and yanked him off his feet. The Hawkeye's plane captain ran in dangerously close to the spinning propeller. His arms were up and his fingers clutched at the air as if he wanted to grab Larry and pull him out of that awful machine. And the blood, the goddamn blood, was in the engine. The prop spun, its vortex vaporized the red into tiny droplets and busted off links of Larry's chains. Blood and gore instantly splattered everyone nearby. Busted links flew like bullets. One beaned Steven Oaks' helmet so hard it shattered. The young men could only duck down in the catwalk for fear that those broken links would pummel them. Lengths of chain, scraps of Larry's clothing and an explosion of gore sprayed over the side of the ship. Blood painted the loudspeaker on the railing red. Christopher Marlow clamped his eyes shut so tight tears couldn't leak out. Angelo kept yelling, "Oh my God! Oh my fucking God!" so loud it distorted his voice and sent pins and needles down the backs of Christopher Marlow's legs.

Chapter 1: Land Ho!

A salty breeze fluttered their black neckerchiefs, ruffling the bellbottom cuffs of their dress white pants, threatening to blow the white hats off their heads. The sun rose and burned off the morning mist, revealing the jagged contours of Diamond Head Crater on the horizon. Sailors hooted at the sight of land.

They stood in a ceremonial formation, spread out in single file along the edge of the flight deck—a Navy tradition for ship's entering Pearl Harbor.

"Land ho," Christopher Marlow whispered as he glanced from the catwalk below his feet to the islands in the distance.

The men to his right and left, he'd never seen before, their skin white from working down below. They'd not seen the sun since leaving San Francisco eight weeks earlier.

But working on the flight deck every day had tanned Christopher Marlow's face and shoulders to a leather-brown. His fingertips still tingled though, from handling steel tie-down chains in subzero winds on the Bering Sea. At twenty, Christopher had been a deckhand aboard the Enterprise for three years. And he'd been carrying chains, drums of aircraft cleaner, dragging fuel hoses and electrical power cords across the black steel as it pitched and rolled on oceans around the world. All that and strong-backing bombs under jet wings had roughened his hands, broadened his shoulders.

Christopher's polished shoes, his white jumper and a Dixie cup hat crimped over his freshly trimmed crew cut made him look squared away, but the truth was he felt like shit. Doctors had been jerking him around. He thought about the times he'd sat on an examination table at sick call with a corpsman looking at him with disinterest. Christopher pointing to his tan muscular chest, near his heart, saying, "I finished the vial of pills you guys gave me last time but it still hurts, right here."

They never looked him in the eyes; just held a pen in one hand and his medical record in the other, inventing a new way to write the same diagnosis: "Changed patient's meds, ordered back to work on full duty." They scribbled nonsense hieroglyphics and moved on to the next ill sailor in the long line at sick call. And Chris added another vial of antacids, muscle relaxers or painkillers to the pharmaceutical collection in his locker.

And there he stood at the edge of the deck with the tips of his polished shoes against the scupper, looking down at the catwalk. He started thinking about Larry Tynan, but quickly he looked away at the near horizon where green mountains loomed over the white hotels on Waikiki. He took a deep breath of fresh sea air and felt the anxiety in his chest ease.

Seagulls rode the breeze, flapping their wings, swooping and cawing. Beams of sunlight penetrated the dark green depths, slanting through kelp beds. A steady hush from the ship's keel as it pushed aside the water, cutting like a knife through the breakers close to land. And then white sand surfacing through the dark green and now transparent blue water. Land! He'd not seen it in eight weeks. Vibrant green palm trees—so green they burned a sailor's retinas—leaned lazily in the Pacific Ocean breeze. All the sailors standing along the edge of the flight deck blinked at the brightness, and on the black backs of their eyelids they saw green ghosts shaped like palm fronds. And there among the palm trees were rows of little houses, with cars parked in their driveways. A woman holding a small child shielding her eyes from the sun watched the big ship enter the mouth of Pearl

Harbor.

And now a stiff breeze came across the deck and dozens of white hats took flight to leeward. Many men put their hands on their heads and felt their hair. Surprised looks appeared on their faces as their hats twirled and spun on the breeze and fell eighty feet to the water where the mighty ship plowed them under its frothy white spume.

"Attench hut!" a voice snapped from the deckedge loudspeakers. A line of marines standing on the bow and sailors along the ship's rails snapped to attention. Tugboats came alongside. On the water's surface, cement memorials like floating tombstones appeared. Chris read the old battleship names painted in neat navy blue letters, USS California, USS Tennessee, USS West Virginia, USS Maryland, USS Oklahoma, and USS Nevada. These marked the ships sunk on Battleship Row when the Japanese attacked Pearl back in December of 1941.

As the Enterprise came alongside the Arizona Memorial, a voice crackled from the loudspeakers. "Hand salute!" There below the surface all beheld the hull of the once mighty battleship, now sunk in the mud on the floor of the harbor. Her superstructure, rails and stacks cut away. All the holes torn in her hull by Japanese torpedoes, welded over with steel plate patches. And there built right over the sunken hull, the white memorial appeared to float on the water—a memorial to all who lost their lives that day.

Forward on the ship's bow, a marine barked a series of commands. Bolts slid, triggers clicked and rifle fire pierced the morning air. Three times a marine gave the commands and three times seven rifles fired, rendering a 21-gun-salute in tribute to our shipmates lost so long ago on that day that lives in infamy.

A stroke of rainbow rose from the plush green mountain and a light rain began to fall. "To," banged from the PA, and everyone dropped the salute. The sun slipped behind a cloud, a thrusting cat's paw caressed the deck, and Christopher's Dixie cup hat flew away like a wingless gull. With one hand on his freshly clipped crew cut, he watched his hat spinning towards the water along with many others. For a moment, it floated like a tiny, empty life raft and he imagined a tiny person sitting in it holding on for dear life, helpless before the ship, a gray wall of steel bearing down on it.

A bolt of lightning split the sky and thunder rumbled over the green hills. Big cool raindrops fell, soaking through the shoulders of Chris's white crackerjack blouse. The wind blew more hats over the side. Sailors fidgeted and held their hats on their heads as gusting winds swept the harbor. The marines stood fast until a shrill whistle blew.

The formations broke, and sailors scrambled between the jets on the deck to find their way to hatches leading into the ship.

Chris walked aft between the fighters and bombers, helicopters and ground support equipment. He lifted his feet over tie-down chains securing aircraft to the deck.

Far aft, he paused at the edge of the flight deck before jumping over the scupper and landing several feet below in the catwalk. Through the mesh under his feet, he saw 80-feet to the water below, and then he hopped down the metal steps welded against the hull and went through a watertight door into the ship.

*   *   *

Upon entering the living compartment someone yelled, "Get out of the way, Marlow!" Chris's head blocked the TV, where a show never seen at sea appeared on the screen. He turned to look, and there saw a beautiful young blonde woman in a white string bikini performing deep knee bends. Blooming flower gardens surrounded her and a tall white hotel towered in the background. What captivated Chris wasn't her flat bronze tummy or her long firm thighs but her soft yet commanding voice steadily counting, "and two and three and four—" He hadn't heard a real woman's voice since leaving San Francisco eight weeks ago. Sure, he'd heard women on the television, talking in movies, but this live broadcast reminded him that today they were going ashore, and he might have a chance to meet a girl and talk to her. His heart raced as he caught himself inhaling sharply.

"Marlow! Get out of the way of the TV, man!"

Chris   pushed   through   the   crowd   and   into   the compartment's center aisle. Every few feet to the right and left there were cubicles packed tight with bunks and lockers and men in every stage of dress, every phase of conversation. Eighty aircraft mechanics lived in the compartment. Forty worked nights and forty worked days, but today the ship was pulling in for three days of liberty, so no one was at work. Everyone was in the compartment. Cigarette smoke and cologne were overpowering. Men talked excitedly about going out on the island as they pulled on jeans, shirts, tennis shoes.

Chris shook a Marlboro from his pack and lit up as he entered his cubicle. His friend, Steven Oaks, stood in the florescent shine of the overhead lights.

"You manned the rails." Steven was a handsome, well-built 20-year-old from Boston. He wore blue rubber sandals and tighty-whitey underwear. He had well-proportioned muscles on square shoulders and chiseled chest, tight buttocks and bulging calves. Steven stood there dragging a comb through his brown hair. After a moment, he put down the comb and plucked the cigarette from Chris's fingers.

"Our hats blew over the side," Chris said, as he kicked off his shoes and climbed into his bunk, the middle one in the tier of three on the left side of the cube.

Chris glanced across at the bunk above Steven's. It was Larry Tynan's old bunk. The mattress was stripped and folded over, the locker emptied and the curtains removed.

"We ought to go out and see the Arizona Memorial," Chris said. "I mean, we've been here like six or seven times and we've never been out there. A thousand guys are buried inside the sunken hull you know, and after forty years it still leaks oil."

"Right," Steven said. "I bet maintenance guys row out there at night and refill it." He wrapped a towel around his waist, locked his coffin locker under his bunk and picked up his mesh bag of toiletries.

"Well, we really ought to go see the Arizona on Sunday."

"You going to that Army hospital today?"

"Yeah, what are you doing?"

"Me and Angelo are going to Waikiki." Steven said. "First I was thinking we'd get some steaks and a big order of real fries, you know the ones with the skins still on 'em, and wash it all down with a gallon of cold draft. And then for dessert I'm gonna order a big bowl of vanilla ice cream and a jigger of cream de mint." Steven stopped and smacked his lips savoring the thought of his first meal ashore. "Then we're gonna get a pint of Johnny Walker, that one with the special black label, and a cold case of Molson Golden Ale." His eyes rolled up, a finger went to his chin and a look of deep contemplation came over his handsome face. "Or Grolsch, yeah maybe Grolsch, I gotta make up my mind! I kind of like the doohickey top on those beers."

Steven handed the cigarette back and Chris took a drag.

"We'll find a grove of palm trees and a couple lounge chairs," he said, "and we're gonna spend the afternoon getting fucking stoned, you know, a good old liquor picnic. You want to meet up with us?"

"Sure," Chris said without conviction, still contemplating a trip to the Arizona Memorial.

"Tonight Angelo wants to go to that nightclub the Wave," Steven said. "You know that joint?"

Chris imagined himself doing something adventurous, like taking a windsurfing lesson or going out on a charter boat for some deep-sea fishing. So many things were possible when the ship entered port, but when a gang of sailors went ashore they usually resorted to the least common denominator and ended up in a bar talking shit and trying to meet girls.

"Let's meet at the Wave around eight," Steven said as he left to go take a shower. "Hey," he turned back, "how long until the gangway is down?"

"Any minute, we're alongside the pier now." Chris clamped the cigarette between his teeth and swung his legs out of his bunk. He opened his locker and took a last drag before snuffing the butt in an ashtray.

He reached into his locker and pulled out a cellophane packet, squeezed out two chewable Mylanta tablets and popped them into his mouth. He crunched them into frothy foam between his teeth and swallowed. As he leaned back, looking up again at Larry Tynan's empty bunk, he recalled the detectives who came with the bolt cutters and snipped Larry's padlock. They tossed

Larry's stuff—his coveralls, uniforms, underwear, toiletries, civilian clothes, paperback books and letters from home—into an evidence bag. And then the detectives left without saying a word to Chris or Steven Oakes, and that was it.

Larry was gone. Dead.

The dull ache in Chris's chest flared anew, and he wondered if Steven was right. Would a gallon of cold beer bring greater relief than chalky Mylanta?

Chapter 2: The Doctor's Eyes

Amidst the hurly-burly of stevedores, officers and roughneck bosuns, cranes hoisted nets full of cargo, forklifts belched smoke between the clattering, grinding of their gears. Bails of green bananas, burlap sacks, drums of aircraft cleaner, crates of oil and grease stacked shoulder-high along the pier. Across a gangway that spanned from the Enterprise to the pier, a steady stream of sailors in civilian clothes came ashore.

As soon as the ship had tied up, men armed with fire hoses lowered over the side in baskets to blast sea slime off the carrier's steep, gray hull.

Across the pier from the Enterprise, the USS Sacramento was tying up. A streamer of bright colorful signal flags flapped in the breeze atop her superstructure. The tugboats steering her in churned up the water with their powerful props and their foghorns bellowed through the air. A loud POP cut through the busyness, as a man on the pier fired a rifle that shot a ball of twine up to a man on the Sacramento's main deck. He scrambled after the ball and grabbed it and pulled with gloved hands to hoist up one of the six-inch hemp lines used to tie the ship to the pier.

On the periphery of all this commotion First Class Petty Officer Redburn lay couchant, sunning himself on a pile of dunnage. His rotund belly bulged under the front of his dress white jumper, and his fingers interlocked behind his head pushed the Dixie cup hat forward over his eyes. Emulating the pose but not so well endowed with girth or shaveable whiskers, Airman Christopher Marlow lay beside his superior officer. The third patient, a marine in camouflage pants, white T-shirt and rubber

9

sandals, sat in a wheel chair occasionally extruding a low moan of pain. In order to accommodate his inflamed left shoulder, the marine craned his neck at an odd angle. A white band of gauze circled his brow.

"Tell us, marine," said Redburn, "What catastrophe has befallen you?"

"Befallen?" the marine asked.

"What happened to you?" Chris asked.

"I was sleeping on the hangar one night and a forklift came along and dropped a crate on me."

"You don't seem to be in much pain," Redburn said without opening his eyes. "Is anything broken?"

"My collar bone is broke, but it only hurts when I move," the marine said. Even with his head bent to one side, appearing disjointed, he still seemed courageous and strong. His bandaged skull shaved in a tight crew cut and a bulldog, tattooed on his well-developed forearm sneered sharp fangs. Chris imagined that even with a broken collarbone the marine might still beat most sailors in a wrist-wrestling match.

"It only hurts when you move, you say?"

"Yeah."

"Does it hurt real bad?" Redburn persisted.

"Only when I move," the marine repeated, wincing.

"Then just sit still because our corpsman went to the motor pool to get a van."

"How far is the hospital?" The marine grit his teeth.

"Actually, you could see it from here but I don't advise you move your head. It's that huge, pink edifice nestled up there in the foothills. Can you see it there, Marlow?"

"Sure can."

A few minutes later, the corpsman showed up in a Ford Econoline 15-passenger van. He wheeled the marine over to the side door, and as the marine unsteadily climbed into the van, he said to the corpsman, "Hey, take it easy on the bumps while you're driving, okay? I'm sure my collarbone is broke."

But while exiting Pearl Harbor's main gate the corpsman accelerated to make a right on red but suddenly slammed on the brakes to avoid hitting a pedestrian. The marine yelped like a whipped dog, sobbed, swallowed hard and sniffled.

Gawking at the marine in the rearview mirror the corpsman said, "Oh, dude, I'm really sorry, like this thing's got sticky brakes."

Every time the corpsman stopped at a light or curved along the twisting road, the marine whimpered. In the corner of his eye, Chris saw the guy's jaw tensing and his lips wriggling as tears ran down his rugged cheeks. Outside the emergency room, the corpsman sped off after instructing Redburn, "Take the marine inside, you can get a bus back to the ship outside the hospital's main lobby."

After walking through miles of hallways and asking for directions a couple times, they got in an elevator and went up.

"That corpsman didn't even put the van in park to let the marine climb out," Chris said.

"Don't worry," Redburn said, "marines can't feel pain."

They checked in at the gastroenterology clinic and the receptionist told them they'd have to wait because the doctor was away performing an emergency surgery. Chris scanned the magazines strewn across a table in the waiting area and the 1980s rushed back to him. Ronald Reagan, AIDS, Cocaine, MTV and starving African children. He flipped through an issue of People and pictures of Boy George, Mr. T, Stephen King and Valley Girls jumped out at him.

After a while, a corpsman called for Redburn to see Doctor Burkham.

Chris went out onto a patio balcony to smoke.

Honolulu International Airport was just out of view behind a mountain ridge. Every few seconds a jet airliner circled down out of the sky. The jets were gigantic, and Chris imagined hundreds of tourists over from the mainland all belted snugly into their cushioned seats.

He loathed the tourists who saw Oahu through the windows of air-conditioned tour busses, rental cars and from the balconies of their luxury hotel rooms, but he knew he was no better for having seen Hawaii so many times through the bottom of a cocktail glass. The fact that he'd been eight weeks on the Pacific coming over from San Francisco and had worked twelve hours every day of the passage prevented him from thinking of himself as a tourist. In every port of call, he came ashore without any hotel or rental car reservations. Arriving on land thirsty for cold beer and longing for female companionship, he didn't know quite what he was, a sailor he figured, certainly not a tourist.

"Hey, kid, Major Burkham wants to see you," Redburn said through the screen. Chris pitched his cigarette into a tin can on the floor and went inside. "Down the hall, room three," Redburn said.

Major Burkham had a touch of gray in her short brown hair, sharp eyes and a determined jaw. Her runner-lean body stood Army-straight in an impeccable light green shirt. Golden oak leaves pinned to her collar points. Her piercing gaze and confident tone made Chris straighten up and throw his shoulders back.

"Tell me what's going on with you," she said.

A twinge, something between dread and optimism, shot through his innards each time a doctor pressed him with this question. His thoughts polarized. His mind split in a schism. On one side a mass of worries, fretting over the possibility that he was just a sissy, a hypochondriac—was he making it up? But these thoughts were at odds with the simple yet regrettable fact that he did feel pain in his chest. Somewhere in the middle of his mixed up head, in the balance, he thought maybe this doctor could actually tell him what was wrong and set him up with a cure.

"Well Ma'am, uh, Major," he picked his words carefully. "It hurts right here," pointing to the left side of his chest. "Sometimes after eating, or when I wake up in the middle of the night, or in the morning," he paused. Unlike the ship's doctors who read his medical record while he spoke, Major Burkham looked him in the eyes. "When it hurts it isn't too bad, sometimes it goes away in an hour." Her apparent concern caught him off guard, and he had an urge to downplay the pain, to buck up and be tough. Rub some dirt on it and walk it off. But he told the truth. "There's times it hurts pretty bad for a few days and when that happens it gets hard to breathe."

"What kind of pain is it?"

He'd seen several doctors on the ship, and they wrote prescriptions for painkillers and antacids when they saw him coming, but she was different. Clearly, she wanted to get beyond the symptoms and find out what was wrong.

"When it lasts a short time it's piercing like something is jabbing me, and when it lasts a few days it feels more like a cramp and my left arm starts to hurt."

She kept her concerned gaze pinned to his face, examining his voice and expression for sincerity. "Remove your shirt and sit on the table," she said, skimming through his record.

"What's it like on your ship?"

"What do you mean?" he asked, because life aboard ship was a completely alien experience compared to day-to-day life on land. He didn't know where to begin.

"The food, living conditions, the work you do."

"The food isn't bad. They serve a lot of stew, pot roast and potatoes in the main galley. On the speed line I eat hamburgers and pizza."

"How long after you eat before going to sleep?"

Chris thought about it. "A couple hours, I guess. I usually eat, lift weights and then go to sleep."

"That might be part of your problem," she said. "That type of food, gravy and fatty meats, can sit in your stomach for several hours after you fall asleep. What kind of work do you do?"

"I'm a plane captain on the flight deck. I have an airplane, an A-7 Corsair, and when it lands the directors park it, and I chain it down to the deck. I top it off with fuel and work with the mechanics and bomb loaders."

"You said chains. Tell me about these chains."

"They're tie-down chains, about six feet long. I carry three over each shoulder. They weigh about seventy pounds total."

She walked behind him, and the cold disk of her stethoscope contacted his skin. She listened for a moment at several spots on his back. Then she traced his shoulders and backbone with her fingers and explained how nerve bundles run down the spinal cord and the heavy chains might be pinching a

13

nerve in his shoulder.

When her fingers touched his back, a load of stress and tension rolled off. With the exception of a few high fives and handshakes, another person's skin hadn't touched his in months.

*   *   *

Back in the late 1960s, Janet Burkham graduated from college and entered the US Army with the rank of second lieutenant and the title of medical doctor. She went immediately to the hospital ship USS Sanctuary off the coast of Vietnam, where she performed surgery over two thousand times. She did amputations to finish the work started by land mines. She put stomachs and intestines back together after bullets and grenades exposed and burned them. Then she worked in the emergency room at a veteran's hospital in San Francisco through most of the 1970s, and now in the 80s—here in paradise, on Oahu where living was easy—she saw how tough young military men behave, even when there isn't a war on. A steady stream of them sat on her examination table with hernias, ulcers, sexually transmitted diseases, PTSD, cracked vertebra. Her patients were typically young men with early signs of cardiovascular disease, cirrhosis of the liver, cancer and all manner of psychological problems.

Airman Marlow's heartbeat sounded a little too heavy, and the muscles in his neck and back were tight like ropes.

"I'm sending you downstairs for x-rays, and I want you back here in two days."

He put his shirt on and said, "Thank you, Ma'am."

*   *   *

At the radiology department, he stripped and put on a thin cotton robe. It hung open in the back. A technician handed him two cups; a small paper one with crystals the size of kosher salt in the bottom, and a large plastic one filled with a milkshake-like substance the technician identified as Barium.

Anchored to the ceiling and the floor, a huge stainless steel wheel filled the white room. An examination table mounted horizontally on the wheel. A robotic arm with actuators attached to metal appendages extended from the wall. Mounted on the arm, Chris marveled at a globe covered with a variety of lenses that looked like fisheyes, wide angles and zooms.

"Lay on the table," a voice came from behind him.

Chris slid up and lay on his back on the table, careful not to spill his crystals and Barium. Suddenly the room began tipping as the table spun quarter way around. His feet began descending. His head began to rise. He was afraid the apparatus, spinning on its axis, would pinch him in half. The robotic arm extended, and the globe of lenses rotated until a wide-angle pointed at his belly. Everything stopped, and he was standing on a metal shelf with the tabletop behind him and the lenses in front of him. Across the room, the x-ray technician stood at his control panel behind a green tinted window.

"Now I'd like you to turn around, stand up straight and lean your head slightly forward."

Chris complied, self-conscious because a draft blew on his bottom through the gown's open back.

The optical ball snapped several images of his hips, spine and skull.

"Now turn around and face me. Stand as still as you can. You are going to toss the crystals in the small cup to the back of your mouth and then wash them down with the Barium in the big cup. Whenever you're ready, go ahead. And remember to stand as still as you can."

Upon tossing the crystals into his mouth, they contacted his saliva and crackled. One popped out of his mouth and shot across the room. He gulped the Barium, a gray paste the consistency of pancake batter with a gluey taste.

The lens focused and shuttered, capturing the up and down movement of his Adam's apple, flap like epiglottis, peristalsis of the esophagus and the opening of the stomach's cardiac sphincter. The muscular walls of his stomach began writhing to accommodate the crackling crystals and the pint of Barium. The high-tech camera captured the turgid unfolding on X-ray.

He held the pose until the technician said, "Okay, step

down and get dressed."

                              *   *   *

In the Tripler Army Hospital lobby, Chris waited, hoping Redburn might arrive, but the two men never saw each other again. That's how it is with sailors. Shipmates know each other for an hour or a year, and then they're gone forever.

Outside the hospital, he waited at a bus stop thinking about Larry, his former best friend. They'd gone ashore together in ports around the world but now he was gone. When the bus pulled up, Chris asked the driver if she went to Pearl Harbor.

"Sure do," she replied. "I stop at the Navy Exchange, Arizona Memorial, Makalapa gate, main gate and the shipyard."

                              *   *   *

Back on the Enterprise, Chris pulled on shorts, wiggled his toes into a pair of sandals and buttoned a floral print luau shirt that he wore only between the tropics. The loose fitting casual clothes were an extreme change from his flight deck gear. Eight weeks of wearing black leather steel-toed boots, greasy green canvas pants, a sweaty long-sleeve turtleneck jersey and a cranial helmet made his civilian attire feel wispy, made him feel practically naked.

He splashed on cologne and inhaled the aroma with a gusto he hadn't felt in eight weeks, since San Francisco. He slipped two crisp hundred-dollar bills into his wallet and snatched a fresh pack of Marlboro from the carton in his locker.

When he glanced at Larry Tynan's old bunk, and saw the bare, folded mattress that had been his friend's home for several years, memories flickered in Chris's mind.

He remembered standing in the catwalk, helping Larry heave tie-down chains onto his shoulders. He remembered Larry trudging up the ladder. Then Larry stopped and leaned over because one of his tie-down chains caught on the scupper. Larry looked Chris in the eyes, a plea for help, and Chris unhooked the stuck chain from the scupper. Chris watched Larry take two steps—

At that, a chill shivered along Chris's spine and he gasped for breath and put his hand to his chest. But the memory persisted. He saw the back of Larry's cranial helmet and the back of his brown flotation vest. The chains heaved over Larry's shoulder jangled down his back. Those chains always were too heavy for him. Chris remembered the scene as if it were five minutes ago. He wanted to reach out and grab Larry, stop him from taking another step. That fatal step.

The metal door banged shut as Chris ran from the living compartment, ran from the memory of his dead best friend.

Chapter 3: The Wave

The constant gray water, gray steel and blue sky surrounding a sailor on the high seas habituate his mind to celibacy. Long periods at sea inflict sensory deprivation and encrust the sailor's lusts and vices under a shell of boredom. The steel walls and floors of the ship trap the seaman's mind, force it to lay dormant under days of boring routine while at sea. But when he comes ashore, it's like waves rushing in, suddenly animating his life with all the vibrant colors of shore leave. The act of walking off a ship in civilian clothes and stepping on dry land fills a sailor with equal parts delight and danger.

When Chris stepped off the bus at the corner of Ala Moana Boulevard and Kalia Road, the Hilton Hotel stood before him. The white concrete escarpment towered up from the beach higher than the sun. The Fort DeRussy Hotel, a 14-story rampart of balconies and sliding glass patio doors sat next in the great wall of luxury skyscrapers lining Waikiki beach.

He followed the smooth sidewalk between manicured gardens and towering palm trees until he reached the beach. He flipped off his sandals and held them in his hand as he walked across the white sand. He'd been eight weeks on top of the Pacific but hadn't felt a drop and all he wanted to do now was cool his tired feet in the warm water.

He stood in the crystal blue knee-deep breakers and gazed at the sunset burning up the sky far off on the horizon. He waded along the shore toward Diamond Head Crater. Eight weeks of hard labor melted off his shoulders as he felt the sand squishing between his toes.

At the Royal Hawaiian, a pink adobe palace with blue awnings and courtyard gardens full of stunted palms, Chris slipped his sandals on.

He walked up the steps to the hotel's entrance and saw two strikingly attractive women in elegant strapless dresses coming out of the lobby. He held the door for them. Their resemblance said they were mother and daughter, and when the mother turned to him and said, "Thank you, young man," he was unable to utter a reply. Chris simply smiled and felt completely overwhelmed by the perfection in the way they both had applied red lipstick. They glowed like angels, the way their hair parted and held back behind their ears with white and orange orchids. They descended the steps to a waiting limousine, and Chris could only stare after them, stunned by two sets of bare smooth, shoulders.

The sailor had been too long at sea.

The host led him to a table on a green lawn ringed by palm trees and took his drink order. Minutes later a waitress brought him a Fog Cutter; a slushy concoction with lots of rum and fruit juice. A couple of sips had him unwinding until his mahi-mahi, sliced pineapple, asparagus and rice arrived. For the first time in over 60 days, he chewed his food slowly and savored every bite.

Muscular men, surfers during the day, set up bongos and torches. When the tables around him began filling with diners for the evening luau, Chris paid his bill and left to meet his friends at the Wave.

The rum lit a wonderful feeling in his mind, and back on the street now, he admired the beautiful people in vacation clothes walking and driving in shiny rental cars and jeeps. Suddenly in the crowd shined the face of his shipmate Ordnanceman Goblat. He was red faced after being rummied away in a pier bar with Pabst Blue Ribbon on tap all afternoon.

"Marlow!" said Goblat, extending a handshake at the end of a huge forearm tattooed with a golden anchor, outlined in black and emblazoned with USN. A black-haired hula girl swayed her ample hips each time he flexed the sinewy bulk of his left forearm. Goblat's jaw, hinged like a bear trap beneath a furry red beard. He stood a stalwart five foot five, wore brown topsiders, white creased pants and a pink dress shirt.

"Hello," Chris said.

"I'm going to dinner. Will you join me?"

"I just ate at the Royal Hawaiian," Chris said, a hand on his satiated belly. "I'm meeting Angelo and Steven Oaks at the Wave in a little while."

"So you're drinking at the Wave tonight?" Goblat asked.

"Yeah, you should meet us there."

"I'll eat my dinner and head over."

"See you later," Chris said.

* * *

The Wave sat on a busy street beside a drawbridge, across from the Waikiki Marina. Yacht masts like sparsely lit Christmas trees filled the rows of docks. The block-long building completely covered with a gigantic florescent mural of a tidal wave about to crash on the steep slopes of snowcapped Mount Fuji. A mob of tourists dressed for a night swilling cocktails and reveling on the dance floor moved slowly past three muscular bouncers who checked IDs and collected a five-dollar cover charge.

"Chris!" Angelo shouted as he floated above the crowd. Chris pushed through to the curb and there sat a glossy jade Suzuki Samurai jeep with Steven Oaks at the wheel and Angelo standing on the front passenger seat holding onto the windshield. Chris leapt in as Steve stomped on the gas and darted into traffic.

"Where we headed?"

"Cruising!" Angelo said. He had dark skin and a tight black afro, and he was stocky with a barrel chest. Steve wore mirrored Ray-Bans. A cigarette hung from his lips. "You like this ride?" Angelo asked.

"It's fine!" Chris shouted and sat back.

Steve turned street corners and accelerated onto a

highway entrance ramp. Big signs loomed overhead. Koko Head 8, Kaimuki 4, Pakalolo 1. The temperature dropped a few degrees as they climbed into the Koolau Mountains.

Angelo indicated a brown bag on the floor and Chris pulled out a bottle of Beck's from the six-pack. Angelo handed him the opener and a second later passed back a bottle of Southern Comfort.

Chris swigged some SoCo—the familiar hot-candy flavor electric in his mouth. He raised the Becks to his lips and glanced at the empty seat beside him. Larry should have been there. And just as Larry's smiling face materialized in his imagination, Chris chugged a great long guzzle of beer and attempted to wash him away. But it wasn't enough. Larry persisted smiling and Chris tried to wash away the ugsome memories with another hit of Southern Comfort. The beer fizzed in his belly and the warmth from the syrupy liquor radiated into his guts and upward through his chest, rising right up through his neck and directly into his brain. It felt so good; it made him smile back at his dead best friend. He lit a cigarette, inhaled a drag and came alive for the first time in eight weeks.

In a short while, they were on the King Kamehameha Highway traveling along the shore. The black ocean spread out to their right and the steep mountains rose to their left. Steve slowed near a sign that said Wawamalu Beach. He turned onto a sandy trail through a copse of palms, banyans and tropical monkeypods. Bristles of saw grass and taro grew knee high up to the tire tracks. On the crest of a low dune, Steve stopped and cut the engine. With the headlights off, they sat quietly in the darkness for several minutes. No light marred the seamless night. Not even the moon showed it celestial face. A belt of pinprick stars collected themselves across the heavens.

"Let's take a swim!" Angelo shouted, leaping from the jeep as if jettisoned on an ejection seat.

It became a footrace to the surf. All three men disrobed and then dove on the purling waves and recklessly swam out over a sandbar and beyond a reef where the ocean floor fell deep away. They swam out so far the coast became a dark silhouette on the horizon far behind them.

The long, hot workdays on the black steel melted away. The high decibel whine of jet engines singing soprano on the fragile follicles of their inner ears became muffled splashes in the murky water.

Chris drew a breath and plunged below. Pointing his head straight down, he kicked his legs powerfully, and reached out, cupped his hands and pulled himself into the black depths. As the salt water became noticeably cooler on his skin, he kept kicking and pulling, descending deeper. Cool thermoclines turned the water around him brisk and at first refreshing, but then the saltiness scrubbed away his memories.

He remembered water blasting from a fire hose. And he saw the water surging from the hose's brass nozzle and blasting the black steel, washing away blood and chunks of flesh and bits of bone and what? He didn't know; but he did know. It was a pink tube, a hose, likely a length of Larry Tynan's small intestine.

Christopher reached down and scratched at the water, trying to claw his way further into the abyss, but something held him. He realized what it was and he blew all the air from his lungs and descended further into the wet and the dark.

When he finally surfaced, he gasped for air, and then plunged under again. He swam down, down until his lungs ached and his ears stung. He shivered in the cool water, shivered because he almost remembered what happened right after Larry died.

* * *

They collected driftwood in the dunes and built a fire.

"Hot nurses at that hospital, yeah?" Steve asked.

"They made me swallow Pop Rocks and chug a bucket of pancake batter while they took x-rays."

"What'd the doctor say?"

"I'm going back in two days for test results."

"Are you gonna stay here?" Angelo asked. "They got the best rec' center in the Navy, so you better keep lifting weights you pussy."

"She's not gonna keep me here," Chris said.

21

"She!" cried Angelo. "She! My boy, we're in paradise, the best rec' center in the Navy and you got a lady doctor! Oh, man!" Angelo was having a fit. "You should stay here; get some of that luau booty!"

"I don't know," Chris said, grinning. "I have to go to the IO."

"Why go to the Indian Ocean when you can stay here?" Angelo asked.

"I need money."

"For the college fund?" Steve asked.

"What?" Angelo asked.

"My dad gave me three grand to put in the Navy college fund but I spent it," Chris said.

"What'd you spend three grand on?" Angelo asked.

"Paid off my motorcycle and took a road trip to Vegas."

"Smart." Angelo laughed.

"So how's this college fund work?" Steve asked. "I'm thinking about making a deposit."

"They give you two dollars for every dollar you put in, so I'm putting in three thousand and getting back nine."

"Not a bad deal," Steve said.

"Fuck college," Angelo said. "If I was you, I'd take the luau booty now."

"You can catch up with the ship in the Philippines in a month or so," Steve said.

"I'm not staying here," Chris said. He'd spent an hour with a calculator and a pencil working numbers on a legal pad. He had no choice but to save every paycheck during the Enterprise's upcoming three-month line period on the Indian Ocean. He knew it meant working the flight deck every day and saving every dollar he earned for three months, but he had no choice. His Dad had given him three thousand dollars but he blew it, so now he had to work his ass off to earn that money back and deposit it in the Navy college fund.

"Let's toast to Larry." Steve hoisted his beer.

"To Larry fucking Tynan," Angelo said and drained the last of the Southern Comfort.

"That son of a bitch," Angelo said.

"When we get back out there," Steve said, "we gotta keep a better eye on each other."

"There's nothing we could've done," Angelo said. "He walked right into the damn thing!"

"Let's go do some drinking at the Wave," Chris said.

*   *   *

The block-long mural of an ominous tidal wave about to crash on Mt. Fuji glowed in the streetlights like vaporized silver. Suntanned girls with smooth beautiful faces like seashells and eyes like pears, fresh clipped hair and subtle eyeliner captivated the sailors. Myriad lines led from the club's entrance and clusters of friends stood around talking, smoking, surveying the crowd.

Goblat was close to the door, so they cut in.

Above a pulsing mass of partiers, projector screens suspended on invisible wires, broadcasted M-TV music videos. Goblat and Chris parted the mob, pushed through to the bar.

Someone paid for the first round.

A band came on stage and jammed through dance hits, oldies, new wave and surfer jams.

Everyone's attention fragmented between talking, laughing, dancing, smoking and drinking. Dancing at a nightclub is like drinking liquor at an aerobics workout. The sailors joined a group of sorority women from Kansas and combined their efforts in an attempt to drink the Wave dry. When the band, which had a three-piece horn section, took a break, the sisters and the sailors gathered upstairs in an air-conditioned lounge. They bent backwards over the bar to have shots of Slippery Nipple, Kamikaze, True Religion and Screaming Jesus mixed right in their mouths.

Fun.

Blind drunk.

*   *   *

Chris snapped out of a black paralysis.

Standing between two beds, his vision unable to focus on

23

a lamp on a nightstand ringing like a convenience store's burglar alarm. He stared at the lamp so hard his head hurt. Inside his eyes burned with hot liquid that might have been blood. He couldn't understand why the lamp rang, but holy shit it was loud.

That's when he saw the phone and picked it up.

"Hello," he croaked.

"Aloha," a cheerful female voice. "Wakeup call for Mister Marlow."

"Wake up call?" His brain refused to function.

"It's six am. Is Mister Marlow there?"

Chris glanced around the dim room. Sleeping bodies strewn here and there. He remembered a drunken girl insisting you could run faster in a hotel hallway. It didn't make sense, but she swore to it, so they all tried it and discovered it was true. Drunk off their asses, they sprinted through the narrow space. Someone started banging on doors. All kinds of people came out in the hall. Parties started in random hotel rooms. He remembered his reflection under lines on a mirror. Purple-haired Hawaiian refer smoked in a bong had them all laughing at Goblat and an Australian sailor—both stripped naked and comparing their tattoos. He liked the Aussie's accent. A confrontation with hotel security after someone complained. And then outside in the warm night air, on a balcony under the moonlight, kissing his friend from the Kansas sorority. Later in the bed, she let him unbutton her shirt. But she wouldn't let him take her belt off even though he tried.

"This is me," Chris said into the phone, not quite sure.

"Have a wonderful day, Mister Marlow." She hung up.

He pushed aside the curtain and stepped onto the balcony.

A deserted beach thirty floors below. Another dirge of images flashed in his head; a tattoo parlor where a guy with a Camel no-filter hanging between his lips, breathing ashes and smoke as he buzzed the big flank of Goblat's deltoid with a tat' gun. A ferocious orange and black striped tiger broke through the foliage with sharp claws on its big front paws. And one of the sorority girls got the Egyptian Eye of Ra printed on her scapula.

Chris slipped back into the room and almost stepped on Goblat who slept with his face planted in the carpet, shirtless, a bandage taped over his new tattoo. Steve and Angelo were in the other bed, under a sheet, with a girl spooned between them.

And there alone on the mattress, slept the shirtless sorority girl with the chastity belt. A sniffling snore whistled through her nose. Brown locks across her face, her body half covered by a blanket. Chris remembered her great boobs. Reality snapped back, when he pulled out his wallet and found a single dollar; not nearly enough for a cab and he had to muster for duty section in an hour, at seven.

"Wake up." He shook Steve's shoulder.

"Dude?" Steve groaned.

"Can I have some money for a cab?"

"Sure, take twenty." Steve rolled his bloodshot eyes toward his wallet on the nightstand.

Chris waited for the elevator and wondered what hotel he was in. Right before the doors slid open the impossibly loud ding of a bell, like a nail being hammered into his brain. And as the elevator descended his stomach dropped out and he swallowed hard to keep from barfing. His brain spun, woozy between his ears, like a chubby ballerina. It was hopeless. His stomach bucked alcohol and acid into the back of his throat. He pressed a hand on the wall, sank to his knees and vomited hard twice.

The bell clanged again and the doors slide open on the lobby. He stood up and wiped the back of his hand across his mouth. Something angry gnawed beneath his ribs like a rodent trying to eat its way out.

He wondered about the exact meaning of the word lousy.

Look for

SAILOR'S DELIGHT

By Malcolm Torres

Available at www.amazon.com in 2014

www.ingramcontent.com/pod-product-compliance
Lightning Source LLC
Chambersburg PA
CBHW020240180626
46810CB00006B/2280